BIG BIG TRAIN

BIG BIG TRAIN

Between The Lines

The Story Of A Rock Band

Grant Moon

KINGMAKER PUBLISHING

First published in Great Britain by Kingmaker Publishing Limited in 2022

© 2022 Kingmaker Publishing Limited

www.kingmakerpublishing.com

Front cover photograph by André Wins

Proof-read by Professor Geoff Parks

ISBN 978-1-8384918-2-6

Printed in Great Britain by
Biddles Books Limited, King's Lynn, Norfolk

Contents

Author's Note

This book began to take shape in 2020, as the Covid-19 pandemic kicked truly in, the world we knew ground to an unprecedented halt, and an eerie silence fell. These really were what a wise, talented man would soon be calling 'The Strangest Times'.

With Big Big Train's history stretching over 30 years, there was much to cover in any biography, and their engine was still running hot as the book neared completion in 2021. Their thirteenth album, *Common Ground*, was finished, and destined to go Top 40 in the UK. Some major players had departed from the ranks, but, with new faces appearing, there was a fresh energy and a definite buzz within the band.

At the risk of dropping a spoiler, our story originally concluded as Gregory Spawton and David Longdon raised a glass together at Real World Studios, with the *Common Ground* sessions drawing to a successful close, and thoughts turning to their own next chapter. There were exciting opportunities coming their way in the live arena, with a palpable sense that Big Big Train were about to take things to the next level (a recurring theme within these pages, as you will see).

And how I wish, with all my heart, that this had been where we'd written 'To Be Continued', and gone to print.

But, as you surely know, it was not to be. David Longdon's tragic death in November 2021 robbed the world of a good man, and a great artist. It also cast a long, dark shadow over the band he had helped bring to the forefront of the modern progressive rock scene.

But despite this terrible turn of events, considering Big Big Train's achievements over the past three decades, the wonderful music they make, and the contributions of the many people involved in their development (David being one of the key names among them), their story is rich, and ongoing, and still worth the telling. I spoke to my publishers at Kingmaker – Big Big Train's own Gregory Spawton and the band's manager Nick Shilton – and also to David's fiancée Sarah Ewing. They all agreed – he would want this story to be told.

While David is no longer with us, to stay in keeping with the style of this book his quotes (honest, insightful, fun – a mark of the man) remain in the present tense. His voice – and what a voice it is – is one of many here, each adding their valuable recollections of this remarkable band's journey so far.

And, ultimately, what better way to pay tribute to David Longdon, to honour his memory, than to celebrate the band that made his name, to tell the story of Big Big Train.

Grant Moon
Cardiff, March 2022

I

'Let us begin where it all began...'

NESTLED IN THE WEST MIDLANDS SOME 40 miles from Sutton Coldfield is the village of Cleobury Mortimer, where Gregory Mark Spawton was born, on Monday 17th May 1965. At the time Roger Miller had the UK number one single with *King Of The Road*, the country's best selling album was *Beatles For Sale*, and down in London a fledgling rock band began referring to themselves as The Pink Floyd Sound.

Gregory Spawton's parents were both from Leicester. His mother Doreen had grown up in a railway cottage there, and her dad and brothers were all rail workers. Gregory's father Barry was a sales rep for Findlaters, a major wine merchant, and the job meant the Spawtons moved around the country for a while, finally settling in the Maney area of Sutton Coldfield in 1970. Their house was in Moss Drive, a cul-de-sac built on the site of an old quarry, and where Gregory and his brother Nigel – his elder by five years – were raised in a home littered with the products of their father's trade. They played soldiers and flew Airfix fighters amid bottles of Campari and Black Tower.

Proper Jack Froster: Gregory outside his Moss Drive home in 1975.

Barry was a good woodworker, and built his younger son elaborate forts and castles that his beloved toy knights could guard and battle for, his vivid imagination running wild. One Christmas Gregory was given his first railway set. Produced by the Tri-ang company, the Big Big Train had gauge zero red plastic track for its fleet of tiny, battery powered locomotives to trundle over. The boy played with that train set until it almost fell apart.

The Spawton boys enjoyed one of those long lost, free range 1970s childhoods, real *Bash Street Kids* stuff. When not in school Gregory would bomb down the steep slope of Maney Hill on his racing bike, and into the wide open space of Sutton Park, where he would spend most of his free time with his friends. On snowy winter days (Doreen called them 'Proper Jack Frosters') it was the perfect place for sledging. In the summer, he would leave the house in the morning, spend the day firing bows and arrows and catapults in the park, then in the fading evening light wheel his bike back up the hill, mud and a smile on his face, in time for his tea.

But at home, life was less idyllic. Having always been an avid social drinker, Barry slid into full blown alcoholism over time. Spawton remembers him reeking of whisky, even when picking the family up from town in the car. "My dad was a horrible drunk," he says. "He was violent towards my brother and my mum. They got into some nasty fights – Mum was tiny and she would throw things at him. She worked for a taxi firm, and some of the drivers were big lads. I remember her arriving home with some of them for muscle when Dad was being especially difficult. Moss Drive was a great place to grow up, but their divorce eventually made it horrific."

His parents split in 1977. Barry moved out and slowly drifted to the periphery of his sons' lives, seeing them once a month or so thereafter. Doreen moved with Gregory and Nigel to a two-bedroom housing association flat nearby, and she got together with Will, one of the cab drivers at the rank, who became the boys' stepfather. "And they're still together now," says Spawton. "He was a good, decent man, with a Kevin Keegan hairstyle back then. He did an amazing job with us – he's the father I never really had and I am proud to call him my dad."

By then, music had become a regular part of Gregory Spawton's life. When he was seven, his whole class at Town Junior School was made to learn the recorder, and later he would learn to read music. As a boy, he had an angelic voice, and willingly took his place in the school choir. He donned the obligatory ruff and over the next few years got some early touring experience, performing with St Peter's Choir in cathedrals throughout the UK.

"I'm certain that this is where my whole musical background emanates from," he says now. "John Wetton, Geoff Downes and others have made the same point about

St Peter's Church, Maney, Sutton Coldfield.

church music before, but when I started getting into rock it was the church background that made me gravitate towards music that featured great melodies and strong, powerful chords. The better hymns are sing-able but have elaborate chord sequences and big moments, with the organ's bass pedals kicking in. Our church had a really good organist and an old school organ. We used to sing carols and hymns, and works by Handel – stuff that made the hairs stand up on the back of your neck."

But nature took its course, and, around the age of 12, Spawton's voice broke. When he was unceremoniously ejected from the choir pews he was a little devastated, but his fascination with music was set. At home the family turntable had been altogether more secular, the Spawton record collection comprising The Beatles, Glen Campbell, Rod Stewart and Barbra Streisand, and a Barry Spawton favourite – *The Planets* by Holst.

❖❖❖

Growing up 180 miles away in Dorset, Andy Poole lived with his mum, dad and younger brother in Bournemouth.

His home life was, he says, "unremarkable, really. We didn't go on many family holidays – we would just go down to the beach or to the New Forest. My mother's family were farmers on the nearby island of Purbeck, so we'd go and visit them. I only remember lots of happy times."

Poole was born on 15th March 1963 in the town, just an hour and a half before his childhood best pal, Ian Cooper. Their mothers had met at the ante-natal clinic at the local hospital, and the two families were both close neighbours and close friends. On school fancy dress day the two boys went in together as Bill And Ben, the Flower Pot Men. Growing up, they would head out into the countryside, hunt for eels in the local river, chase each other across the fields, play Spock and Kirk, locked in fierce phaser gun battles. On weekend mornings they'd sit together in front of the TV, rapt by *Captain Scarlet And The Mysterons* and *Thunderbirds* (to this day Cooper's mobile ringtone is the *Thunderbirds* theme).

But when it came to music, their tastes diverged. The Poole family music centre was dominated by The Carpenters, James Last, Simon & Garfunkel, Manfred Mann and – Poole's particular favourite – *Hold Tight!* by Dave Dee, Dozy, Beaky, Mick & Tich. The boys were just the right age for the '70s glam rock scene, and Poole's imagination was fired by Slade, David Bowie, T Rex, and particularly The Sweet. He loved their 1974 album *Sweet*

Andy and Ian as the Flower Pot Men, late 1960s.

Fanny Adams, and during that same year he saw Queen perform *Seven Seas Of Rhye* on *Top Of The Pops*. He rushed out and bought its grandiose, proto-progressive parent LP, *Queen II*, and fell under the spell of the band's subsequent work, including *A Night At The Opera*, the record that gave the world *Bohemian Rhapsody*.

Like most music mad teenagers, Poole devoured the pages of *Melody Maker*. One week, while leafing through the magazine, he found his curiosity piqued by the striking visuals of a band – a new one on him – called Yes. "Their album covers intrigued me," he says, "because of the Roger Dean artwork. Nobody at school was into Yes and they were never played on the radio, so there was an air of mystery to them. I remember going to WH Smiths and buying one of them without even having heard it."

With just three songs on the track list, *Close To The Edge* appeared to be pretty poor value for Poole's pocket money. But Yes were one of the biggest names on what would later be called the 'progressive' rock scene, with that 1972 LP regarded as one of its milestone recordings. Poole reluctantly parted with the cash, went home, dropped the needle on his new vinyl, and swiftly fell in love: "I'd never heard anything like it before. I was completely blown away by it, totally captivated."

From there he was hooked on progressive music. He would get home from school, quickly settle at the family's

Sanyo music system, encase himself in a pair of huge headphones, and get lost in this new musical world. "I'd immerse myself in all these prog albums," he says now, "I wouldn't even listen to bands like ABBA or even ELO because they weren't prog enough for me. I was a bit sniffy, and missed out on people like Neil Young and Joni Mitchell until quite a while later."

Instead, Poole worked on building up his progressive rock collection. He amassed Yes's back catalogue, then a friend's brother played him *Supper's Ready* by another major name in the genre, Genesis. Their dramatic, magisterial instrumental *Los Endos* had a profound effect on Poole too, and he quickly added *A Trick Of The Tail* to his rapidly expanding prog shelf, with the works of Pink Floyd following soon after. When he was 15, he attended his first gig in 1978, seeing Hawkwind at The Wessex Hall, Poole Arts Centre. "And it was awful! A cacophony that wasn't exciting at all. They only said eight words all night: 'What do you want us to play now?' And of course the crowd shouted for *Silver Machine*. So it was just a load of noise with *Silver Machine* as an encore. I just didn't get it."

His gig life improved though. Steve Hackett performed at Bournemouth Winter Gardens while promoting his album *Spectral Mornings* in '79, and returned a year later during his *Defector* tour. Genesis played Southampton's Gaumont Theatre on their 1980 run for *Duke*, and that year Poole also saw Yes at the same venue, on their *Drama* tour. Poole usually went alone to such events – none of his immediate circle of friends shared his passion for prog, especially not Ian Cooper.

For his part, Cooper's main musical love was – and remains today – ABBA. At home his family had an organ, and his mother played piano well. "I was given a few piano lessons," Cooper says, "but quickly got bored of them. I never learned to read music but found that I had a pretty good ear – I was always more mathematical than musical, but I could listen to something and more or less play it back, not very well admittedly."

When Cooper passed his O Levels in 1979 his parents bought him his first keyboard, a Yamaha CS-15 synthesiser, which he affectionately nicknamed 'Squeaky'. "I never claimed to be a very good keyboard player, but I did enjoy it. Synthesisers and keyboards have always been my passion."

Synths were also key to the new wave of music at that time. As well as ABBA, Cooper was heavily into the electronic heavy sound of Ultravox, Tubeway Army and the latter band's enigmatic leader, Gary Numan. With his good mathematical mind, Cooper was headed for the local college that autumn to study for an HND in Mechanical Engineering. Over the summer he used his brain and a good ear to navigate his way through tunes by Ultravox and Numan, and to systematically work out what Squeaky's many knobs, faders and oscillators actually did.

There was at least a partial overlap with his mate Andy Poole's preferred music. Prog had its share of superb keyboardists, and Cooper would come to love the work of Yes man Rick Wakeman (whose later solo albums *White Rock* and *Rhapsodies* remain among Cooper's favourites). Equally, the early synth era was epitomised by artists including Jean-Michel Jarre, Tangerine Dream and Kraftwerk, all of whom had an experimental, avant-garde approach that chimed with prog rock's own grand, adventurous aesthetic.

Unlike Cooper, Poole was an unenthusiastic student. He scraped six O Level passes in '79, and got onto a BTEC course in Business Studies at Bournemouth College, starting that September. In the summer he worked at the West Beach Café on the seafront near Bournemouth Pier, saved £160 and bought his first electric guitar, a Japanese copy of a Gibson Les Paul, teaching himself to play a few chords and licks. He played Cooper one of Genesis's defining albums, *The Lamb Lies Down On Broadway*, and while his friend liked the songs *Hairless Heart* and *Counting Out Time*, much to Poole's chagrin the rest left Cooper cold. Nevertheless, they both now had instruments, and the pair decided to become a duo, and formed their first band together.

Squeaky was a relatively primitive synth but still offered up some decent sounds. Also in their arsenal was the Coopers' family organ, Poole's guitar and a recently acquired Boss Dr Rhythm drum machine. "We had two cassette tapes," Poole remembers, "and we would record a backing track, then dub over that. Then I got a little four-track portastudio, which freed us up to layer things. Out of necessity there was quite a lot of experimenting with sound, textures and exploring different chords and interesting ways of playing things."

"And there was some very dodgy singing too!" adds Cooper. "Andy's was just talking really, and I did what I could. We made up songs, and eventually came up with an album, *The Friend Inside*. It was a fun hobby which we both enjoyed. We would get together at least one night a week and put stuff down on tape. We spent many hours on it and got some quite good recordings, given we were recording onto cassette."

Their name, Arcshine, was a partial anagram of the Sea Urchin, another beach café where the young Poole had worked one summer. By 1981, after almost three years of on and off noodling, the pair felt ready to unleash themselves onto the music world. On a scorching summer's day, Arcshine played their first gig to a tiny crowd – a sixth form school leavers' party at the nearby Tarrant Hinton Village Hall. Arcshine were the main event, and when the time came the stage curtains were pulled back to reveal Cooper and Poole behind banks of keyboards. Faced with two nervous strangers playing weird original tunes (titles included *Picture Of Disguise*, *Tears Of Dust* and *Dancebeat 6*) the crowd's curiosity soon waned, and by the end of their set Arcshine were playing to an all but empty room, partly for the love of it, mainly for their pride.

Arcshine at Tarrant Hinton Village Hall, 1981.

Their biggest booking came two years later. Bournemouth's Starkers Royal Ballroom was a beautiful, Grade II listed Victorian theatre with a 1,500 capacity, and through a college friend Cooper got Arcshine on the bill at a big Christmas party there. The first act on, the pair played to a respectable, 600-strong crowd, and by now had learned some lessons.

They played through the venue's huge PA and had a backing tape to beef up their sound. The original numbers were peppered with such floor fillers as Tubeway Army's *Are 'Friends' Electric?*, Gary Numan's own *Complex*, and *I Remember (Death In The Afternoon)* by Ultravox. But, due to the heat coming from the stage lights, their backing tape began to speed up, and as Poole recalls, "we had to keep tuning our keyboards as we went to stay in key, and the electric drums we were using kept being triggered totally at random by the bass coming out of the PA. It was embarrassing. There were 600 people there but they weren't terribly into it. It was mainly our own stuff after all. But we got some great photos out of it, and it was a great experience. For me playing on a big stage through a proper PA was a real revelation."

Despite these mixed successes, the duo continued their musical collaboration throughout their college years. Ian Cooper began work at a local engineering firm, and Andy Poole went into local government, taking a job in the summer of 1984 in Bournemouth Council's Housing Department.

Arcshine at the Royal Ballroom (now the O2 Academy), Bournemouth, 5th December 1983.

•••

Up in Birmingham, prog and punk rock had co-existed affably in the Spawton household. In the early 1980s, Nigel Spawton had been the drummer in a punky, new wave band influenced by Buzzcocks, Sex Pistols and Elvis Costello. They never gigged but did jam regularly in the basement of a mate's house, focusing on their own musically banal yet lyrically meaningful songs. When Nigel's younger brother started sitting in on rehearsals, he was transfixed. In a rite of passage every musician knows, Gregory was watching real, original music being made by actual people, and people he knew at that – his brother, and his mates Pete McDonald, Steve Lugg, Tim McCarty and their frontman, Ed Serafinas. Music moved from the ineffable realm of the spiritual world and into the physical, while losing none of its magic.

When the band were searching for a name, Gregory thought back to one of his favourite childhood toys. "What about Big Big Train?" he asked the older lads, who looked around at each other, considered it as good a name as any,

and shrugged in approval. For nearly three years the punk band Big Big Train led their angry, unheard revolution in a Birmingham basement, finally fading out in 1982, when Nigel left for Oxford Polytechnic to study for a Master's in Architecture.

In the same year, on his seventeenth birthday, Gregory Spawton got his own first guitar – a black replica of a Gibson Les Paul, made by budget instrument manufacturer Kay. It was hard to play but still an adequate piece of kit for a beginner, and those musical channels opened up in his adolescent brain.

"I was interested in writing, not playing," he says. "I had had a fantasy of writing music before I got the guitar. I would imagine a song, give it a title, write words, sing it onto a tape recorder and then it would go on a pretend album. Every musician I know who writes started off learning their instrument and went on to write later, but it was the other way round for me. I wrote a piece of music on my birthday, as soon as I got the guitar, just single note stuff. I picked it up and made noises – I had this five watt plastic amp that rattled like mad, but was enough to put stuff onto tape.

The original Big Big Train, 1981 (Nigel Spawton on far left in left photo and on drums in right photo).

I remember one of the first things I learned was the E major chord – slide it up a few frets and you get Rush's *Xanadu*."

In the confines of their two-bedroom flat Spawton drove his mum and stepdad crazy over the following year, as he learned to really play guitar via books and cassettes. He worked on his technique, got to know the fretboard, familiarising himself with the mechanics of chords and scales. "One of the problems for me throughout my life has been an inability to play at a very high level," he says, "and what always interested me was using my limited technical skills in a Peter Hammill way. He's a brilliant writer and I idolise him for that – he's very much focused on the writing side, and lets others do the musical heavy lifting."

Though a relatively late starter, Spawton was also a fast learner. He acquired an acoustic guitar, and took lessons from a tutor in nearby Erdington, who helped him with the basics of song structure and ran him through intermediate guitar pieces such as *Angi,* the essential fingerstyle workout by English folk legend *manqué,* Davey Graham. The elements of composition really began to sink in for Spawton when he decided to learn *Horizons,* Steve Hackett's beautiful, Bach-inspired guitar piece from Genesis's 1972 album, *Foxtrot.* "That was the first time I realised, 'Ah, so *that's* how it's done!' *Horizons* helped teach me how chords worked together, and I began to unpick it from there. I know it was stupidly ambitious, but most rock musicians short-circuit the training and go for broke, and that's what I did."

Just a few years earlier, Genesis had been Spawton's gateway band into the vibrant, phantasmagorical otherworld of progressive rock. His brother Nigel was a keen and broad-minded music fan himself, his tastes happily extending beyond the world of punk and rock 'n'

roll. He loved nothing more than to sit in a hot bath in the house at Moss Drive, his bedroom door wide open across the hallway so he could enjoy music emanating from his cranked-up record player. In 1977, after a day spent record shopping, he was in the bath and letting his newest vinyl acquisition soak in. His mates had urged him to buy that year's must-have punk album, the Sex Pistols' *Never Mind The Bollocks.* But Nigel had chosen something from the opposite end of the musical spectrum.

"I can picture it now," says his younger brother. "I got in and the house was *shaking* with this loud music. I was at the bottom of the stairs, I didn't know what it was, but I loved it. There was a particularly lovely guitar figure that stopped me in my tracks and captured my imagination instantly. In Nigel's room I looked at the album cover – it was *Selling England By The Pound* by Genesis, and the song was *Dancing With The Moonlit Knight.* Nigel explained that some Genesis songs were ten minutes long, which was baffling to me. So that was my epiphany about this particular type of rock music. I became the kid at school who had Genesis written on his bag, as a badge of honour. I was probably one of two or three kids out of 800 in school still listening to progressive rock in 1978 to '79. Everyone else had gone down the new wave or punk route, so I was an oddity. Probably still am, I suppose…"

Having listened to his brother's copy of *Selling England* repeatedly, a year later Gregory fell in love with a song he heard on the radio called *Follow You Follow Me.* When he twigged that this was also by Genesis he bought its parent album …*And Then There Were Three…,* and from there began hoovering up the band's entire catalogue in earnest. He read *I Know What I Like,* Armando Gallo's acclaimed biography of the band's early days. In the book, Gallo mentions a band called Van der Graaf Generator and a long song of theirs called *A Plague Of Lighthouse Keepers*. Thus Spawton discovered another of his lifelong favourite acts, and he began exploring other pioneering prog groups too – from Italy's PFM to Pink Floyd, the band created the same year he was.

All this made him part of the ideal audience for what was coming as the new decade dawned. The 1980s saw a fresh slew of bands inspired by Genesis and other '70s progressive bands, and the weekly music paper *Sounds* picked up on this 'New Wave Of British Prog Rock'. "They featured these bands every other week or so," says Spawton. "Twelfth Night were on the front cover, and then Marillion. I read about Solstice, who became a very important band to me. I had missed the '70s scene, so this was my era of prog rock, and I got heavily into it."

By 1982 Spawton, all six foot two of him, was armed with his cheapo Kay electric guitar and a whole new rock 'n' roll attitude. He had grown his hair long – an egregious offence at Bishop Vesey's Grammar School, where he was studying for his A Levels. Halfway through sixth form he was pulled aside and issued with an ultimatum by his intimidating headmaster, Mr Harvey: 'Get your haircut or get expelled.' The shaggy hair remained and, good to his word, Mr Harvey booted him out. "It was pathetic of me really," Spawton admits now. "It was an identity thing. I was 17, rock music was my life and I was a bit of a hippie. But my mum was brilliant. She marched in and gave Mr Harvey a right old piece of her mind. She immediately got me into Sutton Coldfield College next door. There was no school uniform there, and nobody gave a shit that I had long hair and wore a denim shirt every day."

One of Spawton's fellow students at the college was Phil Hogg, a keen drummer whose claim to fame was that he had taken lessons from the brother of Carl Palmer, one third of superstar prog trio Emerson, Lake & Palmer. Spawton met Hogg through two of his former fellow Veseyans, budding guitarist Simon Kirby and – Spawton's best friend to this day – Richard Williamson. With Williamson assuming lead vocals and Kirby switching from guitar to bass, the four of them began horsing around in their very first band.

Equus took their name from the cult 1977 film starring screen legend Richard Burton and (far, *far* more importantly to the teenaged lads concerned) the transcendently beautiful English actress Jenny Agutter. Spawton was the band's prog head, Hogg had that ELP connection, and Kirby and Williamson shared Andy Poole's affection for Queen, along with the work of then-relevant Canadian rocker, Aldo Nova. Put together, these influences made for a chaotically eclectic set list. "We were doing ludicrous covers," Spawton recalls. "We would try ELP's *Karn Evil 9* on guitar. We played a few Steve Hackett things, like *The Steppes*, Genesis's *Abacab*, Pink Floyd's *Comfortably Numb*, and we'd also do Queen's *Crazy Little Thing Called Love* and *Dragon Attack*, from their album *The Game*."

And among this incongruous morass were some self-penned Equus tunes. In the main these were written by Hogg, but Spawton submitted one too. *Rainbow Warrior* was, in its writer's words, a "dreadful piece of music" inspired by Greenpeace's flagship vessel, sunk by the French intelligence service in '85.

Equus would practise above Hogg's father's tailoring shop in Aston, where they played also two small gigs for friends and family. Spawton fondly remembers Hogg's bass drum pedal being on its last legs, and Richard Williamson's

Equus friends & family show, Aston, Birmingham, 1983.

mother smiling through gritted teeth throughout, her fingers firmly planted in her ears.

These were actually warm-up shows for Equus's big break, at the YMCA in Sutton Coldfield. They were scheduled to be the support band, but when the headline act heard Equus soundcheck they generously offered to swap places on the bill. "I remember looking out," says Spawton, "and suddenly the room filled up with about 50 people really watching us. It was the first time I engaged with an audience, and I thoroughly enjoyed it."

In the summer of '83 Spawton got his A Level results: a B in both English and History, and an E in British Politics & Government. The night before he was due to sit one of the exams for the last of those subjects, Equus had taken a band trip to the Stonehenge Festival. Hawkwind hit the stage at 4am and – with Dave Brock and band's sound bouncing his head off his tent floor – Spawton got no sleep at all. The following morning he made it back to school just in time for the exam, and promptly fell asleep at his desk for a grade-critical hour.

But no matter. By then he was enthused by how quickly Equus had developed, and was convinced that music was

Equus at Sutton Coldfield Rugby Club, 1984.

going to be his life. He decided to take a year out to focus on the band before going to university. He signed on for unemployment benefit, and over the year Equus rehearsed regularly and played a handful of gigs, notably to a grand total of 40 people at the Sutton Coldfield Rugby Club Open Air Festival.

Spawton also made a weekly trip down to London for a gig fix. The Marquee on Soho's Wardour Street was a Mecca for rock fans like him. It was here that the next generation of progressive bands were braving the headwinds of punk, pop and new wave, and carrying the prog rock torch into the new decade. "It was really happening down there," says Spawton. "You could see Solstice, Twelfth Night, IQ, Marillion, Pallas, Pendragon. It was great, though I would often just miss the last night bus from the centre of Birmingham, and end up getting in at 4am. But that's how obsessive I was about the music."

Equus split amicably in 1984 when its members dispersed to various colleges, with Spawton securing a place at Reading University to study Archaeology. He had been obsessed with history all his life, and at the time was smitten by the trendy TV historian, Michael Wood. "He was incredibly influential," says Spawton. "Just ask any historian of my age and they'll say the same thing. Michael made history sexy. It was a dry subject back then, learned from Ladybird books or stuffy textbooks. But in the late '70s Michael Wood was there in his jeans and leather jacket and long hair, in a helicopter looking at old battle sites, talking about the history of England, with great incidental music behind him. It was revolutionary. That's why I ended up in college doing Archaeology."

At Reading he dug deep into his studies, and though he still played guitar and jammed with new friends, he buried his musical ambitions for the duration. For six months he struggled with a serious bout of glandular fever, and lost three stone in weight. And he fell head over heels in love with a girl. Joy was in the year above him, they became a couple, and on graduating she moved back to her parents' house in Bournemouth, with Spawton vowing to follow once he had completed his degree.

While love was blooming, it felt to Spawton that the happening prog scene centred around The Marquee was dying off. Then, while home for the holidays in the summer of '86, Phil Hogg and Simon Kirby raved to him about this great new band, It Bites. "I heard *Calling All The Heroes,*" says Spawton, "and thought it was just a bit of pop music, but then I heard the live version with Francis Dunnery going off on this crazy guitar solo. I got heavily into the band and saw them a lot during my last year at uni, and I followed them around the circuit. They were a great live band. At The Marquee they were so close you could almost touch them, and I watched Dunnery closely. He had this fluid legato guitar style, this Allan Holdsworth thing going on, but in a rock/pop context. I craved that technique, but just knew I couldn't do it. It Bites reconnected me to going to gigs, and to thinking about doing music again. If it wasn't for them, I would never have got back into it."

◆◆◆

That same year Andy Poole had seen It Bites too, at Bournemouth International Centre, on their tour for their album *The Big Lad In The Windmill.* He thought they were incredible, but by then he was heavily invested in another band on the prog scene. While Poole was at college, a mutual friend had introduced him to Dave Paddock, the lighting engineer and roadie for a rising Southampton band called The Lens. Paddock played him their demo, *No TV Tonight,* which harked back to the music of Genesis, and the music pushed all Poole's buttons. He went to see The Lens at a Southampton show and, impressed, he began attending as many of their gigs as he could. Paddock introduced him to their guitarist Michael Holmes and keyboardist Martin Orford, and soon Poole was crewing for the band.

In 1981 he ended up at the Stonehenge Free Festival with The Lens, which, he says, "was a real eye opener for me aged 16. Hippies walking around naked, and Hell's Angels – it was a real culture shock! The Lens had been promised a slot on the main stage, but instead they were offered a place on a smaller stage, at two in the morning. Mike and Martin disappeared and I think they had a discussion about The Lens not working. My understanding is that that's when they decided to disband The Lens and move on, and they conceived IQ."

IQ formed that year and, with shows across the country and regular slots at The Marquee, they soon became one of the leading names on this new, or 'neo', prog scene. When they released their 1983 debut album *Tales From The Lush Attic*, Michael Holmes presented a chuffed Andy Poole with a signed first edition on vinyl. What a trophy this was, a gift that surely only a true prog connoisseur could appreciate.

◆◆◆

On graduating in 1987 Spawton got engaged to Joy. He moved home to Sutton Coldfield but, as per the plan, he sought work in Bournemouth, and applied for a position as a Trainee Housing Officer for the local council. In the 'Other Interests' box on his application form he mentioned that he liked music and was a guitar player. This was true, far more so than some of the other information he supplied.

To imply he was local, he gave Joy's parents' address as his own, and he also claimed to own a car. He was interviewed on a Friday and was offered the job on the spot, to start on the Monday morning. He was actually based 180 miles away, and didn't have a vehicle to make that, or any other, journey. Over a frantic weekend Spawton dashed back to Sutton Coldfield, his stepdad Will bought him a battered second hand Ford Fiesta Kingfisher, and then, with all his belongings crammed into the boot, Spawton

hightailed to Bournemouth for his new job, and a new life.

On that Monday morning, some of the female members of staff in Bournemouth Council's Housing Department were hoping that a Harrison Ford/Indiana Jones type would be swinging into their office. "I swear that there was an expectation that some guy would come into the office wearing a fedora and carrying a whip!" says Spawton with a laugh. "The air was sucked out of the room when I walked in – they were so disappointed, and quickly disappeared."

His archaeology background earned him the office nickname of, not Indy, but Digger, and it stuck. He was shown round, and was introduced to his new colleagues, including one Andy Poole. Poole had been told that the new recruit was also a music fan and – in the middle of their open plan office, their boss within earshot – the pair got involved in a long, detailed conversation about music.

They discovered their mutual love of progressive rock, and got into the time-honoured duel of name-checking all their favourites. They began with the obvious – Genesis, King Crimson, Camel – and headed down the prog pecking order, the references getting more obscure as the conversation deepened. Spawton was an IQ fan himself, and was confident that they would be his trump card. He was staggered – and just a little annoyed – to learn that Poole actually knew Michael Holmes and Martin Orford well. And he had the signed vinyl to prove it.

"Greg was so taken aback that I knew about IQ," Poole recalls, laughing. "I remember that one lunchtime we went to do some house visits together, but a lot of the time we were just sat in the car talking about prog. We had the same passion for Genesis, but Greg was more passionate for *Selling England By The Pound* and I was more for *The Lamb Lies Down On Broadway*. I was a bit more into Yes, while Greg was into Van der Graaf Generator and Peter Hammill. I hadn't touched Van der Graaf, but after Greg introduced me I developed a passion for them. For my part, I got Greg into XTC and Prefab Sprout. We broadened each other's horizons."

This was years before the term 'bromance' was coined, but that's what this friendship became. The two men got along well from there on in. Beyond music they had plenty in common, bonding over the small, important stuff like movies and TV – *Spinal Tap, Monty Python, The Comic Strip Presents*, even the gently nostalgic TV show *The Wonder Years* and then-hot yuppie drama *Thirtysomething*. But music was their main thing, and eventually the inevitable jam happened.

Poole was living at his mum's house, just two minutes away from Spawton, and had a studio set-up in his room – two tape recorders, an electric 12-string, some other guitars and a bank of keyboards. At the time the pair were both listening intently to *Private Parts & Pieces*, an eclectic selection of solo music by original Genesis guitarist and 12-string maestro, Anthony Phillips. Suitably inspired, the pair would sit and improvise long, rambling instrumental pieces of their own, proudly inspired by Phillips' work.

Arcshine was still active too, and, for fear of alienating his pal Ian Cooper, Poole kept clear blue water between the two musical relationships. "Andy was kind of two-timing Ian with me," says Spawton. "He would spend a couple of days a week working on Arcshine with him, then a couple of evenings a week working with me on these acoustic things. I used to say to Andy, 'This is ridiculous – Ian plays keyboard, we could be a band here.' Andy was wary as he'd known Ian a long time."

After a year Poole and Spawton were making a decent

sound and had some solid original material. A nervous Poole took a breath and passed a tape on to Ian Cooper, who liked it, and the three began playing together. "I just thought, 'Let's get on with it!'" says Cooper. "Greg's influence dramatically changed what Andy and I were doing, and I like to think we had some influence in the opposite direction as well. It seemed a natural progression to me in terms of the musical complexity and the equipment we were purchasing, or borrowing. It progressed into a much higher quality outfit, a big progression from Arcshine. And we got on extremely well."

With the synth geek at one pole, the prog nerd at the other, and Poole the warm water in between, the trio quickly found a pleasing musical middle ground. While uncertain what they were aiming for, by early 1990 they were making music regularly enough to consider themselves a band.

By then Spawton and Joy were nearly two years into their marriage, Cooper was in a serious relationship, and Poole had bought a flat with his then girlfriend, Jane. She was away much of the time studying in London, so Poole could sequester the whole living room and use it as a rehearsal studio, complete with a camcorder to record the trio's early efforts. With Cooper on keys and Spawton on guitar, Poole happily assumed the role of bassist, investing in a blue Ibanez bass from Bournemouth's leading instrument emporium, Eddie Moors Music.

"There were some really good times," says Ian Cooper. "I always got on really well with Greg. It was evident from very early on that he was the leader, and that was cool because his musical tastes were slightly different to mine, and although it wasn't necessarily the sort of music I would go out and buy, it was enjoyable to play something that stretched my keyboard skills."

But what to call their band? Spawton suggested Commanding Heights, but Poole and Cooper demurred. Kingmaker was also mooted, but the name had already been claimed by a hotly tipped indie band from Hull. There was another name that Spawton had brought with him from the Midlands. He had never thought much of it really, but his brother's basement rockers had been defunct for almost a decade now, so it was up for grabs. He suggested it, his bandmates thought it was fine, so in 1990 Arcshine was dissolved and Big Big Train officially rolled into service.

The first line-up of Big Big Train in Andy Poole's home studio, 1990.

II

*'Hit the ground running hard,
upon hard broken shattered stone...'*

THAT SAME YEAR, 1990, lifelong rock fan and Anglophile Martin Read landed in the UK from his native Canada. He was 28, good looking and bright eyed. Eager to begin a new life in England, he settled in Bournemouth. Back in Vancouver Read had sung for a few bands that hadn't amounted to much. "One of the reasons I moved to the UK," he says, "was to find a band I could sing for, and hopefully go somewhere with. The bands I loved, like Yes, Genesis, Pink Floyd, all hailed from England, so I felt that was where I would find a band that did the music I wanted to do. I wanted to be a rock star! Strangely enough, I found Greg and Andy really quite quickly."

The three members of the newly plated Big Big Train had swiftly realised that none of them could sing. They placed an advert for a vocalist on the large, flyer-strewn noticeboard of Eddie Moors Music. This shop was where Andy Poole had bought his bass, and where he and Ian Cooper had spent a lot of money on keyboards during the Arcshine years. "Eddie Moors was *the* music shop in Bournemouth," Poole explains. "It was old school –

Eddie Senior had the shop since forever, selling brass and string instruments, and his son Eddie Junior ran the guitar and synthesiser section."

A few candidates responded to their ad. One was a schoolteacher who sang well but whose gentle voice wasn't ultimately suited to the band's rocky sound. Another was a Dorset lad who turned up in a tasselled leather jacket and sunglasses, affecting a cod American accent throughout his (brief) audition. Another wannabe fatally insisted the band should play a gig on top of a building dressed in pink tutus, 'to get attention'.

So it was a relief when Martin Read showed up at Poole's flat. Personable, presentable and age-appropriate, he looked the part and could hold a tune better than any of the others. He sang through a few things, including a song he had written, a lament for the Native American population called *Indian Souls*. To Spawton, Read's Canadian accent and roots made him feel exotic, a little alien even. And he could even play some guitar, too. The vote was unanimous – he was in.

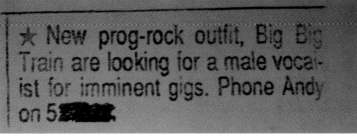

★ New prog-rock outfit, Big Big Train are looking for a male vocalist for imminent gigs. Phone Andy on 5▪▪▪▪▪

*The advert placed in Eddie Moors Music and in the
Bournemouth Advertiser.*

Read had enjoyed the occasional spliff with his musician buddies back home, but was trying to get away from that whole scene, so the abstemious Big Big Train suited him fine. "I was definitely looking for a non-smoking band," he says, "and Big Big Train were the only ones I contacted. I felt I had something to offer, and when we met it all fell into place. I got on really well with Greg, Andy and Ian. They played me what they had done so far, and I liked it."

Poole, Cooper and Spawton had been writing together for a year, both instrumentals and songs, with Spawton emerging as the band's lead songwriter. "I was writing a lot, so it fell to me," he says. "I'm not precious about it – my songs were crap back then. I was a late starter and there was no real quality there. I was just the only one putting things forward."

As Cooper remembers it, "Greg's stuff was the stuff he wanted to do. I suppose the stuff I wrote was never proggy enough, and whatever he came up with was better than what Andy and I did. It was certainly way more complex."

Now a four piece, Big Big Train assembled at Poole's flat to make their first proper demo tape. Spawton's mother had lent the band £3,000, which was invested in a Fostex R8 reel to reel tape machine. This was hooked up to an Atari ST computer – enabling them to run some simple sequencer parts too – and they had that Dr Rhythm drum machine too. An engineer by day, Cooper proved adept at programming that box's fiddly parameters. When his bandmates suggested he was making rhythms no human drummer could possibly play, he took it as a compliment.

All this gear guaranteed a sufficient level of sound quality. "I'd never done any recording before," says Martin Read. "Greg, Ian and Andy were full steam ahead with it, and seemed to know what they were doing. They did most of the work, and I just sang what they wanted me to sing. I had a little book of ideas I'd written down and Greg re-worked a few of those for me."

Completed in 1991, the demo, *From The River To The Sea*, was a formative combination of It Bites-style pop-prog, Hackett-inspired rock and quasi-*Horizons* classical guitar parts. With Read on vocals, Poole ably kept the bass parts flowing, Spawton's guitar playing belied his late start on the instrument, and Cooper's burbling synths and fiddly drum parts kept the whole thing ticking in tricky time. They were proud of their work.

Promo photo for the first Big Big Train demo tape.

"By and large *From The River To The Sea* was really quite good," Andy Poole contends now. "There were some decent ideas there, but we weren't yet capable enough to deliver them, although we had a good stab at it. There were songs about relationships, some political stuff – *Downhilling* was an anti-Thatcher song. We only had eight channels to play with, so that was quite limiting and the sound palette was fairly restricted. We didn't do any backing vocals, partly because we didn't have enough tracks left, and also because we didn't have a clue how to! We were playing harmony parts on instruments but didn't know how to write harmonies with vocals. We weren't that confident in ourselves."

They sent a copy of their new cassette to *Making Music*, a magazine distributed in music shops across the UK, and aimed mainly at fellow musos. The mag gave the band their very first review, awarding the demo three out of five stars, praising the group for their prog savvy, their 'grasp and execution of this obtuse form of expression'. The four members pored over that short review for hours together, reading and re-reading it, looking between the lines for deeper praise and crueller slights. "I was really excited," says Spawton. "Andy was more realistic about it and reined me in, saying they probably gave us an extra star just for being candid about being a progressive rock band!"

Another significant moment came when the band met fellow Bournemouthian Stuart Nicholson, frontman of local prog band Galahad. They had formed in 1985, and by '91 were on a roll. They had played The Marquee with enduring '80s proggers Pendragon, and were featured on Radio 1's prestigious weekly rock show, presented by legendary DJ Tommy Vance. The band recorded a live session for it at the BBC's famous Maida Vale studios. This was all to promote their first proper debut LP, *Nothing Is Written*, which had been praised by Deep Purple's Ian Gillan, no less, in *Metal Hammer* magazine. Coverage for prog bands like Galahad was usually the preserve of fanzines – small circulation mags produced on a shoestring, and lovingly written and curated by the music's staunchest supporters. Galahad were thus relatively high profile. Along with that mainstream radio play and celebrity endorsement, they earned valuable

column inches in *Kerrang!*, that era's kingmaking rock and metal weekly.

"*Kerrang!* were a little sarcastic about us," says Stuart Nicholson now, with a veteran's chuckle, "but it was still publicity, and it helped us. In those days prog really was a dirty word. It was the rock equivalent of buying a porn magazine – real under the counter stuff! There was no internet back then of course, and I basically looked out for all the fanzines that were sympathetic to prog rock. A lot of them printed lists of other fanzines and magazines with addresses, so I gathered those and tried to network. I'd listened to a few bits of Big Big Train's music and thought it was okay, but what really struck me was that Greg and I were kindred spirits. I liked what he was trying to do, and that he was passionate. Not many new bands were trying to do this kind of stuff – I wanted to help out."

"Stu had an address book to die for," adds Spawton. "He knew everything there was to know about the fan magazine scene at the time, so we had places to send our demo tape. We produced a few hundred copies and sent many of them out. The reviews we got were ridiculously glowing; we didn't deserve them."

Plundering Nicholson's generously volunteered black book, the band sent *From The River To The Sea* to numerous prog-friendly fanzines. One was *Feedback*, a publication that had grown out of the newsletter for Mensa's Rock Music Special Interest Group. In 1990 progressive fan (and walking musical encyclopaedia) Kev Rowland became that group's secretary, and began covering prog extensively in the pages of what would evolve into *Feedback*.

"*From The River To The Sea* was the first tape I ever received that I didn't pay for," says Rowland, who has been writing about music ever since. "There was a photo and a letter from Greg. I didn't know anything about them. I worked out that they were from Dorset, so Stu must've told them about me. There had been an explosion on the progressive scene, and at that time a lot of fanzines were coming and going. *The Organ* was probably the most important independent magazine at the time, there was *A Flower*, and *Silhobbit*, run by people who were mad on prog and took the piss out of it. I look back on that as a time we'll never have again. It was a very close knit community. I used to bump into Greg a lot. He was young and keen and, like all of us back then, he was a fan. In '92 I went to a Pendragon gig at The Astoria with Galahad and Mentaur, but missed Mentaur's set because I was outside talking to Greg, who was flyering for Big Big Train."

Rowland reviewed *From The River To The Sea* in the December '91 issue of *Feedback*, and judged the tape to be 'very good'. He singled Poole out for praise for his 'great bass runs', selected *Downhilling* as the musical highlight, and recommended the band to fans of 'Genesis (prog not pop), Galahad or Marillion'. The band leapt on that last line for use on subsequent advertising for their tape. *The Organ* also offered their approval of Big Big Train's 'complex, melodic, mellow prog', and generously praised the demo as 'a healthy, well produced, well recorded debut […] Somewhere in between Jadis, later Freefall, little bits of It Bites and Galahad'. Most prog fanzines assessed albums with this supportive, often forgiving tone, and would diligently print each band's postal details at the foot of their review. Thanks to such coverage and the band's extensive flyering, *From The River To The Sea* sold a few hundred copies via mail order. Spawton and Poole dutifully posted out cassettes from home, though usually completely forgot to cash the cheques they received.

Some listeners even suggested that the album should be released on compact disc. In the days before every PC came with a CD burner as standard, this was a tall, expensive order. Again, Stuart Nicholson came to their aid. "We had used some companies to get our own CDs pressed," he says, "so we helped Big Big Train put their record out on CD. They used our label, Avalon, the idea being to make it look like a proper label release, as opposed to a home-made thing."

The band rejigged the track order and added a couple of new songs to the CD version – the crunchy pop rocker *Returning To The Fold* and Martin Read's *Indian Souls*, by now a mournful acoustic piece. They remastered the music from the original source tapes, a new cover was designed by a student from Bournemouth Art College, and the CD version of *From The River To The Sea* emerged in 1992. "At the time that wasn't that easy to do," says Ian Cooper, still with a certain level of joy. "To this day I'm proud, personally and for the band, of what we achieved there. In the very early days in my office we had a computer running [word processing program] WordPerfect. Out of hours we used it to do the inlays, the foldout lyrics sheet, all ourselves. I remember waving the completed CD around to all my friends and family – 'We made an album!'"

In the wave of reviews for the CD some publications praised the two new songs – especially *Indian Souls* – and reiterated the band's potential, though a few pointed out how low tech and basic the recording was. Reviewing for *A Flower*, Chris Frost bemoaned the poor production, Read's weak voice and the lack of musical contrast over the 12 tracks, but Frost (himself the keyboardist for Stoke-on-Trent neo proggers Epilogue) still managed to conclude that it was a 'very promising first release from

Big Big Train. If they can maintain and develop their own style, resisting pressure to be something more proggy, then they should appeal to a wider market and achieve success.'

"I think the CD showed the record's failings," says Gregory Spawton, "and exposed how crude it was. It was actually less well reviewed than the tape. People had higher expectations of an album on CD, and we singularly failed to meet those." The 1,000 disc production run was spectacularly optimistic at the time, but much later – when the band had evolved into an altogether different beast – these CDs would change hands for high prices among more avid collectors.

◆◆◆

By this time, Big Big Train's first human drummer had breezed into the ranks, bringing a burst of youthful energy with him. Steve Hughes had moved from London to Bournemouth with his parents in 1991. He was just 15, and from an even earlier age had been into jazz, fusion and prog, idolising Chick Corea and a list of elite drummers topped by Vinnie Colaiuta and Rush's Neil Peart. Understandably, he'd always felt different to the other kids in school. His father – himself a drummer in his youth – would happily keep Hughes home during term time so he could practise his snare drum rolls. The lad was obsessed, wanting nothing else than to be the best drummer in the world.

So he was raring to go when he opened a local Bournemouth rag and saw Big Big Train's advert, which seemed tailor-made for him. "It said 'Drummer wanted for polyrhythmic rock band'," Hughes recalls. "It had been my dream to be a top drummer from an early age, and I was overconfident. I was very young, still at school, and to get into the band I lied about my age. I said I was 18 and at college."

Six feet tall, cocky and with a cheeky charm and maturity beyond his years, Hughes immediately struck Spawton as a real breath of fresh air. "Steve pricked our balloon of pomposity," he says. "He was young, he didn't take himself too seriously and had a good sense of humour. He added a lot of fun to the band."

With both vocalist and drummer now in place and the first CD under their belts, Big Big Train could finally play live. They rehearsed in the back rooms, basements and storage rooms of local pubs. Some landlords banned them along the way for being too loud and 'putting the locals off their pints'. One regular rehearsal haunt was Holdenhurst Village Hall. King Crimson's Robert Fripp grew up in the small Dorset town of Wimborne Minster just 20 minutes away, and Crimson had used the hall in 1980 while preparing their album *Discipline*. "There were pictures there of Fripp, Levin, Bruford and Belew rehearsing there," Andy Poole remembers. "We couldn't believe it! It was a bit away from everywhere, so you could make as much noise as you liked. It was a popular rehearsal venue for bands.

An early rehearsal at Holdenhurst Village Hall, 1991.

"We probably spent too much time rehearsing. We kept putting off playing live, but of course you need to play in front of an audience – we learned more from two or three gigs than we did from 30 rehearsals. There wasn't much of a progressive rock scene, but we did what we could. Some shows on the local circuit of pubs around Bournemouth got us started."

Big Big Train played their first gig on 3rd December 1991 at The River Park, a pub in West Parley, just a few miles north of Bournemouth. That same Christmas they also appeared at Gander On The Green, a favourite haunt for students at Bournemouth College. Gregory Spawton remembers the unlikely moment that two girls hit the dance floor in front of the stage, gamely trying to groove along to Big Big Train's progressive rhythms. "They were completely drunk," says Spawton fondly, "and when we finished they told us: 'You're just like one of those professional London bands!' I just said, 'Thanks!'"

Mr Smiths was another hot venue in the town. Galahad could sell out the 100-capacity club, and Big Big Train supported them there a few times. However, when the band – still unknown in the local area – played there as the

headliner in January '92, they performed to just a handful of people. They endured plenty of those rite of passage gigs that year, to one man and his dog in otherwise empty pubs, but Steve Hughes really enjoyed those times: "I was naïve and young and just wanted to be in a band," he says. "Big Big Train's music really resonated with me; it was life-changing for me. They were fantastic times and a big part of my formative years as a teenager and aspiring musician."

That same year Hughes was obliged to move back to London with his parents, but still made the journey to Dorset to play for Big Big Train at every opportunity. In September they even ventured north to Stoke-on-Trent, to

The first ever gig at The River Park, 3rd December 1991.

20

take the foot of the bill slot at 'An Autumn Night's Dream'. Headlined by Pendragon, this prog mini-festival took place at the Theatre Royal Hanley, and also featured Galahad, Framework and Grace. Stoke lads themselves, Grace had organised the whole event, and Spawton remembers their soundcheck taking the other performers aback. "They did their *whole set*, doing the poses and everything. The other bands were getting increasingly irate. I think we just had enough time to do a line check. My amp wasn't working, then to top it all my brother Nigel turned up with my dad, Barry. There were about 400-500 people there and it was our first proper light show, but them being there threw me off. I played really badly and was very embarrassed. I bristled for years afterwards whenever I saw Grace mentioned."

The following month Big Big Train supported Galahad at the College Of Arts & Technology in Rotherham, Yorkshire. That event was organised by Martin Hudson, who had formed the Classic Rock Society in October '91. The CRS fanzine *Wondrous Stories* was a respected publication, later to turn into the authoritative and affectionately held magazine *Rock Society*.

"The CRS gang and I were still finding our feet in organising gigs," says Martin Hudson now, some three decades later. "We soon learned there were a lot more bands out there besides Yes and Genesis et cetera, bands such as Galahad. Possibly on the recommendation of Stu Nicholson, Big Big Train had sent me a cassette tape of *From The River To The Sea* to review in *Wondrous Stories*. Both bands hailed from Bournemouth, so it made sense to promote them together. About a hundred turned out at the Rotherham show and enjoyed the evening. I remember Big Big Train sounding a bit different to how they would years later, but progressive rock was in the doldrums back then – it is easier these days for a band to

20

A NIGHT AT THE OPERA, OR A DAY AT THE RACES?

On September 5th, some of the best U.k Progressive rock bands on todays scene converged on Stoke for the Official U.K Progressive rock festival at the Theatre Royal. With five bands playing one after the other on the same stage the whole thing was frought with complications and problems and could easily have been a massive disaster. However the show went almost too smoothly with at most only a five to ten minute gap between each band.

After a long day of frantic backstage work the festival kicked off at around six thirty, with comparitive newcomers **BIG, BIG, TRAIN.** The band were there to promote their debute album, **"FROM THE RIVER TO THE SEA"**, playing tracks such as **"JAS"** and **"TO THE SEA"**, in their rather short set. Unfortunately the theatre was not too full at this point, as many people had yet to arrive, and the band played to a disappointingly small audience, leaving a number of people saddened that they had missed the band when they arrived towards the end of the set. However they gave a spirited performance and received a warm welcome, definately picking up a few more fans.

Next on came **FRAMEWORK** to a salvo of bright lights and a barrage of noise. What was perhaps the most spectacular beginnig of the evening was made yet more attention grabbing by the entrance of frontman Adriam Peddie, wearing what can only be described as a cross between Andy Pandy's romper suit and the garb of the famed Marillion jester. Hitting home straight away with the enegetic, **"TAKE ME INSIDE"**, the band played a set which consolidated their hold on the audience. Performing tracks from their CD, **"PICTURE GLASS THEATRE"**, and airing prospective tracks from their forthcoming CD, **"CONFIDENTIAL WHISPERS"**, the high points of their time on stage were the numbers, **"BIG MACHINE"**, **"CLOSE TO THE WATER"** and the wonderful **"QUEEN OF THE MOORLANDS"**.

After a short pause that wound the continuation of the narritive that wound it's way between each band all evening, it was the turn of **GRACE** to tread the boards. Although they were the most well established band of the night, there were many who had never heard their music or seen them live. They were in for a surprise. **GRACE** received one of the most enthusiastic receptions of the whole event. As the set progressed they just got better and better, even though Mac Austins vocals were occasionally shakey. Old classics such as **"CYRIL DINGLE"** and **"THE SQUARE"** were played, along with newer material from the new **"THE POET, THE PIPER AND THE FOOL"**, CD: **"THE PIPER"**, **"THE POET"** and **"HOLY MAN"**, for instance. The show brought out all of Harry Davies' exhibitionist qualities and the bands loyal following of fans came along to rally the audience and make sure they did the correct motions for **"RAIN DANCE"** and **"THE HOLY MAN"**. Dib - dob.

Nevertheless a large percent of the crowd had come primarily to see the ever popular, **GALAHAD** and **PENDRAGON**, and the first of this

Review of the show in Stoke-on-Trent, in the A Little Angry *fanzine.*

find an audience. Hopefully we did our little bit back in '92 to further their cause."

"Galahad were a good live band," says Spawton, "and we weren't. We paid their lighting guy a tenner to give us lights. In his mind that meant one spotlight in the middle of the stage. So Martin and I spent the gig edging each other out of the way to get into it, with the rest of the band in darkness. I really didn't like gigging in those days. I was very nervous, but I felt that, as the lead guitarist, I had responsibilities to play flashy solos, to strike poses, and I was never comfortable in that role. Plus it was bloody tiring – we were young men but all working full-time. If we played The Royal Standard in Walthamstow, we'd get home at four in the morning, and then have to unload the van."

Playing Walthamstow's prog-friendly (and sadly now defunct) Royal Standard involved a round trip of five hours and 240 miles for Big Big Train, but they endured the journey a few times. In July 1992 a show there led to a life-changing stroke of luck, not that it felt like it at the time. The band had secured a support slot for Jadis, a more

established Southampton prog band, who were promoting their strong second album, *More Than Meets The Eye*. Martin Read in particular adored their eponymous 1989 debut, and admired their charismatic lead singer Gary Chandler.

Loading the gear into their rented van was always a Tetris-style challenge. Numerous gig bags, guitars and keyboards were wedged tightly into place around Spawton's Marshall stack and Poole's 500 watt Peavey bass amp. After the long drive, that particular show went pretty well for them. As they packed up afterwards they discussed their performance and enjoyed the after-show glow, pleasantly surprised by how easily everything fitted back into the van. Some 70 miles later, halfway home on the M3, Poole realised why. They had left his bass amp back at the Standard.

Thankfully, Jadis had noticed and kindly brought the amp back with them to Southampton. Poole arranged to pick it up from them a few days later at a Jadis show at The Joiners Arms, one of the town's most vibrant music venues. When Poole showed up that evening, Jadis bassist John

Outside The Royal Standard, July 1992.

Big Big Train in action at The Royal Standard, 1992.

Loading up for a trip to The Royal Standard.

Jowitt introduced him to the band's sound engineer. Born and bred in Southampton, Rob Aubrey had played bass in bands since he was a kid, but always had an engineer's ear for the technical aspects of sound. In the past he had worked in the local university's Physics Department, as a stage technician at Southampton Guildhall (where he helped stage IQ and The Enid, Robert John Godfrey's revered prog ensemble). The Jadis gig at the Joiners was one of Aubrey's first jobs as a live sound engineer, but he was well placed to do it. By day he was the resident sound engineer at Parklands Studios, a professional, 24-track recording facility in the village of Denmead, near Portsmouth.

Onc of Aubrcy's rcgular gigs at Parklands was for a local radio station called Power FM. They paid him to record songs by bands from the area, and these were then broadcast to promote the local music scene. "I happened to mention this to Andy that night," says Aubrey, "and he sent me a few Big Big Train tracks. I chose *Far Distant Thing* for them to come in and record."

Far Distant Thing was just one of the songs the band had been working on for their next tape, *The Infant Hercules*. Steve Hughes turned out to be a wise hire – recording his real drum kit live at Bournemouth club Mr Smiths, he could knock out his parts pretty much in one take. The drum machine was gladly consigned to the shelf, and on record Big Big Train started to sound like a proper band.

Spawton still saw himself as a slow starter in songwriting terms, but began to gain a certain level of confidence. "I was writing a lot, and most of it was awful, but that was the first time I felt I started to write reasonably. A bit of the song *Kingmaker* was written with my friend Richard Williamson back in the Equus days. *Lincoln Green* had terrible lyrics but was a good tune. *The Infant Hercules* started to show a little more of our prog backstory. The songs were stretching out a bit, there were more 12-string guitars and Mellotron sounds."

Andy Poole agrees. "Our sound moved forwards. We were starting to get more adventurous, exploring instrumental ideas and themes. *Dismounting Tigers* had political lyrics, and *The Infant Hercules* includes the original version of *Kingmaker*, which we were playing live at the time."

Once again, the album was recorded in Poole's front room, but Aubrey's production of *Far Distant Thing* sparkled brightest by far. Owing a big debt to the glossy pop-prog of It Bites, it was a hint of what the band could produce given the right setting and guidance. While they were at Parklands for their Power FM session, Aubrey could see that "Andy and Greg were the driving force. Greg was always painted as this intense fellow who was very nervous about recording. On the day they arrived he wasn't going to be there until later. I told Andy – with my producer head on – that part of the song needed changing, and he was a bit scared to do it because it was Greg's song. But once Greg came in, it worked well. I always really try to make recording fun as well as getting it right. I used to take the piss and mark off the amount of times they got takes wrong on the desk."

"We were like rabbits in the headlights," admits Spawton. "It was the first time we had been in a 24-track recording studio, working with a professional recording engineer – somebody telling us how to get the best out of our instruments, suggesting we vary a certain part the second time through, asking Andy to apply more damping to his bass strings. All these useful little tips. He could see a mile off that we were wet behind the ears, but Rob always tries to lighten the mood. He knows recording can be stressful, so he keeps it light and jokey. He's good at reading who needs what to get the most from them. You begin to see the value of an outside set of ears."

"We were like kids in a toyshop," adds Poole. "The sound we accomplished doing *Far Distant Thing* was way better than anything we had ever achieved at home. Working with Rob was so easy, but it was also the acid test for our playing. He had played bass too and coached me, and we realised that there was a discipline to recording – once that red light is on, can you perform?"

Spawton got a bad case of the 'red light fever', physically shaking with nerves and adrenaline as it came to his turn to put his guitar parts down. The session really mattered to him. The band were developing quickly together, and to him their home demos weren't keeping up with their progress as a unit. "This was the first hint of light for me, the moment I realised that we could move this forward. In those days there was a big difference between recording at

home and in a professional studio environment – it was expensive and most bands didn't get the chance to do it. It increased your aspirations to do more."

Much to the band's delight, when Power FM finally aired *Far Distant Thing* a few weeks later, the DJ segued it with Kate Bush's *Wuthering Heights*. *The Infant Hercules* was released in January 1993 and sold a few hundred copies through mail order, generating some much needed band funds. In the March issue of *Feedback*, Kev Rowland was surprised by 'how much the band has grown in stature [...] They have developed further than could have been imagined.' He even ventured that 'Big Big Train are going to be a Big Big band.'

In the melodic rock fanzine *Boulevard*, writer Peter Sims liked the 'slow majestic *Lincoln Green*' and marked out *Dismounting Tigers* and *Show Of Strength* for attention. 'Simple melodies combined with skilful musicians and techniques are their hallmark. While they may lack the production values of some of their contemporaries, Big Big Train have a good deal more to offer in the long run. If they can get Rob Aubrey to produce their next album then the results should vindicate all the praise they have been getting.'

European publications had picked up on the band too. In Dutch fanzine *Background* writer Jan Schoenmakers commended the band's blend of prog (on *Kingmaker* and *Red Five*) and modern mainstream rock (*Dismounting Tigers*, *Show Of Strength*). Schoenmakers also compared them favourably to IQ, going as far as to say that 'Big Big Train are one of the most interesting new British prog rock bands.'

"Musically and quality wise *The Infant Hercules* was an improvement," thinks Ian Cooper. "For me the satisfaction came from recording at home and developing a song's detail and concept. That was the exciting element that rewarded me, not the live shows. We all had input, but Greg in particular would have a very strong view of how the arrangements should be. We got on extremely well but, in a nice way, we accepted Greg's ego into the band."

Early on, Cooper and Poole had nicknamed Spawton 'The Ego Monster', and Spawton would play along, sportingly roaring and beating his chest. "Greg's a large character," says Cooper, carefully. "He's six foot two and his personality's big too. You accept him for what he is and what he isn't. His passion runs very deep, so when he wants to do something you end up doing it. And, you know what? He's usually right. There were a few times over the years where you'd say, 'Greg the guitar's a fraction too loud'. And he'd say, 'Yes, but it has to cut through.' I'm fairly risk averse and I like harmony, both in the work place and my private life. If there's a compromise then I will go out of my way to achieve it. So, okay!"

Despite Cooper's 'oil on the waters' approach, he couldn't hide his growing frustration with gigging. After a long day at his engineering company, the last thing he wanted was to drive hundreds of miles in an uncomfortable van to perform to a sparse scattering of another band's fans. "My partner at the time had no interest in the music at all," he says, "and travelling up to Stoke-on-Trent to play for three people wasn't doing it for me. The stuff we did at home or locally – rehearsing at Holdenhurst Village Hall in the middle of a freezing winter and trying to play keyboards with gloves on – that was fun. The rest of it was becoming incompatible with my family life."

◆◆◆

In the glow of the Parklands session, thoughts turned to the first Big Big Train album proper. The band were keen to work with Rob Aubrey again, and £5,000 bought them a fortnight of the engineer's time and the studio slots needed to record and mix a full LP. Spawton spent six months writing what would become 1994's *Goodbye To The Age Of Steam*, during which time he began to feel the first inklings of his own unique voice as a songwriter. "I had drifted away from the It Bites influence and was beginning to find my own sound, my own chord vocabulary in particular. I don't have the musical language to explain it, but there were just particular patterns I found pleasing to the ear, and the recognisable Big Big Train sound was beginning to emerge. You can draw a line from a song like [*Age Of Steam*'s] *Expecting Snow* to the music we make today.

"I wrote most of the songs on classical guitar, then I'd dismantle them and allocate certain parts to the bass, the keyboards, the vocal. Anything before *Age Of Steam* was teenage frippery. *Edge Of The Known World* still has a bit of It Bites to it, but I was influenced by Steve Hackett – in his *Defector* and *Spectral Mornings* era – and I was listening to *Wish* by The Cure, so there's some jangly guitar stuff in there. It was a happy confluence of things."

And along with the more confident musical direction came a lyrical aesthetic, conveying the romance of the early industrial world. Spawton had been on holiday on the north coast of Cornwall and the landscape had made a major impression on him – the old tin mines along the coast, the engine houses studding the moors, the exhausted pits below the surface. "I was beginning to get interested in this contrast of mankind's infiltration of the landscape, and then his withdrawal from it, leaving something behind, something that seems noble and with a beauty of its own.

'Goodbye To The Age Of Steam' was a phrase I found in a book, and it sounded like a farewell to the Industrial Revolution. Of course, there are massive contradictions to that. Much of what happened during that era was appalling, and I feel deeply for those local communities damaged in the Thatcher years. But there remains a nostalgia for that sense of community, that pulling together which emerged from those times."

With Steve Hughes' drums recorded first at the nearby Denmead Community Centre, the band convened at Parklands Studio in July 1993. The two-week window to get the album done was ambitious. Rob Aubrey was determined to squeeze the most out of their studio time for them, and so the band ended up working long days, sometimes 20 hours straight. One morning, while driving from Bournemouth back up to Denmead for another session, an exhausted Spawton fell asleep at the wheel of his car, narrowly avoiding a serious crash at 60 miles per hour. To

Steve Hughes recording drums at
Denmead Community Centre, July 1993.

this day, when he finds himself on that stretch of road he gets twitchy.

Spawton played all the album's piano parts, using a Roland GR1 guitar synth. Ian Cooper considered himself a synth player, not a pianist, and didn't mind. "It's a rare breed – like Mr Wakeman – who can do both," Cooper believes. "You need more feeling than I could give it. That first proper recording session at Parklands was fun, but I wasn't particularly fussed about spending long nights in the studio. Again, that was beginning to impact on my family life."

Martin Read had long wrestled with Spawton's convoluted lyrics, struggling to articulate lines like *Downhilling*'s: '*Hidden behind the dust that you raise/Are abuses of power so silently countenanced*'. The singer's job was made tougher by the unconventional time signatures and vocal phrasing being thrown at him, and, as other parts of the Big Big Train sound were becoming refined in the studio, the singer's limitations were also becoming more apparent.

"Some of Greg's lyrics were quite a mouthful," says Read now. "He's very intelligent, with quite an imagination and lots to say. He would ask me to give my delivery a bit more oomph, and I just never seemed able to do it. My voice never really had the edge to it I would have liked. I've never really enjoyed listening to what I did on *Age Of Steam*, which is why I don't listen to it now, and haven't heard it for years."

Sometimes the rest of the band would go to the pub while Read slaved away in the booth for Aubrey, trying to nail certain lines. Andy Poole says that Read had a way of singing that suited him, "but I think we pushed him too much out of his comfort zone. Greg was writing melodies that were a bit too technical for him and were tripping him up. At Parklands Martin was cursing Greg because he couldn't nail some of the vocals."

In fairness to Read, Spawton now accepts some of the blame for this: "As an inexperienced songwriter I was writing all the words I thought needed to be said, rather than thinking about the melody or the song. Martin was left with mouthfuls of words at times that were hard to sing. But I remember those sessions were exciting. Rob was relatively new to it as well, and worked his arse off."

Poole says he clicked with Aubrey from day one. "He was of our type – similar age and background, very easy going and with similar humour. Rob would adapt his approach depending on who the client was, but with us he seemed very relaxed and natural. Rob wasn't really into prog, but I think he found it interesting and challenging as an engineer."

"What I liked about prog at that point," says Aubrey, "was that when you're involved in a song you really can get your teeth into it. It wasn't something that I would listen to, but something I would really like to work on. Working with Jadis and IQ and later Big Big Train was fun. We'd always try to push the boundaries, like going to school halls to record the drums to try to get big sounds. They would also work to any suggestions I had. I liked them as people."

For *Goodbye To The Age Of Steam* the band wanted to bring in some extra singers to add harmony and depth to the sound. Aubrey knew some session singers – Mandy Taylor, Sally French and Ken Bundy – and also offering their talents were Galahad's Stuart Nicholson and Jadis's Gary Chandler, who was handed the very last line of the record on grandiose closer, *Losing Your Way.*

Aubrey perceived that arranging backing vocals didn't come naturally to Spawton, so he invited IQ's Martin Orford to the studio to help out. Orford remembers it fondly. "They had asked me to work out harmony vocals, and said they would get me a whole range of vocalists. When I turned up there was a minibus full of them! I spent a couple of days devising vocal arrangements and then we recorded them, and I did a bit of singing myself. It was tremendous fun and it ended up quite a lush sounding album vocally."

"That was the value Rob was adding," adds Poole, "bringing in all these people. Martin [Orford] came in to be master of ceremonies, co-ordinating the whole thing, and between them they layered up all these vocals, and it was fantastic. It transformed the whole thing."

But Aubrey also had an ulterior motive for inviting Orford to Parklands. IQ had just founded their own record label, Giant Electric Pea, mainly to release their own independent album, *Ever.* Along with IQ themselves, GEP's roster included Jadis and rising prog metal band Threshold, and they were looking to expand. Aubrey suspected that, with his record executive hat on, Orford might be interested in releasing Big Big Train's record on the label.

Orford had found the band's earlier material a little too quirky for his taste, but did think they were promising. "They have a strange way of writing," he says. "The songs go off at funny tangents. I liked them with reservations in those early years. I always thought they would do something really interesting one day. As it turned out, they did it much later on."

When Orford heard and saw potential in the band at Parklands, he invited the band to his house in Bishop's Waltham, and over a few glasses of his formidably potent homebrewed beer, he pitched GEP to them as a label in the mould of Charisma, Tony Stratton-Smith's own famous prog imprint. It would be a good home for them.

However, GEP wasn't the only record label in the frame at this time. Music impresario Malcolm Parker ran a successful music mail order company, GFT, specialising in underground prog rock albums, and was launching his own label, Cyclops. Grey Lady Down, Credo and Hawkwind would all soon have releases on the label, and in '93 Parker expressed an interest in adding Big Big Train to his growing stable.

But it was GEP who won out. They offered Big Big Train a one album deal, with the label fulfilling the basic tasks of pressing, distributing and promoting *Goodbye To The Age Of Steam*. "This was quite a big thing for us," says Spawton. "We were big IQ fans, slightly in awe of them in fact. They had been through the whole thing – they'd signed a major record deal, lost it, then were doing things themselves. GEP was new and *Ever* was hot off the press. We'd read about Charisma and that 'family feeling' the label had, so when Martin offered us a deal we were on cloud nine. We felt like we'd arrived."

Big Big Train's debut album proper, *Goodbye To The Age Of Steam* was released on 31st May 1994. Comfortably superior in sound and material quality to their two previous demos, it

earned mainly positive reviews in the prog press, both in the UK and beyond. One French magazine, *Harmonie*, called it 'a record that demonstrates notable progress since their last opus', and praised 'the beauty of the melodies, the excellence of the guitar parts and the musical intelligence of the ensemble.' However, another Francophone magazine, *Musicmania*, was less convinced by their 'soft, unsurprising rock' with 'no strokes of genius to titillate the ear. [...] Sometimes they come close to excellence, but just a little something extra would permit Big Big Train to go to the next level.'

At home *Feedback* was kinder, with Kev Rowland opining that 'an album this good is crying out to be heard' and commending Martin Read's improved vocals. The eccentric, lovingly irreverent *Silhobbit* picked up on Read's performance too, and also complimented Andy Poole's 'thumping hot bass' and the drumwork of one 'Steve Huge'. With trademark playfulness they concluded: 'It's great to see this band develop, and develop like a Polaroid picture of your loved one.'

With the GEP deal came the band's first taste of real distribution. Big Big Train could feel the thrill of going into HMV, Virgin Megastore or Tower Records, finding their very own slot among the other B's and seeing their

Goodbye To The Age Of Steam.
Cover artwork by Kevin Thompson.

tangible album there – a genuine mark of credibility for any group at that time. Over the following year *Goodbye To The Age Of Steam* sold a respectable 2,500 copies, a significant shunt forward commercially for its makers.

"*Goodbye To The Age Of Steam* is actually one of my favourite albums full stop," says Ian Cooper. "I think it hangs together really well. There are themes throughout it, and it works as a whole piece, rather than individual songs. I love albums like that."

Andy Poole remains fond of it too. "It's one of those albums where, if you start it, you'll finish listening to it. The songs are connecting pieces and by the time you finish the fourth song [*Landfall*] you're involved in the whole album. We were using and re-using musical themes on there; there's an ambient section of pad chords, like a sorbet between prog songs to cleanse the palate a bit. At about 2am during recording we were listening to those pad chords on their own, and they had a great atmosphere. They were from the verse of *Wind Distorted Pioneers*, we put them at the beginning of *Blow The House Down* with some rain effects."

Call it an omen, but during the first print run the pages of the accompanying booklet were printed in the wrong order. Martin Orford spent a finger-shredding evening physically extracting and re-applying staples. Despite this laudably hands-on approach, Gregory Spawton soon saw flaws with the record deal itself. "GEP promised more than they delivered, as I'm sure all record labels do. We were sold on the Charisma side of things, but it soon became apparent to me that IQ were clearly the most important artist on the label. After all, the band members were the directors, which meant it was difficult for them to separate the interests of IQ from the interests of the label."

It rankled that, while Big Big Train had paid for the recording of the album themselves, their royalty rate was a minimal £1 per copy sold. "The whole deal didn't do much for us," says Spawton now. "They were very good hearted people, but it was a bit of a disappointing outcome from our perspective. I was calling them trying to hustle for gigs and for a second album, and it started to feel like they weren't returning our calls. We quickly began to tire of not being masters of our own destiny, which I think had an impact on us later. Then a licensing deal came in for Japan, and that changed their opinion of us almost overnight."

Based in Tokyo, the Marquee label contacted GEP and offered to license *Goodbye To The Age Of Steam* for the Japanese market. GEP pressed and freighted 500 copies, which were quickly snapped up. For a thrilling moment the band thought they were becoming big in Japan, and might even get to play there. "That did peanuts," Martin Orford states, soberly. "The royalty statements for that were nothing you would buy even a small round of drinks with."

Though the returns were low, this international interest helped convince GEP to give Big Big Train the go-ahead to begin work on another album. But not before the band's first line-up change. Ian Cooper had made no bones about his qualms around gigging, and the prospect of more driving – more disruption to his family life – meant he could compromise no more. "I used to be a bit grumpy," he says, "and they knew my feelings about playing live, so me quitting shouldn't have been a bombshell. I don't remember any significant or even vaguely serious arguments. Everyone was passionate about the music, everyone really cared about it and any debates we had were because of that. But it was becoming too time consuming, travelling was a pain in the arse, and for me the enjoyment factor was way down. It came to a head and I had to stop, for my sanity."

It was tough for Andy Poole to see his childhood pal and constant musical companion leave the band. When a tearful Cooper gave him the news, Poole was shocked, but could understand. And so could Gregory Spawton. "Ian was a little further on in his life," he says. "He was losing the will to live on those long journeys to Stoke and Walthamstow. He understandably didn't want to be a weekend rock 'n' roller, he wanted to get on and settle down."

The band had two shows scheduled – one local, one at The Royal Standard. They cancelled the first, but when they contacted the latter to let them know their predicament, they were told in no uncertain terms that if they didn't fulfil their commitment then they would never play the venue again. Spawton begged Cooper to honour this last show, as a favour, but he refused. "I was furious," Spawton says. "I could understand him leaving, but I was angry that he was leaving us in the lurch."

The four remaining members powered through the Walthamstow show as a quartet, with Poole gamely taking on the dual role of bassist and keyboard player. Despite the Dunkirk spirit, Spawton says the gig was dreadful. "We couldn't get off quick enough. Then we had that epic drive back home, and everything was miserable. It all ended with Ian on a very sour note, but looking back now he

was sensible and I was young and dumb. I've never had a problem with people being direct, and that's what he was. He wanted to have a family and that's what he went away and did."

In June 2020, Ian Cooper pulled his trusty Yamaha CS-15 synth down from his attic. Squeaky had been up there untouched for over two decades, along with other keyboards and a stash of Arcshine and Big Big Train cassettes. To Cooper's surprise, the synth still worked just fine. He's still in touch with good mate Steve Hughes and lifelong friend Andy Poole, and recently he spoke to Spawton about that very last Royal Standard gig. They found they could both laugh about it.

"I'm proud to have been a part of the Big Big Train story," Cooper says, "and pleased and proud that Greg stuck with it. He went on to achieve what he wanted to, and without his enthusiasm and drive that wouldn't have happened." Lately Cooper has even started composing new instrumental music, albeit on a newly purchased keyboard. "Sadly," he says, "Squeaky can't keep up with modern recording technology."

Back in 1994, the positive experience of *Goodbye To The Age Of Steam* galvanised that enthusiasm and drive for the four remaining Big Big Train boys. Clinging to the dream, they pinned another ad on Eddie Moors' heaving noticeboard.

III

'You still dreaming?
Your fingers burned from falling stars...'

Up to the moment he saw the 'Keyboardist Wanted' notice at Eddie Moors, Tony Müller's only brush with progressive rock had been the occasional, highly casual listen to Genesis. Living in Poole in Dorset, he had started playing piano aged 14 and focused on classical music, jazz and blues, passing his Grade 6 exams within just a few years. While studying for Grade 7 he discovered the joys of the pub, and the opposite sex. Combining these interests, he played in various groups in Bournemouth, providing the piano skank for a local reggae band, and channelling his inner Ian McLagan playing Faces covers with a pub rock outfit, Wild Turkey. By day he worked at a hospital, and Andy Poole took him to be "quite the ladies' man, working his way through the nurses!"

If he came across as a Jack The Lad, at the piano Müller was a gentleman – a naturally talented player with taste and tone beyond his 17 years. Despite his newly discovered distractions, for the Grade 7 exam he would be delving deep into jazz, and wanted to find a good band to join, to keep his chops up. Progressive rock hadn't featured in his life but, intrigued by Big Big Train's advert, he thought he'd give it a go, and dialled the number.

"Musically," he says, "and in terms of skill, Big Big Train's music was very in depth compared to what I was doing with the other groups, which was usually just three chords. Their music was like modern classical, in a way. Prog rock wasn't my thing at all, so it was quite a challenge practically, but I got into it. I loved *Wind Distorted Pioneers* [from *Goodbye To The Age Of Steam*] and some of the other early songs. Greg and Andy were really easy to get on with too. I liked to go down the pub with girls and enjoy myself and do the music as well. They were probably a bit more focused on the music, and less on the going out."

Despite being nearly twice his age and cut from a different dispositional cloth, Gregory Spawton was taken with Müller, and happy to have him join the ranks: "Tony was a younger guy, a very gifted pianist – decent looking, quite vain and very successful with girls. He was sweet but much more streetwise than we were. I was probably a bit pretentious and up myself – and bringing in personalities like Tony and Steve Hughes, who saw life a bit more lightly, helped the mood within the band. They were great guys to have around."

By 1995, Andy Poole's relationship with Jane had morphed from romance into friendship (they remain close), and he had found love with new girlfriend, Delphine Asprey. Between him and Spawton there was a nagging sense that adult life was starting to crowd out their youthful musical dreams. Ian Cooper was gone, and Spawton's own work responsibilities had become more onerous.

He had moved to New Forest Council and was now managing the 25 staff on the Homelessness Team. At home, things had taken a bittersweet turn. In '94 Joy had given birth to their first child, Ellie, with their second, John, born in '96. But over this time the Spawtons' marriage was unravelling, and they were heading for divorce. "That probably was a period when I should have done what Ian did and just focused on my career and family," Spawton says, "but I had something to say in music and a wish for the songs to be heard. Any success we've had is nine tenths stubbornness, or maybe an inability to recognise when we should stop."

Coming together quickly, *Goodbye To The Age Of Steam* was a consistent and focused record, but its follow-up had a long gestation period, and emerged as a more scattered, uneven affair. Eventually released in 1997, *English Boy Wonders* came together piecemeal over a period of two years, with the band's attentions divided and funds scarce. As and when Spawton or Andy Poole had a few hundred pounds to spare, they would book time at Parklands and work on the new material for a few days. Creatively they were in the thrall of newer influences alongside their classic prog roots. Chief among these were Prefab Sprout's complex, 19-track art pop album *Jordan: The Comeback*, and *The Bends*, the second, career-making LP from Radiohead. This latter was one band who – in the face of the more regressive Britpop scene prevalent at the time – was bringing forward-looking (some might even say progressive) rock music back to the masses.

Halfway through the recording of *English Boy Wonders* Parklands was taken over by an advertising company,

and Rob Aubrey found himself surplus to requirements. He needed another studio, and found one, in slightly less formal surroundings. The father of Jadis drummer Steve Christey lived in the remote Hampshire village of Nomansland, an hour's drive from Parklands. With no neighbours in sight, there were big, noisy parties at the house, and Mr Christey was very happy to let Aubrey use his garage as a makeshift studio.

Ironically, given the basic room, that's where the engineer made the move from two-inch tape to digital, linking three 8-track ADAT machines to create a 24-track digital studio. The first album recorded there was IQ's 1997 release *Subterranea*. Aubrey was the sound engineer for John Wetton on his 1998 European tour, and the accompanying live album went through post-production at Aubrey's new garage home. Released in '99, the record was even entitled *Nomansland*.

A year after the *English Boy Wonders* sessions at Parklands, this was where the second half of this album was recorded. This relocation, and the forgiving ease and capacity of the digital medium, added to the disjointed, kitchen-sink-'n'-all feel of this 75-minute album. "There are probably too many ideas on there," concedes Andy Poole. "If it had been recorded all in one block, I think we would have condensed things down and related tracks to each other. But we were doing them in isolation and then sticking them all together on an album – we lost that cohesiveness. It would probably have been better as a shorter, 45-minute album, focusing on the heavier pieces. We could have dropped things like *Brushed Aside*, which sounds a bit contrived and fiddly. *Pretty Mom* was about our friends having children and being pretty mums – literally. It was of its time."

❖❖❖

Early into the recording for *English Boy Wonders*, Big Big Train were offered their biggest gig to date. Chris Alexander, the promoter at The Astoria in London, called out of the blue to offer them a slot on a bill opening for Jadis and IQ. In what were wilderness days for all but the biggest prog rock bands, this was to be the second of Alexander's 'New Progressions' concerts, bringing together known and upcoming prog acts onto one stage. It's a trick he would repeat in the 2000s with his successful 'Progeny' events – prog weekenders hosting such genre stars as Fish, Carl Palmer, Arena, Mostly Autumn, Pallas and The Enid.

Today, Chris Alexander's candour is refreshing, if a little withering: "There was a plethora of fairly mediocre bands in that period, and having listened to their debut, Big Big Train fell firmly into that category for me, showing no inkling of what they were to become. However, the idea of 'New Progressions' was to try and light a fire under a dying genre, and putting three such bands on the same bill in central London seemed to attract a fair audience. The bands I thought would flourish – Jadis, Grey Lady Down –

have been far surpassed by their contemporaries. Good job I didn't work in A&R!"

The fire was to be lit at The Astoria on 2nd February 1996, and the 'fairly mediocre' Big Big Train would be first on. They were given a strictly limited slot of 25 minutes. One second over and, they were told, the plug would be pulled. Knowing full well that most of the audience would never have heard of them, the band elected to concentrate on the new *English Boy Wonders* material. They prepared a set timed down to the minute, opening with the fast and fiddly *Boxgrove Man*, then segueing carefully into the much more stately ten-minute piece, *The Shipping Forecast*.

Rehearsing for the Astoria show, January 1996.

With around 500 people attending, the Astoria show represented a big opportunity. On the night the band got a proper line check, the venue was winter cold but the staff were warmly welcoming and – best of all – in their shabby dressing room they had been given their very first rider, a case of Red Stripe lager all their own. Drummer Steve Hughes had got a boozy head start on the others. He had come into town on the train from his home in Hayes, west London, and had brightened his journey with a can or two of Stella Artois. "By the time I got there I felt a bit pissed," he recalls. "Not slurring my words or unable to do the gig – I'd just had a few."

When their stage time rolled around, Hughes was nowhere to be found. After a frantic search Andy Poole eventually spotted him. There were a few female prog fans in the club that day (that rare and treasured breed) and Hughes was happily chatting one of them up in the bar. Poole grabbed and all but frog-marched the drummer to the stage, where the rest of band were waiting, and raring to go with *Boxgrove Man*'s fast, funky intro. Hughes shambled to his stool, counted in *The Shipping Forecast*, and was away. Wrong song. Wrong tempo.

There's an unwritten rule in live music: whatever goes wrong on stage, you plough on – you never, ever stop. For a few bars there was confusion and panic, with the band bravely trying to adapt *Boxgrove Man* to *The Shipping Forecast*'s slower beat, but it all soon ground to a confused halt. In the Astoria's silence, they could hear laughter echoing up at them from the modest crowd. Spawton glared back at Hughes, hissed at him to concentrate, and they started again.

"I was embarrassed and furious at the time," says Spawton, "but looking back it's funny, and the show was pretty good after that. We played too fast and it was a bit of a rollercoaster, but we went down okay. I remember Andy hitting a low bass pedal note in *The Shipping Forecast* and the whole stage shook, which seemed really cool. We'd had our 25 minutes of fame, or so it seemed."

In good voice, Martin Read had a particularly good time. "That was probably the best show we did," he says. "My biggest complaint about the 10 years we spent together was that in the whole time we only did a dozen gigs. I never really got a chance to hone my performance because the gigs were so few and far between and I was usually scared witless when we did get on the stage. So I never really got comfortable."

Among the loyal progressive fraternity at the show was artist Jim Trainer, an avid fan of the band who had come down all the way from Newcastle to see them play. He was so shy that his wife had to drag him over to meet the band. Nevertheless, he, Poole and Spawton hit it off, and swapped contact details. *Feedback*'s Kev Rowland was there too, and in his generous review in that fanzine he said of their gig: 'After a shaky start, Big Big Train proved that in the concert setting they are as good musically as they are on CD […] What they are sadly lacking is live practice, as when the keyboard player needs sheet music and the vocalist looks out of place when not singing, then the rust shows, but these faults can easily be cured with more live work and I look forward to seeing them again.'

Neither Rowland nor the band themselves could have known that Big Big Train wouldn't be seen again in England's capital for nearly two decades. The next time they would be playing across town, a stone's throw from the lines of King's Cross Station, and in altogether grander circumstances.

◆◆◆

As 1996 progressed the band continued to whittle away at *English Boy Wonders*. Rob Aubrey was notably less enthusiastic about the album and still had misgivings about Martin Read's performance. "He really was a bit lazy," Aubrey claims. "On that album I was struggling to produce the vocals and, again, Martin Orford came in to help. Having another singer there really focused Martin [Read], and made him buck his ideas up a bit. He performed better."

If Read still struggled with some of Spawton's more ornate melody lines on *Boxgrove Man* and another 10-minute prog opus, *Albion Perfide*, the singer hinted at his potential on the short yet sweet acoustic piece *28 Years*, a song he wrote himself and presented to the band. Andy Poole still likes that one. "Martin sounds much more comfortable on *28 Years*," he says. "There were vocal parts he was given which he didn't have the freedom to play with, and that was becoming increasingly uncomfortable for him. He was then uncertain about how he fitted into the band."

"We were just drifting

along by that stage," reckons Read. "I brought a collection of songs to the guys initially, but the problem is I'd never finished any of them properly. I've always been a bit shy playing in front of people, but I was quite good once I got going. I'd listen to myself playing my own songs and I'd come to life more than when I was singing one of Greg's songs."

Tony Müller had joined the group halfway through the recording, and if he never felt fully comfortable with the Wakeman-esque multi-tasking required of a prog rock keyboardist, he brought in a valuable new pianistic element to the band's sound, something beyond Ian Cooper's synth-centric range. "There's a difference between a prog

The English Boy Wonders *line-up outside the studio in Nomansland, 1996.*

rock keyboard player and a pianist," muses Gregory Spawton. "The '70s keyboard players were pianists who played organ and Mellotron. Many of the '80s players, the neo prog ones, were just keyboardists, so there were more 'pad' sounds. They couldn't really play advanced piano arrangements. Tony was a proper pianist, and hearing him play on our music made a deep impression on me."

To record Müller's piano parts to the standard they deserved, Spawton and Poole splashed out £600 for three hours at RG Jones Studios in London, a high-end facility that had its own grand piano. "There was a lot of piano and keyboard work for me in the band," Müller remembers. "I always had the music in front of me because there was such a lot to compress. It was hard work because my sight reading isn't amazing, so it was a lot of practice." The odd time signatures of tunes like *A Giddy Thing* and *Two Poets Meet* were a challenge,

Counting in sevens – Tony Müller at RG Jones Studios, 1996.

and he would often have to count them out loud to keep the rhythm. "Because it was all mic'd up, all they could hear was me going, 'one-two-three-four-five-six-seven' – which meant I was spoiling the takes!"

Comprising 13 tracks in various styles, *English Boy Wonders* was eventually judged to be finished, and appeared on GEP in 1997. That year the label also released IQ's *Subterranea* and Threshold's *Extinct Instinct*. Elsewhere in the prog universe Dream Theater offered up *Falling Into Infinity*; Genesis carried on without Phil Collins with *Calling All Stations*, which featured Nick D'Virgilio, the highly capable drummer for US prog prospects Spock's Beard; and Radiohead upped the creative ante with *OK Computer*, a visionary, dystopian work that brought ever more experimental, multi-layered music to the attention of the younger, hipper, alt rock crowd.

As Thom Yorke's band earned plaudits everywhere from the *NME* to *The Times*, Big Big Train's new release garnered a few supportive, if mixed, notices in the prog press. Some reviewers were enthralled by *English Boy Wonders'* promiscuous mix of catchy rock (*Big Empty Skies, A Giddy Thing*), jangly pop (*Pretty Mom*) and ambitious pure prog (*Reaching For John Dowland, Albion Perfide, The Shipping Forecast*). Others were flummoxed by it.

"I think it was fairly reviewed," says Gregory Spawton. "It was a weird combination, there were odd songs next to each other – sometimes that works, but not here. Also the songs were under-arranged. I wrote the best stuff – *The Shipping Forecast, John Dowland, Fell Asleep* – very near the end. That's when I hit the sweet spot in songwriting. There were some musical parts that we added for the 2008 re-issue that should have been there originally. We didn't have enough money at the time, so Rob wasn't given enough time or budget for mixing – he did what he could. It was a damp squib of an album really. GEP promoted it, but they hated it."

Recording guitars for English Boy Wonders, *1996.*

Martin Orford recording flute for The Shipping Forecast, *1996.*

"*English Boy Wonders* is a great title," says Martin Orford, "but I never gelled with the album at all. There were lots of things on it that didn't feel quite finished to me. It needed a bit more work and filling out – perhaps fewer songs realised to a more expanded level."

As well as helping Rob Aubrey with the vocal production, Orford had added some extra keyboards and played flute on grand centrepiece *The Shipping Forecast*. But his initial interest was waning. "I drifted away from Big Big Train at that point. I liked the idea of the band and very much liked the people involved. I did my best for that album, but from a record company point of view you could tell it was falling on stony ground. To this day I don't often play it."

GEP deleted the album not long after release. To the label, the band's observers and Gregory Spawton himself, there was a nagging sense that Big Big Train weren't quite making good on their early promise, not quite finding their niche or really nailing their sound on record. They were beginning to run out of momentum. So when the phone rang and they were offered their very first European show, it was just the shot in the arm they needed. Or so they thought.

◆◆◆

As with the Astoria date, the offer to play The Netherlands came unexpectedly. Dutch band Flamborough Head had just launched ProgFarm. This small progressive rock festival was sited on drummer Koen Roozen's farm in Bakkeveen, a village in Frisia, near the Dutch/German border. Big Big Train would be one of five bands playing the festival's second year – Flamborough Head would headline a bill featuring Swedish group Twin Age, Slovakians No Name, and Dutchmen Sinister Street. Seduced by the exotic prospect of their debut European show, Big Big Train gratefully agreed to play, but Steve Hughes declined to go. He was way too busy.

Since his return to London, Hughes' career as a drummer had picked up considerably. He had joined The Enid in 1994 and played with them until '98, appearing on the albums *Tripping The Light Fantastic* and *Sundialer*. "That was a crazy time," Hughes says. "I did at least 100 gigs with The Enid, and I was in about five other bands too. I'd got a little frustrated that Big Big Train didn't do gigs – it was never really a 'band' as far as I was concerned, more a recording project."

Steve Hughes (top left) with The Enid.

Recruited to replace Hughes for the show, Peter Hibbit was a talented, enthusiastic and seasoned player who performed regularly around the Bournemouth area. He absorbed the band's complicated set well over just a few rehearsals, and in November 1998 he joined the band for their 500-mile drive to Bakkeveen. On the way, on a Belgian motorway, Poole recalls that "Tony was so desperate to pee that we made what was probably a highly illegal pit stop, the massive relief of which he declared as 'better than coming!' Greg scoffed about it, I remember."

Spawton would soon eat his words. Roozen's farm was remote and the area would have been idyllic in the warmer summer months. In the winter, however, Spawton found it "windswept and desolate, like something from a Scandi-noir series. The stage was built in one of the farm's barns, the organisers and the fans were lovely, but it was unbelievably cold and very 'Dutch' – there was a lot of wacky baccy."

"I thoroughly enjoyed that trip," enthuses Martin Read, "although I haven't got the greatest memory of our set. We kept having technical problems and I was scared shitless. There were quite a lot of heavy metal fans from Germany,

Pre-gig practice in the dorm at Bakkeveen, November 1998.

and I felt our songs weren't quite what they were looking for. But then I got nice feedback from various people that evening who said differently."

With a whole hour allotted to them the band had considerably more time than at the Astoria show, but their set was beset by gremlins. Spawton's guitar processor kept failing. Every time Hibbit struck his bass drum pedal drum too hard, the whole PA seemed to power down. Müller remembers playing *Blow The House Down* from *Goodbye To The Age Of Steam* and the sound disappearing completely. "It was a rubbish gig," he says, and jokes: "I think it was a conspiracy – they didn't like the English!"

All these problems threw off their performance and, slowly, the 150-strong crowd began to peel away and out of the barn. "It was horrible," says Spawton, grimacing at the memory. "I remember watching the audience dwindling to about half. But they were still enjoying it, I think, as we battled our way gamely through it. It was a happy moment for me to get off stage. What a horrendous experience."

Once they were off, the band bunked together in their glamorous festival accommodation – a spartan dormitory on the farm. Their sleeping bags were no contest for the bitterly cold Frisian weather, and they slept in their clothes in a vain attempt to preserve a degree of heat. "It was like 'BBT Does Spinal Tap, or Bad News'," says Poole. "After a freezing, sleep-deprived night, you dared not leave the modest relative comfort of your sleeping bag – layered on top with every other item of clothing – for a wee. But Greg eventually succumbed to an urgent early dawn dash to the latrine and returned declaring, "Tony was right – it *is* better than coming!'"

Such joys were in short supply for the band on this depressing weekend on a cold farm far from home in the

On stage at Bakkeveen, 7th November 1998.

middle of nowhere. The gig was ultimately a shot in the foot rather than the arm, and only compounded the growing disgruntlement within the ranks. Not only was Hughes' commitment to the band in grave doubt but Spawton – recently divorced and miserable himself – sensed that Read had begun to lose interest. And after the lacklustre *English Boy Wonders*, they had slid way down GEP's priorities list, if they hadn't fallen off it altogether. "I was a broken man coming back from ProgFarm," says Spawton, "physically, emotionally and mentally, thinking that I'd never play another gig again, and that the band was pretty much over."

Between them, he and Poole now concluded that the band had probably peaked, but they decided to have one last hurrah. They crafted some new songs and reheated some leftover material from the *English Boy Wonders* session until they had enough for one more album. *Bard* would be their swansong. Once it was done, they would decommission Big Big Train once and for all.

◆◆◆

"By *Bard* they were happily recording some of the stuff at home," says Rob Aubrey. "They didn't have a great deal of money and they weren't going to be on GEP for that third album, so I made what I thought was a tough decision. I told them not to come to me to record, but to invest the money in their own equipment and then maybe come to me to mix. And that's what they did, apart from recording the drums with me at Nomansland."

Instead of paying £5,000 for two weeks in the studio, Spawton and Poole bought some good microphones and their own copy of Pro Tools, the industry standard audio production software at the heart of most professional studios. They reasoned that, when everything was finally done and dusted, they could at least sell off the gear and recoup some cash.

They set all the gear up in Spawton's dining room, where the pair had regularly convened for what they still called 'band practice', but which was actually less about practice and more focused on writing and demo recording. Ian Cooper had been the real equipment boffin – programming the drum machine, managing the mixer – but now he was gone that role fell to Andy Poole, who was more tech-savvy and more patient in these matters than Gregory Spawton.

Poole embraced Pro Tools, and with Aubrey helping him get his head around the rudiments of the software he took to it very well. Spawton gave Poole a key to his house so he could come and go as he pleased, tinkering at their music on Pro Tools whenever he had a spare moment. Poole spent so much time in the Spawton dining room that Spawton's daughter Ellie thought he had moved in. She called it 'Andy's room'.

Once done, the demos for *Bard* were sent to the other members. Steve Hughes disliked what he heard so much that he refused to play on the album altogether. "I do really regret that to this day," he says now, "but when the demos came through I thought, 'Bloody hell, is this the best they've got?' The quality wasn't great, they sounded twee to me. But my mind was a bit scrambled. I didn't have a lot of time – I'd been playing so much music, doing sessions and depping in various bands, having so many late nights. I was young back then and wanted to make a break. I felt they were holding me back a bit I suppose. But looking back I don't know what came over me, because when *Bard* was released I absolutely loved it."

The band's line-up during this period was, at best, fluid. Spawton's old Equus bandmate Phil Hogg was drafted in to play drums, and – reassured that no gigging would be involved – Ian Cooper was back to add some synth. Spawton and Poole played most of the instruments, and they coaxed Tony Müller to step up to the microphone. "I don't consider myself a natural vocalist," says the pianist, "but Greg and Andy asked me to sing because they'd heard me do my own stuff. I wasn't totally comfortable – I listen back to some of it and think I didn't have a good voice. I thought Martin Read had a lovely voice."

In the album credits, Read was demoted to 'Additional

Vocalist' along with talented backing singer Jo Michaels. "Even Greg sang one on *Bard*," says Poole. "There was real uncertainty around the vocals, and *Bard* became… unusual."

With overwhelmingly minor key, mid-tempo music and frequently melancholy lyrical themes, this 'unusual' album was largely borne of Spawton's bleak personal life. All too aware of the effect of marriage breakdown on children, he was fighting to get custody of his own for half the week, not just weekends. Sung by Jo Michaels, *Broken English* was a break-up story from the female perspective. The achingly sad *This Is Where We Came In* reflected Spawton's own dislocation ('*Come and see us any time you want/How does it feel to be moving out of the real?*'). On *A Short Visit To Earth* his own tentative, whispered vocal added fragile poignancy to lines like: '*When did the colours start to fade?/The kids are young/And we are old/I loved you*'.

It was a far cry from the Big Big Train that would come down the track a few years later, but there were also flickers of the historical angle that would inform some of their best future material. *Broken English* referred to the polymath astronomer Ptolemy; *The Last English King, Harold Rex Interfectus Est* and *Malfosse* drew on King Harold, the Battle Of Hastings and the brutal melée that raged after it.

As usual, Rob Aubrey was also sent the demos for the songs so he could see where they were headed, and he was with Steve Hughes. "I think I turned round and just said, 'This is a pile of crap!' And Greg went and wrote some more. I never listen to lyrics though, so I don't know what it was all about. My mind drifts because I'm too involved with the music and hearing production things, rather than following the lyrical avenues."

For all the flaws in the album, Spawton and Poole were pleased with the technical achievements they'd made in the dining room, in 'Andy's room'. The music *sounded* good. *Bard* eventually surfaced in 2002, five whole years after *English Boy Wonders*. The GEP deal was a distant memory and other record label interest was non-existent, so the pair created their own homespun label, Treefrog, on which to release *Bard*.

While progressive rock was still perceived as an under the counter genre, there was still a spark at its heart. That year saw albums that would later be lauded in prog circles, like *Snow* by Spock's Beard and *In Absentia* by Porcupine Tree, but *Bard* wasn't destined to be one of them. In the press release Spawton and Poole described it – with cheeky semantic accuracy – as their 'definitive' album. The aptly titled closing track *A Long Finish* faded out slowly with strummed acoustics and Hackett-like guitar swells. It could well have been Big Big Train's final, mournful whistle.

But as it turned out, Classic Rock Society founder Martin Hudson rather liked the album. In his critique for their *Rock Society* magazine he bemoaned the band's lack of live work and had a dig at Martin Read's previous vocal performances, but he once again sang the praises of Spawton's agile guitar playing, and enjoyed this new, 'come one, come all' vocal approach. '[*Bard*] isn't going to change the world,' Hudson concluded, 'but it is pleasant, melodic and has a selection of songs to please the socks off any 21st century neo prog fan!'

Another generous review sticks in Andy Poole's mind, which posited that the album was 'pleasant listening for a Sunday morning'. (Presumably neither this critic nor Hudson had scanned the lyrics too closely.) "We were actually fairly proud of *Bard* at the time," Poole says, "but we weren't objective enough about what we were doing.

Again it was probably too long and with too many ideas, there was an edge to it but a lot of it was very laid back. I don't think we were especially excited by it."

"I hate *Bard*," says Spawton flatly. "But I've only disowned it subsequently, because at the time I thought it was great. Mostly though it's a terrible plod, and shows inexperience in recording. It's wallpaper music, nothingy, and I feel nothing about it."

In the early '90s the band used to produce their own newsletter, enigmatically titled *Ventilator Four* (the name's significance now lost to time). This was dutifully posted to previous mail order customers to inform them of news, upcoming releases and ever rarer live dates. Over time their mailing list had accrued to over 500 names, and they let this core fanbase know that their new, 'definitive' album was now available. With no distribution, it was once again down to the two of them to get the CDs produced and mailed out.

They kept flyering outside concert venues, putting leaflets in people's hands as they left other bands' shows, tucking them under windscreen wipers in the car park. Big Big Train's friend, fan and 'contact in the north', artist Jim Trainer would do the same thing for them around Newcastle. But they also went one better, handing out free CD samplers of their music – burned on their own home computers – hoping to attract some new listeners/customers.

They did this to push *Bard* in 2003, hanging outside shows by bands such as Galahad, handing out a free disc called *The Last English King*. Along with that *Bard* track, the disc included *The Shipping Forecast* from *English Boy Wonders*, *Blue, Silver, Red* from *Goodbye To The Age Of Steam* and an unreleased demo, called *Powder Monkey*. In another vote of confidence for Big Big Train, *Rock Society*

reviewed this sampler in its own right. Writer Steve Ward called it 'brilliant' and highlighted *Powder Monkey* as 'a taster for the band's new album set for September release, and on this evidence it promises to be an album well worth investigating.'

That was yet to come, but in its release year *Bard* did little to further the band's creative cause, and marked a downturn commercially too. *Goodbye To The Age Of Steam* had sold over 2,500 units, *English Boy Wonders* achieved about half that, but only 300 copies of *Bard* were sold of its original 1,000 disc run. (The remaining units quickly sold out years later when the band's fortunes changed.) As those sales petered out, now – surely – was the moment to call time on the band?

Clearly not. "Those 300 copies told us that there was still an audience," says Spawton. "We could pay off the Pro Tools kit, and the reviews weren't great but they were okay. We knew we'd never make a living at this, but Andy and I decided to carry on. Don't ask me why – I suppose it's partly because it's what we'd always done for our entire adult lives."

Another reason for optimism was that Spawton's personal life was looking much brighter. His divorce was behind him, he had bought his now ex-wife out of the family home, and he was sharing custody of his children Ellie and John. And with his new partner, Kathy, he felt he had finally found his soulmate.

And in this state of new found domestic bliss, Spawton was also rekindling his affections for the shimmering sound of his Takamine 12-string acoustic guitar. He had written the band's recent material on electric guitar and keyboards, but of late he'd been sitting down with his 12-string and revelling in its familiar, consoling sound. It was one evocative of earlier, more hopeful days, a portal to the soundworld of Anthony Phillips and Mike Rutherford, of Genesis's *A Trick Of The Tail* and *Wind & Wuthering*. For the first time in a long time, he found himself actually enjoying the writing process: "It really was like going back to my first love. I suddenly remembered a musical world in writing terms where I felt more comfortable. It's where my work sits best and, rather than fight against the tide, I decided to go with it."

"As I recall," says Poole, "soon after *Bard* Greg had plenty of new song ideas that we felt were especially strong." Having brushed up on his bass playing for the albums and the handful of Big Big Train live shows, Poole was focusing increasingly on the recording side. He had a facility for the new generation of sophisticated recording software and tech, and was drawn more and more to the other side of the studio glass/dining room table.

Other changes were afoot too. Things had run their natural course for Tony Müller. He had been living in London since 1999, and was training to be a paramedic. With no fuss, fanfare or big goodbye, he amicably drifted out of the Big Big Train line-up. These days he still plays piano and makes music for his own pleasure, and says he 'looks back fondly' on his brief brush with prog.

Having been sidelined on *Bard*, Martin Read's time with the band had also come to an end. "I'd enjoyed myself for 10 years," he says, "and couldn't see any reason why we wouldn't continue. I thought there was still potential there, and Greg and Andy still wanted to plug away recording. I think they felt they'd had their time with me and wanted to search out someone else. Fair's fair – it was Greg's band and he was the brains behind it all. But I just turned up at a practice one day, and then we went our separate ways."

Read subsequently went into the pub trade and by 2017 was running his own place, The George Inn in Portland, Dorset. At the twice monthly jam night, he has been known to uncase his acoustic guitar and treat the regulars to a few tunes. The way he disembarked from Big Big Train did leave a bitter taste for a while, and he hasn't kept up with them much since. "I was a bit peed off with it at the time," he says. "Obviously I could see that they carried on, but I wasn't really interested to be honest. But I must have helped them get on the road to a certain extent, and that's good enough for me."

And so once again Big Big Train was boiled down to just Poole and Spawton. Both agreed that, if they were going to keep going, they needed to be at least perceived as a fully fledged group. The pair could handle the writing, most of the instruments and the engineering/production. Aubrey's mixing expertise was still at their disposal and, despite his *Bard*/ProgFarm wobble, Steve Hughes was still an ally who could be called upon to play drums. But if Big Big Train were going to gather any speed at all in this new, 21st century, they were going to need a new singer.

IV

'He is patient,

in reach of a phrase,

and the end of all time...'

SEAN FILKINS' VINYL COLLECTION reflected his good, catholic taste in music. Steve Hillage and Hawkwind leaned against Holst and Hendrix; Tangerine Dream, Klaus Schulze and Ulrich Schnauss nestled next to Stravinsky and Vaughan Williams. And in pride of place, amid all the prog, rock, kosmische and classical, were the playworn discs of his beloved Yes.

Born in Rochester, Kent in 1962, the singer had always adored those progressive pioneers. Back in the '80s he took to the folk circuit with his acoustic duo Broken Gun, and they'd often throw in *Survival* from *The Yes Album*, along with *God If I Saw Her Now* by ex-Genesis man Anthony Phillips. These were refreshing choices for an audience more used to endless re-treads of hoary staples like Fairport Convention's *Meet On The Ledge*. "We used to do a lot of harmony-based music," Filkins says. "I've always loved harmonies, ever since I was a kid in school and we'd sing in rounds. Mum and Dad were into Simon & Garfunkel and The Hollies. Playing folk clubs is really intimate, you have to get it right – those were the hardest audiences I've ever played to. It was a very good grounding for what I did later on."

Sean Filkins (right) with Mark Williams in Broken Gun, 1985.

44

In the '90s he fronted Hounslow-based rock band Vigilante, and then Soma, a space rock band with whom he could indulge his love for Hawkwind-style space rock. He also fronted neo proggers Lorien, who made a minor splash in 1994 with *Children's Games* – an album that owed much to Marillion and Genesis – and he played the decade out with Lazy Jane, his duo with Lorien's guitarist Darren Newitt. Marillion covers were their speciality – sometimes they'd perform 15 tracks by the band in a night. "I did like some Genesis too," says Filkins, "but I was never a massive Peter Gabriel fan. My favourite three Genesis albums are

from the Phil Collins era – *A Trick Of The Tail, Wind & Wuthering, ...And Then There Were Three...*"

By the early 2000s he had settled in Gosport. By day he worked as an aero engine technician, but, by night, he still liked to rock. In pubs and clubs across the area he channelled his inner David Coverdale as the frontman for Whitefake, quite possibly Hampshire's premier Whitesnake tribute act of that time. He also played with his prog covers band The Indigo Pilots, whose set included Marillion's *Hooks In You,* Pink Floyd's *Comfortably Numb*, and Dylan's *Like A Rolling Stone* – the latter performed in the style of Yes, of course.

Big Big Train popped up on Filkins' radar in 2003 via a 'musicians wanted' website, where the band had posted that they were looking for a vocalist. Filkins was just one respondent. Gregory Spawton recalls that John Mitchell – the guitarist for Arena and Frost* and future founder of successful solo project Lonely Robot – applied too, with a recording of himself singing Peter Gabriel's *Red Rain*. (Though Mitchell didn't wind up in Big Big Train, he would go on to get the gig replacing Spawton's erstwhile hero Francis Dunnery as the singer/guitarist for It Bites.) When Filkins replied to express his interest in the job, he attached some songs recorded with Lorien, and his voice really caught Spawton and Andy Poole's ear. They invited him to audition, sending him some of the material and an outline of the concept behind Big Big Train's new 'comeback' album.

While rediscovering his love for the 12-string guitar, Spawton had visited London's Imperial War Museum, which was holding an exhibition focused on World War II. Among the pieces there was a photograph of a woman bidding a tearful farewell to a serviceman, and beneath

Soma in Berlin, 1993.

it a line that had stuck with Spawton ever since: 'In every goodbye there is a scene of death.' "And that really haunted me," he says. "War intensifies every emotion – everything is felt more deeply, including both love and fear. In fact, that quote was the working title for the album."

The planned record was geared around the Battle Of Britain in 1940, themed on the life and death of a Spitfire pilot involved in the combat. This concept really hit home for the incoming Sean Filkins. His grandfather had been in the Royal Air Force in 1918 and had gone on to fight in the Battle Of Britain, and Filkins' father was RAF too. Just before his audition the singer went on holiday to Norfolk and played the material he'd been given on constant loop in preparation. "I must have bored my wife and daughter shitless playing those songs over and over! I went to Greg's house for the audition and sang those songs as if it was the last thing I was ever going to do."

Even though Filkins was suffering with bronchitis on that day, Poole remembers that "Sean had a good, strong voice and a clear love of prog. He also got really immersed and invested in the whole album, which helped. Previously we'd had vocalists who were singing the words but weren't living the part, but Sean really got into it."

Poole's ear for engineering and production was developing considerably. Spawton was the chief songwriter but Poole had his own good instincts, including a valuable nose for excessive pretension. When his bandmate suggested they call the final album itself *In Every Goodbye There Is A Scene Of Death*, Poole vetoed the idea straight away, shutting it down for being way too pompous, not to mention fatally uncommercial. Poole suggested instead that they borrow the title of the album's last song. *Gathering Speed* worked much better, he felt, as it represented Big Big Train's sense of revival, of things picking up again after the low point of *Bard*.

Looking back, it was partly small tweaks like these that made the pairing of Spawton and Poole work so well for as long as it did. They had known each other for over 15 years at this point, and their friendship and unity of purpose remained strong. "Andy and I were good friends and a good partnership for a long time," reflects Spawton. "He kept me on a level, and chipped away at some of my pretentiousness."

That meaningful quote did still make it onto the album, in the lyrics of opening track *High Tide, Last Stand*. The song opens with the highly evocative sound of a Spitfire soaring overhead, an idea that came from Filkins who, as Poole says, bought into the record whole-heartedly. He would make the hour's drive from Gosport to Bournemouth to Spawton's house on Sundays to listen to demos, lay down tracks, and discuss details and embellishments.

"I added my ten pence worth and tried to make my mark," Filkins says. "I think Greg and Andy were happy because they gave me a writing credit on some of the songs. It was great that they were open to my ideas with the harmonies with [talented additional vocalist] Laura Murch, and all the sound effects – the Spitfires, the man breathing through the oxygen mask [on *Pell Mell*]. I thought those things would help tell the story. On [penultimate song] *Powder Monkey* there's a clock that strikes seven for the album's seven songs, then the ticking stops, and that's the pilot gone, and *Gathering Speed* comes in. That clock was given to my grandad when he left the RAF and I've still got it – it still chimes every hour and half hour."

Bronchitis notwithstanding, Filkins' audition take for *Powder Monkey* was so good that Poole used much of it on the final track as he assembled the album. Like *English Boy Wonders* and *Bard*, once again this happened at BBT HQ – Spawton's dining room (in promotion they called it 'The Garden Room' so the enterprise didn't feel quite so homespun). Unlike its two predecessors, however, this record was well conceived, tightly composed, and came together smoothly and easily.

Gathering Speed was a world away from the bitty, world-weary *Bard*. Poole's engineering smarts were improving. Spawton had reconnected with his musical roots and come up with a strong, cohesive collection of songs with a compelling theme. Sean Filkins introduced a welcome injection of enthusiasm and some long overdue vocal prowess. He also brought that cinematic dimension to the sound and a good ear for vocal arrangement, working well with Laura Murch to add extra layers. Ian Cooper was back again to add keys, and Steve Hughes was in the fold too, making the trip to Southampton to lay down the drums at Rob Aubrey's own, brand new recording facility.

Finally, Rob Aubrey was out of Nomansland, and had

The Gathering Speed *line-up, 2004.*

opened Aubitt Recording Studios. With the help of his planning consultant – Jadis's John Jowitt – he opened Aubitt at the bottom of his long garden in 2002. This modest but highly efficient, bungalow sized recording space would become a great success for the engineer, and would be a hugely significant space for Big Big Train from here on in.

Andy Poole remains rightly proud of *Gathering Speed*. "*Fighter Command* still holds up really well," he says. "It's a good, solid chunk of prog, with a Marillion singalong section towards the end. We were getting more into Radiohead and you can hear echoes of *Planet Telex* from *The Bends* on *High Tide, Last Stand*. There's some real passion in it as well. Being a concept album it had a direction and energy – it works as an album. Having Steve back on board felt right and Sean fitted in well."

"The album was close to Andy's heart," thinks Spawton. "It really was just for the love of the music. To me *Gathering Speed*'s not an earth-shaking album, but looking back some of the writing is quite nice and it sounds okay. It was just Andy and me loving recording my songs, and getting them out to people."

Released on their Treefrog label in 2004, *Gathering Speed* got out to those people through the usual channels, and some new ones too. By then the band had their own website, www.bigbigtrain.com, designed by Robert Zimmer, a German fan who contacted the band directly to offer his services as webmaster. Also they had a page on MySpace, the era's hot new social networking site that allowed artists and fans to connect easily online.

Sean Filkins really believed in the album, and set about promoting it with enthusiasm to radio stations, magazines, the prog friendly corners of the worldwide web – anyone who would listen, really. "I spent literally hours," he says, "speaking to people all across the world online, on MySpace, drumming up support. I'd speak to DJs in the US, Holland, and made a lot of friends in the process. I did a lot of work behind the scenes to push the album.

"Greg and Andy came up with the idea of a promotion where we gave out flyers all about us, with snippets of reviews, what the album was about. If people were interested they could send us their details, we would post them the album on CD, and if they liked it they could give us the money. I remember standing outside Brixton Academy at a Hawkwind gig in the pouring rain, and at the Southampton Guildhall, and especially Wembley Arena, before a Yes show. Me and a good friend were handing out hundreds of these flyers to people outside the arena and I was nearly arrested – they thought I was selling underground tickets and merchandise!"

And when designing the flyers there were plenty of good review quotes to choose from. European prog digest *Acid Dragon* heard some Camel amid the album's 'excellent melodies and arrangements. […] This 'second-rate' band from the UK can now be compared to the most talented outfits such as IQ or Pendragon. This concept album is a must undoubtedly, the big big train is gathering speed for our pleasure.'

In his review for *Exposé* magazine, Paul Hightower also recommended *Gathering Speed* to fans of IQ, and spotted the mid-70s Genesis influence, 'particularly in Gregory Spewton's [sic] 12-string guitar playing that has Mike Rutherford and Ant Phillips written all over it. […] New singer Sean Filkins fits well into the tableau, lending an ethereal and wistful tone to the vocals and overall the collection gels nicely.'

French prog magazine *Koid9* also highlighted the vocals on this 'rich, rather melancholy work full of sonic ambience and atmospheres', praising Laura Murch's 'sensual' contribution and comparing Filkins' tone to that of Steve Hogarth on *Afraid Of Sunlight* (which, as it happened, was and remains Spawton's favourite Marillion album). The British angle also appealed to the French reviewer, who rather poetically concluded that the album was 'as bright as a sunrise after three weeks of drizzle over the English moors'.

Selling over 3,000 copies in its first year of release, *Gathering Speed* became Big Big Train's most successful record so far. Spawton and Poole felt reinvigorated. With their creative juices flowing and a new sense of purpose, they proceeded straight on to the next album.

However, experienced performer Filkins couldn't quite get his head around the pair's reluctance to play live. His previous bands had actively sought to gig when they had an album to push, but not these guys. "I got us a chance to play a rock festival in Cheltenham," he remembers. "They really wanted us, we would've got £1,000, and more importantly it would've been great promotion for us. I was 100 per cent up for it and thought we were capable of doing it, Steve wanted to do it because he'd played live a lot as well, but Greg and Andy simply didn't want to. I was disappointed at the time, but I didn't throw my toys out of the pram. I was told that 'we don't play live', and that was that."

◆◆◆

Coming a whole three years after *Gathering Speed*, Big Big Train's fifth album would prove to be a real curio in their catalogue. Andy Poole's growing skill and boldness with music software, and his investment in an array of plug-ins (digital instruments and effects) meant that the band could experiment more freely with sound textures and developments such as digital amplifier simulation. They could crank up a virtual Marshall stack within Pro Tools, and Spawton's neighbours wouldn't hear a thing.

In this, Big Big Train were chiming with the times. The 2000s was a ripe era for bands bringing more left field musical approaches out of the margins and into the mainstream. Radiohead were still leading the charge. Off the back of their game-changing *OK Computer*, they topped the album charts across the world early in the decade with *Kid A* and *Amnesiac* – oblique, avant-garde and seemingly uncommercial records that appealed to a new generation of listeners, those with an open mind and an appetite for more complex, thoughtful – again, progressive – music. Spawton and Poole loved them.

Another favourite was The Mars Volta, a smart, gutsy Texan group adding layers of new tech to their fresh, punky and deceptively complicated rock. Spawton and Poole witnessed one of their high intensity shows at The Wedgewood Rooms in Portsmouth as the band toured their stunning debut LP, *De-Loused In The Comatorium*. "That was unbelievable for us," says Spawton. "We thought it would be the prog crowd, but it was full of students. Andy and I were the oldest people there by a mile."

Poole remembers emerging from that show completely inspired. "They had a magic way of taking an idea and then turning it on its head and doing weird things to it. That was feeding into my consciousness about how to approach things differently. So on the next record we were reaching for traditional prog stuff but also The Mars Volta and Radiohead. And The Cure again, Crowded House, Del Amitri and Counting Crows."

For a while now, the term 'The Difference Machine' had been rolling around in Spawton's head. "It was this mysterious, ethereal phrase," he says, "and I just loved it. I'd already had an idea for the fifth record. When Kathy's mum Gwen died, I watched the dynamic between Kathy and her sister – two daughters processing the loss of their mum. As they talked there would be tears, but also smiles and laughter as they went through their memories. Gwen was a gentle soul, and there were hundreds of people at her funeral – I realised then that she had a significant impact on a lot of lives. It was profoundly moving. 'The Difference Machine' became a metaphor for such a person. The vague concept is like the butterfly effect, where somebody dies and the ripples they caused in other lives go out further and further, into the galaxy, so that 100 million light years away, they cause a star to die. The song *Summer's Lease* was specifically about that. 'The Difference Machine' is the person who makes a real difference in your life."

By the time Big Big Train came to record *The Difference Machine*, Andy Poole had all but stopped playing bass. Spawton happily took up the slack, getting to grips with Poole's beautiful Rickenbacker bass, and gladly adopting it as his own. At that Mars Volta gig Poole had been particularly intrigued by the band's creative use of the Korg Kaoss Pad, a modish and useful gadget with which – at the move of a finger – sound samples could be treated and modified in real time with equalisation, echo, distortion and other effects. Muse and Radiohead had also used the Kaoss Pad on their own innovative recordings, and Poole now applied it to sections of Big Big Train's own work.

"Andy had some great ideas using what they had," says Rob Aubrey, who admired how Poole had taken on the mantle of engineer, producer and sound designer. "He had an ear for it. They were creative with the instruments given to them. With the Kaoss Pad Andy would manipulate sounds and add sound effects. I don't get involved in that, even now, because you can fall down a rabbit hole and work for hours on something that doesn't end up on the final album. I usually just engineer what they give me."

With their mutual lack of enthusiasm for gigs, Spawton and Poole began to warm to the idea of Big Big Train as an act in the vein of Steely Dan – a musical collective with the two of them in the Fagen/Becker roles. They would be the creative nucleus and a rolling cast of top musicians would revolve around them, performing their songs to the highest standard possible. Also, getting some prog famous guests aboard might pique the interest of existing fans of the genre and draw in some new listeners. In the absence of live shows, they would have to be enterprising to grow their audience. They would have to speculate to accumulate.

Aubrey had been the sound engineer for Spock's Beard on their 1998 European tour, and their bassist Dave Meros was recruited to supply the bass part on the album's 14-minute prog opus *Perfect Cosmic Storm*. For another long, ambitious piece, *Pick Up If You're There*, the band hired Marillion's hugely talented bass player, Pete Trewavas. Whereas Meros recorded his part remotely, Trewavas came to Aubitt with his Rickenbacker double neck, and Spawton watched and learned. "Pete was great to work with," he says. "He was at Aubitt for a day and wrote and recorded the parts on the spot. We weren't used to that ethic really. He's also a genuinely lovely guy, very down to earth. We hoped to get a bit of additional promotional push from

Pete Trewavas recording Pick Up If You're There *at Aubitt Studios, 2006.*

the guest artists. As it was, I don't think we particularly benefitted commercially."

Much of the album's final texture was down to the sublime sounds of Southampton saxophone/flute player Tony Wright. He had appeared on IQ's albums *Subterranea* and *The Seventh House*, and Big Big Train asked him to channel Van der Graaf Generator's own saxophonist, David Jackson. A friend of a friend, Rebecca King added some viola parts across the record. Spawton heard great potential in these real strings, and filed this away as something to explore further later on. But there was one new contributor to *The Difference Machine* who would make a particularly indelible impression on Big Big Train's sound, and their future.

Nick D'Virgilio had been Spock's Beard's drummer since they formed in 1992, and a decade later had also replaced Neal Morse as lead singer. A lifelong session and touring musician, D'Virgilio was born in Whittier, California on 12th November 1968. He got his first drum kit aged just six but didn't take his first proper lesson until he was 18. He was a student at the Dick Grove School Of Music where his teacher was Dave Garibaldi, the hugely respected and technically replete drummer for leading funk band Tower Of Power. D'Virgilio never looked back after that, having grown up absorbing the best stuff there was – The Beatles, Led Zeppelin, Genesis, Bill Bruford, Marvin Gaye, Prince. He began to make his own name as a highly adept player, gigging with his covers band The Neighborhood and other working groups across the Los Angeles area.

Along with Spock's Beard, D'Virgilio's impressive and eclectic CV would go on to feature Zappa acolyte Mike Keneally, Fates Warning, Dream Theater's keyboard master

NDV in 1973 about to sing at his father's business meeting.

NDV at an early drumming gig.

Jordan Rudess, Frost* and Canadian band Mystery. In 1994 he befriended cult musician Kevin Gilbert, who invited him to join him for the ProgFest event in LA. The band – which also included noted prog keyboardist Dave Kerzner – performed Genesis's *The Lamb Lies Down On Broadway* in its entirety, with Gilbert the Peter Gabriel figure, D'Virgilio his Phil Collins-style counterpart.

From there D'Virgilio joined Gilbert's band Thud, and then his other jam-based group, Kaviar. This also featured fellow elite drummer Brian MacLeod, who had just played on Tears For Fears' 1995 album *Raoul And The Kings Of Spain*. MacLeod declined the chance to go on the accompanying world tour the following year, but recommended D'Virgilio for the gig to Tears For Fears linchpin Roland Orzabal. D'Virgilio won the slot, and finally got his break into the big league.

NDV with Tears For Fears, 1996.

In '96 it was Gilbert who also encouraged him to contact Genesis. After all, Phil Collins had left the group, so as well as needing a new vocalist, they'd need a new drummer too. D'Virgilio sent a copy of Spock's Beard's album *The Light* to the Genesis office, which found its way to their engineer/co-producer, Nick Davis. "I remember hearing him and thinking he was really good," Davis says now. "He came along to a drum audition and we liked him and used him. He didn't mention the fact he could sing or play anything else. We

were still looking for singers, so that would have been an interesting thing. Nick is an amazing musician as well."

So D'Virgilio contributed drums to the band's 1997 album, *Calling All Stations*. He shared those duties with fellow sticksman Nir Zidkyahu, and, unfortunately for D'Virgilio, it was the latter whom Mike Rutherford and Tony Banks chose to take on the accompanying world tour, with new singer Ray Wilson fronting the band. (This period in Genesis's career would intersect with Big Big Train's own in another way too, of which more later.)

"We really liked Nick's drumming," says Tony Banks now. "He's a very tasteful drummer. But we also had Nir, who's more of an attacking drummer, which was kind of what we needed and was actually very good for the group [live]. The songs Nick played on on the album were the slightly more tasteful ones, and I think he had a really nice feel."

Maybe it was fate that D'Virgilio hadn't let on he was also a singer. It was only later, when he sent Banks recordings including his take on *The Lamb Lies Down On Broadway*, that it dawned on the star keyboardist that they might have missed a trick: "I only realised then that Nick had such a good voice. If he'd told us, he wouldn't necessarily have been our lead singer, but he would have been an incredibly useful second singer. He would probably have been slightly more comfortable with some of the things Phil sang than Ray was. It would have been quite an interesting combination."

Sadly, Kevin Gilbert – who'd been instrumental in these two huge opportunities for the drummer – died young two years later, aged just 29. D'Virgilio – a multi-instrumentalist and composer in his own right – joined with name producer John Cuniberti to complete Gilbert's second, unfinished solo LP, *The Shaming Of The True*, which was released in 2000.

◆◆◆

Rob Aubrey first met D'Virgilio and Dave Meros while engineering the sound on that '98 Spock's Beard tour, and they had become good friends. The drummer's supreme talent and professionalism had made a huge impact on Aubrey. "On that tour their first show was at the Blue Note in Göttingen, Germany," he says, "and they blew me away. Nick had come off a tour with Tears For Fears and I thought, 'Now this drummer really knows what he's doing'. He was singing and was turning his own mic on and off as needed, which was really helpful to me as the engineer. Later at Aubitt I'd set up sessions so that Nick could come over at the start or end of a Spock's tour or drum clinic, whatever he was doing, and earn pretty good money. Sometimes he would land in the UK from the States and within two hours he'd be in the studio playing drums."

Through this arrangement D'Virgilio supplied world-class drums and percussion to a raft of albums by artists including Steve Thorne, IQ's own Martin Orford, and Lynden Williams and his rock band Jerusalem. Aubrey liked Steve Hughes' drumwork, but instinctively felt that D'Virgilio would be able to take Big Big Train's music on to a new level. "Steve was brilliant in his day," says Aubrey,

NDV with Spock's Beard at The Astoria, London, 2001.

"but I always suspected he didn't know what was coming next in the song, and probably quite often didn't. Nick was far more instinctive. I imagine Nick had often never even bothered listening to the demos – he would just come in and bluff it, but he would still do way better than anyone else could ever do."

When Aubrey first pitched *The Difference Machine* to D'Virgilio, it was just another session to him. "I knew nothing of Big Big Train," the drummer admits. "I didn't hear a single note until the day I met them in Aubitt, which was par for the course with a lot of people that came into Rob's studio. He convinced them that I was good enough to play on their music and we just sat and listened to the song."

D'Virgilio bonded with Spawton and Poole from the get-go, the three of them geeking out over, among other things, their shared love for Genesis. "Nick was just a lovely, genuine guy," says Spawton. "Uber talented and incredibly musical. Drummers can be rhythmically talented, but Nick is talented across the board – a world-class, all-round

NDV's first recording session for Big Big Train, 2006.

he says. "They wanted me to be *busy*. I've played a lot of sessions where they just want you to lay down the beat, and that's what I do 90 per cent of the time in my regular life – I play groove and backbeat stuff. So it was refreshing to be encouraged, to be told to go for it, to go off and play as many notes as I could possibly play. It was a fun experience and they seemed to like it. *The Difference Machine* was challenging, with long passages and odd time signatures. It wasn't a typical session in the end, it was a little more experimental."

musician who played drums and sang. He was bringing more than that though – he was bringing a *vibe* with him. He's an incredibly quick worker, and we locked into a good working relationship straight away. I didn't know it at the time, but it was a very significant moment."

Hughes had already recorded his parts for the album, but as Andy Poole recalls, "Steve had been sent the demos months in advance so he could work on his parts, but we were slightly underwhelmed by some of them. Nick played *Perfect Cosmic Storm* and *Pick Up If You're There*, and he put so much into it we were completely blown away. Those are the two big tracks where Nick made a huge difference."

Perhaps because of their shared musical DNA, D'Virgilio attacked these long proggy tracks with relish. "I sweated my ass off in Rob's studio and played hard,"

The plan was to release the album with Hughes' original drums, with a bonus disc featuring the D'Virgilio versions of *Perfect Cosmic Storm* and *Pick Up If You're There*. But after being completely stunned by the American's energetic, highly accomplished contributions, Spawton and Poole decided to replace Hughes on those two tracks on the main album. The Bournemouth Becker and Fagen tacitly decided that, from then on, D'Virgilio's services would be used whenever possible.

A step towards the modern world, *The Difference Machine* pulled in strands from old favourites like Genesis and Van der Graaf Generator, and also newer ones too – The Mars Volta, Icelandic texturalists Sigur Rós and Danish indie act Mew, whom Spawton adored. The album was very much a studio creation, way too complicated for the band to even contemplate playing live. And that was just how Spawton and Poole liked it.

Tough in parts, languid in others, and pretty out there throughout, *The Difference Machine* was markedly different to its predecessor, and Spawton thinks it's the better album for it. "*Gathering Speed* was pastoral," he says, "with acoustic and 12-string guitars, classic prog rock sounds. Quite derivative, really. *The Difference Machine* was more hard edged and experimental, and probably stands out as more unique. For me it's a successful album – the lyrics are strong and there are some moving moments."

Poole reckons it's a 'weird' album. "People must think we were off our heads on drugs! Even now it astonishes me by its relentless intensity and weird soundscapes. It is a challenging listen, very much our 'Radiohead does proper prog' album. *Perfect Cosmic Storm* is a peculiar track, and others are too. We were back to trying to cram in too many ideas, partly because with the guest musicians we had an embarrassment of riches."

Those riches included swathes of D'Virgilio drum parts, which Poole – flexing his newly hewn editing muscles – cut up and shoehorned into the songs wherever possible. He also took some of Tony Wright's outtakes and shaped them into the mournful lines that colour the long, moody, Mellotron-drenched outro of *Summer's Lease*, one of their most rounded pieces at that point.

"On *English Boy Wonders* we were trying to go with simple, relatable guitar sounds," says Poole, "whereas this time we were going out of our way to find different sound textures, and that appealed to me because I loved the experimentation. I think we probably ended up trying too hard in places on *Perfect Cosmic Storm* and *Pick Up If*

You're There, and I think it was a more difficult album for Sean – it wasn't thematically or lyrically so much what he was into."

Despite unsuccessfully trying to get some of his own songs onto *The Difference Machine*, Sean Filkins is co-credited for the music on *Pick Up If You're There* and *Salt Water Falling On Uneven Ground*. Contrary to Poole's assessment, the singer maintains that he was very pleased with the finished album. "*Gathering Speed* was more on the pastoral side of what they'd done before," he says, "and the production was lighter. *The Difference Machine* moved the band on again, it had a slightly heavier edge, and I think Greg realised I could do that. It gave me a chance to do something different. I like to be pushed. It had Greg's concept about the butterfly effect written into it, which I got into, and I loved the music. Again I worked hard on the harmonies, which take a lot of work to get right, and some of the singing is the best I've ever done. I still think *Salt Water Falling On Uneven Ground* is the best track, and that's with Steve Hughes playing drums."

Hughes could sense that his position as Big Big Train's drummer was now, at best, tenuous. Added to those previous periods of self-imposed exile around ProgFarm and *Bard*, he himself didn't feel he had nailed his drum parts this time. "I didn't record them that well," he says now. "There wasn't the right vibe there, I didn't feel I had what it took to do justice to that album. There was already talk of Nick, who is a fucking amazing drummer. It was a transitional period – Greg had a vision, the band was growing, and for me there wasn't the same close chemistry as before. I just wasn't going the same way they were."

When Hughes emailed Spawton and asked directly if his role in the Big Big Train story had come to an end, he was told that it had. "The fact he had declined to play on *Bard* probably assisted me in being fairly brutal," Spawton says. "Nick was giving us an extra degree of oomph and musicality, and we had reached a stage where potential was beginning to coalesce into something real. I wanted my songs to be presented at the highest level we could achieve, so that they could go out into the world and be heard by as many people as possible. To Steve's credit, he took the news extremely well. I don't think it was a big deal in his life."

"It pricked my pride a bit," says Hughes now, "but we didn't fall out, and there were no harsh feelings whatsoever. They did the right thing and it moved them on to the next level. Looking back, I was so cocky. They were very patient with me, there was a lot of love there – they were fond of me and took me under their wing. Maybe I chucked it in their face a bit when I went and joined The Enid, but I really wanted to get out and do gigs. Big Big Train was a formative part of my early years, and I have lots of fond memories."

Steve recording drums for The Difference Machine *at Aubitt in 2006 – his last session with the band.*

Released in August 2007, *The Difference Machine* went on to sell over 5,000 copies. While the band were still in the red financially, their expensive hobby was beginning to almost pay for itself. Spawton for one began to think that "maybe there was something in this, and that the band could continue in a very positive trajectory. We were on an upwards curve."

And the press attention the album received seemed to bear this out, with Big Big Train now getting noticed by more mainstream music titles. In *Classic Rock*, the UK's biggest rock magazine, two of the country's most authoritative rock journalists both picked up on the album. Veteran writer Dave Ling called it 'Splendidly mellifluous prog'. In his prog rock column, former *Kerrang!* founder and *Sounds* editor Geoff Barton described it as 'finely crafted and acutely moving, especially the chilling *Salt Water Falling On Uneven Ground*.'

Elsewhere, *Guitar And Bass Magazine* described it as 'a tasty slab of pure prog. This is an English garden variety of progressive rock [...] Genesis and Marillion are your references.' Giving it a surgically precise mark of 15½ out of 20, the US magazine *Progression* wrote that 'the distinctive vocal harmonies and instrumental passage resolutions of the long tracks are what make this recording such a special experience'. And, never knowingly understated, UK extreme music journal *Terrorizer* deemed it 'unashamed, unreconstructed PROG FUCKIN' ROCK! *The Difference Machine* is bound to please fans of Yes, The Enid and early Genesis. This one's an epic – sit back and lose yourself.'

Terrorizer was usually the preserve of metal bands like Nightwish and Arch Enemy, but the magazine had been exploring the new frontiers of progressive music. Much to Andy Poole's chagrin, Gregory Spawton was persuaded into paying around £500 to have *Perfect Cosmic Storm* added to the covermount CD of the magazine's November edition. While it wasn't the most productive marketing move, the CD also contained tracks by Dream Theater and Porcupine Tree. Little did the pair know that, just a few years hence, they would be rubbing shoulders with members of these bands, and many others, at a glitzy awards ceremony.

◆◆◆

Some 30 years after they divorced, Gregory Spawton's parents were moving on very different trajectories. His mother Doreen and stepfather Will were living happily in Tamworth, having set up a successful plastics business together, and Gregory and brother Nigel gladly saw them regularly. The boys had seen Barry just once a week as kids, on long, resentful Saturday mornings that invariably ended in an argument, the pair defending their mother against their father's bitter slights. These fractious meetings had become less frequent as the Spawton boys grew up, until eventually they only saw their father once a year.

A heavy smoker all his life, Barry Spawton had continued to struggle with alcohol after leaving the family home, and regularly got into financial difficulty. More than once Gregory and Nigel visited his flat to find unpaid bills among the mess. At first they quietly settled these for him, but he would just get mired in debt again, until it became clear he was in a desperate cycle. His boys insisted that he take responsibility, and he did eventually achieve a modicum of balance in his life. He met a new partner, Violet, with whom he had an on-off relationship, and he was drinking less than he had.

But the years had taken their toll. His hacking smoker's cough got progressively worse over time, he was ultimately diagnosed with emphysema, and in 2007 Violet called Gregory with the news that his father had died.

The day before the funeral, Spawton drove north to Tamworth, where he would be staying with his mother and Will while back in Birmingham. He had decided beforehand that he didn't want to see his father's body, but once he arrived he changed his mind. He drove in a daze to the funeral home in Sutton Coldfield, and got badly lost there in his home town on the way. When he eventually arrived it was late afternoon, and the funeral home had closed.

He knocked on the doors and called through the letterbox, but there was nobody there to let him in. With his hand resting on the brick of the Victorian building – and despite all that had passed between father and sons – Spawton began to cry. "I sat in the car park very upset," he recalls, "knowing my dad was on the other side of the wall. Within minutes that started to come through in the lyrics for the song, and the phrase, 'Victorian Brickwork'."

The next day, after the funeral, Violet told Gregory and Nigel that, a couple of days before he died, she had asked Barry whether she should call them. And he told her, 'No – they will call if they want to'. "Given we spoke once a year," Spawton says now, "that was never going to happen. I looked at her in absolute shock and was very angry about it. I wish she had tipped us off – we could have had a farewell. It all fed into the song. I went home, picked up a guitar and wrote the chorus for *Victorian Brickwork*. The words just tumbled out of me."

Happier inspiration struck Spawton around that time during a train journey from Bournemouth to Bristol. He was reading *The Hidden Landscape: A Journey Into The Geological Past* by British palaeontologist Richard Fortey who, Spawton says, "described the journey I was making as a journey back through geological time, because the rocks get older the further west you go. I thought this was incredible. It got me thinking about the railway engineers who built the Great Western Railway, who were literally digging back through time, then I thought about the great Victorian engineers, linking it all to deep [geological] time. And that's when I started to think about The Underfall Yard. People see it as a historical dock in Bristol harbour, roughly on the same site as the engineering feature designed by Brunel. But it was the otherworldly sound of the words that attracted me – the combination is beautiful, mysterious and odd. In my scattergun way I did some reading about it, then set about continuing to write the next album."

Master James of St. George was one of the great architects and castle builders of 13th century England and Wales. Spawton channelled fond early memories of his father, who had constructed those fantastically intricate castles and forts for his son's toy soldiers and knights. Beneath the song's historically literate title, Spawton was burying something very personal. And he came across other characters from British history who, while lesser known, were utterly intriguing.

Perhaps the most incredible was William Walker. A highly experienced and courageous deep water diver, between 1906 and 1911 Walker worked six hours a day, in 20-feet-deep pits of pitch black water beneath Winchester Cathedral. With the building in clear danger of collapse, he single-handedly bolstered its two supporting walls, adding tons of concrete beneath them. This ensured that the groundwater could be pumped out, then essential restoration could be done safely, preventing the beautiful building from collapsing into rubble. Walker's story inspired *Winchester Diver*, which contains, in Spawton's opinion, "my best set of lyrics to this day, comparing things above ground to the bleakness of his working conditions."

And so with the band's stock high after *The Difference Machine*, Spawton, Poole and Filkins began work on the follow-up, with Nick D'Virgilio due to swoop in on drums once again. There was a new stability, rhythm and semblance of a plan within the ranks. The band was trundling along nicely. And then Spawton received a call out of the blue from Rob Aubrey, who told him he had found the perfect singer for Big Big Train.

Gregory, Andy, NDV at Aubitt Studios, 2007.

V

'We speak a while of the old days,
years ago in times so far...'

BY THE TIME HE POPPED UP on Rob Aubrey's radar, David Longdon was sure his long held dreams of a life in music were fading. And it wasn't for the lack of trying. He'd had numerous chances – with bands, as a solo artist, and there was even a near miss involving one of prog rock's giant acts – but nothing had ever fully panned out.

Music had always loomed large in his life. He was born David Ashley Longdon on 17th June 1965 in Nottingham, to mother Vera and father Eric. "My dad liked lots of easy listening," says Longdon, "artists such as Bert Kaempfert, James Last and the organist Klaus Wunderlich. My Uncle Jack was a collier and a bright, well-read man who liked poetry. He was into Grieg, Rossini, Tchaikovsky, Mozart, and the big gift he gave me was the music of Johann Sebastian Bach, which is like gifting someone an ocean of possibility. It was great to be exposed to that as a young musician. But Jack also listened to artists like Johnny Cash, Marty Robbins, Jim Reeves and Glen Campbell. The symphonic rock that you find within a

David with his friend Simon Withers ('Sam' in the song Make Some Noise) *and Pippa the dog at Sutton on Sea, Lincolnshire, probably 1978. David is wearing his Rainbow On Stage badge.*

John Henry Herring (Uncle Jack).

David with home organ, mid 1970s.

progressive rock band plus the storytelling from country? Jack gave me that. The classical music showed me how to extend and musically develop themes and variations. The country music has the storytelling aspect – it would draw the listener in. Jack would think nothing of putting on a Puccini opera and then listening to Johnny Cash. It seemed entirely natural to do so."

As a boy Longdon had piano lessons, practising at home on an organ his parents had bought him. Though he had a natural ear for melody, he struggled with the theoretical side of music, especially notation – 'the dots' – which he found to be restricting. When required to play a piece of music for class Longdon would craftily ask his music teacher, Margaret Burchinal, to play it first. Then, rather than sight-read the music, he would just copy her by ear, and usually got away with it.

Having done his music O Level, Longdon was obliged to learn an orchestral instrument in order to move on to A Level. "My teacher wanted me to play a tenor horn, which I absolutely hated. It was heavy, and it stank! I deliberately left it on the bus once, but nobody was stupid enough to steal it. So shortly after that I changed to flute, which was light enough in weight that I could put it in my bag." Along with the flute he went on to learn the guitar, bass and mandolin, and could keep a beat on drums too.

This eclecticism was reflected in his musical tastes. Early record acquisitions included Beethoven's First Symphony and The Who's two LP compilation, *The Story Of The Who*, and he thrilled to the music of The Beatles and The Rolling Stones. His very first concert was Whitesnake in 1980, at the De Montfort Hall in Leicester. This was during their *Lovehunter* period, with Deep Purple's Jon Lord and Ian Paice in the line-up – an irresistible draw. Longdon's friends, and their elder brothers, helped him expand his musical palette, introducing him to the likes of The Sweet, Rainbow and Todd Rundgren's Utopia. He revelled in the

David with Simon Withers and friend Ian White, in the place in Nottingham known to locals as Door One.

sheer drama and dynamics of Led Zeppelin, David Bowie, Steeleye Span and Pentangle. He relished the mod fashion of the Small Faces and The Kinks.

Normally Eric Longdon would whistle along to cassettes by the likes of Sky and ABBA in the car, until one day a colleague gave him a tape of Pink Floyd's *Dark Side Of The Moon*, assuring him it was the best album ever made. As his son listened to the record more and more, its unusual, mysterious soundworld made a lasting impression upon him. Poring over his well-thumbed copy of *The NME Encyclopaedia Of Rock 'n' Roll*, Longdon came upon a band he had never heard of: King Crimson. Included in their

entry was a quote from Longdon's hero, Pete Townshend, about the debut album, *In The Court Of The Crimson King*: "He called it 'an uncanny masterpiece'," Longdon recalls, "and that made me curious. I like all periods of Crimson, but their first album is my favourite."

The early works of Genesis appealed to his literary artistic sense: "I loved *Foxtrot*, and the storytelling, the way it all unfolded. With *Supper's Ready* the extended song format was like reading a book." Later he would find himself in the thrall of other experimental artists, from the fiery fusion of The Mahavishnu Orchestra to the bucolic, very English progressive folk of Fairport Convention. He particularly admired their self-titled debut from 1968, thrilling at the guitar work of Richard Thompson and the cut-glass English tones of their enigmatic female singer, Judy Dyble.

In 1982, after a brief stint as a young teen in an amateur folk rock group, the 17-year-old Longdon joined some school friends in a more serious band called Greenhouse. They played local pubs and the occasional club, their set comprising covers such as The Velvet Underground's *Sweet Jane*, Free's *Wishing Well*, *Substitute* by The Who and *Afterglow* by Genesis.

He recalls he was the only member with aspirations as a songwriter: "The first song I ever wrote was called *Curtains For You*, and it was terrible. But it was a start – the wise man dies many times before he is born. You write a few terrible songs and keep going somehow until you manage to write a half-decent one, and on it goes. The more you write, the better you become at doing it."

He briefly studied music at college, but the formality and orchestral nature of the course didn't suit him, so he switched. After a foundation year at West Bridgford Art

Greenhouse in action: on a truck at Castle Donington, 2ⁿᵈ October 1983, and at Old Malt Cross, Nottingham, 4ᵗʰ January 1984.

Local gig guide from the Nottingham Evening Post, *1983.*

College, he studied for a BTEC qualification in Art & Design. Greenhouse continued for just a few years, but by 1983 another Nottingham musician, Charlie Stephenson, had spotted Longdon's nascent talents. Stephenson had himself been in bands in his own heyday in the '60s and had a decent home studio. With Stephenson inviting him to record there, Longdon made two demos, *Another Look* and *Up On The Plateau*. When Stephenson later formed his

own studio/label, Frontier Studios, Longdon was among his first signings, and when he opened a record shop, Frontier Records, right next door to the studio, Longdon was recruited to manage that.

After Greenhouse split he had continued to develop his writing and performing skills, singing and playing guitar and flute with O'Strange Passion, a quartet featuring drummer Dave Hill (later to play for Neil Finn and '90s alt rock band Arnold). "I was into [classy Australian indie pop outfit] The Go-Betweens at the time," says Longdon, "so O'Strange Passion was wordy, arty, and I was on acoustic guitar so it was quite jangly."

In the 1990s he started another group. The Gifthorse were, he says, "a bit more polished. We were going for an indie art rock thing, though somebody once described us as being like Simply Red and Talk Talk. Maybe it's because my voice was soulful, though obviously I don't sound anything like Mick Hucknall."

This first incarnation of The Gifthorse played a pivotal role in his career. In 1992 they were asked to stand in last minute for a friend's band at The Grand Central Diner, a restaurant/bar/music venue converted from a disused railway station on Nottingham's London Road. Among the audience was A&R man Michael Stack.

Stack had already been tipped off about this great singer called David Longdon by a journalist friend, who had passed him a cassette of The Gifthorse. A Longdon-penned song on there, *Crying Out*, particularly grabbed Stack's interest: "Two things leapt out," he says now. "Firstly David's voice, because it was so distinctive. I'm a big fan of soul singers and David has so much soul in his voice. It's the old cliché – that guy could sing the telephone directory and it would sound like he meant it. But what really got me were the lyrics – I still think he's one of the most underrated lyricists this country has

Following the fashion in 1985...

ever produced, because he gets the craft. He's one of those rare writers; I'd put him in the same class as Tim Booth [of the band James] and Paul Weller in terms of the attention to detail, the craft of writing, structuring and arrangements, from top to bottom. There's nothing in a David Longdon song that doesn't belong there."

Stack attended the Gifthorse show specifically to see Longdon in a gig situation, and his abiding memory is that he did not pay much attention to the other band members. "I was totally fixated on David and his voice. There was something about him – it was almost as though he was lost in the songs. There may as well have been nobody in the room because I'm pretty sure he didn't see anybody while he was singing. He seemed to be completely absorbed in the moment and just owned whichever song he was singing."

A few months after that '92 show Stack was offered a job at Rondor Music Publishing, and Longdon was his first signing. This was a development deal, so Longdon was contracted to deliver a certain number of songs within a defined period, with a view to him and/or The Gifthorse performing them. "Rondor had kudos," says Longdon. "They used to be the publishing arm of A&M Records and were the largest independent music publisher, with the rights to people like Joe Jackson, The Doors, Rick Wakeman, Supertramp and Joan Armatrading. But they were looking to do more than publishers used to do. They were nurturing songwriters to work on their own material and then try to get recording deals for them. The head of Rondor, Stuart Hornell, listened to my stuff with Michael, and signed me. He told Michael that when my album was produced [legendary producer/engineer] Glyn Johns had to produce it. That was music to my ears, but it never happened."

"We had a studio in Parsons Green in London," Stack recalls, "so we gave David about a week's recording time. He recorded a song called *Moon & The Stars* which I loved, a beautiful ballad, and he may have re-done *Crying Out*."

"There were several recording sessions done at Parsons Green," Longdon recalls. "One of the first was with Dave Dix, who was a music producer. He'd been a member of the band Black with Colin Vearncombe, who had a hit with *Wonderful Life*. I also brought The Gifthorse to record a session with Gary Bromham."

Gary Bromham had produced Andrew Ridgeley's post Wham! album, *Son Of Albert*, and had also written for a diverse roster of artists including George Michael, Sheryl Crow and Eddie Money. He and Longdon had met through their mutual manager at the time, Paul White. They were

paired up to co-write songs, and hit it off, with Bromham going on to produce demos for The Gifthorse.

"The first thing we did," Bromham recalls, "was to go out and have quite a few drinks and get to know each other. I'd just gone through a breakup of my marriage and Dave was a great counsellor, as well as this resource of ideas – such a creative person."

They wrote numerous songs together, the first being called *OK Sean*, and a notable piece entitled *Hieroglyphics Of Love*. But 18 months into Longdon's contract Stack moved on from Rondor, and the singer-songwriter was, as he puts it, "left to the wolves, and in the end I got dropped."

Bromham was close to him at the time: "I saw a disillusion in Dave after that, in that whole period where it didn't quite go to plan. It all kind of switched for a while, and I had to kind of sit him down and try to persuade him that he had this innate talent, and that he should never lose that as his focus. Weirdly enough, we drifted apart for a couple of years after that, because I was off on my own journey trying to get my own record deal."

Then in 1994 real tragedy struck, when Longdon's beloved father Eric died of acute myeloid leukaemia. "The death of my dad hit me very hard," he says now. "He died at the age of 63. I thought the way in which he died was very unfair, and it altered the way that I viewed the world. I felt great anger. It was after his funeral that I decided to shave my hair. It was a cathartic act. His death was a major catalyst, changing the way I wrote songs. I was performing songs in a far more cathartic way."

The Gifthorse carried on, playing locally around Nottingham and making an occasional trip to London. They supported Kirsty MacColl, Blur and The Pogues, with Longdon's performances fuelled by this new, nihilistic

The Gifthorse, outside Nottingham Playhouse.

energy. His way with an astute and acerbic turn of phrase was evident from their set list, which included songs called *The Quintessential Englishman Abroad*, *Your Favourite Bastards* and *Swallowing The Pop Myth Whole*.

"The Gifthorse gigs were very intense at this point," he remembers. "The music was uncompromising, entirely on its own terms. The shows were dramatic and I would throw myself entirely into them. I was against the world, channelling Jackie Leven's band Doll By Doll, and John Martyn. I'd gone through the mill with the record industry, and felt like it was the wrong thing at the wrong time continually. I was in the right place sometimes, but it never really clicked. My favourites around then were bands like The Waterboys and The Lilac Time, but I was just doing my own thing. It was acoustic music, and, at that time, people didn't really want to know."

He also joined another band in '94. The artist Louis Philippe was signed to él Records, a subsidiary of Cherry Red, and Longdon had been in communication with him because he liked Philippe's style, and particularly admired his 1986 album *Appointment With Venus*. "We became friends," says Longdon. "He saw me with The Gifthorse at [London club] The Borderline and invited me to join his live band, doing backing vocals, playing flute, a bit of guitar and keyboards."

He contributed to Philippe's classy 1996 art pop/chanson album *Jackie Girl*, and, while in London for the recording sessions and live rehearsals, Longdon met and befriended two other notable artists contributing their talents. These were XTC's erstwhile guitarist Dave Gregory, and Philippe's musical director, Danny Manners. "Danny had been Philippe's MD for many years," says Longdon, "playing French chansons and baroque pop. He was

producing *Jackie Girl* and I was struck by his attention to musical detail. He and I got on well from the off. Danny has a good, downbeat and silly sense of humour too."

And in that same year, opportunity knocked in an unexpected and rather proggy way for David Longdon. By then Gary Bromham was half of a synth duo called The Big Blue, who were signed to EMI. In '96 they were working on an album at The Farm, the plush Surrey recording studio owned by Genesis and run by that band's engineer/producer, Nick Davis. Phil Collins had recently left Genesis apparently for good, and Davis mentioned to Bromham in passing that Tony Banks and Mike Rutherford were looking for a vocalist to replace Collins for an upcoming album and tour.

"I put David forward straightaway," says Bromham, "I knew he was right for it. I told Nick, 'I've got a singer for you'. It wasn't even like, 'Oh maybe you should check out this guy' – I just went, 'Nick, I have the singer that you need.'"

Bromham gave Davis a cassette of the song *Hieroglyphics Of Love*. "I listened to it," Davis recalls now, "and thought, 'This is good'. So I played it to Mike and Tony and they both said, 'Oh yeah, this *is* good!' And we were actually struggling for singers. It was a hard slot to fill – I don't think we knew what we were looking for particularly."

In May that year Genesis manager Tony Smith invited Longdon to The Farm to audition for the vocalist vacancy. They wanted to hear him sing their repertoire, and had prepared 'Top Of The Pops' mixes of nine Collins-era Genesis hits. These mixes featured the original instrumentation minus Collins' lead vocals, and among the tunes for Longdon to tackle were *Land Of Confusion*, *Mama*, *No Son Of Mine*, *Throwing It All Away*, *Turn It On Again*, *I Can't Dance* and *Tonight, Tonight, Tonight*.

Longdon initially found this test intense, because of Banks and Rutherford's lofty status, but he says they were "very welcoming and friendly – they tried to put me at ease. They were all in the control room looking at me and I was standing just next to the live room with headphones on. They kept me in quite a long time because they didn't know anything about me. I didn't have any recorded work or videos, so they were trying to get to know me."

For a second audition in late October, Longdon was asked to go back to The Farm and jam with Banks and Rutherford. When he saw the pair there, with their equipment set up and ready to go, the singer remembered seeing them jamming with Phil Collins in that same environment on an *Old Grey Whistle Test* episode: "It was when they were recording *Abacab* – it was very reminiscent of that. I got excited rather than nervous, and just went for it. The first time I went down to The Farm had been a bit weird – thinking about what I was going to do, having seen Genesis in the past performing live at the Six Of The Best reunion concert in 1982, then suddenly being faced with these people in the flesh. It helped that Tony and Mike weren't nostalgic at all – if anything they were quite nonchalant about their past and their achievements. They weren't resting on their laurels or waxing lyrical about their heyday. It was all about moving forward. It was a great opportunity to work with people I'd admired for a long time, but a job had to be done."

Banks and Rutherford asked Longdon to come up with ideas for a batch of tunes they were working on for their forthcoming album, *Calling All Stations*. They played pieces that would later appear on the record (including *Congo* and *Shipwrecked*), wanting Longdon to improvise melody lines as they performed together.

"We liked David's voice a lot," Tony Banks remembers, "which is why we got him down to audition. But I think he was quite green. We did some old songs, which are easy enough, then we were on to some other newer things we were doing, we hadn't really written any final lyrics. We wanted him pretty much to just improvise along, and he was uncomfortable with that. So he sat down and wrote a lyric for one of the pieces."

By this point other auditionees, including (Gregory Spawton's guitarist *fétiche*) Francis Dunnery and Cutting Crew's Nick Van Eede, had dropped out of the running. The shortlist was narrowed down to Longdon and the powerful, gravel-voiced singer Ray Wilson. In '94 Wilson's post-grunge band Stiltskin had scored a hit across Europe and a UK number one single with *Inside*, which had also featured on a TV advert for Levi's 501 jeans. With all this buzz around Stiltskin, the Genesis team could view plenty of video footage of Wilson in performance, whereas with Longdon they had no way of seeing how he was live. "Previously whenever I'd fronted a band I'd always had a guitar," he says. "The only two times I haven't are when working with Genesis and, later, in Big Big Train. Then I wanted to be the singer and frontman. I wanted to establish myself as a classic 'stand and deliver' vocalist like Robert Plant or Roger Daltrey."

Genesis owned a company called Vari-Lite, which manufactured the state of the art lighting system which the band used in their live shows and also licensed to others. They invited Longdon and The Gifthorse down to their premises on Hanger Lane in London to perform a set. Longdon was specifically instructed not to play his guitar (Bromham stood in on the instrument). "They wanted to see how I moved around," says Longdon, "how I spoke and whether I looked confident. I thought that, out of the whole process, this would be where I came unstuck. But it wasn't – they started negotiating contracts."

So by 1996 Longdon's life was gathering speed. Throughout the Genesis experience Carol Willis, one of Tony Smith's assistants, worked closely with him. "Carol and I became good friends," Longdon says, "and I asked that if Mike and Tony decided not to go with me, then she should be the one to give me the bullet. Which she did, bless her."

That bullet came in late November when, after much deliberation within the Genesis camp, Ray Wilson won the role. "Carol said that they had to have a singer who could sell the material," Longdon says, "and they felt Ray would be the best person to do it. I suppose they felt he had more experience, and they were right. He was the more seasoned performer. He had also had a number one single and had seen the machinery of the music business, and I guess that made them more comfortable. They were probably concerned that the pressures of it might be too much for me, which is fair comment. Ray and I have never met or corresponded, but I thought he did a really good job considering the task he was charged with."

"It's a difficult thing fronting any group," says Tony Banks now. "You work your way into it a bit. When Peter Gabriel first sang with us he was very unsure of what to do, and was not at all confident. If we'd been just starting out it wouldn't have been a problem, but in the end we couldn't really see David as the frontman of Genesis as it was at that stage. He didn't have the confidence necessary, hadn't done much before he came to see us. By contrast Ray had much more experience and was the more obvious choice, given that we were established and aiming to play to reasonably large audiences. But David was certainly down to the last two, and was definitely a good singer."

Equally impressed, Willis suggested to Tony Smith that she should manage Longdon herself, but Longdon says that Smith balked at the idea because "to establish an artist from scratch would be a costly labour of love rather than a sensible idea. So Carol sent me to speak to Simon Draper, the head of Virgin Music at that time, and he advised me to forget the whole Genesis thing had ever happened. And that's kind of what I did. I put it to the back of my mind and tried to move on, but it was really difficult. Had I got the job, it would have been like winning the lottery.

"The whole Genesis thing is odd. It's something I'm noted for *not* actually having done. I'm pleased I didn't blot the Genesis copybook. When I was younger I had no reason to talk about it, because it meant nothing to the people in my life or indeed to me, and it had no currency in my wilderness years. But it's quite another matter when you're fronting a progressive rock band. I think the Genesis DNA is present in the timbre of my voice. It's most likely why I got the audition in the first place, and it was a useful thing for Big Big Train when I arrived."

The Gifthorse disbanded after the Genesis audition process, and it was a disconsolate Longdon who, somewhat wearily, returned to the local music scene in 1997. "I played various gigs around Nottingham and Derby, either on my own or with small ensembles, with a flexible band of musicians that were known as The Magic Club. But I felt that my heart wasn't in it. I knew I wanted to write music, so I just concentrated on that."

He bought some home recording equipment and, with contributions from The Magic Club, set about recording a solo album, *Wild River*. With its title track written for and about his late father, the album exercised Longdon's singer songwriter muscles, but he was entering his mid-30s and real life was encroaching on his musical dreams. In '98 he took a job as Workshop Manager and Theatre Technician at South East Derbyshire College. While there he met a new partner and it was, he says, "a new beginning. We committed to having a family together. Our first child, Amelia, was born in 2003, and I applied for a job at New College, Telford, teaching Music Technology. We moved to Shropshire in order to make a better life for our family. Initially it was great – Shropshire is beautiful and we had a lovely time there. But being a father and a teacher was demanding, and after a few years I began to burn out and became unwell."

Wild River was finally finished and released in 2004. He travelled back to Derbyshire from Shropshire to play an album launch show, at The Red Lion Hotel in Wirksworth. But what should have been an affirming event instead became a moment of real reflection for Longdon. In the context of his new life and responsibilities, the record's eventual, modest release represented a line being drawn under his musical aspirations. "I decided then," he recalls, "that, actually, perhaps it was time to let go of those dreams."

His partner gave birth to their second daughter, Eloise, in 2007 and, while Longdon found joy in

family life, by that point he felt that, artistically, he had reached the end. "I really did think that music was done with me. But then I read an article online about Martin Orford. He was speaking frankly about his experiences in the world of progressive rock and I liked what he had to say. He was preparing to ship out of the music industry because illegal downloads were making his life a misery. On a whim, I decided to call him on the GEP office number. I was leaving a message on the answering machine, but when I mentioned my Genesis audition, Martin picked up the phone."

Orford had left IQ in 2007 and – despairing of what he perceived as the devaluation of music in the download era – had decided to retire from the business entirely. When he and Longdon had their first conversation, Orford was working on his swansong album. Recorded with Rob Aubrey at Aubitt Studios in Southampton, *The Old Road* featured an array of guest artists, including John Wetton, Jadis vocalist/guitarist Gary Chandler and one Nick D'Virgilio.

The Magic Club at the Off The Tracks Festival, Castle Donington, 2ⁿᵈ September 2006.

Orford told Longdon that he had a couple of tracks that he might let him sing on *The Old Road*, if Longdon could perform them better than he could himself. On 28th July 2008 Longdon travelled down from Shropshire to Aubitt and, in one morning, recorded the songs *Ray Of Hope* (featuring D'Virgilio on drums) and *Endgame*. "He blew us away as soon as he opened his mouth," says Orford with a laugh. "I remember Rob and I looking at each other and thinking, 'This guy's really got it!' David did a wonderful job for me."

For Longdon, this was a rare moment of artistic hope and belonging: "Suddenly I was appearing on an album alongside people like John Wetton and other luminaries of the prog world. I felt I was finally in the right place."

Aubrey had been openly sceptical about all of Big Big Train's singers up to that point, and he remembers that first recording session with Longdon very well: "It was instant. David had been chatting away, then suddenly he got behind the microphone, and his voice was zinging, a beautiful sound, and there was a little buzz that I was totally hooked into. I thought this guy had something special. Greg, Andy and I were going out for a curry that night – I called and told them to listen to the six vocal takes David did, because the passion in the voice and the ideas were phenomenal."

Big Big Train was a name that had previously passed Longdon by, but Aubrey began gently sounding him out about potentially doing something with them. As a rule, Longdon had kept an open mind on progressive rock music over the years, but had also kept it at arm's length. "When I turned 40 [in 2005], for my birthday I bought a few new prog albums that had caught my attention – *The World*

That We Drive Through by The Tangent, which I liked very much, *Octane* by Spock's Beard, which was good, and *Adam & Eve* by The Flower Kings, which I also enjoyed. But 'prog' was most certainly a four-letter word back in the '80s and '90s. I was trying to have a career in music, and having overtly progressive rock influences at that time would have been career suicide. Having a tonal resemblance to Genesis vocalists was always a double-edged thing for me. I don't think the vocal similarities did me any favours."

A few months after Aubrey's enquiries, the singer saw that the August 2008 copy of *Classic Rock* came with a covermount CD called 'Prog Spawn'. There, among tracks by known contemporary progressive acts like The Pineapple Thief, No-Man and Mostly Autumn, was a song called *Summer's Lease* by that 'Train' band Aubrey had talked to him about. Out of curiosity Longdon bought the magazine, played the CD, and was intrigued by what he heard.

But by this point, he had little hope of anything happening, whether with Big Big Train or indeed with anyone else: "I was beyond hope. I just wanted to be involved with something musical. Working with a band was a good option for me because I was tired of making things happen on my own. I didn't have any expectations that something would happen because I'd been in very similar situations many times before. There was no sense of 'maybe this is the one'. I just thought that it would be great to be involved with a musical project."

"I wasn't expecting Big Big Train to achieve the success it has," he says today, "because where we are now is a million miles away from where we were back then."

VI

'Chasing a dream of the West,
made with iron and stone...'

WHEN GREGORY SPAWTON GOT THE CALL from Rob Aubrey about the fantastic new singer he had met, Big Big Train were proceeding full steam ahead with *The Underfall Yard* album. The demos had been recorded with the highly capable and engaged Sean Filkins, *The Difference Machine* was selling well and getting the band wider exposure, and Spawton had no plans to change the status quo.

But while taken aback by Aubrey's suggestion, Spawton did also trust the engineer's instincts. After all, he had been right about many things in his 15-year association with the band, most recently regarding Nick D'Virgilio. The way Andy Poole sees it now, "Rob had seen we were pushing

An early recording session for The Underfall Yard, *2007.*

forward in certain ways but, vocally, we weren't playing to our full potential."

Poole and Spawton headed to Aubitt, where Aubrey played them Longdon's performances from Martin Orford's *The Old Road*. "They weren't earth shattering in themselves," says Poole, "because they were fairly modest parts. David wasn't being pushed to the limit and there were no backing vocals."

Spawton also found the songs straightforward, but heard the potential in Longdon's rich, characterful voice, and quietly contacted him about doing some work with Big Big Train. "I was painfully shy at the time," Spawton says, "and picking up the phone to a potential new singer was genuinely very difficult for me. I nervously spoke to David, perhaps ten times over the course of three or four weeks, and we started to develop a rapport, just sounding each other out. First we talked about music, about Genesis – I didn't ask about his experience with them at that time; that would have been like prodding a wasp's nest. We're both Midlanders, so that was a connection, and we both shared a love for history, with David more into the history of art. It turned out that, between us, we had a lot of common ground."

"I don't think Greg had been so communicative with Sean," offers Longdon. "We were trying to foster a creative relationship. Greg wanted Big Big Train to appear as a group when, actually, it was really just him. He was shy and needed the strength of having at least the *idea* of a band around him. Greg would say that I needed an organised band and, yes, I definitely needed that."

Longdon was sent a copy of the title track to *The Underfall Yard,* and was asked to see what he could do with it. To ensure he wasn't swayed by Filkins' previously recorded vocal, Poole removed it from Longdon's copy, with Spawton himself supplying a guide vocal in its place. Longdon sent back his interpretation of the song, and Spawton was impressed with what he had done, and how well he had negotiated its tricky 19/8 metre. "It was clearly very rough," says Spawton, "but what David had done was beautiful. I could hear that there was a tone and a soul that I had never had from previous singers. And what I didn't understand at the time was that, with two young kids and a busy job, David only had about 15 minutes a day for music before going to work."

Highly reluctant to change up the band's effective existing line-up, Spawton was now faced with a real dilemma. Longdon had turned in an excellent audition tape and clearly had an extraordinary voice. But moreover, Spawton felt the two of them had a real sense of *simpatico,* even though they had only ever spoken on the phone. Remembering that his ultimate goal was to get his songs across to the widest possible audience, Spawton wrestled with his thoughts long and hard, and came to the tough conclusion that the best option was to proceed with David Longdon as Big Big Train's singer.

"To Andy's great credit he was much less sure about it," says Spawton, "and really didn't want to sack Sean. He felt it was very hard-nosed. I suppose it was. It was certainly

the hardest decision I've ever made with Big Big Train. But I didn't want to bring David down behind Sean's back either – that would have been really unpleasant."

"Greg didn't want to sit on it," says Poole, "and emailed Sean the next day. He was pretty unhappy about it, and said he realised then that he had never been more than a session guy, a hired hand."

"I wasn't very happy," says Filkins now. "All of sudden I got an email telling me they had got someone else and I wasn't going to be involved. I was pissed off because of the work I'd done on *Gathering Speed*, which lifted them out of the doldrums. Then *The Difference Machine* lifted them again and we had a lot more interest, some fantastic reviews, some good interviews and we could do some gigs. Again, I'd done a lot behind the scenes. And now I wasn't going to be on the next album."

"Sacking someone by email is really bad," Spawton admits, "but I knew if I called him we would just get into a shouting match. In any case, Sean called me as soon as he had read the email, so I only postponed the argument by a few moments. But I really don't blame him for being extremely angry and upset. He had every right. It was a stressful period, both for him and for me, and I'm not proud of it. I was brutal, but it was all about getting the songs heard."

Sean Filkins is more sanguine about it all nowadays. If anything, the final version of *The Underfall Yard* only confirmed his suspicions that he and Spawton were on different wavelengths. "They were going a different way. I knew Greg was a big Genesis fan, but I'm a massive fan of Yes, Uriah Heep, Robin Trower, and the music on *The Underfall Yard* wasn't going that way.

"With *Gathering Speed* I was enjoying it, so I added loads

of stuff, and the same with the social networking – I just believed in what we were doing and what Greg had written. I would've liked a bit more involvement in the music on *The Difference Machine*, but I really enjoyed it and put loads of harmonies in. But maybe I didn't put enough into my performance on those *Underfall Yard* demos, because I wasn't overly enamoured with the musical direction they were taking. When you've been doing this long enough you *know* when things sound good, and I wasn't happy with what I was doing, and they probably sensed that. Then later, when I heard the brass band, that wasn't my thing at all.

"But I'm still proud of the fact that I was a big part of them getting back on their feet again and turning their fortunes around. Bands make changes for a reason. You stand back and look at what Big Big Train went on to do, and I think it was the right decision. There's no point in holding grudges about it."

In 2015, Filkins and Spawton met again at the wedding of a mutual friend, music writer Alison Reijman. There in that happy atmosphere the two put the past behind them and caught up over a few drinks. They had plenty to chat about. After leaving Big Big Train, Filkins recorded his magnum opus, solo concept album *War And Peace & Other Short Stories* (2011), an acclaimed prog epic co-produced by another English prog notable, Lee Abraham. Ten years later he released this digitally, with Big Big Train helping him set up his first Bandcamp page, and putting him in contact with their own vinyl contact, Plane Groovy's Chris Topham, for the album's release on good old wax.

In 2012 Filkins joined IQ, Pallas and The Tangent on the bill of the inaugural Celebr8 Festival in Kingston upon Thames, also playing Summer's End Festival, and taking his band on a tour of the Netherlands. His catalogue of

Sean Filkins signing vinyl copies of War And Peace & Other Stories, *2021.*

guest slots as singer and writer also accrued over time, with Abraham, Corvus Stone, and Minor Giant among the artists with whom he recorded. And in 2015 he supplied lyrics and vocals for *Tales From The Silent Ocean*, the accomplished debut album by none other than his mate, Big Big Train's original drummer, Steve Hughes.

◆◆◆

David Longdon was sent the rest of the material for *The Underfall Yard*, and was invited down to Aubitt Studios in Southampton for a two-day recording session (16th – 17th July 2009), with a view to recording the vocals for the entire album. In hindsight, this was a risky gambit. Longdon was living in Shrewsbury, some 200 miles away. He hadn't worked directly with Spawton or Poole yet, nor had he even met them in person. With Filkins fired, had the three not clicked then the gamble on a new singer could have backfired badly.

The naturally cautious Poole had been more circumspect about the move, but on meeting Longdon he immediately felt "a kinship and chemistry – it's corny but true. When he first started delivering these amazing vocals, he was very relaxed about it. He's not a method actor – he'd go in and sing a brilliant line or two but between takes be joking and laughing, then just click back in the zone."

From the vocal booth Longdon was supplying plenty of useable material for the band to work with – long, coherent takes that didn't need patching up or editing. Also, Longdon impressed with his efficient, professional approach to backing vocals, which had always been a weaker part of Spawton's game. The singer could work up rich vocal arrangements with relative ease, and this opened up a whole new horizon for the band. "Suddenly the way he was working with Rob building these vocals was incredible," says Poole. "He'd have some stuff worked out in advance but he'd do other stuff on the fly. It was phenomenal."

"Sean was a good vocal arranger," says Spawton, "but David was at a completely different level. He gave us some incredible, sophisticated multi-layered vocal parts. He had clearly done a lot of prep before coming to the studio, but he was also thinking on the fly. I knew he was a songwriter and multi-instrumentalist, but I had no comprehension he was able to do that too, so it was an unexpected joy."

With Longdon on board *Master James Of St. George* truly came alive. Though the song has just 26 words of lyrics, it builds ever upwards, thanks largely to the singer's abilities as both vocalist and vocal arranger. He could also embrace the freedom afforded by Big Big Train's dim

view of live work. "Because we weren't going to play gigs we could really go for it," says Longdon. "It was a bit of a Beatles, *Sgt. Pepper* thing – we could be more experimental in the studio than possibly we would have been if we'd been a standard gigging band. At that point there was no thought of playing the songs live at all."

Though largely instrumental, the album's opener *Evening Star* begins with Longdon a cappella – his thickly produced, tightly harmonised 'ahs' and 'ohs' setting the tone. This leads into *Master James Of St. George*, another showcase for him. That sequencing was no accident – it was by Andy Poole's design. "Andy wanted to get the new singer heard as soon as possible," says Longdon. "The a cappella section that starts *Evening Star* was recorded for the middle of the song. It was Andy's idea to copy that and move it to the front, so then I started recording and layering vocals, whooshing noises. We tried to make it sound like an extraordinary opening to an album. I work fast in the studio and they saw me build these soundscapes and layer vocals and sounds and noises. When we played it back, the results were clearly there and we could hear it was working."

Longdon had arrived at Aubitt with a car boot stuffed with an array of colourful instruments. Over those two days he also laid down parts on flute, keyboard, mandolin, glockenspiel, psaltery (a zither-like instrument) and dulcimer. His taste for such exotica would inform the band's sound from here on in, but the biggest moment for Gregory Spawton arrived when they began work on the album's monumental 23-minute title track.

"I'd written it in two halves," he says, "and I'd worked out a way to get back to what we call the 'Twelve Stones' section in the middle of the song. But I felt it needed something else – if you're going to invest 20 minutes in a song you rightly want it to blow you away – and so I asked David to improvise over it at the end. Thinking on his feet, he dove into the words and gave this beautiful, soulful improvisation over the last 20 bars and, Christ, it took the song to a different level. I was brimming up in the studio, thinking that this was completely beyond how we had worked before."

In video footage Poole recorded during these sessions, you can see Longdon singing his heart out in the booth, while, in the control room, Spawton and Aubrey are marvelling at the sheer quality of what he's doing. "Sometimes recording vocals is a real chore," Aubrey tells Spawton on the tape, "but this is just joyous." And Spawton agrees, as he soaks Longdon up: "I think he's a real talent, to be honest. He's dragging us out of our 'bedroom', isn't he? It's just the way he sings a word like 'far' [in the line '*He could still see far*']. The tone of it, it's just beautiful."

Over the years a useful word, an acronym, had emerged among Big Big Train's two key members. If a musical passage, a line or a sound just wasn't working for Spawton, he would tell Poole that it was 'BTFOOM' (pronounced 'bee-tee-foom'), or 'Bugging The Fuck Out Of Me' – and had to be fixed. There were no major BTFOOM moments over Longdon's first weekend, but another telling moment did emerge. At one point Spawton was getting himself in a knot about the chorus for *Winchester Diver*, fretting that it wasn't finished, loading it with extra chords and adornments in search of a fix. "David turned to me and just said, 'Greg, it's a fucking *chorus*! Stop fannying around trying to make it more complicated.' I immediately knew what he meant. A chorus should simply bring people together, in a way that something over-complicated just

won't. I said, 'Yeah, that's fair enough.'"

Longdon's character was clearly chiming well with that of the others. And above all, he finally imbued Big Big Train's music with the rare quality that A&R man Michael Stack had spotted in him over a decade earlier. He added soul. "I brought David in as a singer," says Spawton, "and found out that I had a singer with exceptional vocal arranging and instrumental ability, and with real soul. Peter Gabriel, John Wetton, Jon Anderson – they all have soul, they're not mechanical. Progressive rock is difficult music, and if you can convey emotion among the time signatures and stuff, that's when you start to achieve things. Music is about moments, and David can deliver those moments."

Aubrey's instincts had been spot on again, and Spawton's gamble had paid off. But that first day of hard work took its toll on Longdon. He was staying at Spawton's house, and on the drive home from Aubitt Spawton found the singer a little dark, brusque, even argumentative. But he quickly realised that "David was just dead on his feet. He'd been up since four in the morning to drive to us, he had burned the fuse all day and then it just went out."

"Those sessions were very heavy," Longdon confirms. "I was tired. I had a lot to do, and my temper would fray. Also I thought I'd put the Genesis experience away, but there was still a lot of anger around it. When it started to be reawakened, there was stuff I hadn't dealt with, and Greg was on the end of some of that as well."

On the long drive home to Shrewsbury after his second, intense day, Longdon had time to stew over all this. His exciting experience at Aubitt had stoked the embers of that lost Genesis dream, but had also sparked some new ones, deep down. "I was a starving man and I'd just been given a banquet. I had this huge toy emporium and a brief to go in and make the music brilliant. In those days we had very little time in the studio – money was tight and Big Big Train were in the red. But we were all hungry for it. By the time I came in, *The Underfall Yard* was written, it was done. I just tried to make it more extraordinary with the embellishments and arrangements I put on it."

Despite the success of that two-day recording session, the plan went no further at that point than to see how this one album went. With Longdon back home, Spawton and Poole reviewed the material, and knew they were onto something.

Back on the Big Big Train drum stool for *The Underfall Yard*, Nick D'Virgilio had approached his own two-day recording session as just another gig. "I knew I was getting paid to record some drums," he says, "I liked the guys, and the music was interesting and challenging to play. There's some really hard stuff in there – they were pushing their

The first promo picture with David at Throop Mill, Bournemouth, July 2009.

boundaries, and they would get more adventurous by the record. At the start I'd record lots of parts for them, not knowing at the end of my session what the finished product is going to be – the guys figured that out later after I'm gone. So I just played off what I heard, the groove and the vibe of the song, and also what Greg was trying to explain to me, without knowing what it would sound like in the end."

This recording method meant the band made the most of D'Virgilio's unlimited talent and limited time. He would play to the song's demos with a click track, breaking each one down into manageable sections and laying down several takes for each one. On his last take Poole and Spawton would exhort him to really go for it, to go all out prog. Later, Poole and Spawton would listen to the plentiful material he had given them and, as the demo developed into the final version of the song, Poole would edit D'Virgilio's drum parts in accordingly, often stitching together just the most complicated parts, those 'just go for it' moments. That was fine when Big Big Train was a studio project, but would be a different story years later, when D'Virgilio had to learn the parts for live shows. "I don't know how I pulled some of them off!" he says. "The way Andy edited them was a bit 'left of centre'. We didn't even talk about playing live then, so I didn't worry about that, and went for it. Having to learn the parts later was insane. Parts of the song *The Underfall Yard* are crazy, and *Victorian Brickwork* is very strange, particularly the beginning section."

Hungry now, Poole and Spawton looked for other ways of enhancing the music. On a walk through the city of Bath with his partner Kathy, Gregory Spawton passed a bandstand where a brass band was playing an adagio. He found this strong yet gently stoic sound to be profoundly moving, loaded with pathos, and evocative of the industrial towns and mining communities that fascinated him. He immediately called Poole to say they simply had to have a brass band on the album. Poole saw the point, and suggested adding this to the climax of *Victorian Brickwork*.

Both he and Spawton knew that, unlike strings, brass was hard to emulate well digitally. Only the real thing would do, and they brought the topic up with Rob Aubrey. It was beyond the band's finances, and Aubitt's modest floor space, to accommodate a full colliery band of around 20 brass players. Instead, Aubrey suggested that a four- or five-piece section would be more workable, and he had a lead on a local Southampton musician who could make this happen.

As a trombonist in the Band of the Coldstream Guards, Dave Desmond had regularly participated in the Changing of the Guard at Buckingham Palace. He had played with the band at ceremonial and state events, at impressive venues like the Royal Albert Hall and St Paul's Cathedral, and he was a skilled brass arranger too. He wrote and

Dave Desmond at the Queen's Diamond Jubilee Concert,
June 2012.

arranged the fanfare that opened the Live 8 charity concert at Hyde Park in 2005 (an event so significant that David Gilmour and Roger Waters put their differences behind them for a Pink Floyd headline set). Aubrey made contact with Desmond through mutual friends.

"Rob said they were after that brass band feel," says Desmond, "which is epitomised by that deep vibrato and has that almost melancholy style. For reference Greg sent me a couple of things by [Yorkshire folk artist] Kate Rusby, including her song *My Young Man*. That was right up my street, and not only that – the players I planned to draft in had actually played with Kate Rusby before."

When he was sent a simple demo of *Victorian Brickwork*, Desmond felt something of a Proustian rush. As a kid, he used to listen to his brother's Genesis albums – *A Trick Of The Tail*, *Selling England By The Pound*. "I'd forgotten all about them over the years, and the song evoked those strongly for me. It was almost like coming home, in a strange way. Then they sent me a very basic demo of *The Underfall Yard*, with no drums and a single line melody of how they heard the brass. I wasn't sure from that if it was going to work."

He set about composing the parts, assembled his players and, just a few weeks later, Desmond, Rich Evans (cornet/trumpet), Nick Stones (French horn) and Jon Truscott (tuba) crammed themselves into Aubitt's hot, cosy live room. Over a few hours they created the very textures Spawton had in mind. By that time there was more meat on the bones of the song, and it was only then that Desmond really understood how his parts fitted. "Once we heard what was behind it," he says, "we thought, 'Oh wow, this is going to be *beautiful...*'"

It Bites' Francis Dunnery was approached to add a guitar

solo to the title track, with Spawton seeking the blisteringly fast legato work that punctuated It Bites tracks such as *Turn Me Loose* and *Plastic Dreamer*. "But he wouldn't do it," says Spawton. "Francis was going through a period where he was rejecting progressive rock, so luring him was very difficult. He had played guitar with Robert Plant in the '90s, Robert is rootsy, and that had a big impact on Frank – he was in a different place. He did a decent solo for us though." Dunnery's honorarium for his part was a contribution to The Charlie and Kathleen Dunnery Children's Fund, his charity dedicated to the wellbeing of children in his native Cumbria.

At this time Jem Godfrey was making waves in the prog world with *Milliontown*, the 2008 debut album by his progressive band Frost*. A gifted keyboardist and writer, Godfrey had previously enjoyed lucrative success as a producer and songwriter for big pop artists such as Atomic Kitten, Blue and *The X Factor* star Shayne Ward. Spawton and Poole had been honoured to have him endorse Big Big Train around the time of *Gathering Speed*, predicting that they would 'do something great one day'. "The playing on *Milliontown* is amazing," says Spawton. "For *The Underfall Yard* I wanted something showier than usual, so we approached Jem and he quickly came back with a solo played on a [state of the art] Roland V-Synth."

And another large piece of the Big Big Train puzzle was also falling into place. Back when David Longdon had contributed to Louis Philippe's 1996 album *Jackie Girl* he had met and befriended guitarist Dave Gregory. For 20 years Gregory had played guitar for XTC, the British band that Gregory Spawton, Andy Poole and millions of others consider to be one of the finest of their era. Gregory had appeared on every XTC album from 1979's *Drums And*

David Longdon in 1999 recording a full-length version of Supper's Ready *for Dave Gregory's* Remoulds *project. The song has never been released.*

Wires up to '99's *Apple Venus Volume 1*, including 1992's *Nonsuch* – one of Spawton and Poole's all-time favourite records.

Outside of XTC, Gregory's turn with Philippe was just one strand in a long and varied session career. His proggier credits included guitar on Peter Gabriel's third self-titled solo album from 1980 (known as *Melt*) and, in '97, Steve Hogarth's extra-Marillion *Ice Cream Genius* LP with his all-star h Band.

Released the same year, Porcupine Tree's modern prog classic *In Absentia* featured string arrangements by Gregory too. He had also contributed to his share of pop – sugary

Steve Hogarth's h Band in 2000.

hits by Lulu, Take That's Mark Owen, and TV soap star turned pop star Jason Donovan. He had even played guitar and Mellotron on *Wild River*, the solo album by his good mate David Longdon.

The singer called the guitarist in 2008 to talk about this promising band from Bournemouth he had become involved with. At that point Gregory was 56, and at something of a loose end. "I was doing absolutely nothing at that moment," he recalls. "Having been idle for such a long time, I'd put a covers band together with some friends in Swindon, but had basically resigned myself to being 'retired' – staying at home, listening to music and not playing professionally. The phone had stopped ringing. I had assumed I was too old to be rocking and rolling. But I got the calls from Dan and David almost within the same month."

The Dan in question was Daniel Steinhardt, with whom Gregory would form the prog rock/pop quartet Tin Spirits that year. They would come to notice with two excellent, critically lauded albums, *Wired To Earth* (2011) and *Scorch* (2014), before disbanding amicably in 2018. Once David

Longdon was firmly ensconced in the recording of *The Underfall Yard* in 2009, he reported back to Gregory that the album was shaping up nicely, Big Big Train had some great star guests on there and – hint, hint – they were looking for some more.

Gregory Spawton had written the song *Last Train* to accommodate a long guitar solo, and this was sent to Dave Gregory. "I had never been asked to sustain a solo for that length of time," he says. "I didn't know what Greg was expecting to hear, and that was liberating – I was flattered that they would want to hear that much from me. I followed my instincts."

As well as a guitar player, Dave Gregory was a collector and tinkerer. He had recently acquired a new toy, a Fender Custom Esquire, a Korean-made budget guitar he had souped up with a high-end Gibson humbucker pickup. Plugging this Esquire into his home studio in Swindon, he set about working up an inspired two-minute guitar salvo that was some way beyond even Spawton's considerable skill with the instrument.

When this recording arrived in Bournemouth it surpassed all expectations. "We were euphoric," says Andy Poole. "Dave was unproven doing a long solo – he'd never done that with XTC, and was used to 18 years of indifference to his parts from Andy Partridge – but this solo was stunning. And having Dave Gregory on the album felt like a big deal for us. Soon after that we met him in Bristol, and it really was like meeting one of your heroes."

Gregory remembers the encouragingly positive response. "They were over the moon with what I'd done. I thought they would book a studio so I could come down to record it properly, but they wanted to use the demo itself. And that was my entrance into the band. Then they sent me *Master James Of St. George, Evening Star, Victorian Brickwork, The Underfall Yard.*"

In that title track's latter moments, Gregory's tasty, bluesy guitar lines snaked around Longdon's expressive improv. The guitarist recorded all his parts at home, where he would lay down the vast majority of his Big Big Train work over the next decade. "It means you can spend as long as you like selecting your sounds," he explains, "and you can take as long as you need on 16 bars of music until it's right – poor Rob would be driven out of his mind. It also means you can call your own takes. When satisfied, I can send it in, happy in my own mind it was the best I could have done. Nobody had to sit and listen to all my mistakes, and I didn't have to turn a blind eye to people's grimaces when I fucked up!"

There were no mistakes in what Gregory sent in, and his consummate, often sublime guitar contributions were yet another scoop of coal into the Big Big Train engine. Dave Desmond's brass band was a big milestone too, an unusual sonic trademark in the world of progressive rock, one that gave the record a very British warmth, depth and gravitas. Nick D'Virgilio was now on board as their 'permanent guest drummer', and they had also stumbled upon a stellar vocalist who could bring the whole picture together. This had driven

The Underfall Yard *cover painting by Jim Trainer.*

Gregory Spawton to fine-tune his songs to the very best of his abilities, until he felt that *The Underfall Yard* comprised his most accomplished set of songs to date, and made him determined to do even better. Add to that Jim Trainer's striking, thematically apt artwork for the album, and, to Spawton, the band's offering was stronger than ever.

Andy Poole knew the new record was good, but not at the expense of their back catalogue. "When we finished it I didn't think, 'Here's this, forget everything else'. But I knew it was good and had moved us on to another level. *The Underfall Yard* was a sea change album in that it heralded the arrival of David, and we again embraced the traditionally tried and tested prog approach with a wealth of 12-string guitars and Mellotron. So it didn't seem like a shift in direction, more business as usual with bells on."

The Underfall Yard's release date, 15th December 2009, was another hint at the band's relative naivety. Christmas is a graveyard shift for the music industry, a period reserved mainly for festive cash-ins, greatest hits compilations and gift-friendly boxsets. The album got a little lost in the seasonal shuffle, but in 2010 sales took off, helped by a raft of positive reviews. *Classic Rock*'s venerable prog columnist Geoff Barton once again enthused about the band. They were, he said, getting better and better by the album, and he judged *The*

Underfall Yard to be 'an Anglo-prog masterclass packed full of tall tales and deep laments. The brilliantly melancholic *Victorian Brickwork* is a standout.'

And prog rock's horizons were widening with the publication of a brand new glossy magazine. *Classic Rock Presents Prog* was an offshoot of the well-established *Classic Rock,* and the UK's first mass market publication dedicated entirely to the progressive rock genre. It was the brainchild of Jerry Ewing, the battle-hardened British rock journalist who had founded *Classic Rock* back in '98.

While also a devotee of classic bands like AC/DC and Black Sabbath, Ewing's passion for progressive rock went back to the early '80s, when as a teenager he fell under the spell of Marillion circa *Market Square Heroes*. At one of that band's Marquee shows he picked up a copy of their newsletter, *The Web*, and was inspired to dabble in music writing for the first time himself. Lasting for seven issues, his own fanzine *Court Jester* was dedicated to Marillion, Pendragon, Twelfth Night and other 'Marquee names' of that decade.

Progressive rock had enjoyed a boost in the late '80s and early '90s through the rise of the prog metal scene, with bands such as Dream Theater, Queensrÿche and Tool proudly bringing a symphonic depth to their chugging guitar riffs. By the late 2000s, Ewing for one could see that the progressive scene was flourishing in the internet age. As printed fanzines slowly became fondly remembered vestiges of times passed, prog was finding a home online. Fans were sharing their appreciation for – and plentiful opinions on – this music through chatrooms and forums, such as the popular Progressive Ears (progressiveears. org). Enthusiasts curated websites dedicated to the cause, among them The Progressive Aspect (theprogressiveaspect.

net), and – with *Feedback*'s Kev Rowland one of its main contributors – Prog Archives (progarchives.com).

It was standard practice for bands to have their own sites to maintain contact with their listeners and sell records and merchandise. Social media – especially Facebook and Twitter – played an increasingly crucial role in the interaction between artist and fan. Online music stores – from Bandcamp to Tim Bowness's Burning Shed – served this loyal audience, who existed largely under the radar of the mainstream media. By 2008 then, Jerry Ewing sensed a real sea change.

"There was something happening in prog around then," he says. "There seemed a slight resurgence of interest, and less of a sneery attitude from the mainstream media. The hangover from the *NME*'s line that 'punk killed prog' had waned, and the people who thought like that no longer occupied positions of power in other media. Then the BBC made *Prog Britannia* as part of their excellent *Britannia* documentary series on various genres of music. I thought, 'Right, this is the optimum point – if we don't go now this is never going to happen.'"

That same year he pitched the idea to Future Publishing, whose diverse portfolio included *Classic Rock* and leading heavy metal monthly *Metal Hammer*. With the world in the grip of a crushing recession, 2008 was hardly an ideal time to launch such a risky new venture, but Ewing's paymasters saw that the idea had legs, and the first edition of *Classic Rock Presents Prog* appeared in March 2009. Months later, when it was clear the magazine had a momentum all its own, its title was shortened to *Prog*. The demands of sales targets and shelf appeal dictated that recognisable, big-name acts – Pink Floyd, Genesis, King Crimson, ELP – had to go on the cover, but this new title was also a boon for the ever growing crop of upcoming artists, including Big Big Train.

"*Prog* was tailor made for our audience," says Gregory Spawton. "When it came out I remember thinking it felt utterly bizarre that a mainstream magazine dedicated to this music would be in high street stores. There was a slight turning of the tide, and we felt more positive. We were doing better, and now there was a magazine in the UK for our audience, which made it easier to connect with them."

"Some of the old guard were actually suspicious of us at first," Ewing recalls, "but the smaller bands said, 'Thank god – we've got a mouthpiece!' It's easy to dismiss the Big Big Trains and Galahads of this world as being plankton in a giant ocean, but we didn't treat them like that. They were and they remain important in the scene because it's not all about the memory of Yes and Genesis. The prog community – the little, prog-centric labels and individual bands – all supported *Prog* from the off. They put their hands in their pockets and bought ads, bought space on the cover CD. We're a commercial entity, but I see us a service for that prog community as a whole. That's why there's more of a personal connection between the magazine and the bands and the people who buy it. Perhaps that's why it's seen as important for bands like Big Big Train."

The Underfall Yard was warmly received in the progressive ecosystem online, and in print. In his flattering half-page review in *Prog*, Ewing called it the band's finest album to date, and honed in on how they 'mine a rich and rewarding seam through the heart of an England gone by [...] conjuring up wistful tales that spring to life thanks to the boundless musicianship and Longdon's emotive delivery.'

Soon after that the band were the subject of a page long feature in *Prog*'s 'On The Threshold' section, which puts the spotlight on notable new artists. Here and elsewhere in the prog-related press, Longdon's brush with Genesis level fame was a newsworthy angle, as was Nick D'Virgilio's own stint with that band on *Calling All Stations*. Longdon and D'Virgilio knew it and acquiesced to countless questions about the hows and whys and could have beens. For Gregory Spawton and Andy Poole it looked like their years of hard work, patience and tenacity were finally paying off, but they were about to have their first major disagreement.

❖❖❖

CD sales had reached an all-time peak in around 2000, then stagnated year on year as the internet era unfolded. While the taste for tangible albums remained (and remains) strong among the progressive community, vast swathes of music fans switched away from the format, preferring to buy music as digital files, from sites such as the market leader, iTunes. Then, in the late 2000s, the model began to shift again, with the advent of subscription streaming services. Through companies like Spotify and Apple Music, consumers now had access to a colossal library of recordings, effectively renting them without ever actually owning them. Through 'free' sharing sites such as YouTube, millions of uploaded songs and albums were available to all. And piracy remained a stubborn problem, with an unpoliceable number of file sharing sites allowing less scrupulous listeners to obtain any music they wanted for no money down.

This tough new landscape had been the final nail in the coffin for the likes of IQ's disheartened keyboardist Martin Orford, but Gregory Spawton was committed to finding the best route through it for Big Big Train. The terrain could be hostile, but there were also opportunities if you were shrewd. Spawton proceeded to read everything he could about the new paradigm of the music business, and he wanted to try an experiment: "We weren't gigging, so I thought let's offer up something radical. Let's put *The Underfall Yard*'s title track on our website. No 'tip box' payment system or anything like that – let's put it online as a proper, high-end WAV file, so people could download it for free. It was our magnum opus at that time, and it was so good that it needed to be heard. For me it was a Trojan horse – it was a way of breaking through to more people. But Andy was totally opposed to giving away stuff for free, as he saw it."

"So much blood, sweat and tears to produce that title track," says Poole now, "and then to have it seemingly relegated to the status of a giveaway. There was an emerging trend of artists doing likewise, and even giving away a complete CD with some daily newspapers. But then that same artist was gigging the London O2 for a couple of nights…"

There was no possibility of Big Big Train recouping money through gigging, but David Longdon still thinks Spawton's 'giveaway' was a masterstroke: "We were selling the album for five or six quid, something ridiculous like that, because we wanted to sell a shitload of them, and we did. The download got the word out, and people then saw the album was affordable. You have to speculate to accumulate, which we did. And it spread like wildfire."

Over 2010 alone *The Underfall Yard* sold around 20,000 copies, a pretty staggering figure for what was still very much an underground studio project. "It took off very quickly," says Spawton, "and we were completely blown away by it, particularly because we weren't gigging or doing any other promotion. People just seemed to like it and think we were doing something different. When I look back on it, I suppose we were."

Many years later, a poll on the band's own Facebook page (established in 2009) revealed that the download of the song *The Underfall Yard* was a gateway moment for many longer term listeners; it was their way into the band's world. Spawton felt utterly vindicated: "It strengthened my instinct that all my reading and thinking about how we could navigate the music industry maze was making my judgement of more value to the band than Andy's more cautious judgement. He wasn't doing any of that research – he just didn't seem that interested in it. In my opinion our partnership was becoming unequal, even back then."

But for all the success, and the importance of the album in the group's story, Nick D'Virgilio wasn't overly enamoured with *The Underfall Yard* at first. "I didn't hate it," he says, "but maybe listened to it just once. It was interesting and I liked David's voice, but I didn't think of the future. I had so many other things on my mind – it was just another project. I didn't see the day to day building that was actually happening, and that could be because I'm 3,000 miles away and not in the UK where a lot of the groundswell was really happening. I just thought it was another cool album to be on."

David Longdon was paid a princely £199 for his work on *The Underfall Yard*, but his future as Big Big Train's vocalist was assured. For him the success with the band had come immediately, "but obviously for Greg and Andy it had been 20 years getting to that point. When the positive reviews came in for *The Underfall Yard* – and there were waves of them – it was a real shot in the arm for all of us. It is an extraordinary sounding album, but that was the whole point. We wanted to make a striking record. It remains a dramatic, exciting listen for me. It has a lot of emotion and heart. It was a very lucky album for us – the momentum and energy from it stayed with us, and helped to propel us onto the new phase. I remember Rob had finished mixing it and wrote a very emotional letter to Greg and Andy saying what it meant to him. For all of us it was a crowning achievement. It's definitely our *Deep Purple In Rock*."

Jem Godfrey had once suggested that Longdon was the missing piece in Big Big Train's jigsaw puzzle. But the opposite was also true. In Spawton and Poole he had found brothers in arms, and together the band was, at last, truly gathering speed. "We were doing well and we were getting on well," says Longdon. "The creative decisions Greg and I were making were working. There was a strong element of trust between us that nurtured very quickly because we were on a roll. The fact that *The Underfall Yard* was doing well made us braver. We could reach and dream."

New horizons: Andy, David, Gregory on 17th July 2009.

VII

'And shadows are cast by the stones,
along the road that leads us home...'

DAVE GREGORY HAD LONG BEEN DUBIOUS about much of the music that passed for progressive rock. He found that most of the 1980s second-wave, 'neo prog' bands he had heard in his time weren't actually that progressive at all. They often valued style over content, he thought, with too few good tunes and too many noodly solos, and they cleaved too closely to the tropes of the genre's pioneers.

"All the successful prog bands from the early 1970s had good songs," he says, "melody and proper musical skills. They weren't just a platform for soloists, and if you're going to make an instrumental album you'd better be bloody good, and not just average. So I was suspicious of the term 'progressive', but when I heard Greg's songs I knew they definitely had something. Thought had gone into them, with proper lyrics that had been researched – little history lessons in places. It took me back to what I loved about Bob Dylan and Robbie Robertson in The Band in the late 1960s. All of Robertson's songs were like little pocket history lessons too. The lyrics really drew me into the music, rather than the music drawing attention to the lyrics."

Gregory was aware that the unsigned Big Big Train barely broke even and, on paper at least, was a hobby band. He had accepted a lower, 'mates rates' fee for his services on *The Underfall Yard*, due to his friendship with David Longdon. It had been an enjoyable gig, but he also assumed it would be a one off. "I thought *The Underfall Yard* was brilliant. It was great music and I did wonder if they would ask me back, but I wasn't really expecting them to. Having made the album, I thought another nation of musicians like Francis Dunnery would be willing to contribute, and I would go back to being retired. I didn't think I'd be called a second time."

Gregory and David Longdon's mutual friend Louis Philippe was, like Rob Aubrey, a magnet for talent of all stripes. Take his musical director/double bassist – a tall, considered man whose musical tastes had, compared to most, matured in Benjamin Button-like reverse motion.

Danny Manners was born in Edgware, north London in 1958, into a musical family. His mother had trained to be an opera singer but hadn't pursued the calling. His father loved to play accordion at parties, and would happily teach his young son some boogie woogie piano licks on the family joanna. The boy showed promise and took piano lessons from the age of 8, and, just like his future bandmate Gregory Spawton, Manners was made to learn recorder with his class in primary school.

"My secondary school had a really good music department," says Manners, "and that's where I first

The Louis Philippe band featuring Philippe Auclair, Dave Gregory, David Longdon and Danny Manners.

Bowie passed him by. He loves *The Lamb Lies Down On Broadway* now, but back then Genesis weren't for him either. "I suppose it was the theatrical delivery, and I didn't really like Peter Gabriel's voice. My huge prog love at school was Gentle Giant, whose music was really interesting and advanced. I saw them at the New Theatre in Victoria in '75. Glam rock was in at the time and musically that was a return to rock 'n' roll – not for me. I got into Yes too, the classic *Close To The Edge* era. The classical influences in Genesis were more from the Romantic era, but in some Yes and a lot of Gentle Giant I could hear they had listened to 20th century classical like Stravinsky and Sibelius."

BBC Radio 3 informed his classical tastes, and through the station's few shows dedicated to jazz he cottoned on to Charles Mingus, Miles Davis, John Coltranc. His love affair with the form continued at King's College, Cambridge, where he played in numerous jazz ensembles while studying for his degree in English. He turned his nose up at the 'three chord crap' of punk, and while the post punk/ new wave explosion eluded him in school, it eventually caught up with him at university.

picked up the double bass. I composed a few things – chamber pieces, stuff for carol concerts – then in 1972 the headmaster got us tickets for a memorial concert at the Royal Albert Hall. It was Leonard Bernstein conducting *The Rite Of Spring* and other pieces by Stravinsky, who had died the year before. I became a Stravinsky nut after that, and started really getting into him and other composers like Debussy, Ravel and Bartók."

As a teenager in the '70s Manners was most likely to be found enjoying a record by these past masters, or maybe his favourite fusioneers Weather Report. With no interest in the visual side of the musical arts, even greats like David

Jazz odyssey: Danny Manners in 1977.

to graduation, he sheepishly told his careers advisor that what he really wanted to be was a jazz musician. Instead, he was pointed to the burgeoning world of computing. Once established – the advisor suggested – Manners could go freelance, make his own hours, which would allow time for his musical ambitions. Manners saw the logic. His lifelong career in IT began at a London software house, and when not at the keyboard (the QWERTY kind) he spent much of the '80s onwards playing double bass in conventional and contemporary modern jazz outfits across town.

Manners usually found himself on the outskirts of the scene, usually on its left periphery. He went on to perform

Ideal Home, 1980.

"I thought you either had stuff that was very complex and expansive and interesting, or you had stuff that was very stripped down and boring. In Cambridge they had a record library with lots of rock and pop. I borrowed *Go 2*, the second album by XTC, purely on the strength of the Hipgnosis cover. It had these weird dissonant chords in it, but the whole thing was stripped down. Then I discovered all these other bands like Wire, Scritti Politti, Pere Ubu, Gang Of Four. It was a revelation – you could do something raw, but it could be weird and interesting too."

His college band, Ideal Home, was inspired by XTC and Talking Heads, but jazz was still his real love. Prior and record with some truly maverick artists: Stuart Moxham, songwriter for Welsh post-punk outfit Young Marble Giants; Sandy Dillon, the hard-living New England firebrand who once played Janis Joplin off Broadway; The Fatima Mansions' darkly intense singer Cathal Coughlan, a Scott Walker type with a louring Celtic broodiness to him. And, in an old railway building outside of Camden, he fell in with the London Music Collective.

This rag-tag collection of young bohemians and old hippies made music together and played vibrantly anarchic gigs, often to near-empty rooms. In '87 Manners moved into the ranks of The Happy End, an often 20-strong ensemble whose 'swinging socialism' saw leader Matt Fox's Maoist lyrics set to intoxicating big band arrangements. Freighted with tracks like *The Red Flag*, *The Oakey Strike Evictions* and *Rhumba Por Nicaragua*, their 1990 LP *Turn Things Upside Down* still sparkles today, its theme song sung by Soft Machine's legendary linchpin, Robert Wyatt.

"I enjoyed Soft Machine and the Canterbury sound," says Manners. "I discovered Hatfield And The North and National Health a little later, but I'd forgotten about prog in the '80s. I knew nothing about the second and third waves, other than Marillion because they had a hit single."

If prog had fallen by the wayside for him, he finally got into pop when he met Louis Philippe in the late '80s. At the start of their fruitful and still ongoing relationship, the Frenchman set Manners right on a few things. "Louis told me, 'You need to listen to The Beach Boys – Brian Wilson is a genius!'. I had that stereotype, sun and surf image of them, and had never really listened to them before. But Louis was right, he changed my mind totally."

Starting as Philippe's bassist, Manners soon became his arranger too, and in the run-up to the 1996 album *Jackie Girl* Philippe enthusiastically played Manners a tape he'd been sent by a fan, a talented singer called David Longdon. The three met, got on well, and played some shows together. Longdon then appeared on *Jackie Girl*, performing backing vocals, slide and acoustic guitar, and flute.

He and Manners became fast friends, and even recorded their own song together the following year, *Dreams Of Harry Beck*, inspired by the designer of the iconic London Underground map. In 2010 Longdon mentioned he was singing for an upcoming Bournemouth progressive rock band, and invited his friend to play double bass on a moody ballad for their forthcoming EP. Long out of touch with the progressive world, Danny Manners was rather intrigued.

◆◆◆

To Gregory Spawton, *The Underfall Yard* album had represented a significant step forward for Big Big Train, with a satisfying recording experience and the revelation of David Longdon's diverse talents. Despite this record's success, the band's finances were such that Big Big Train was still more a costly passion project than a viable business. The band had been on the verge of petering out several times, but now there was a new impetus to forge ahead. With still no thought of playing live, there was now pressure on two fronts to get new material out there. The band had to keep the Big Big Train story rolling and maintain their rising profile among their growing fanbase. Also, given the extra value David Longdon had brought with him, it was vital to keep him interested.

With a full-time job and a busy family life in Shrewsbury, Longdon had little scope to get down to Bournemouth for the protracted writing sessions needed for a full length album. Andy Poole – with his producer hat on – suggested an alternative approach: an EP based on existing, unused material.

Spawton had an old instrumental demo called *The Wide Open Sea*, a small excerpt of which had featured on *The Difference Machine*. It was loosely based on the colourful life of Belgian chanson master Jacques Brel, but Spawton had run out of steam while writing it, and parked it, considering it a ramshackle series of ideas rather than a coherent composition. Poole fished it out of their hard drive and sent it to Longdon to see what he could do with it.

Poole also sent him *Brambling*, a half-written song shelved in the lead-up to *The Difference Machine*, and *Fat Billy Shouts Mine*, which in its original form hadn't made the cut for *The Underfall Yard*. Also on its way to Longdon was Spawton's Christmas break-up song *British Racing Green*, originally written for *English Boy Wonders*, but vetoed by Poole on the grounds that it was just too depressing.

Again, the work that Longdon returned on these songs thrilled the pair. And whereas previously Spawton had been resistant to others getting in on the songwriting, Longdon's way with things, and the almost contrapuntal talents he and Spawton possessed, made their de facto co-writing very smooth.

"Greg had a very tight grip on the songwriting," says Poole, "and he and I had a tight grip on things overall. David knew that. He didn't try to change any lyrics on *The Underfall Yard* – he was singing them as written. Had he come in and tried to re-write things or present himself as a package deal with his writing, that might have put a different complexion on him joining the band. There had been a couple of occasions where Sean Filkins had tried to change or write lyrics and was completely knocked back by

Greg. Sean had presented a couple of songs for us to do, and they were diplomatically kicked into the long grass. But once David had sung on *The Underfall Yard*, Greg realised he was adding a lot of value to the songs, and taking them up another level."

"I didn't want to give up chief songwriter role," admits Spawton, "but David had skills I didn't have – he completed my skillset, and when that happens you do have to open yourself up to it. I can't recall having any concerns about him contributing. I trusted him implicitly with my chord sequences, and it took some of the pressure off me. I couldn't see how I would get *British Racing Green*, *Brambling* or *The Wide Open Sea* finished in a way that would satisfy me, and I was interested to see what David would come back with."

By the time the 2010 Big Big Train line-up finished with it, *The Wide Open Sea* had risen from a patchy demo into a monolithic epic over 17 minutes long. Longdon had picked up on scratch lyrics Spawton sang on his sketch recording, intended just to indicate where the melody would be. "Some of it didn't make sense at all," says Longdon, "and I liked that. I tried to put that into the story. When I was listening to the music my elder daughter said it sounded like ghosts, so I thought it could be a ghost story, and it started making sense as a supernatural tale. When we did the title song of *The Underfall Yard* I remember saying we'd probably never record anything as long as it again. Lo and behold, the next time we were in the studio we recorded this huge, sprawling piece. I think it's a bit under the radar amongst our audience, but it's a real gem. It doesn't hurry and takes a long time to get to its climax. We've got that squall of noise that sounds desperate and terrifying – it's quite a dark piece."

Longdon took Spawton's music for *Brambling*, adapted some of the melody and wrote a tender new set of words. "It's about sex," he says, "that period when young people discover the erotic side of their nature as they go through puberty. I think it addresses that quite poetically, and it was fun to write. It's the idea that you need to be wounded in order to grow – that's how we reach emotional maturity. Writing about sex is odd – the song is quite explicit if you read the lyrics. Someone kindly said they thought the lyrics had something of DH Lawrence in their feel. I'll take that!"

Longdon's approach to *British Racing Green* taught Spawton a lot about the craft. "It was an incredible lesson in how a song can be transformed by arrangement," Spawton says. "David had ideas about these layers of vocals, like a 10cc thing. I'd never seen that before – reimagining songs from the ground up while keeping the structure the same. He sweetened it, so it changed from being just miserable to being beautifully sad. Thanks in large part to him, it became one of the strongest things I've ever done."

"I don't think Greg could see the wood for the trees with *British Racing Green*," Longdon reckons. "I acted like a producer on that one. I put in more instruments and gave it the claustrophobic synth pads in the middle and the double bass part. I like using external stimuli: if you imagine a video for the song, it would be a couple sitting in a restaurant just looking at each other, but with everything around them exploding, and they're just unmoved by it."

The sad, slow sleigh bell in the song's refrain, '*We tore each other's hearts out*', was just one lovely nuance that this new, collaborative spirit brought about, along with Longdon's soul-wrenching '*Baby baby*' improvisations towards the end, and his beautiful flute lines. Tony Müller had recorded a gorgeous, moody piano part for the song's

English Boy Wonders iteration, and that was retained in the new version.

Later, Spawton wondered more than once why this incongruous ballad didn't annoy the band's stauncher, prog-centric fans. "Sometimes when we've done music which clearly isn't in the progressive rock genre it has caused concerns. But there's so much soul in there, it doesn't really annoy that part of our audience. Perhaps it's because it's a classic break-up song and so many people have experienced that. It's universal, it resonates."

And when the band decided the song needed a double bass part, Longdon knew exactly who to call. "I liked the track," says Danny Manners. "It was more like Prefab Sprout than Genesis, and as I would discover it was a very atypical song for Big Big Train. I also really liked the drummer, he had a great feel."

The fact Manners didn't know Nick D'Virgilio's name spoke to his remoteness from the operation at the time. Manners recorded his bass part at Regal Lane Studio in London's Primrose Hill, overseen by its owner Ken Brake. Brake was a long-trusted, high-pedigree producer who had been another part of Louis Philippe's talented coterie, and from this point both he and Regal Lane would become another fixture in Big Big Train's recording life.

❖❖❖

To Andy Poole, Big Big Train was starting to look and feel much more like a real band. Much of this was down to David Longdon, who had earned his respect and confidence. "David solidified his position in the band," says Poole. "As well as mopping up viable unused material, he was having ideas and wanted to use real instruments rather than samples. He was pushing us slightly out of our comfort zone, or at least getting us to release control of certain things. He was so comfortable in the studio and had good instincts. We'd gone with the brass band, and now we needed to go with David on some of his ideas too."

Longdon's eclectic taste in instruments and his facility as a multi-instrumentalist was opening up new avenues for Big Big Train. Above the embellishments on zither and accordion, glockenspiel and Theremin, Longdon's flute would provide the band with yet another sonic trademark. He could make it sing, rasp and flutter, all the while tapping deeper into the band's sense of English tradition. In this context the instrument had inescapable echoes of prog rock's flautist in chief, Jethro Tull's Ian Anderson, and the genre's pastoral heritage.

While working on the EP, christened *Far Skies Deep Time*, Longdon requested a real vibraphone. When Rob Aubrey duly acquired one, it turned out to be a hefty unit that they couldn't quite angle into Aubitt's little live room. Longdon ended up recording his vibes in the kitchen. "David would turn up for a session," remembers Andy Poole with a smile, "he'd pull all these instruments out of the car and we wouldn't know what half of them were. But then you'd hear these things – like the vibraphone – and you could see where he was going. He was confident, it was in the way his ideas were working and how he could follow through and deliver on them with conviction but humour as well. And he can be a good objective judge of what's working or not – he would try things in the studio and reject them. He can be very intense but he's very engaging, and you get carried along with that."

And contrary to his own expectations, Dave Gregory was indeed called back for a second time. His atmospheric guitar work helped take *The Wide Open Sea* in its ultimate

David recording at Aubitt Studios in 2010.

grand direction, even if he wasn't overly enamoured with the song when the preliminary sketches were first delivered to him. "I thought it was 20 minutes of sheer boredom. An attempt to do a *Supper's Ready* but without the basic ingredients. But the more I listened to it, the more I thought it was like a musical cinema short, and that we had to find some atmosphere and conjure up a picture.

"David had given me a rough outline of the story, the death of Jacques Brel, about which I had known nothing. We needed some musical ghostly images of dark night on still waters, and then this turbulent storm erupting towards the end. I'd go up to my room with a 12-string electric guitar and play some atmospheric things. Then I'd get stuck and leave it for a couple of days before coming back to it. It took a long time but gradually took shape. It doesn't grab you by the throat straight off – you have to live with it, just as I did. I like the ebb and flow of it and the cinematic aspect. I do remember the first mix Rob and Andy did was *dreadful* – a great wall of sound with no peaks and troughs. I did send a rather sarcastic email outlining my dislike of what they'd done, and making some suggestions for improvement."

Gregory Spawton remembers Gregory's own 'BTFOOM' email well: "Dave got *very* upset. He has incredibly sensitive ears, and is very alert to overly compressed mixing and mastering. He – rightly – felt *The Wide Open Sea* had been mastered too hot [too loud and with minimal dynamic range], and he had a bit of a strop about it. To Rob's credit, he did not get defensive, but invited Dave down to Aubitt to help steer a new mix."

"I want to please everybody," offers Aubrey, "and I might have huffed and puffed a bit at the time, but I pulled the faders down and rebalanced the mix, and it pleased Dave. As a result we pulled the faders back a lot more on subsequent albums, so they sound a lot less ploughed [the tracks now mixed so they are not all loud and competing with each other]. That pleases Greg."

"The more I listened," adds Spawton, "the more I thought Dave was right, and our releases have become progressively more 'audiophile' over the years. The episode really helped with our overall approach to audio. It got us tuned into dynamic range issues, and The Loudness War."

A recording session at Aubitt Studios.

This so-called 'Loudness War' reflected a modern production trope that was anathema to audiophiles. To make a song stand out on CD, on radio, or online, the trend was to pump up its general volume and let a compression unit bring up any quieter moments and flatten out any louder spikes. On a Pro Tools screen the waveform of, say, XTC's *Senses Working Overtime* curves over time with the song's amplitude – the quiet verse drawing thin lines, which get thicker as the song builds up in its louder chorus. At the extreme, a pop or rock song with everything cranked up and heavily compressed looks like a thick rectangular block – three and a half minutes of uniform amplitude. For a sophisticated listener (and vinyl lover) such as Dave Gregory – sensitive to the stirring peaks and lulling troughs that give music its true dynamics – that's kryptonite. "Rob's remix vastly improved *The Wide Open Sea*," he says. "I don't think my email went down well, but I was being cruel to be kind."

Kingmaker was something of a Big Big Train deep cut. It had originally appeared in rougher form on *The Infant Hercules* 17 years previously. Spawton's skills had improved inordinately since then, and the song was revamped completely for this new record. The good parts were retained, the weaker ones re-written, with some knotty 11/8 and 7/8 prog moments added for good measure. Poole re-edited the piece with a long introduction to push it over 10 minutes, cannily ensuring that anyone wanting to hear *Kingmaker* via iTunes would have to purchase the whole EP, rather than just pay the standard 79p for that one track. Whereas they had 'given away' *The Underfall Yard*'s title track, this was the other extreme, and while Spawton thought this was somewhat sharp practice, he didn't dig his heels in.

Dave Gregory absolutely loved *Kingmaker* from the off, but just as the guitarist had initially struggled with *The Wide Open Sea*, so David Longdon at first resisted getting on board with this one. "*Kingmaker* sounded incredibly derivative to me and initially I threw my toys out of the pram about it," he says. "It seemed a step backwards, like we were letting the side down. But one Saturday night I sat down and programmed the marimbas in the middle bit, which then got moved to the front. In the end we transformed the song and got there."

Finally weighing in at ten and a half minutes, *Kingmaker* didn't appear on the original issue of *Far Skies Deep Time*, and first emerged on the covermount CD of the July 2011 edition of *Prog* magazine. Instead, the EP initially opened with Big Big Train's cover of a song by Spawton and Poole's early hero, Anthony Phillips. The pair had recently heard Phillips' well-rendered demo of *Master Of Time* on the 2008 reissue of his 1977 debut *The Geese & The Ghost*. They really took to this bonus track, and thought they could do something interesting with it.

Through EMI and Genesis's dense carapace of management and 'people', they had sent Phillips their version of *Master Of Time* and obtained his blessing to release it on *Far Skies Deep Time*. When Russian label MALS offered Big Big Train a distribution deal for the EP in that country, one of their stipulations was that the cover version was removed, to avoid any costly copyright niggles. It was thus replaced by *Kingmaker*, though both tracks would appear subsequently on the EP's digital version and its 2017 remaster.

The song also marked the first contribution to the band by Andy Tillison, the highly talented keyboardist for and leader of prog stalwarts The Tangent, of whom Longdon

was a fan. Martin Orford was back at Aubitt too, supplying a fast and furious keyboard solo on *Fat Billy Shouts Mine*. Orford's honorarium for the gig was the usual – a curry. Big Big Train would often pay people for their services in curry, and these boozy meals would become something of a band ritual over the years, with sometimes over 20 people crowding around their table at Southampton's Coriander Lounge or Namaste Kerala.

❖❖❖

With *The Underfall Yard* having done well, expectations were high for the follow-up. *Far Skies Deep Time* ran for over 40 minutes, comfortably LP length, and had all the makings of Big Big Train's next official album. But Spawton was unsure about this rather diverse, scattergun recording. Between them the straight-ahead, melancholic ballad *British Racing Green*, the ornate, classic era prog cover *Master Of Time* and sprawlingly cinematic *The Wide Open Sea* represented the three points of their musical triangle. But Spawton saw the disparate record as not quite on a par with *The Underfall Yard*, whose solid thematic architecture underpinned its artistic and commercial success. "For me an album isn't just a collection of songs," he says, "it's a cohesive body of work. I don't think *Far Skies* was necessarily that, so we released it as an EP to relieve some of that pressure, while keeping the Big Big Train name out in the progressive marketplace."

Longdon didn't quite see it that way. "The whole EP is quite quirky. It's got a different character to it than *The Underfall Yard*, and that's what I like about it. I thought it was a really interesting moment in the band's development and I wish we'd spent more time in that phase, but then we were onto the next album. Greg wasn't concerned about me getting involved in the writing, but he was certainly wondering what that might mean. We're very different as writers and that's good, and *Far Skies* is a really good example of Greg and I writing together. We've hardly done that since then, and we're probably missing a trick."

The singer's increasingly significant role in the band also stretched to the visuals, for which he had a flair. As a studio project, Big Big Train risked becoming faceless, anonymous. In photographs it was all too easy to default to rock 'n' roll cliché, and find yourself standing in a field in your best leather jacket and jeans, staring meaningfully into the middle distance. When it came to taking photos for this CD's inlay, Longdon suggested a fresh approach.

"I was very conscious that the band didn't have an image, so I asked them all to dress up as if we were in the 1960s, to make it look a bit different and make a statement. The idea came from the black and white photographs we'd seen of Jacques Brel. I know that Greg felt uncomfortable with the shoot at first, but the pictures were evocative and made a statement. It let people see what we were about and made them curious."

Andy Poole reckons it wasn't just the fact that Spawton was told to tuck his shirt in that made him ill at ease: "That photo shoot definitely pushed Greg a bit out of his comfort zone. I think he began to realise that it wasn't just his band anymore." Along with the photos, artist and loyal fan Jim Trainer – who had excelled himself on the artwork for *The*

Underfall Yard – supplied the EP's classy cover, and *Far Skies Deep Time* was released in 2010.

One person now monitoring Big Big Train's development closely was prog critic Nick Shilton. In his review for *Classic Rock* he commended the record's 'sheer craftmanship' and 'thoughtful, cliché free lyrics', calling it 'one of the prog year's indubitable highlights from a band that seems set to go from strength to strength.'

The sales figures bore out Shilton's prophecy too. *Far Skies Deep Time* quickly sold over 10,000 copies, and with the physical version re-pressed several times it has kept selling well for the band ever since. "It was a successful piece of work for us," Spawton remarks. "The nucleus of the band was coming together. And it did start to feel like a band rather than a project, but it was still a studio band in the same way that Kate Bush and XTC were predominantly 'recording artists' rather than 'performing artists' – though obviously at very different levels to us."

It wasn't on the cards yet, but within just a few years the band would be moving from the studio to the stage, as their fortunes continued to shift and their popularity grew. By the time the EP was released Spawton and Longdon were separately writing material for the next LP, one that would prove to be a career changer and a highlight in their catalogue. To build up the anticipation, they even announced its title in the *Far Skies* liner notes with the James Bond-like teaser: 'Big Big Train will return with *English Electric*'.

VIII

'Took a little time to find the past,
to walk the roads we used to know...'

THE STARVING MAN who had been given a feast, David Longdon had been fully sated by *Far Skies Deep Time* and *The Underfall Yard* before it. But he was also working on his own solo material, his new friends had recording equipment and record label infrastructure of sorts, and they had agreed to help him realise his individual artistic vision. At least, that was the plan.

But as Big Big Train's success grew, so priorities changed. Gregory Spawton and Andy Poole were keen to push on, rather than have that good progress derailed by a distracting side project. And though Longdon had his own musical ambitions, he could also see the track ahead clearly. "The original idea was that Greg and Andy would help me record my solo work," he says, "but there was good sense in continuing with the band, and obviously I was complicit. I could have said I wanted to stick to the original deal and have them focus on helping me record my solo work. But it's good being in a band because it's a gang – suddenly you're no longer alone. Writing an album on your own is a big undertaking, and with me alongside him Greg suddenly had a musical partner in crime, and that took the pressure off."

On the way home from a holiday in Wales, Andy Poole dropped in on Longdon at his house in Shrewsbury. The singer ushered him into his converted loft space and man cave, and played him two songs he ostensibly intended for his next solo album. One was a demo recording of a tune with a breezy, country waltz rhythm and sweet melody that belied its acidic lyrics about mealy mouthed liars in love: '*When leopards say they can change/They don't mean a single word that they say/Because leopards promise the earth/For all they're worth/Swear blind they feel the same*'. "It's about whether people can really change," says its writer. "I think you can, but you really need to know and watch yourself."

For the other, Longdon reached for his banjo, and performed a jaunty folk tune, inspired by his own dear Uncle Jack, the poetry loving, classical music aficionado who had introduced him to Bach and Johnny Cash as a boy. As Jack had been a collier in Derbyshire, deprived of the natural world during his working day underground, he valued it all the more when returning to surface. The seasons, the hedgerows, the flowers and the leaves and birds and seeds – these were all manna from heaven for Uncle Jack.

"I think David might have been sounding me out," says Poole, who immediately thought the songs would fit nicely into the Big Big Train soundworld. "I hadn't heard either of them before, and I adored them both. It was another

David's Uncle Jack with his dog, Peg.

went on to write *Judas Unrepentant*, which made me think, 'Right, in that case *I'm* going to write a big prog rock song too.' David's got that Brill Building approach – he can write anything. And so our pot of songs was starting to grow."

The framework and presentation for these tunes was something Spawton had been nursing for a while. Founded in 1918, English Electric was an industrial manufacturer whose output included aircraft, locomotives, steam turbines and diesel motors – the very objects that fascinated Spawton, and had helped define aspects of the Big Big Train aesthetic since *Goodbye To The Age Of Steam*.

"I knew English Electric since boyhood," Spawton says. "They turned their hand to everything from fridges to fighter planes – the English Electric Lightning was a fighter and looked like something out of *Thunderbirds*. 'Frightening Lightning', they called it. I thought the name, the phrase, seemed to convey a spirit, and – as with 'The Difference Machine' – I liked the association of the words."

Serendipity struck when, while scrolling through the photo sharing website Flickr, Spawton happened upon a striking shot taken by photographer Matt Sefton. "It was the most evocative thing," Spawton recalls. "A rusting English Electric nameplate Matt had found on a little crane in Tanfield, near Newcastle. Someone in the comments below the photo said it would make a nice album cover, and I contacted Matt to buy it. I had that cover image for a year or two before we finished the album, and having it at the start was cool – it gave us all a point of reference."

Over those two years the *English Electric* project came together steadily, always predicated on that *Sgt. Pepper* 'studio' idea Longdon had alluded to: the band's collective imagination would dictate the end product, with no

breakthrough point to have David's original songs on an album. Greg was completely comfortable with *Uncle Jack*, probably less so with *Leopards*."

"I was really pleased that Andy went to David's house," recalls Spawton. "At that stage the bond between the three of us was important. As songwriters David and I had a natural bond, and I suppose we were working out what sat in our world, or what one review would call our 'Big Big Terrain'. The term 'prog' covers a vast amount of ground and doesn't limit you, so we began finding out what band we were now, and David's role in terms of songwriting. Andy felt *Uncle Jack* and *Leopards* suited us, then David

Matt Sefton's English Electric *cover.*

concessions made to potential public performance. They would record whatever they could hear in their heads, and if they needed to draft in extra players to realise *English Electric*'s full potential, then so be it.

With the band's songwriting engine fired up, the material became more broad-ranging than ever. The versatile Longdon enhanced the XTC-friendly side of their sound with *Uncle Jack*, but, as *The Wide Open Sea* had proved, he also had a flair for progressive rock's dramatic, rhapsodic forms. "The idea of me in a non-prog band doing something progressive would have been preposterous," he says. "I like artists like Prefab Sprout, Richard Thompson and Thomas Dolby, so I veered away from prog to be honest. If I'd turned in *Tales From Topographic Oceans* at Rondor I wouldn't have been a writer there for very long. Prog was a dirty word, and in some quarters it still is. I can be more objective if I'm working on more than one song at

a time. Like I read three books at the same time, I usually write in threes. Usually I like to write one folky thing, one kick-arse thing and one more experimental thing."

If *Uncle Jack*'s jolly, elegiac banjo arpeggios represented the folky side of the Longdon coin, *Judas Unrepentant* was the experimental flipside. The song was inspired by the story of lovable rogue Tom Keating – a 20th century English art restorer turned prolific forger. With its ever-shifting metre, puckish organ-led riff and singalong chorus, the song brought Keating's tale to vivid musical life.

For Spawton's part, his nimble bass lines showed how his skills on the instrument were aligning with his notable guitar chops. "David wanted to get some grit on the bass," he says, "and to make it a Chris Squire-y thing. *Judas* is a bugger to play, it moves from 3/4 to 4, then to 5 and 6. I don't count it out, I just worked very closely to Nick's drums and then learned it. If I lose my way, I'm in trouble."

An altogether bleaker work, *A Boy In Darkness* was a sophisticated, minor-key piece from Longdon, with another big chorus plus speedy flute, violin and growling guitar solos. The song's sombre mood came through in the sparse verse, the tolling bell and ominous string arrangement, supplied by Louis Philippe. As Longdon wrote this one he was brooding over the tragic story of Peter Connelly. Referred to in the press as 'Baby P', Connelly was a toddler who had died from injuries arising from repeated physical abuse at his family home in London. "I'd not long become a father at that point," Longdon recalls, "and I remember watching the news with tears rolling down my face, and then thinking about those conditions and children's rights and people speaking out about it. *A Boy In Darkness* was an experimental song, a hard hitting one, and I didn't think Big Big Train would go for it because of the subject matter."

In fact, not only would it feature one of Nick D'Virgilio's all-time favourite Longdon vocal performances, but Gregory Spawton loved the song from the day he heard the demo. He saw it as "a clever piece of writing from when David was adapting himself to the Big Big Train style. We both needed to give a bit of ground, and to find some common ground as well."

The Midlands represented literal common ground for Spawton and Longdon as they were first bonding, and this took musical form beautifully on *Summoned By Bells*. Written by Spawton, the song centred on change, conservation and stasis in the Highfields area of Leicester, where his mother grew up and the men in her family worked on the railway. Musical echoes here of Genesis, Talk Talk and the Beach Boys, as, again, Spawton's traditional prog was enriched by Longdon's impeccable vocal embellishments.

Spawton could feel the songwriting gauntlet being thrown down. Not to be outdone, he wrote *The First Rebreather*, his second piece (after *Winchester Diver*) inspired by a heroic English aquanaut. Diver Alexander Lambert's incredible bravery saved the Severn Tunnel from a terrible, life-threatening flood in 1880. His story became the source for one of the band's most overtly prog rock pieces to date.

At home in Swindon, Dave Gregory couldn't believe the amount of quality material coming at him from his friends in Bournemouth and Shrewsbury. He was genuinely amazed that part-time musicians, holding down day jobs and with families to support, could find the time to write this many quality songs, let alone demo them. "With *English Electric* I felt I'd officially become a band member," he says, "and it appeared I was the only guy playing electric guitar. Greg was still playing acoustic guitar but left all the electric stuff to me. He told me there were no plans to recruit any other guitarists, that I was Big Big Train's guitarist, and his endorsement gave me the encouragement to work harder."

Once again Dave Gregory sent in his parts from home, and Spawton and Poole worked on their parts and pulled

Station Masters: Big Big Train in January 2013.

Rob Aubrey accepting some well-meaning mixing advice from band members.

The Covent Garden String Quartet with Louis Philippe, Andy and David.

the record together mainly at the Spawton house. In their album credits 'English Electric Studios' was a catch-all term for any music recorded by members of the band outside a proper facility, such as Aubitt. There, it was down to Rob Aubrey to mix and master the album, shepherding in and conforming all the parts coming his way.

It took a broad span of contributors to make the *English Electric* dream a reality. Louis Philippe's strings for *A Boy In Darkness* were performed by the Covent Garden String Quartet, recorded in London at Regal Lane Studios with Ken Brake. (Longdon approached both Deep Purple's Jon Lord and Uriah Heep's Ken Hensley to play organ on the track; Lord expressed an interest, but ultimately nothing came of these enquiries.)

Dutch player Jan Jaap Langereis laid down sweet recorder parts for the song *Summoned By Bells*. In a cold blast from the past, these were recorded at the studios of Edo Spanninga of Flamborough Head, hosts of that ProgFarm event all those years ago. Meanwhile in Southampton, Dave Desmond and his colleagues once

again stood cheek by jowl in Aubitt's live room to add the brass, fast becoming another sonic signature for the band. And, among this extended coterie of musicians, there was another, notable new face.

Rachel Hall was a talented young violinist who had caught Rob Aubrey's ear at Aubitt a few years earlier, while recording for prog/psych artist Lynden Williams. She had graduated from Bath Spa University in 2009 with a degree in Music, and while her main focus had been classical music (with some jazz violin instruction from noted teacher Nina Trott), Hall was also a lifelong folk fan.

She had just played violin on Fairport Convention singer Judy Dyble's comeback album *Talking With Strangers*, with Robert Fripp also among the contributors. While at uni Hall would travel up to Liverpool on odd weekends for club and festival gigs with Irish born songwriter Anthony John Clarke. She had also had local success as half of a violin/guitar duo with fellow student Tim Graham, and since 2007 she had occasionally played with re-formed oddball '70s hippie rockers Stackridge, with shows at The 100 Club,

Cropredy and Glastonbury. When avid Stackridge fan Lynden Williams spotted her obvious talent at one of their gigs, he invited her to record with him at Aubitt.

"Rob kind of liked what I was doing," Hall recalls. "About two years later he recommended me to Greg and he got in touch via Facebook and said, 'Would you like to do some violin on a couple of tracks for us?' I didn't really know a lot about progressive rock and I'd never heard of Big Big Train, but when I first listened to the demos I instantly thought, 'Okay, this is really good – I really want to do this'."

Just prior to taking the Big Big Train session Hall had been on a gruelling six-month tour of Europe with folk rock band The Wishing Well. Busking for coins on streets across Germany and Switzerland, they were often moved on by the police, and snatched a few scant hours of sleep in youth hostels between cities. The experience had dented Hall's enthusiasm for a career in music, to the point that when she arrived at Aubitt from her home in Norfolk, "I was thinking that music really wasn't going to be a part of my life anymore. Going to that Big Big Train session was probably really scary because I felt I was going back into an environment that I'd sort of just got myself out of. It actually meant a huge amount to me to be doing it."

Turning up at Aubitt for a day's recording, Hall laid down her violin parts for *Judas Unrepentant* and *Hedgerow*. "Saying 'Okay, here are my ideas' is actually quite a hard thing to do at first," she says, "when you don't know the people. Obviously as I got to know them, I became more comfortable doing that."

Gregory Spawton had demoed the *Hedgerow* violin melody on keyboard and, he says, "Rachel ran with it, and it really evolved. She had prepped well for the recording day and played really beautifully, but at that point we had no inkling we'd be having her in the band. She brought us a folky side, more of a classical feel, and a good singing voice. Rachel was a real find."

That other, earlier Aubrey find Nick D'Virgilio was back again too, laying down his drum parts for the album. By 2010 his commitments to Spock's Beard were winding down, and he finally left that band the following year. His main employment at this time was as the drummer (and, later, assistant musical director) for Montreal-based contemporary circus troupe Cirque du Soleil. "And thank God I got that gig," he says. "I was still technically in Tears For Fears, but they were gigging six weeks every other year. I was struggling financially and my wife Tiffany was working her butt off. The kids were young and we were in debt. The Cirque gig really turned my life around – money and stability got fixed because of it. I left Spock's basically because I got the Cirque gig and wasn't able to commit to Spock's anymore, and they didn't want to wait around for me.

"But it was Big Big Train that allowed me to stretch my wings musically, drumming-wise, and to stay current. From the mid-2000s there were guys taking drumming to the nth degree technically and physically – guys like Mike Portnoy, Jojo Mayer, Virgil Donati, Thomas Lang – and Big Big Train gave me the opportunity to be at the level of these guys. The music let me do all the fancy stuff and play all the chops and still groove. They not only let me do that, they *wanted* me to do that. So it was a real personally fulfilling thing. The more I was hanging out with the band, the more fun I was having, and that made me try harder. That's when I started really listening back to the music that I was recording. It brought a lot of joy back to me as a musician."

Through their experiences with Genesis, D'Virgilio and Longdon were still in contact with producer/engineer Nick Davis. He came down to Aubitt for a day to hear the band's progress on the new record, and suggested some tweaks that Rob Aubrey – at his open-minded best – gladly adopted. At one point Tony Banks was invited to play keyboards on *The First Rebreather* but declined, on the grounds that the song reminded him too much of *Stagnation*, from Genesis's 1970 album *Trespass*. "It's a fairly straightforward musical theme in the keyboard solo," Gregory Spawton reasons, "and I guess does remind some people of *Stagnation* – certainly it wasn't written with that in mind. We were disappointed at the time but in the long run it meant we focused more on getting a keyboard player in."

Spawton and Poole had been covering keyboards for years, but with the sheer calibre of talent now in the ranks they didn't feel they were sufficiently proficient anymore. The Tangent's Andy Tillison was invited to return to play keys on the *English Electric* sessions, and his contribution to the project was considerable. Poole remembers how they would send Tillison the tracks requiring his skills and "two days later Andy would send it back with all the keyboard parts done. If we did want to change something he wouldn't tweak it – he would do all his parts all over again. He did some brilliant stuff, he was really adding value. On *The First Rebreather*, the way the end fades out is all Tillison."

Danny Manners was back too, recording double bass for *Uncle Jack* and the lilting *Upton Heath* with Ken Brake at Regal Lane. Tillison's entrenched commitments to The Tangent meant that the band's keyboard stool was still, in theory, unoccupied. Longdon pointed out to Spawton and Poole that, as well as playing double bass, Manners was a highly accomplished pianist, and talked up his friend's deep knowledge of classical and jazz theory, and his arranging skills.

"I'd never played in a prog band," Manners says, "so understandably they were wary. My entrée was double bass, but they could hear from my work with Louis that I could play piano, so they brought me in to play some of the parts that Andy [Poole] or Greg couldn't manage, and it was mission creep from there. I didn't have any expectations really. I was excited by it, it was a chance to expand my skills. I'd put an organ down here, then I did some arranging on *Summoned By Bells*. Greg was thinking about a whistle blowing at the end of a factory work day, and he wanted everyone to extemporise, but it was a mess. He said, 'You're into jazz, can you edit this into something?' I put down a piano and bass part based on a sequence of Greg's, then at home I assembled about ten tracks of brass, so that established my arrangement credentials."

The first piano part Manners laid down was for Spawton's beautiful, building ballad *Curator Of Butterflies*. "I really didn't like it to start off with," Manners admits with a laugh. "It took quite a while for that piece to fall into shape. The original version had an extra, up-tempo instrumental proggy bit in the middle that had been on Greg's original demo. I think Greg decided it was detracting from the song, so it was completely excised. Later on I remember there was some idea of an opening that was a bit more Tom Waits-y."

If the prog sceptic Manners wasn't initially convinced by *Curator Of Butterflies*, he enjoyed the complex *Winchester From St Giles' Hill* much more, at one point rising to Spawton's challenge to evoke a 'babbling brook' with his playing. Slowly and surely, Manners wandered deeper and deeper into that 'Big Big Terrain'. "Two things really pulled me in," he says. "I put some piano and organ down for the song *Worked Out*, and said I could hear the possibility for a synth solo. I asked if I could have a go at it, which I did, but I thought it was too proggy. I didn't know what the reaction was going to be, but they loved it. That was the point I thought, 'Maybe I *am* a prog keyboard player! But the clincher for me was *East Coast Racer*. As that came together I thought it was something special."

"Danny came back with some great piano parts for that song," enthuses Andy Poole. "As far as Greg was concerned the song was finished, but I was concerned there were certain sections that were too driven by the rhythm section, which suited Greg because there were some fairly prominent bass guitar parts. I felt we needed some more detail and, because we had time, we could do more work on it. It was good that we held it over because it became a more complete song."

"Danny contributed massively to *East Coast Racer*," agrees David Longdon. "By *English Electric Part Two* he was adding a lot to the arrangements. Danny's thing is jazz and he's great at musical voicings; he's a consummate musician, a force, and he started coming into his own. He'd got his hands on the reins by then so his presence is felt more on the second part."

Though she had been gigging since she was 13, Rachel Hall was working as a waitress in Bath at this time. But Big Big Train was inspiring her, and she found herself drawn back into music, and becoming more and more immersed over time. "It certainly didn't feel like just another gig. There was something about the music that really connected with me at that point in time. I have vivid memories of escaping to my room above the Foresters Arms in Combe Down on my day off, and sometimes during the small hours of the

morning [to write]. Additional parts for the album would pour out of me – it wasn't a controlled effort but more of a need within me to capture the lines I could hear.

"I remember I was approached by Mike Tobin, the Stackridge manager, who was keen to put in a word for me for some up and coming band in London, but in my mind I was already thinking, 'No, I'm not going traipsing around right now trying to be the session player people want me to be. I've found the band I'm looking for.' I guess as *Part Two* unfolded, some of those songs would have been on my second recording session with the band, and I became more confident putting forward ideas or trying out improvised sections, like at the end of *The Permanent Way*, for example."

The decision to split *English Electric* into two parts was made at some point in the two-year recording process, as the songs just kept coming and the album running time just kept growing. "Once we were past the 80-minute mark we thought it was getting silly," says Spawton. "CDs meant that album lengths could inflate to 74 minutes, but as we well knew that's not always a good thing. But also as we weren't playing live we were thinking of ways we could keep in the public eye. If we released two albums six months apart that would give us a longer period of coverage over that time – so we thought that was a clever way of building the band's profile. But all the music was done in the same stretch of time – we didn't want *Part Two* to feel like a bunch of leftovers. I think the balance worked."

Rob Aubrey strongly felt that the monolithic showstopper *East Coast Racer* should take pride of place on *English Electric Part One*. The band knew they needed to make a big impact with the first record, but Spawton felt a 15-minute prog opus might cast too long a long shadow over the other songs. Besides, they needed to keep at least some of their powder dry to ensure the second part was as strong as the first.

Also, certain internal themes and references had emerged throughout the recording that gave the records a natural flow and logic. Written by Spawton and Longdon, *Hedgerow* was selected to close the first *English Electric* album, neatly reprising Uncle Jack's story from earlier in the work. Spawton says that Longdon's songcraft here strongly reaffirmed his faith in his talent. "There's a repeated theme in the keyboard solo of *The First Rebreather* that reoccurs in *Upton Heath*, but the masterstroke for me on the first record was David's ability to bring the nursery rhyme element of *Uncle Jack* and put it into *Hedgerow*. How he even conceived that and to make it work melodically, harmonically and scan, I don't know. It feels preordained, but it wasn't."

As for Spawton's own writing, Danny Manners came to see why he was able to keep coming up with interesting, unusual moments. "Greg always says he's got no idea about it, but he writes a lot on guitar, these simple lines, but he adds slightly unobvious notes which he's found on guitar, and these give the music a subtle colouring. Greg wanted certain things that I was able to provide, but the classical element in Big Big Train's music was always latent. Sometimes he and I would butt heads a bit if a chord was really ugly to me, but it is all totally subjective – sometimes I persuaded him to change it, sometimes I didn't."

"Danny and Dave Gregory have incredible musical brains," offers Spawton. "While David and I are more instinctive, those guys really understand music – they really gave us more gravitas. For example, Danny's incredibly evocative piano motifs on something like *East Coast Racer*.

English Electric had more depth and range than anything we'd done until then. Those two albums probably have four of our top tunes: *East Coast Racer, Keeper Of Abbeys* is great fun, while *The Permanent Way* seems to be the aficionado Big Big Train song, and *Curator Of Butterflies* too."

"It was brilliant having Danny on board," enthuses Dave Gregory. "His piano playing was out of this world. As I said to David at the time, we had found our Tony Banks. Two of my favourite songs are on those records. *Summoned By Bells* is a beautiful song and *The Permanent Way* has me almost in tears. A lot of it was down to Danny's piano playing and the way he interpreted what Greg had written."

The guitarist also very much savoured the way *English Electric Parts One* and *Two* were at once complex, yet also lean and efficient: "There's no spare flesh on them. Even though the songs are long and quite involved, to my ears it all works musically. If there's a change of time signature, it happens for a reason and is all mathematically correct.

"One really important element in all these records and that drives the band forwards in a literal sense is Nick's drumming. What a fantastic drummer he is! I can't imagine that there can be more than a handful of people on the planet capable of doing what he does. And he's not just a drummer – he plays great guitar and sings. Later on, when we played live, he would be the all-American cheerleader before the show. To us stuffy English folk, it comes as a bit of a shock. But it works. The band just wouldn't have been as successful without him."

Billed as 'a celebration of the people that work on, and under, the land and who made the hedges and the fields, the docks, the towns and the cities', *English Electric Part One* came out in September 2012 and quickly earned Big Big Train acclaim and even wider press coverage. They did in-depth interviews in Dutch magazine *iO Pages* and French fanzine *Koid9* (which also ran a long Q&A with Louis Philippe about his exquisite string contributions) and, in the UK, *Prog* magazine. In his astute review for *Prog*, music writer Rich Wilson picked up on the English whimsy, the sentimental, almost Victorian feel and the album's rich cast of characters. He called Big Big Train an 'enormously talented and imaginative band' whose music was 'at times simply sublime'.

All this heat was generated by what was, once again, a self-released album. To ensure the album was on the shelves of HMV and Virgin Megastore, a distribution deal was struck via GEP, with the band making a tiny profit per CD sold in the shops. Selling through the band's website was more profitable, but also involved much more work. At home in Bournemouth Gregory Spawton and his partner Kathy could barely keep up with demand. They sat in their lounge amidst boxes of freshly pressed *English Electric* CDs, feverishly stuffing copies into Jiffy bags, printing off address labels and running the packages through their newly acquired franking machine. Andy Poole was tasked with heaving sackfuls of orders down to the post office, to send out to an audience who over the next few years would buy the CD in the tens of thousands.

In another first for Big Big Train, *English Electric* would be available to fans of the retro, resurgent medium of vinyl. A commercial airline pilot by profession, Chris Topham was a music obsessive at heart. He set up his record label Plane Groovy in 2012, with the goal of releasing vinyl editions of albums by progressive acts such as Francis Dunnery, Echolyn and Glass Hammer, and also more mainstream artists including Squeeze's Chris Difford.

Topham had been pleased, if not surprised, to see the popularity of the format rising again as compact disc sales waned. Produced properly, vinyl was not only a highly effective means of faithfully capturing recorded sound, it was also a medium with an aura of tradition, romance and nostalgia that no CD – and certainly no computer file – could match. From the sound quality to the design-friendly size of its cover, there were plenty of good reasons that listeners and artists alike were falling in love with vinyl once more.

Over the years Topham had heard some of Big Big Train's previous albums and felt lukewarm about them, but then he happened to catch *Kingmaker* on the covermount CD accompanying *Prog* magazine. He loved it, and eagerly got in touch with the band with an offer to release *English Electric* on vinyl. "I got the sense they were uninterested," says Topham now. "Dave Gregory was a vinyl nut but the others weren't really. But GEP were happy and the band were happy to do it, so we went ahead.

"I spoke to Rob Aubrey, who is really, *really* good at mastering for vinyl. I don't particularly like the sound of CD, and the whole 'Loudness War' thing, I find it tiring to listen to. It's one thing when it's digital – if you're listening on a computer or an iPod you don't want to be changing volume track to track. But when it's analogue – one album, on vinyl – you've got a volume control, you can turn it up or down. To that end, when mastering you can take off all but a tiny bit of compression for the peaky stuff like cymbals, and you get a massive dynamic range and a better sounding product. Some engineers get it and others don't, and Rob really gets it. Keeping the dynamic range is the be all and end all for me, and he knows that."

All individually numbered, the 500 copies of *English Electric Part One*'s initial vinyl run sold out quickly (and in later years would change hands for serious money among collectors). One found its way via a big fan – Marc Catchpole – to legendary British DJ Bob Harris, and over that year Harris supported the release and that of its *Part Two* companion on his Sunday show on BBC Radio 2, with plays of *Uncle Jack, Winchester From St Giles' Hill, Swan Hunter* and *Leopards*. Through exposure like this, numerous positive reviews and healthy sales, the vinyl did well for both the band and Topham. A relationship and friendship was formed, and Plane Groovy would go on to release all future Big Big Train albums on the format.

In all, Gregory Spawton thinks that *English Electric* served the band extremely well. "It got people to notice us. It has always been my goal in life to leave behind a substantial body of work, and by the time we got to the end of *English Electric* I felt that we were getting there, that we had some strength and quality of writing and production, down to the delivery of the artwork, and the vinyl too."

"I still really like that album," adds David Longdon. "It's really strong, and a bit rugged for Big Big Train. There was a big difference when Danny came in as the full-time keyboard player. I love Danny to bits, he's great. When he plays everything becomes sophisticated and beautiful, but it can lose a lot of the edge. Andy Tillison's got edge. He can play beautifully, but there's real attitude to his playing too. One isn't better than the other, they're just different, and I like a mixture of the two. You can hear it on *English Electric Part Two*. The songs were done around the same time as *Part One* but had longer to steep. Danny was suddenly all over it – he makes quite a statement."

English Electric Part Two emerged in March 2013, with Big Big Train's audience larger than ever and very keen to hear what the group would come up with next. Culled from the same fertile stretch of work that ran from 2010 to 2012, it made good on the promise of its counterpart.

Opening the album, *East Coast Racer* didn't so much cast a shadow over the album as cast it in a fresh new light, a mythos. Soon to become a fan favourite, it was both a confident statement of intent and solid reassurance that the previous record hadn't been a fluke. Dave Desmond and his brass unit excelled themselves on the catchy, harmony-rich *Swan Hunter*, and *Worked Out* featured Danny Manners' boldest foray into the land of prog rock synth. Making more of an impression on Spawton, Poole and Longdon over time, Rachel Hall had added further work to the records after her first session. Once again she made her mark with a standout, folky violin solo on *Keeper Of Abbeys* (with Dave Gregory's electric sitar infusing it with some spice).

From that early demo David Longdon played Andy Poole at home, *Leopards* had been fleshed out into a fully realised piece with sweeping strings, glockenspiel, contrapuntal vocal harmonies and clever dabblings in various unconventional musical scales. Decorated with plangent strings and mannered piano arpeggios, *Curator Of Butterflies* closed the record in epic, tear-jerking style, but perhaps it was the penultimate track, *The Permanent Way*, that pulled the entire *English Electric* project together. Reprising themes from *Part One*'s *The First Rebreather* and *Hedgerow*, it reflected the kind of thematic unity Spawton and Poole had always admired in the prog albums they loved. It was a device they had long tried to make part of their own work, and now it was being achieved at a higher level than ever. And people were noticing.

Prog magazine had been very good to the band. In the magazine's 2012 end of year Readers' Poll, Nick D'Virgilio and David Longdon both made it into the Top 10 lists for Best Drummer and Best Male Vocalist respectively. *English Electric Part One* was voted the second best album of the year, losing out only to *Sounds That Can't Be Made* by Marillion, a band of near unimpeachable status among the magazine's readership. Then, in the April 2013 edition, *English Electric Part Two* was given the coveted, double-page lead album review slot. Once again, writer Rich Wilson caught the mood of the record and was fulsome in his praise, concluding: 'The fact that this is their second release of such a calibre within a year can only reinforce the opinion that what we're dealing with here is an act of rare, often indescribable brilliance.'

"That was a big one for us," says Spawton. "It was a big leg up for us to be in WH Smiths, and *Prog* gave *Part Two* that big review with a lovely illustration alongside it. I was so excited when I opened it. I was there in Smiths in front of the checkout girl saying, 'Look – it's me!'"

Spawton was going to have to tuck his shirt in again later that year, as the band he and Andy Poole began over 20 years previously began to break through. Joined by David Longdon, the pair would very soon find themselves in London, mingling with some prog rock legends, and winning their first, highly prestigious award.

IX

*'We're gonna crank it up to give you our love –
come on, make some noise!'*

ON THAT PARTICULAR TUESDAY EVENING in September 2013, London was unseasonably warm. The floor to ceiling glass of Kew Gardens' elegant Nash Conservatory – relocated here brick by Georgian brick from the grounds of Buckingham Palace in 1836 – gave out onto Kew's immaculate grounds, bathed in the gold of the late summer sunset.

The reception for the second Progressive Music Awards ceremony was abuzz. The first one, held here the previous year, had been a notable success. Given the niche status of the genre, the fact that the BBC, Sky and other major news outlets were once again present in force was another sign that something was going on.

This curious, renaissant scene was having a moment, was coming in from the cold. With champagne flowing, veteran prog stars – Genesis guitar great Steve Hackett, Jethro Tull's Ian Anderson and Hawkwind's Dave Brock – rubbed shoulders with prog's blue-eyed boy Steven Wilson, Dream Theater drum maestro Mike Portnoy and other latter day torch bearers.

Conversations were charged with excitement and a little surprise that, in the 21st century, their patch of musical ground – loved by those within it, often reviled by those without – was being recognised and celebrated in such fine style. Was prog rock finally becoming unshackled from the lampoonish clichés that surrounded it – the wizards, the goblins, the gold lamé capes? Those in attendance – including Yes keyboard legend and noted cape enthusiast Rick Wakeman – thought that, on balance, it probably was.

It had made sense for *Prog* to host its own awards ceremony. Its sister titles, *Classic Rock* and *Metal Hammer* both held their own successful star-studded events, and *Prog* had proved to be a hit with its target market, becoming a mainstay in the community's conversation since its 2009 launch. "The magazine was big enough to have its own awards," says *Prog* editor Jerry Ewing. "We kept it industry, we tried to hit the right tone, and we got lucky. The first one had been a resounding success."

At the second event, some fresher-faced nominees mingled with the established names. Won by prog metallers TesseracT at the inaugural ceremony the year before, the Limelight Award (originally the 'New Blood' award) was to be presented to the most promising newcomer on the scene. In 2013 those in contention were instrumental proggers The Fierce & The Dead, Sound Of Contact (featuring Simon Collins, son of Phil), Cosmograf (a rising one-man band comprising a certain Robin Armstrong) and Tin Spirits, the other new musical project to feature Dave Gregory.

The guitarist had attended the year before, and had been blown away. "It was the great and the good. I couldn't believe that Keith Emerson was *in this room*! I met Steve Hackett, shared a table with Peter Hammill, and [Gong/Knifeworld's] Kavus Torabi came up and embraced me and said, 'I've been a fan of yours for years!' Steven Wilson introduced me to Martin Barre. Friendships were formed there."

The 'Breakthrough Artist' category was a new addition for 2013. With a shortlist curated by *Prog*'s editorial team and voted for by the magazine's readers, this honour would be bestowed on an act who had been at the coalface for a while but, after years of toil, was now making significant commercial and creative progress. Among those in contention were Polish proggers Riverside, Lifesigns (the latest project from much respected keyboardist John Young), neo Canterbury hipsters Syd Arthur, Finnish adonises Von Hertzen Brothers and, squeezed together somewhat self-consciously on a table near the back of the room, Big Big Train.

"It was David, Andy and me," recalls Gregory Spawton. "We were so excited to be there, this really was the golden ticket to us. We got there so early that the gates to the grounds were still locked. It was a really hot evening, and walking into that reception in the conservatory was one of those moments. We just stood there and marvelled at all the people we looked up to being in that one room. It also reinforced what a broad community prog is. It very

much wasn't just a bunch of '70s rockers. It was much more vibrant than that. I remember how irritatingly young and handsome the Von Hertzens were!"

"We were in awe," says Andy Poole. "It was a particular pleasure to meet Andy Tillison for the first time, who had remotely provided wonderful keyboard parts for *English Electric*. But it was so hard to stay cool – 'There's Rick Wakeman! There's Ian Anderson! Steve Hillage! Steve Hackett!' It was one of those 'pinch me' moments. I couldn't believe we were there. It felt like fantasy."

Of the three of them, David Longdon was the most in touch with the reality of the evening, and was determined to make the most of it. He marched straight up to Gong's Steve Hillage – with whom he shared a mutual friend – and entered into conversation. "Andy and Greg were so timid about speaking to people," the singer recalls. "I said to them, 'Have a look around. Where are you? The Progressive Music Awards. Where are you going to be tomorrow night? You don't know. And the night after that? And after that? This is a moment, this is an opportunity – take it!' We've all done that for each other over the years. I can think of many instances where we've had each other's back."

And Big Big Train weren't just nominated in the Breakthrough Artist category. They were also in some seriously talented company on the illustrious Album Of The Year shortlist. *English Electric Part Two* was in the running alongside

With Andy Tillison at Kew Gardens.

Steven Wilson's *The Raven That Refused To Sing (And Other Stories)*, Marillion's *Sounds That Can't Be Made*, Steve Hackett's *Genesis Revisited II* and *Brief Nocturnes And Dreamless Sleep*, from Nick D'Virgilio's former crew, Spock's Beard.

The ceremonial three-course meal was followed by a beautiful recital of the classic Genesis ballad *Ripples*, with Steve Hackett accompanying vocalist Amanda Lehmann on 12-string guitar. In a thrilling, full circle moment for Spawton, Hackett also treated the room to a performance of *Horizons*, the classical piece from which Spawton had learned so much when he was first getting to grips with the guitar, and composition.

Commencing the awards ceremony itself, *Prog*'s editor Jerry Ewing offered a speech about the state of prog, the balance of promoting new bands as well as celebrating the old. *Newsnight* host and avid progressive rock fan Gavin Esler was the evening's MC, and just two awards into the evening he was calling Big Big Train to the stage. Those hard yards were finally beginning to pay off. By popular demand the band had won the Breakthrough Artist award.

"I just remember walking to the stage from our table near the back," says Spawton, "and there were lots of beaming faces. Marillion were there and were happy for us, which was very cool. I was nervous – we still hadn't done any gigs and I hadn't been on a stage for years. I didn't drink much, and was just careful not to trip up. David spoke, and thanked everyone. He has the confidence to feel like he should be there, whereas Andy and I can be prey to Imposter Syndrome. I quietly wondered if we deserved it."

There was no shame in their losing out to Steven Wilson when the Album Of The Year announcement rolled around. Wilson's stock was unassailably high, and he took the

trophy for *The Raven That Refused To Sing*. Tellingly, this defining record in the modern prog catalogue had glanced just shy of the Top 30 in Wilson's native UK, but did hit the Top Three in Germany. Big Big Train had been happy just to be nominated and invited to the night, but now they had their first major award, and were getting known in all the right places.

"It was a no brainer," says Jerry Ewing of their Breakthrough Artist win. "The reader vote for them was massive. I remember them being incredibly polite and shy that night – they had never encountered anything like that before. They weren't the bunch of rabble rousers they became later. They've won a slew of awards since, and rightly so. They're a marvellous figurehead for what modern progressive music is. If you want to understand how that classic prog sound of the '70s has evolved into something modern, I would point you in the direction of Big Big Train."

And it meant all the more to the band because they'd got this far under their own steam. Certain labels circled them that night and afterwards, gauging their interest in a possible deal. But early experience had left a sour taste and strengthened the band's resolve to remain, for better or worse, masters of their own destiny.

"It was an arrival moment for sure," says Spawton. "Over the years awareness of the band grew seemingly by osmosis and then, at some point, that reached a level where it all came spilling out like floodwater. It was huge for us, being in a room with fellow progressive rock musicians, some of them very high profile. We began to feel there was massive love for the genre, *and* we'd won an award. Every time something has gone well, you reconfigure, make an adjustment, and set your sights a bit higher and further.

That's what happened with *English Electric* for me, and then winning the Breakthrough Artist award. It enabled us to start thinking, 'How far can we take this, and what are we going to do next?' At that point I decided it was time to start aiming for the stars."

When that evening ended, Spawton, Longdon and Poole settled for aiming for their B&B, a mile down the road in Kew. They spoke to Nick D'Virgilio and Danny Manners, who had been following the evening's events via the awards' live stream online. Then, still flooded with adrenaline, the three friends saw in the dawn, drinking, talking, setting a course for the stars.

◆◆◆

With coverage of their win earning them fresh interest, Big Big Train released their second EP just three weeks later. *Make Some Noise* was intended as an accessible primer for newcomers to the band, for which they selected some of their more immediate recent material – *Uncle Jack*, *Leopards*, *Swan Hunter*, and edits of *Keeper Of Abbeys* and *Curator Of Butterflies*. "The four extra numbers we recorded for that EP really were the clincher for me," says Danny Manners. "I'd become emotionally invested by then. I did a lot of keyboards and got involved in the arrangements and edits."

These tracks indeed showed Manners' impact, and proved the band's expanding range. *Seen Better Days* was an elegiac piece partly in 7/8 time and rich with Gregory Spawton's signature imagery of rivers, fields and hills, of shipyards, mining towns and mills. With musical quotes from *East Coast Racer*'s plangent opening, Manners' own *Edgelands* was a solo piano showcase for his achingly beautiful, jazz-inflected playing. David Longdon's prog

mini opus *The Lovers* featured a fiery reverse-recorded guitar solo from Dave Gregory (credited as Lord Cornelius Plum, his alter ego in the XTC spin-off band, The Dukes of Stratosphear). The bittersweet lyrics also attested to its writer's hard won insight into matters of the heart ('*Silver-tongued, the lovers' eloquence cuts this relationship to ribbons*').

Also penned by Longdon, the EP's title track proved surprisingly divisive among the band and their more established fans. *Make Some Noise* was an uncharacteristically upbeat and infectious pop rock track conveying the power of youth and music, the unalloyed excitement of adolescent rock 'n' roll dreams. With nods to Queen and The Beatles, it came tooled up with knowingly blunt lyrics to express its theme ('*We're gonna crank it up, 'cos it makes you feel good, come on make some noise*') and a huge singalong chorus to boot.

Longdon had written the song during the *English Electric* sessions, but not for that project. "*Make Some Noise* wasn't meant to be a Big Big Train song," he says. "It was a solo music thing that I wanted to sound like [cult '90s power pop band] Jellyfish. I was working on it with Rob and he said, 'This is great. This is a catchy song.' Then Greg and Andy heard it and asked to use it for Big Big Train. We needed a quick song to do a video for, so I said okay."

Aubrey loved the song and had pushed for it to go on *English Electric Part One*. But while Spawton liked it, he wasn't sold on how squarely it sat with the other material, or indeed how well it suited the band, the rest of whom were also ambivalent. "*Make Some Noise* was an attempt by David to write a single, a crowd-pleaser," says Dave Gregory. "Well, some of the crowd were pleased and others weren't! I thought it was okay but it's not my favourite Big

Big Train song. I do have some sympathy with those who felt it was a step backwards or wasn't quite as prog as they would like."

A lukewarm Danny Manners considered the song a pastiche, but the ever-positive Nick D'Virgilio saw the good in it: "It's fine. Is it the best Big Big Train song in the world? No, but it's got energy and vibe – sometimes you need that straight backbeat to get the crowd clapping, and it's a nice change of pace from all the other technical stuff."

The band's fans gladly expressed their diametrically opposing views on the song via Big Big Train's Facebook page and YouTube channel, posting comments beneath the accompanying video. 'An otherwise great band tries to write a hit single… and fails hard,' lamented one. 'What a breath of fresh air! Awesome!' enthused another. "It got a pasting," concedes its writer today. "It's about kids – it's meant to sound like a young band making a load of racket, a bit three chords and the truth. It's not typically Big Big Train, so it fell on stony ground… but some people like it."

Recorded on 2nd January that year, the *Make Some Noise* video was the band's first promo film. Andy Poole was inspired by *Great British Railway Journeys*, a TV travelogue/history show presented by the former MP, now gaudily attired broadcaster, Michael Portillo. Poole came up with the idea of the band performing the song at Eastleigh Works, a fully operational railway carriage building/repair shop in Hampshire. He and Spawton visited Eastleigh to speak to the manager who was, Spawton recalls, "a bluff old railwayman. He wasn't Mr Health & Safety and wouldn't accept a penny from us for using the works as a backdrop. It was beyond bitterly cold on the day we filmed and we had a whole day in there. The guys were just back off their Christmas break, and it was like being a fly on the wall for

some of the people we had written about, in terms of the industries and their communities. It was fascinating."

By now D'Virgilio had happily accepted the role as Big Big Train's permanent drummer. Flown in especially for the shoot, the Californian zipped up his fleece jacket to the neck and joined his bandmates in the freezing cold Eastleigh depot. Hardened to the cold themselves, the railway workers were happily curious about this rock band turning up at their office. They obligingly helped band and crew get the best shots, moving equipment out of the way, shifting a huge, wrecked car and an engine block with their bare hands. Under the supervision of video director Peter Callow and with Rob Aubrey managing live playback, Big Big Train then ran through the song a number of times. Their performance was later intercut with old photographs and vintage video footage of the members playing as younger men and boys, each in their own separate past, to illustrate the song's nostalgic lyrical theme.

D'Virgilio's drums boomed through the workshop's chilly space. While the others mimed, Spawton and Gregory played along live through their amps, and the bassist looked around at the group in action. At David Longdon leading from the front. At Danny Manners, channelling his inner Jerry Lee Lewis as he slammed his elbow down on his piano keys. At Dave Gregory, resplendent in frock coat and stovepipe hat, his hand almost frozen to the neck of his Gibson Flying V. And at Andy Poole, strumming his acoustic guitar and singing his heart out. Spawton got his first real inkling of what it might be like for this incarnation of Big Big Train to play together live for real. He realised that it would be, at the very least, good, and in that freezing space he began to warm to the idea.

Making some noise at Eastleigh Railway Works, 2nd January 2013.

"The video set that hare running," he says, "together with winning the *Prog* award. Being on stage in front of our peers and betters at Kew made us think there was something in this, and that it was time to move on from being a studio project. This was more like a real band than ever, and people now needed to start seeing us as such, because that's what we had become."

Released that same September, the deluxe compilation *English Electric: Full Power* brought together both parts of *English Electric* and the original songs on the *Make Some Noise* EP, with a tweaked running order. This release did cause some disgruntlement among the more completist ranks of the fanbase: they had been hit in the wallet for the EP, then with *Full Power* were being asked to fork out again for music they'd just bought? Spawton gets it. "If I had my time again, we would have kept *Make Some Noise* off *Full Power* and just on the EP that featured the new songs. Our strategy was to be in the spotlight for as long as possible for the *English Electric* period, but we really didn't want anyone to feel like we were employing sharp practices. We were very explicit about our intentions all the way along, but it did piss some people off. It's always going to be a bugbear for some people."

And yet the original 5,000 strong limited edition run of *Full Power* quickly sold out (it would be remastered and re-pressed in 2016). *The Underfall Yard* had sold well, as had the individual *English Electric* albums, the band line-up had coalesced solidly, and there was that *Prog* award on the band mantelpiece. Most importantly of all, they now had a solid and incredibly loyal and engaged fanbase. Spawton had set up the Big Big Train Facebook page in 2009, and it soon had thousands of followers. The hardcore among them came to be known as 'Passengers', people from all over the world united not just by their enthusiasm for the band and their music, but also with plenty of other common ground between them. Unlike other more combative parts of the web, conversations were constructive and convivial, and Spawton for one was delighted to see friendship groups growing within that community.

The same question regularly popped up on the message feed: when will Big Big Train be playing live? And every journalist also asked when the band would finally be touring. The road-hardened Nick D'Virgilio was champing at the bit for them to play live. 'They're going to fucking *love* us, man,' he reassured Gregory Spawton, more than once. And they also had their not so secret weapon, David Longdon – a charismatic, confident and talented singer with live experience, a man who was once on the cusp of touring the globe as frontman for Genesis.

But it wasn't as straightforward as that. Making an album is one thing, but the logistics of live music – the rehearsals, the travel – are tough on musicians, and their families. Longdon's friend Danny Manners had seen it over his years in the business, and it was in the back of his mind too when, around the time of the *Make Some Noise* video shoot, he was formally asked to join Big Big Train. "When I joined we were just a pure studio band, and if live work had been on the agenda from day one I would still have joined, but not if it had meant weeks and weeks of touring. It wouldn't have been practical at that stage in my life. As it was, it was the perfect balance for me."

And so the band began to discuss in earnest what form a Big Big Train live show might take. Would they involve the brass section that was now such an integral part of their sound? Or would they strip things right back? Between them they decided that before making the leap (and the investment), the best approach would be to have a dry run, to play live with the entire line-up, brass included, but without an audience. Then if they did hit the buffers, at least it wouldn't be in public.

David Longdon suggested that if they were going to do this, then they shouldn't do it by halves, and should once again speculate to accumulate. Rather than booking some gloomy rehearsal room they should find a nice location to rehearse and film their performance. "David said, 'Let's make it an event,'" Spawton recalls. "He maintained it should look like a Rolls Royce operation, even if there was a Reliant Robin engine under the bonnet. It should be at a high-end studio, and we should sell the film we would make to pay for it."

Rob Aubrey had seen Steely Dan play a TV studio in front of an invited audience of 100 people, with the music mixed in 5.1 surround sound. He thought the results were magnificent, and that a similar setup would suit Big Big Train well. Abbey Road was briefly considered, but quickly ruled out as prohibitively expensive, and not quite right for such a tentative experiment. Longdon suggested that a more suitable venue might be Peter Gabriel's place.

Just outside the village of Box near Bath, Real World Studios is set in the picturesque Wiltshire countryside near the Bybrook River. It's a state of the art facility run by top-end engineers and technicians, and housed in a beautifully converted old mill. Usefully, it's also one of the UK's few remaining residential studios. The band would be able to live there during their stay, removing the need for separate hotels and meal arrangements, and thus mitigating the cost. And all the recording gear they would need was there in-house, except for the video cameras, so they would just have to turn up with their instruments and backline, and play the songs live.

On 1st July 2014 Gregory Spawton, Andy Poole and Rob Aubrey headed to Real World on a recce. "And we were blown away," says Spawton. "It was hallowed ground. It's different from Abbey Road. It's a beautiful location, and it does exactly what Peter Gabriel designed it for – it's this world outside of the world, where you can focus purely on the artistic pursuit. The other nice thing is it's family-run, like Rockfield, and it's more homely than Abbey Road; you don't feel quite so on the clock there."

Spawton and Aubrey left Real World highly enthused and excited at the possibilities, but, on the drive home to Bournemouth, Poole wasn't quite so convinced. "My concern was we'd built up a head of steam with *English Electric*," he says, "and that sales were good and healthy. I thought this could be a big diversion of time and money and we would lose momentum for studio albums."

A heated argument ensued between Poole and Spawton right there in the car. As Aubrey remembers it, "Greg basically said to Andy, 'Don't be so negative. We need to do something to push this band forward. I don't *want* to spend that money, but if you have a better idea than the one we've had today, then let's have it!' I don't remember any other ideas coming from him. It was a defining moment – at that point I saw a divide in the band. I for one really wanted it to happen. I knew Real World would be fantastic, as it turned out to be."

"In his mind Andy was Mister Realistic, rooted in reality," says Spawton. "But in mine he was becoming an anchor weighing down the ambition of the band. A lot of our songs were mine, and my songwriting side wanted those to be heard by as many people as possible. I wanted them out in the world, and playing live was a way of making that happen. Andy didn't have an interest in that side of it. His approach was, 'We're making a fair bit of money now doing albums. Let's just be cautious and take one step at a time.' He wasn't totally against the idea of playing live, but I was just frustrated that Andy didn't want to move forward."

In the end Spawton won the argument. Poole acquiesced, Real World was booked for a whole week that August, and preparations began in earnest. One thing that this pair could agree on was that, of all the people who would be onstage at a Big Big Train show, they would be by far the least experienced performers. Their last gig had been that iffy set on a Dutch farm over 15 years ago. Spawton had been a guitarist then, but would now be playing bass. Writing and recording the parts was one thing; memorising and executing 90 minutes of bass material in front of his bandmates – and possibly a room full of paying customers in the future – would be something else.

For Real World he would need to get his head, and feet, around not just the bass parts but also his bass pedals. Along with the Mellotron, Moog Taurus pedals are one of prog rock's trademark gadgets. They've been a vital weapon in the arsenal of – among others – Genesis's Mike Rutherford and Rush's Geddy Lee, allowing these artists to augment their guitar/bass parts with sustained bass notes played with their feet. Much like a big church organ, it adds a powerful lower stratum to your sound, but operating the pedals while playing a bass guitar is the musical equivalent of patting your head and rubbing your stomach at once.

"It's hard," Spawton confirms. "Everyone underestimates the Rutherford gig. For the albums we'd used samples, but I wanted to do it live like he would. Andy had used MIDI pedals in the old days, like at the Astoria gig all those years ago, so we bought a Moog Minitaur [an analogue bass synth], and hooked it up to the MIDI pedals to get the Taurus sounds. We had a top drummer now, and I was sweating to get to a level where I wasn't going to get weary sighs from him – I didn't want to let Nick down. So I went into the live work with incredible trepidation on the personal side, but by this stage it was becoming a career. I felt we had to do it in order to move the band forward, beyond just reasonable CD sales, and into something more out there in the world."

That top drummer had found himself growing more and more connected to Big Big Train as time went by, and he knew that live was where it was at. "We needed to do it," D'Virgilio says. "Once we made the second *English Electric* and the *Make Some Noise* video there seemed to be propulsion forward with the band, with them wanting to do more stuff. I was really seeing and hearing momentum, and each album was sounding better. It was time to give this music to the world, and not just on CD."

To conform to the new demands of live performance, the songs had to be deconstructed and rearranged into a form playable by the current iteration of the band. "A lot of work went into that," says Andy Poole. "We had to home in on all the individual parts. Some of them weren't being played by the original players, so had to be re-written, or

new parts created, such as the Jem Godfrey and Frank Dunnery solos on *The Underfall Yard*. We had to make sure that people were on board and that it was feasible with the brass guys."

With the band going all out, Dave Desmond excitedly agreed to join and, at his suggestion, the brass was bumped up from a quartet to a quintet for the Real World experiment. On *English Electric* euphoniumist John Storey had replaced French horn player Nick Stones (the soldier was on assignment in Afghanistan at the time and therefore unavailable), but for Real World both players were brought in.

Poole and Danny Manners proceeded to divide the keyboard parts, though any other help would be welcome. While Poole would also cover some guitar too, it quickly became apparent that there would be more guitar parts than one guitarist, even one of Dave Gregory's calibre, could handle live. And then there were David Longdon's densely harmonic vocal arrangements – it was crucial to do those justice. They concluded that they really would need another pair of hands.

The previous year, Rob Aubrey had been the sound engineer and de facto tour manager for Spock's Beard on their European tour. The support acts for the tour were Sound Of Contact and Swedish proggers Beardfish, and Aubrey had been particularly taken with the latter band's warm, laconic and highly capable vocalist/guitarist/keyboardist. Rikard Sjöblom was a classic triple threat: he had a powerful voice, and his guitar and keyboard playing were both at an equally high bar, to the point that it wasn't immediately clear which was his primary instrument.

Born on 23rd February 1982 and raised in Gävle, Sweden, Sjöblom's first instrument as a child had actually been the

The young Rikard Sjöblom with his first instrument.

accordion (which would come in useful for David Longdon many years later). As he grew up he soon discovered the heavy metal charms of Iron Maiden and Helloween, and fell in love with the sound of Jon Lord's Hammond organ on Deep Purple's classic album *Burn*. Taking up the keyboard and guitar, he was brought into the progressive fold through such albums as Frank Zappa's *Roxy & Elsewhere*, King Crimson's 1974 live release *The Night Watch* and Jethro Tull's own *Benefit*.

By the time Aubrey found himself pushing faders for Beardfish across Europe, that band's stock was rising through their impressive live presence and their acclaimed 2012 album *The Void*. So, when the guitarist-shaped hole appeared in the live Big Big Train set-up, Aubrey was quick to suggest the Swede.

As it happened, David Longdon was already a Beardfish fan. In 2013 he had contributed some vocals to The Tangent's album *Le Sacre Du Travail*, and Sjöblom was on there too, having toured with Andy Tillison's band himself. Gregory Spawton was unaware of Beardfish, but a quick look at their work on YouTube was all it took. Aubrey made the call.

"Rob asked if I'd be interested in joining Big Big Train for live work," Sjöblom says. "I said, 'For sure!' I had only heard a few songs off *English Electric* and *The Underfall Yard*. I'd heard the buzz going around about *The Underfall Yard*, which came out at the same time as Beardfish's *Destined Solitaire* [2009]. People actually compared those albums a couple of times, which was funny. I really liked what I heard but hadn't become a geek about them yet – that happened later."

Spawton sent him the selection of 12 songs they would be playing live, and Sjöblom says he "fell in love with it. I could tell from hanging out in the English countryside and reading Greg and David's lyrics that there's something really British about the band. The hedgerows and brickwork

A multi-instrumentalist in the making.

Beardfish on tour in 2013.

have an enticing vibe to me and lured me in. And I was immediately struck by the complexity of the music itself. There was a lot to learn, both guitar parts and keyboard parts and lots of vocals. And on top of that, for Real World I also had to learn Andy Tillison's amazing goddamn organ parts for *Judas Unrepentant*!

"I've been playing prog rock for my entire adult life, but it still takes time to learn someone's style of writing, all their little quirks. When you're first hearing someone else's songs and trying to learn them it's unfamiliar territory. Later on I'd get to know their styles pretty well and what to expect, but they'd still take me by surprise. Back then everything was brand new and I had my nervous little twitches about doing *The Underfall Yard*. There was a lot of counting. I had my hands full, but I made that playlist, learned them as well as I could, and flew over to the UK."

Rachel Hall had made such an invaluable contribution to both *English Electric* albums that Spawton called her and asked her to join them at Real World. "Of course I was very excited to be involved," she says. "The music of Big Big Train kind of chose me at that time, rather than the other way around. I felt an immense connection with it, in terms of what I wanted to contribute and the melody lines already there that I'd be covering in a live form. I nearly missed my chance when a few months before, still working in cafés and restaurants, I'd had a nasty accident involving one of the fingers on my left hand. At the time I suggested

perhaps if it hadn't healed in time that they seek out Clare Lindley, my replacement in Stackridge. But they had faith it was going to get better in time, and luckily it did."

And as Andy Poole worked on his chops and prepared for the week at Peter Gabriel's place, he promised himself that he wouldn't lay awake at night worrying about the cost of the venture. He resolved to make the most of the experience, to enjoy it, and to see what lay further down the track.

Andy and Rachel preparing at Aubitt Studios for the Real World sessions, July 2014.

X

'Castles of stone, steel and blood,
but lines get broken down...'

THIS WASN'T NICK D'VIRGILIO'S FIRST TIME at Real World. In 1995 he had rehearsed in a side building there with Roland Orzabal and band, as they prepped to tour Tears For Fears' *Raoul And The Kings Of Spain*. Two years later, he was in nearby Dyrham at Orzabal's studio, Neptune's Kitchen, working on the singer's solo LP, *Tomcats Screaming Outside*. A call came through from Tears For Fears' former producer Chris Hughes: if Orzabal was okay with it, would D'Virgilio like to make the ten-mile drive to Real World and record something with Peter Gabriel? The drummer was a huge Gabriel fan and, of course, had some Genesis form of his own already. Eager to take the

NDV with Peter Gabriel, Real World Studios, 1997.

opportunity, he got the okay from Orzabal, grabbed his car keys, and excitedly made his way to Box.

After a good dinner and numerous games of ping pong, D'Virgilio and Gabriel entered the star's own private writing/recording room on the grounds, and set to work. The song to be recorded was *In The Sun*, a moody tune by the highly respected singer-songwriter and Real World label signing, Joseph Arthur. Arthur wouldn't even record his own version for another three years, but had assented to Gabriel covering the tune for *Diana, Princess Of Wales: Tribute*, an all-star charity album for release that December, in memory of the late Princess.

"I was in the drum booth," D'Virgilio remembers, "and through the glass Peter was playing keyboard and singing along and I was thinking 'Man, this is just awesome!' We went through the song a couple of times then jammed on the outro, and it was really cool. None of that is on the track that made it to the album – what I played was changed up a lot and mixed in very low, if at all. But I was there! I got that experience."

By 2014 the Big Big Train drummer was coming to the end of his four-year tenure with the lavish Cirque du Soleil touring show. He was living with wife Tiffany and their children in Fort Wayne, Indiana, and was about to start a new day job there with Sweetwater, the biggest online musical equipment retailer in the United States. D'Virgilio would be creating online content for them at their Fort Wayne campus – reviewing gear and writing articles ('Gig Survival: Sitting In' and 'How To Listen' were among his early ones). His other duties would include running drum masterclasses and playing as one of the many session musicians linked to Sweetwater's elite in-house studio.

Now, in August 2014, he was back again at Real World Studios, and had needed to sharpen his game to get his limbs around the Big Big Train drum parts, his every fiendish roll and fill having been stitched together by Andy Poole on the records. "If we were going to play live," he says, "I'd have to really start thinking how to perform the music, and have the stamina to get through a whole show. I wanted to be energetic and play the parts with passion live, to pull off what was on our records and make it sound confident and good. Real World was the start of that."

"We were spoilt rotten at Real World," says Dave Gregory, as if he can smell that fresh Wiltshire country air again. "It couldn't have been a more perfect and comfortable setting in which to rehearse." Not long ago Gregory had considered himself semi-retired. In the early 2000s he had toured as a member of Steve Hogarth's h Band, and then Tin Spirits had come along, playing Marillion's Weekend Convention in 2011 and a handful of subsequent dates. Other than that, his only live experience of late had been a few gigs with his Swindon covers band.

Now, as Big Big Train set up for their first live run through, he was in Real World's stunning main recording space – 'The Big Room' – uncasing some of his most treasured guitars – his 1965 Gibson SG Junior, '65 Gibson Firebird 5, his Les Paul Gold Top. He'd even brought along the Jerry Jones electric sitar he'd used on *Keeper Of Abbeys*. "Sometimes I'd break into The Delfonics' *Didn't I (Blow Your Mind This Time)* on it," he recalls now with a laugh, "but nobody joined in! No one got it."

Andy Poole had picked up Rikard Sjöblom from the airport the day before, and that evening he was welcomed to England with a traditional Big Big Train curry night. To Poole's delight, Sjöblom was something of an Anglophile, complete with the prerequisite sense of humour. "We were talking about British sitcoms we were all into," Poole remembers, "like *Blackadder*, *Father Ted* and *Monty Python*. I immediately thought that this was a guy I could really get on with."

Sjöblom's progressive rock adventures had long been subsidised by giving piano lessons, playing in bars, and hammering Sweden's covers circuit. At times during that first day of set up and soundcheck he would serenade his new band, sitting at the studio's grand piano and breaking into singalong tunes like Elton John's *Goodbye Yellow Brick Road* and *Tiny Dancer*. "Real World was a pleasure from the get-go," he says now. "I'm anxious by nature, especially with something I haven't done before, but there was a nice, friendly but serious vibe right from the start. Everyone is after a great result, but also there to have fun. They wouldn't be doing it if they didn't enjoy it. To me everyone was new – until then I'd only had email contact with the band. So you were meeting people and working out who they are, but straight away you had to be like a team who's been working together for years. There was never a dull moment."

The week was to be documented by *Make Some Noise* video director Peter Callow, and that first day he and his camera crew got organised as the band prepped for the rehearsals and recordings – no mean feat given the large band's considerable technical requirements. When Dave Desmond's brass section arrived later in the week, Rob Aubrey would eventually stretch the studio's state of the art SSL mixing desk to the limit of its capacity, using all of its 72 available tracks at once.

Ahead of time there had been some warm-up rehearsals at Aubitt, to ensure elements such as Danny Manners and Andy Poole's keyboard parts were meshing well and that the adapted vocal harmonies were working. "Everybody was excited about playing and the filming," says Aubrey. "They'd all learned their parts really well, they had their sounds down. We were doing it all to a click track, and we had the original backing tracks for the songs loaded into Pro Tools, so if any of them they needed to check something it was there for them. I had sent them all a stem [an isolated track] of their instrument so they could check their tone and what they played, and also a mix of each song with their part removed, so they could play along. If they rehearsed it well, it should sound like the band."

As well as her fiddle parts, Rachel Hall had plenty of vocal harmonies to remember too, and had been woodshedding hard in preparation. For her, the Real World experience would typify how the band worked from here on in: "It was a strange situation. You have an idea of what being in a band is like, you've been in other bands, and you've done rehearsals and gigs. But the scale of Big Big Train is such that you have to be rehearsed before the rehearsal. You've got to be prepared that it might well be filmed or it might well be used for something. A lot of rehearsal is done separately, and I think that's pretty good. It gives people the time to actually think about what they're playing, to fine-tune their parts before they really play them together. We were so used to practising in isolation – it was such a

great feeling to all be in the same room playing together for the first time."

Once ready to go, the plan was for the eight musicians to run through the songs, then focus on any areas that needed ironing out. David Longdon would use the opportunity to work out some choreography, including some moves that would become live rituals in themselves. "Stuff like the tambourine work in *The First Rebreather*," he says. "They were worked out in those run throughs. As all the music had been made without a view to playing live, the band hadn't had to consider the visual practicalities of performing live. But I knew that was my role, and I don't think anyone else was thinking about the visuals."

Spawton and Poole were preoccupied with practicalities of their own, namely playing all their parts for all the songs all the way through live without making too many cock-ups. There were nerves. For the first time they would have to hold their own with some road-savvy musicians: Sjöblom, Manners, Hall and D'Virgilio.

Longdon had years of experience on the pair too, but he himself hadn't gigged properly for years. His last two live appearances had been particularly soul destroying. "In Shropshire I played an open mic night at a pub in Ironbridge," he remembers, "and it was dreadful – badly set up and hardly anyone there. I just used it as a rehearsal in the end. Then I did one in Newport in Shropshire, at a soldiers and sailors pub, because I thought if I didn't then I might never go back on stage again.

"That made me think about what I'm prepared to do and what I'm not. I realised that I'd rather not play live at all than play in terrible places. I've paid my dues, I did loads of gigs in my formative years, but in my mid-40s a line was drawn. There had been thick and thin, but an awful lot of thin and not much thick. I was getting to a point where I started to think, 'Fucking hell, is this *it*? Is this going to be *it*? If this is it, then I don't want it!' But, you can't stop – that means you've packed away all hope. I needed to be recording, and Big Big Train was committed to being a recording band, until this opportunity came."

There was little in the way of set dressing at Real World, bar one notable inclusion. When *Prog* ran their enthusiastic lead review of *English Electric Part Two*, the magazine's art editor Russell Fairbrother commissioned artist Bob Venables to come up with a fitting graphic to accompany the text. Venables created a tableau inspired by a famous railway poster, titled *The Permanent Way*, cleverly interposing the band members as the characters within it. This trophy of arrival thrilled the band so much that Poole and Spawton sprung for a large blow-up print of the illustration, which took pride of place above the Real World stage as they played.

By the evening of day one all the gear was in, Aubrey and the in-house engineer Patrick Phillips were happy, and all the musicians were line checked. The team and band retired for dinner, but were so fired up and keen to hear how they sounded that they returned to The Big Room straight afterwards to finally run through a song properly. Nobody knew for sure how the band would sound as D'Virgilio finally counted them in for the first take of the first song, the tricky *Kingmaker*.

Dave Gregory remembers the overwhelming feeling when the whole octet launched into the tune. "I was quite taken aback – I was astounded at how it all sounded in a room with real people. The music went to another place. I thought it would be damn good, if we could all keep it together."

"*Kingmaker* was the first song, and kind of insane," recalls Sjöblom, "but, as soon as we started playing, it sounded like Big Big Train, which was cool. We realised we could do this."

"I noticed how everything gelled together incredibly quickly between us," adds Hall, "having all been practising our parts at home. Nick's drums were pretty incredible, and I'm sure Greg's bass pedals probably took me by surprise when they came in."

Bright and early on Tuesday morning they were out of the traps, and started rehearsing and recording in earnest with *The First Rebreather*. "There was something magical about hearing these parts played live," adds Danny Manners, "even though we were the band who had put them down."

Manners had been concerned that the atmosphere and colour of the records would be lost in the live performance, and had gone the extra mile to try to include most of the albums' key moments. "I'd taken a purist approach to the keyboards and tried to cover everything. Maybe that was naïve, but I thought, why not? We brought a PA to Real World and were listening to playbacks of the rehearsals and it sounded good – there was energy and it was really together – but it was somewhat crudified. Halfway through Rob said, 'Take half an hour, I'm going to get a proper mix now.' So we then started hearing the playback of the band mixed, and then it sounded really good, as I'd hoped it would. I asked Rob, 'Is that us today, or is that the album?' He told me it was us today, and at that point I thought, 'Okay, this is going to be really good.'

"We went in with quite a lot of uncertainty about whether we could pull it off live at all, and in retrospect that seems a bit odd. Granted, it's quite complicated music and the arrangements are quite dense, but the band is full of good musicians – there's no reason why we couldn't. Greg and Andy were the least gigged of all of us, but they were great as well. And Rikard's very easy to get on with, very laid back with a great sense of humour, and he just fitted right in. He could cover the parts we needed, and add a bit of rock 'n' roll on top."

"I hadn't met Rikard before," says Dave Gregory, "but was really thankful he was the other guitarist. What would have happened if we'd had some egomaniac who insisted on playing really loud, taking all the solos and drawing attention to himself? That's what so many lead guitarists do – most of them are a pain in the arse! But Rikard isn't like that. He listens to the music and to what everyone does – the music comes first with him. He's a joy to have around."

Finally seeing the light of day over 18 months later in March 2016, the *Stone & Steel* film would tell the tale of that Real World week. There are clearly some understandable nerves, but, from opener *The First Rebreather* to closer *Summoned By Bells,* the band simply sound like Big Big Train. Centre stage, David Longdon is revealed as an eye-catching and committed frontman, as well as a rock-solid singer. The elaborate vocal harmonies of *Master James Of St. George* are rendered well by those backing him, and all the discussion and practice Manners and Poole put in beforehand are manifest in the rich keyboard work here. A striking performer with sensitivity and tone, Hall's violin brings verisimilitude and depth to Manners' string samples, and the pair's modern classical interplay on *Wind Distorted Pioneers* rings with class and aptitude. Sjöblom and Gregory soar on *The Underfall Yard*'s monolithic title track, the newcomer taking an exciting solo on *Victoria Brickwork*, as the enhanced brass band work their baleful

magic. Between takes Sjöblom and Gregory can be seen joking over the best way to count the song's challenging 19/8 rhythm. "I hate it," mugs Sjöblom, "and love it at the same time."

Later in the film, the band repair to The Wood Room, Real World's smaller performance space. Manners picks up the double bass for *Uncle Jack*'s cheerful banjo-led folk, and the members line up choir-like behind Longdon for *Wind Distorted Pioneers*. If they look slightly awkward, those precise vocal harmonies still fall nicely into place.

And throughout it all Spawton, the greenhorn, keeps hands and feet under control. "I was nervous the whole week about holding down the bass end," he says now, "but bluffed my way through it and got out the other side, without Nick raising his eyebrows too many times."

"Greg definitely has a 'guitar player's' feel on the bass," says D'Virgilio, somewhat diplomatically. "He's not a typical bass player, but it works for this band and that's all that counts. We'd groove better as a rhythm section as the years went by, but even in those early days he was solid and locking in with me. He was playing the parts, and the more we played together, the tighter it got."

One of the major unknowns had been how Dave Desmond's brass ensemble would fit in. The core Big Big Train band rehearsed until the Wednesday, when Desmond and his fellow players – Jon Truscott, Nick Stones, Ben Godfrey and John Storey – joined, sight-reading Desmond's charts in The Big Room as the band played on. "That was the big road test," says Spawton. "A full-on rock band with a brass band playing in colliery style is almost unique. There was some pressure because we were being filmed, but it was reduced because there was no audience. If any of us cocked up we could bring everything to a halt and start over. But the brass just worked. They're absolutely great guys, and very professional. I mean, they tour, they're blokes in a band, and they could see that Nick, Rikard and Danny were top-end musicians, so there was respect on the playing side. Dave is our fifth Beatle in a way – he went on to do every live show, and he's been instrumental in getting the whole thing to work."

"We were in awe of the band actually," says Desmond now. "We wrote all the music out, but they all did it from memory. I remember brimming over with excitement that week, I was like a schoolkid. Playing this music live had just been a pipedream. I couldn't wait to hear how it would work, how we would all interact." And Desmond also found cause for awe within the ranks of the brass: "Ben [Godfrey] is an outstanding talent. He's been in the London Symphony Orchestra, he's played the West End, and his solo on *Victorian Brickwork* is incredible. I was really struck by the beauty of it live at Real World."

Over the intense, tiring week it became clear that the whole project was slotting into place and that the band – with Aubrey presiding over their sound – could indeed pull this music off on a stage. This was a big deal, and nothing short of a revelation to their stage shy leader. Every once in a while, with the band in full flight, Gregory Spawton would allow himself a glance around The Big Room at what was happening, and take stock.

Some 24 years back in Bournemouth, he, Andy Poole and Ian Cooper had begun jamming in keen but amateur fashion in Poole's front room. Today, through a mixture of talent, luck and sheer bloody mindedness, the line-up had evolved into this set of top players, bringing to life songs he could barely have imagined being within his gift back in the days of *From The River To The Sea* or *The Infant Hercules*.

And all this in Peter Gabriel's own, world-class recording facility. Finally, Big Big Train felt like the band Spawton had always wanted to be in, and now he knew they could deliver live, too. As D'Virgilio's words ran through his head, he could finally dare to start believing them. 'They're going to fucking *love* us.'

From his position at the helm of Real World's sprawling SSL mixing desk, Aubrey could see the change in the band, and particularly in Spawton. "Until that point there was never going to be a gig," he says. "It's only when they physically started playing together that Greg realised playing with people, with great musicians, is really fun. There was still nervousness, but the transformation of the band during the *Stone & Steel* sessions was clear. You could see Greg looking around and thinking, 'I could be on stage with that guy, it's going to be a really exciting future.'"

"The first couple of rehearsals were a little rough," says D'Virgilio, in mitigation, "just because we hadn't played together before, but Danny is an unbelievable musician and listening to him play made me feel comfortable. There was solidness in the keyboard section of the band. Dave has such a great feel, and Rikard is a monster, just stupid good. I knew everyone could play everything fine, but it was whether the arrangements and vocal harmonies worked and the brass band worked. But it all bedded in nicely. When we got everyone in the room and heard the sounds, and the brass guys – all of us making noise at the same time – it was like the clouds parted in the heavens and the choir sang. It was a magical moment."

One thing that sticks with Rachel Hall is that "there was an air of excitement the day that the brass arrived. I remember playing the middle section of *The Underfall Yard* quite a lot. During the filming of the 'Twelve Stones'

Gregory Spawton's view of proceedings at Real World in 2014.

section where we sang vocals in the live room I remember counting on my fingers until someone said, 'Rach, you do know we can see that?'"

"I saw that week that David could deliver the songs," adds Andy Poole. "The thing I was less certain about was the between song banter, which is the downfall of some bands, when it's bland and perfunctory. David would have some pre-written stuff, but I knew he could be very spontaneous and funny and I wanted that to come across."

Previously sceptical about the enterprise, Poole is clearly enthusiastic on the *Stone & Steel* film. "There has been a certain chemistry that has been discovered here," he says in one interview segment. "For Greg and I this has been a long term project and a way of life for us, and for us to come here with all these complementary ingredients and put those together to find they make a very moving and –

for me – a sensational whole has been incredibly inspiring."

Over the years Big Big Train would come to consider Real World almost like a second home, a sanctuary where they could rehearse and record, and get away from the real world itself. Nowadays Poole can see both sides of that heated argument he and Spawton had in the car in the run-up. "I have always thought of Real World as an extravagance," he says, "albeit a mostly necessary one,

given the proportions of the live band and the tech and film crews, who we also needed to accommodate when filming *Stone & Steel*. But it is such a wonderful studio complex and residential retreat that you can but immerse yourself."

And Poole wasn't totally alone in his reservations. Danny Manners shared them, at least initially. "Real World seemed very extravagant, but once I'd worked there I got that it's a fantastic environment – you really can just concentrate on the music and relax in between. You can rehearse, walk one minute to have lunch, then one minute to come back – great food, really nice surroundings, the resident engineers are great. They've improved it since, but when we first went there it had really lousy mobile reception, which was actually rather nice. So it definitely has a monastic quality. It's all geared to enabling you to concentrate on the music and relax in between. Once we'd done it, we saw that, yes, we could do it cheaper elsewhere, but some of the savings would be illusory."

Crucially, above and beyond the music, Real World's residential atmosphere lent itself to the band bonding as a unit, as people, over the week. As Manners says, the main building is a few steps away from the studios. It houses the bedrooms, kitchen and also a canteen area and lounge, which are both highly convivial rooms. Over dinner cooked by Real World's in-house French chef Jerome, and with copious glasses of wine to wash it down, the individuals in the group got to know each other, their evening discussions filled with banter and laughter, often lasting into the wee small hours.

Of course, music was a major topic of conversation. Manners and Sjöblom discovered their mutual love for '70s prog maestros Gentle Giant, and the two fanned out accordingly. Dave Gregory had plenty of tales to tell about his tenure with XTC and their eccentric linchpin, Andy Partridge. Sjöblom would start to collect that band's vinyl as a result, developing a particular affection for 1980's *Black Sea*. Spawton and Poole suggested he should also try out an old favourite of theirs, It Bites. Being in this particular establishment, it was only fitting that D'Virgilio talk about his experience of recording with Peter Gabriel here; and both he and David Longdon had a few Genesis stories for

the table – some funny, a few hair-raising. A big Muse fan, D'Virgilio was knocked out to hear that Manners had played in the string section on the trio's hit 2003 album *Absolution*.

With all those jazz ensembles, socialist big bands and some radical artists on his CV, Danny Manners could add some colour from his days on the London circuit. Dave Desmond's army boys could hold their drink well, and had names aplenty to drop, from U2 to Brian May of Queen to The Queen herself. D'Virgilio actually had some video footage of himself as a tourist at the Changing of The Guard at Buckingham Palace, and broke out his MacBook to show Desmond. As the drummer spoke animatedly to camera about the very English ceremony he was attending, who should march through shot in the background, in bearskin and full regalia, but Dave Desmond himself.

Rachel Hall had her own fondly remembered share of fun experiences, with Stackridge especially. One member of the band used to ride his bicycle down backstage corridors; another would get wheeled onto the stage in a shopping trolley. Another had fallen right off the stage mid-show and, at Glastonbury, one had leapt from their fast-moving van just to grab a goat's milk ice cream. "Exhaust pipes fell off tour vans," she says, "people fell off stages – my oddball family of musicians existed in parallel with university life. I lived my youth, while they re-lived theirs." But still, she was a little reticent at the Real World table, at least to begin with.

Born on 24th May 1988, only two years before Big Big Train was founded, Hall was considerably younger than everyone, even Sjöblom. Moreover, she was conscious that she was less absorbed in the world of progressive rock than most of her bandmates. "When you're with people for a week in the same room rehearsing you do get a bond, and when we were playing, everything felt great. I got more anxious at meal times, when all the guys would be having animated conversations about bands from the past and stuff I just really hadn't had the same experience of. I would be sitting there thinking, 'I know I haven't spoken for ages and I really should say something, but I haven't got a clue what you're talking about!'

"There was a situation where everyone was saying who they listened to as a child. It wasn't too embarrassing because I grew up listening to folk like Fairport Convention, The Levellers, and my dad would play things like The Doors and The Who. But at the same time, when I was a child it was The Spice Girls, B*Witched and Aqua on the menu – and that doesn't really get the same sort of reaction! I think the more we got to know each other, the less self-conscious I felt about that."

Hall really needn't have worried. "The fact is we don't want to be surrounded by just 'prog people'," says Spawton now. "I told Rach at the time, 'Don't worry – nobody is going to criticise you if you don't know the name of Pink Floyd's third album, or who designed the cover for *Foxtrot*.' I think she got more comfortable as the week went by."

For Spawton, Hall was a high pedigree musician and an assured performer who was adding a whole new dimension – and a welcome feminine register – to Big Big Train on record and, now, on stage. He was just delighted she was part of what he remembers as a truly great experience. "We all drank until 4am every night," he says, almost wistfully. "We had the best time ever. That week at Real World was the making of the band, unquestionably. It was a turning point. We were confident that we could recreate the absolute essence of what we do as a studio band. As we were packing up to leave on the Sunday we were all a bit,

'Wow!' But David was in his shell a bit."

You would have to watch *Stone & Steel* very hard to perceive it, but the joy of the Real World sessions had been tainted for David Longdon due to problems in his relationship with his then-partner. Big Big Train's burgeoning success had revitalised him as an artist, but this had caused friction at home, and his mental health was beginning to suffer. "When you look at those Real World sessions I felt that I was literally going through the motions – like a dead man walking. You can see my anxiety when I arrived at Real World. I wasn't well, but I had the music. It was the only thing I was capable of doing, and so I clung to it.

"While I wasn't in a great place, I did find it very liberating. It was nice having the routine and the camaraderie that week, and meeting Rachel and Rikard for the first time. It was good to hear the band come to fruition. I was being a frontman in a band that had never played live, and playing out to Rob, and Patrick Phillips and Oli Jacobs – engineers who became friends over the years. We were all learning at the same time. It would take a small army but, yes, we could do it. I didn't want that week to end. After a few wilderness years I was having such an enjoyable time with like-minded people."

D'Virgilio recalls a deep, late night conversation with Longdon and Sjöblom: "We were getting comfortable with each other, and were talking about more personal things. David was going through some personal stuff and he was in a tough spot. Me, him and Rikard were up drinking and talking about faith and God. Playing together was a beautiful thing, but through these conversations you start to get to know each other, and become closer friends."

As Big Big Train's first sojourn at Real World drew to a close, an emboldened Gregory Spawton knew exactly what needed to be done next. On the last day, the Sunday, he took Sjöblom aside and asked if he would like to join the band full-time. "I was really happy and honoured," says Sjöblom, who accepted immediately. "I loved the music and really enjoyed spending time with all the guys. There's a lot of hanging out and downtime with rehearsing and playing live. I just got along so well with everyone."

And Spawton also asked Hall if she too would consider becoming a fully fledged BBT member. "There weren't any hesitations about it," she says now. "I thought, 'I really like this band, I really enjoy playing their music – it would been silly not to.' We'd all had a great time in the studio and it seemed a worthwhile project to invest time in. Shortly after I moved back in with my parents in Norfolk to escape the long restaurant hours and high rent of Bath, and I got a teaching assistant job in a specialist base for autistic children, and soon became the violin teacher in the main school as well. I was able to spend the time I wanted on the band."

Big Big Train arrived at Real World a studio project, and left it a live prospect. But while the band's musical horizons were expanding, so were the cracks in the friendship between the founder members. Spawton, Poole and Rob Aubrey were back in the car together and headed for home, on what would be their second awkward drive from Bath to Bournemouth.

Highly animated after the week, Spawton was uncharacteristically talkative, brimming with ideas and enthusiasm about the whole new world of potential that had just opened up for them. "I was thinking we were going places," he says, "that we'd get gigging, and Andy was like, 'Come on – calm down!' He didn't read the room, it wasn't the right time to be Mister Realistic.

"Many, many times Andy's judgement had been great. Like when I wanted to record a brass band for *The Underfall Yard*, and he managed sensibly to get that down to a brass quartet. David has ideas that float off to the moon and then it's me who has to be the tether to reality – there's good cause sometimes for caution. But when it feels like a deliberate anchor, a negative reaction without any alternative suggestions, it's frustrating. I was beginning to get really pissed off, and I saw that was the last straw for Rob. I don't think he ever talked to Andy about band strategy again."

The dynamic in the band was clearly changing. From that day on, when it came to discussing his ambitions for the band, when it came to planning the next chapter in their story, Spawton found himself bypassing his old friend more and more, preferring to consult with Longdon and Aubrey instead. And with the looming prospect of Big Big Train's first set of concerts, there was plenty for them to talk about.

XI

*'Made for speed and in full cry,
they gave her the road
and she holds to the line...'*

On 3rd July 1938 at King's Cross station in London, driver Joe Duddington and fireman Tommy Bray boarded the cab of their streamlined, A4 class locomotive called Mallard, and headed off along the East Coast Main Line. Their purpose was ostensibly to test a new braking system, but Sir Nigel Gresley – the train's designer and chief engineer for the London and North Eastern Railway – had an ulterior motive. He wanted to use the test run as an attempt to break the world speed record for steam locomotives.

Sure enough, on the downward slope of Stoke Bank, just south of Grantham in Lincolnshire, the engine hit 126 miles per hour and broke the previous world record of 124.5 mph. Duddington later recounted the moment they passed over the peak at Stoke Box and began their descent on the Bank: "I gave Mallard her head and she just jumped to it like a living thing." The triumph put Mallard into the history books, into legend, and the record still stands to this day.

◆◆◆

A stone's throw from the lines snaking in and out of King's Cross station, Kings Place stands on York Way near the bank of Regent's Canal. It was once the headquarters of Network Rail, and was bought by developers and converted in the 2000s. With its upper levels housing the offices of *The Guardian* newspaper, its lower floor was transformed into a vibrant, modern cultural venue.

You take a long escalator down into the building to reach its two impressive auditoria. The larger, Hall One, is set on a raft of rubber springs, and the acre of wooden veneer covering the room was all sourced from the same, 500-year-old German oak tree. It's a classy place for sure, one that Gregory Spawton had never heard of until Danny Manners mentioned it in passing.

In 2001 Manners and Louis Philippe had worked on *9th & 13th*, an album by bestselling English novelist and ardent prog rock fan Jonathan Coe. Over a decade later Manners had accompanied Coe at a show in Kings Place's smaller room, Hall Two, and as Big Big Train considered where to hold their first series of shows, Manners thought the venue might be a suitable setting.

It was certainly a world away from all those insalubrious venues with poor acoustics that the band members had endured as punters over the years. They didn't want their own audience going through that. David Longdon for one had drawn his line, making clear that his days of playing the sticky floor circuit were behind him. Spawton agreed completely. For Big Big Train's first major foray in the live space they wanted a venue that tallied with the band's higher-end aspirations and need for quality. It would have to have good, clean acoustics suitable for big drums and amped guitars, and be easily accessible for fans. Judging by album sales and the signs of demand from Passengers on their Facebook site, a room of around 500 seats should work. That way they could probably sell out one show, maybe even two.

Kings Place was marketed as a 'cultural hub', with its usual programme heavy on jazz, folk, classical and spoken word events, but by 2014 the team there were looking to expand its remit and stretch out to other audiences. On Valentine's Night that year they'd had a real coup, when the superstar Prince performed an impromptu, two-set show in Hall One to rapturous audiences and rabidly good reviews. So when Spawton and Rob Aubrey turned up to recce the venue just after their Real World week, the place's rock 'n' roll mettle had already been well tested.

The pair liked the 420-capacity room very much, and were impressed with the staff, facilities and the overall set-up. The in-house, 48-track Pro Tools recording system meant they would be able to capture high quality recordings of the shows, raising the possibility of their making a live album. They were provisionally offered two dates in 2015 – 14th and 15th August, a Friday and Saturday. This would give them a year to plan, to sell tickets, and to gird themselves for their next big step.

By this time, Spawton and David Longdon would speak about once a week, between Bournemouth and Shrewsbury, and as their friendship deepened, so would their discussions. Along with band business they would get into everything from their home lives, to the relative merits of Yes's ambitious 1974 album *Relayer*, to the art of British painter Eric Ravilious. And they found they had quirky, human things in common, such as the fact that neither of them could swim. As kids they were both what they'd call 'shallow enders', confined to the safer part of the pool while their swimming friends did their lengths.

But when it came to discussing the mooted live shows, Spawton detected a certain reticence on the other end of the line. "At the time I didn't know why," he says, "but there was negativity coming from David. I had never seen him play live, so for all I knew it was because he was nervous about playing in front of an audience. But we needed a firm yes or a no – time was marching on and I knew we required as much time as possible to prepare for the shows. I told David that the venue needed confirmation of the booking urgently. That wasn't strictly true, but I felt it was the only way I would get an answer from him at that point as he had become very non-committal. I really had no understanding of the ramifications for him of his saying yes."

While reluctant to let the Kings Place shows hit the buffers, Spawton privately came to the view that, if Longdon couldn't commit, then Big Big Train could trundle on as a studio band, and any live plans would be halted for the foreseeable future.

Eventually, late in August 2014, Longdon took the plunge. It hadn't been nerves holding him back at all. "It was a very emphatic move for me to commit. Suddenly Big Big Train had momentum and energy, achieving these things to get to greater goals, and it was incredible. But I knew that committing to the shows would have an effect on my personal life."

He was right. The decision added more strain to his relationship, and soon he moved out of the family home, and back into his childhood home in Nottingham with his mother, Vera. These were dark times for him. "The only thing I was good for was music," he says, "so I just surrendered and relaxed into that and it was supportive – I was buoyant and could float and function. Music was salvation for me."

Longdon set to work, and continued to develop his frontman role. In his childhood bedroom, his wardrobe had tall mirrored doors, and he rehearsed in front of these, building up his voice and his stage persona, his vivid imagination staving off the harsh reality of his personal problems. "I worked on the show bit by bit. I sang through the songs and worked on the breathing and my movements. Eventually stamina builds up, and you also get production ideas."

Just a few years previously, Gregory Spawton had somewhat naively opted to release *The Underfall Yard* at Christmas, a fallow period for album sales. Now the band was entering the world of live performance at the peak of the summer holiday season, when many Passengers may well have already made other plans. Nevertheless, when the two Kings Place shows were announced, the tickets were all quickly snapped up. A third, matinée show was hastily added for the Sunday, and – to Spawton's amazement – that also sold out. He hadn't factored in that, given a Big Big Train show was so rare, some of the band's most fervent followers would want to come and see them more than once. But then, Spawton had zero experience of organising events at this level, and he stood gaping up at the steep learning curve looming ahead of him.

"It's one thing booking the shows," he says, "but then you start to learn about the roles of promoters, tour managers and production managers. You suddenly find out they all do a lot. And we didn't have any of them." There were the band's eight members to consider, plus Dave Desmond's five-piece brass section. They would all have to be rehearsed, accommodated, fed and watered. Then there were the multifarious tasks involved in putting on the gig, from the ticketing to the merchandise, from liaising with the venue and various technical teams to promoting the shows too.

Spawton was still working full-time at the local council in a management capacity, and began to feel incredibly stretched. To Spawton, Andy Poole was conspicuous by his absence during the organisation of the Kings Place shows, which added further to his frustrations about their increasingly splintering collaboration. For her partner's sanity, Kathy stepped in to help. "Kathy was a rock," says Spawton. "Looking back, we should have got some outside help, but the best part is that Kathy and I really learned the ropes. It was a baptism of fire, but it really did help us subsequently. Kathy is very much a 'dot the i's and cross the t's' person, and she was really emotionally invested."

Also invested was Nellie Pitts. A well-known face on the UK prog rock scene, Pitts ran The Merch Desk, a company specialising in band merchandise. With profits from recorded music falling year on year, merch and concert tickets were two vital income streams for the majority of artists in the streaming era. Pitts had perceived that Big Big Train, with its strong brand identity, were missing out on both fronts. "I got involved after *English Electric Part One*," she says. "They were producing really good music, but they didn't even have a single T-shirt at the time. I was trying to build The Merch Desk up, and I had pestered and pestered Greg to play live and also to get merchandise. Eventually he relented, we got 100 T-shirts done, they sold out and I had to get them reprinted three times, each time in bigger quantities."

Pitts would run the band's merch stall in the Kings Place foyer, and bring in a little extra money to help pay for the event. She also happened to be the UK agent for Paul Whitehead, the painter/graphic artist behind such iconic album covers as Genesis's *Trespass*, *Nursery Cryme* and *Foxtrot*, and Van der Graaf Generator's *Pawn Hearts*. Whitehead would come along too, and host his own mini gallery at the gig – a proggy bonus for the many Big Big Train fans who would certainly own the records that his striking artwork adorned.

With Manners and Longdon pitching in, Spawton worked on the setlist. It would be drawn mainly from the Real World set, and by consensus there would be no material harking back any further than *The Underfall Yard*, with the focus on material played by the current band line-up. "You've got to find the right songs that will move people to their core," says Spawton, "and also make them feel part of a communal experience. We tried to tick both of those boxes. Looking back on it I think we chose well, with *Summoned By Bells* perhaps being a surprise."

He was aware that *Victorian Brickwork* had become a particular favourite among the Passengers, so that was a must-have. Nick D'Virgilio pushed for *Master James Of St. George*, but Spawton didn't feel it was a live grabber. Also there was the consideration of balancing the material with brass and without, such as *Uncle Jack*. And they added *East Coast Racer*, the 15-minute evocation of Mallard's historic achievement, which – by pure coincidence and much to the

songwriter's delight – began at the station over the road from their Kings Cross venue.

Some additional arrangement work was required for the song. Its closing section was a re-statement of a musical motif from the brace of *English Electric* albums, and the same chord sequence was already accounted for in the set at the coda of *Summoned by Bells*. Over Christmas 2014 Danny Manners burned the midnight oil, working until 3am on a beautiful and dramatic new chord sequence to allow for a featured guitar solo at *East Coast Racer*'s climax. When Dave Gregory heard the part he loved it, and phoned Spawton to lay claim to the solo.

Then there was the title track of their latest EP, and their only promo video to date. *Make Some Noise* had pleased some of the crowd and bemused others, but it was going to have to feature somewhere. "We knew we had to play it," says Spawton, "but half the audience liked it and half hated it. We thought the audience would assume we'd play it as the encore, so we decided to turn that completely on its head and open with it instead."

◆◆◆

From Nottingham to Norfolk, from Sweden to Swindon, from Bournemouth to London to Fort Wayne in Indiana, the band's preparations gathered pace. After Real World, Dave Gregory had a great deal of confidence in his bandmates' abilities – it was his own playing he was worried about. "I had severe misgivings about whether I would cope on stage in front of an audience, reproducing some of the complicated parts I had played in the comfort of my sitting room. I hadn't played live for such a long time and the music was a lot more complicated than most of the stuff I had ever performed on stage. I went into it as well prepared as I could be, but was very nervous."

Gregory's co-guitarist Rikard Sjöblom had played anything from 50 to 100 shows per year for decades with his covers bands and Beardfish, so he had no such qualms. "For me playing live has always been very natural and comfortable. I could tell that a couple of the guys hadn't played live for a long time. We were all nervous because it was one of those situations – it was conquer or leave."

As for the steely Danny Manners, he wasn't too fazed by Big Big Train's music itself, but in the past he had played as either a pianist or double bassist in the live space; this time he would be drawing on a new set of skills. "These were the first gigs I'd done as a proper multi-keyboardist, having to get everything programmed and with all the patch changes at the right time. Funnily enough I find smaller gigs scarier – you feel a bit more self-conscious when you're in a small room and can really see people watching you."

He practised intensively with Andy Poole, who himself spent the run-up to the show becoming familiar with new parts, new stage software, a protracted process for him. "I'd run through the set at home and find it quite exhausting," he says. "I was unused to the discipline of playing through an hour of music and having that level of concentration. I was learning parts in isolation and then skipping forward. We didn't have a keyboard player on the song *The Underfall Yard* and Greg and I would play abstract parts – trying to learn how those fitted into the song was difficult. If there was something that was more 'written' it was easier. Danny writes more complete parts so you know there's a certain progression; Greg writes with quite a lot of modulation or strange intervals. I was playing parts that didn't always seem a natural progression."

Even the band's most seasoned live performer, Nick D'Virgilio, had to keep sharpening his chops for the shows, while closing out his time at Cirque du Soleil. "When the Kings Place gigs were announced and sold out so quickly a year in advance, it was amazing. It took a lot of practice to prepare for them. I had my own drum booth at Cirque and I would stay after the show was over until one or two in the morning playing Big Big Train songs. That's how I practised a lot of this stuff."

It was in early 2015 that the true scale of the task at hand started to dawn on Gregory Spawton, and the pressure hit him hard. As well as spearheading the planning of the shows, he also had to learn his parts for the songs, stretching his instrumental skill to its limits. He would sit for hours at home running through the set, trying to let the parts sink in, all the while combating the fear of going blank onstage. With all these cumulative tasks starting to appear insurmountable to him, Spawton began to lose his nerve.

"I've always seen myself primarily as a songwriter," he says. "I had not performed at a gig for 17 years and had never played a show as a bass player. I have never craved the limelight and never particularly enjoyed being on stage, so I knew I was going to be nervous. I was still suffering from Imposter Syndrome – I shouldn't be playing bass in front of an audience at all. There were times when I said to Rob that I thought we should recruit a bass player for the live shows, because it wasn't my thing and organising the shows was enough of a job. But, in his inimitable fashion, Rob pulled me back into reality."

Told in no uncertain terms to pull himself together and that he simply had to be on that stage, Spawton endured. He chose to learn the songs by rote and commit them to muscle memory so that, by sheer force of repetition, the parts would be at his fingertips and feet when showtime arrived.

In addition to Kings Place, there was another record release to consider. It had been two years since *English Electric Part Two*, and while the live shows and *Stone & Steel* were on the way, they needed to have product in the pipeline, to stoke the fires of interest in the media and among fans, and also to generate income. Spawton and Longdon had long been cooking up a progressive rock magnum opus to end them all – a concept album that, as Longdon recalls, first developed around 2010, in a pretty rock 'n' roll location: "We were in a jacuzzi at the time. On Rob's recommendation we went to [luxury south Wales hotel] Celtic Manor for a break. It was about the time the big Icelandic volcano [Eyjafjallajökull] erupted, and we mooted a big concept thing for Big Big Train called *Hope.*

"It was going to be a graphic novel, a three-part thing, in the vein of The Who's *Tommy*. One of the songs was called *Edmund Ironside*, and another was *Pagan Times*, about a newspaper and community set in Orkney. I invested so much time in *Hope*, but to put that much work into three albums' worth of music for one release was unworkable really. The band was rising, we were getting lots of attention after *English Electric*, we'd released *Full Power* (which we toyed with calling *Full English* for a while), and after that we didn't need a long-winded concept album. We needed a single volume."

The two songwriters discussed song ideas that fell outside the remit of the lofty three-part opus, and found that between them they had plenty of other material for a separate, single album. They even settled on a concept. "David mentioned the word 'folklore' one day," Spawton recalls, "and we connected on that. The 'F-word' makes people think you've either gone a bit hey-nonny-nonny, or a bit folk rock, but the concept was actual folklore, historical tales. That's what we were focusing on."

One of the early songs typifying this song cycle was *Wassail*, a strident, catchy Longdon piece steeped in pagan lore related to the rituals around the English apple harvest. Andy Poole loved it and thought it would make for a particularly strong release. An EP was planned in the build-up to the Kings Place shows. Nick D'Virgilio had recorded his drum parts for the song during their first Real World visit the previous August (his sessions captured on film on the following year's *Stone & Steel* film). Longdon laid down his vocals, flute and mandolin parts in Aubitt the following March.

The *Wassail* EP was notable for being the first release to feature contributions from the entire Big Big Train live band. A one-woman string trio, Rachel Hall recorded violin, viola and cello at London's Regal Lane with Ken Brake. "I remember Ken was very welcoming," she says. "It was a cosy place downstairs, with a spiral staircase leading to a room at the top. Danny and I often worked closely on string arrangements, and I remember it more for being the first time we had worked together in the non-live studio environment. At my previous studio sessions Rob, Greg and Andy had been present. They'd used Ken's studio for the previous quartet arrangements on *English Electric*, which had worked really well."

From his home in Sweden Rikard Sjöblom sent in his debut guitar and vocal additions. "*Wassail* was the first one I was fully involved with," he says, "and it was tricky. I really just followed the demos. But later on the *Folklore* album itself I felt I should have more of my own ideas."

Also on the EP would be *Lost Rivers Of London* and

Mudlarks, a two-piece suite that Spawton had stored away for a while, and with the *Stone & Steel* Blu-ray release still nearly a year away, the live recording of *Master James Of St. George* gave an early taste of the band's first visit to Real World.

As for the cover, Spawton had been impressed with the work of the artist Sarah Ewing, and contacted her to see if she would be interested in painting something fitting. She was sent a rough mix of the song complete with lyrics sheet, and Andy Poole and David Longdon sent her a loose artistic brief. They were delighted with what Ewing came back with – a wintery scene of a young boy and girl, framed by an apple-studded wreath, crowned by the eerie visage of the Green Man, the pagan symbol of the circle of life and the fertile promise of spring. Ewing was also commissioned to revamp the band's logo, as they moved away from the retro industrial, rail related themes of *English Electric* and on to a more pastoral aesthetic.

From here on in Ewing would shape the band's visual language into a coherent and strikingly recognisable whole. And in the fullness of time she would come to mean a whole lot more besides to David Longdon.

♦♦♦

For Gregory Spawton, 2015 was a busy and varied year. In February he and Longdon went to see King Crimson at Birmingham Symphony Hall. Crimson had been reinvigorated of late. Wimborne Minster's own Robert Fripp finally seemed to be embracing and enjoying his position as one of the few major progressive rock progenitors still standing, and the shows earned the band rave reviews and legions of new fans. With his stock never higher, Fripp's status offered Spawton another object lesson in tenacity.

Now some 25 years into the game himself, Spawton also saw one of his favourite modern bands, Elbow, at London's Hammersmith Apollo. He was struck by singer Guy Garvey's connection with their crowd, and the expertly judged rise and fall of their set list. With the Big Big Train shows coming up, he made notes.

He met up with lighting and projection specialist Sabine Reichhuber, who had worked with other prog bands such as Pendragon and German proggers RPWL, and she was brought in to create the background visuals and light show at Kings Place. All the while Spawton worked on new songs for *Folklore*. One was about The Ridgeway, a prehistoric and richly storied path running from

Sarah Louise Ewing's initial Green Man sketch.

Wiltshire to the Thames. Another was inspired by the Salisbury Giant, a 12-feet tall pageant figure with roots in the 15th century. And in April, a month before Spawton's 50th birthday, Gregory and Kathy finally married in a civil ceremony in Winchester.

Up in Nottingham, David Longdon loved Sarah Ewing's cover design for *Wassail*, and the beautiful accompanying prints of the Green Man illustration she was working on. The figure fitted perfectly with the vibe inspiring Longdon's current crop of songs, and he commissioned mask maker Stephen Jon to work on a Green Man mask. He would incorporate the mask into his live performance of that song. "I wanted the Green Man thing as a link into the paganism thing," he says now. "It was not music hall, but rather this idea of ritual and paganism – a bit *Wicker Man*."

In March the singer had travelled to the Rhondda Valley in South Wales to the studio of Robert Reed, founder of award-winning Welsh proggers Magenta. Longdon had written a set of hopeful lyrics, a new vocal melody and flute parts for a version of Steve Hackett's instrumental *Spectral Mornings*, the masterful title track of Hackett's 1979 album. Credited to Steve Hackett, Rob Reed & Friends, *Spectral Mornings 2015* would see Longdon duet with Magenta's own Christina Booth, herself a much-adored figure in the world of British prog. Reed would be on keyboards, with Hackett himself contributing guitar, and the rhythm

Stephen Jon working on David's Green Man mask.

section comprising seasoned bassist Nick Beggs and, on drums, Nick D'Virgilio. The proceeds from sales of the song would be donated to Parkinson's Society UK, and by way of promotion a Magenta show was scheduled at London club The Borderline, on 27th June.

Gregory Spawton had never seen Longdon play to a proper audience, and finally got a taste of his abilities in this intimate basement venue (which sadly closed its doors in 2019). When Longdon took to the stage as Magenta's guest, Spawton says that he "appeared nerveless and entirely at ease. I knew David was a great singer, but I didn't know he was a great frontman. He was extremely charismatic and up for it, and the performance went well."

The *Wassail* EP was released that month too – a summer release rather at odds with its beautiful yet undeniably festive cover and theme. This wasn't lost on the witty and unyielding music journalist/broadcaster Philip Wilding: 'It looks like a Christmas card!' he pointed out gleefully during a fun, spiky interview with Spawton and Danny Manners on Wilding's TeamRock radio show.

This was fair, and despite its seasonally anachronous release and an initially lukewarm response from Passengers, *Wassail* entered the Amazon folk chart at number one (ahead of The Unthanks, a band that Spawton deeply admired). It also topped Amazon's progressive chart in the US, and when the nominations for that year's

David, Rob Reed and Tina Booth performing live with Magenta in 2015.

the new album. There was a wobble near the time when, after root canal surgery, Nick D'Virgilio came down with a nasty case of strep throat, but by the time he landed in the UK on 7th August he had recovered well enough to perform. Spawton picked him up, they drove straight to the studio, and he recorded drum parts for several *Folklore* tracks, including *London Plane, Telling The Bees, Brooklands* and *Along The Ridgeway.*

The following day the rest of the band descended on Real World along with Rob Aubrey, trusted techs and friends, with Dave Desmond's brass section once again showing up a few days later. The aim was to fine tune the planned two-set show, and over five days they ironed out the live version of *Make Some Noise* and *The First Rebreather,* finally got a handle on the numerous tricky time signatures of *The Underfall Yard,* and bedded in Manners' exquisite new outro to the retooled, 16-minute *East Coast Racer.* Eventually they could play through both sets well.

Progressive Music Awards were announced, *Wassail* was in the running for the Anthem Award (the equivalent of 'song of the year'), along with tunes by artists including Christina Booth, Steve Hackett, John Lodge, Public Service Broadcasting, Mew (another Spawton favourite) and, once again, Dave Gregory's other band, Tin Spirits.

By now the Kings Place shows were hoving quickly into view. In early August the band returned to Real World to undertake final rehearsals, and also to lay down parts for

'So, it's a bar of 19, a bar of 7, then a bar of 11…'
Rehearsals, August 2015.

Sabine Reichhuber brought her slide and film show, and, with Real World's Patrick Phillips setting up a large screen in The Big Room, they played along to her beautiful visuals. On the final day, Kings Place monitoring engineer Dan Pye attended to see what he was in for, and all 13 musicians and their crew worked through from morning to evening, until even Gregory Spawton had to admit that they – and he – were as ready as they would ever be.

And all the while, as showtime approached, David Longdon was working through his moves as a frontman. He had the Green Man mask for *Wassail* now, which would make appearances at all future shows. He had some other moments planned, and also gave thought to that eternal

singer's dilemma – what to do with his hands. In all the many gigs he'd played before with bands like The Gifthorse, he was usually seated behind a keyboard or had a guitar strapped around himself, fingers engaged accordingly. The first time he had sung unencumbered was for that Genesis audition. "And I liked it," he states. "I decided I wanted to be identified as a strong frontman for Big Big Train. My role was to bridge the gap between the stage and the audience, so I'd write songs that would enable me to do that musically and also entertain, rather than just have it as an audio experience.

"In The Gifthorse we would play two hour sets which were pretty demanding and I was singing for most of that.

A new prog rock rhythm section is forged at rehearsals in August 2015.

In *The Underfall Yard* and *Victorian Brickwork* there are lots of lengthy instrumental sections where I'm on stage but not singing. I wanted to be on stage for most of the time – progressive rock isn't just about the singing – it's also about the theatre of it. I wanted to be part of the performance and honour my colleagues within the band, to appreciate what they were doing. It's not hard, they're great musicians. I liked the idea of conducting it, of drawing attention to certain things. You have to embody the music, to do something in sympathy with it, and properly represent the band visually. I wanted to make it the best it could be."

The final rehearsal before the Kings Place shows, 13th August 2015.

Big Big Train at Real World, August 2015.

XII

'She flies!'

Big Big Train and their team pull up to Kings Place at noon on Friday 14th August. Unloaded from the van, their equipment descends to the concert level via the heavy goods lift, and it takes two hours to set up all the gear on stage and throughout the hall.

The band have been supplied with in-ear monitors, specifically moulded at some expense, for each individual's own ears. Nick D'Virgilio, Danny Manners, Rikard Sjöblom and David Longdon are familiar with this modern system, but the clarity of sound and the surreal, earplug-like isolation they give from the room itself take some getting used to. Rachel Hall patiently adjusts to them. For a while now Andy Poole has suffered from hyperacusis: he is unusually sensitive to sound, so needs the music at low level volume in his ears for comfort. The problem then is that when he sings his voice overpowers the mix in his head, and he can't hear the music with which he's meant to be in tune.

Decidedly old school, Dave Gregory won't use these in-ear gadgets at all. Much of his performance depends on his interaction with his guitar and amp, loud and in the room. Not for him the hermetic netherworld the in-ears provide, so he sticks to his classic 'wedge' monitor – an angled speaker at his feet pointed up at him.

It's 5pm by the time everybody's ready and the whole ensemble can play for Rob Aubrey, so he can mix the sound in this bright, rectangular, oak-lined room. In truth it's not designed for a full rock band, and in a venue this size you're at the mercy of the loudest instrument onstage. D'Virgilio's a powerful drummer, and even when he dials down his attack he could easily overwhelm everything else. Dave Gregory's Marshall amp is pretty dominant too – though after Aubrey's finished, it's nowhere near as loud as its owner would like it to be. Because the eight band members are more than taking up the minimal stage space, Dave Desmond and his brass have been relegated to the balcony, and they're a little peeved about it. They'd rather be on stage and in the midst of things with the group.

On the balcony at soundcheck: five of the fairest brass players in all the heavens.

In a lengthy soundcheck the 13-strong outfit play *Kingmaker*, *Victorian Brickwork* and, to line check Manners' double bass, *Uncle Jack*. Stressed but in control, Aubrey adjusts the PA's sound, rejigs microphones, and eventually he, the band and in-house techs are happy. All the while photographers Simon Hogg and Kain Dear buzz around to capture the event, and Peter Callow's film crew discuss sight lines and prep their cameras. The soundcheck takes nearly two whole hours, and the players head backstage with only half an hour until curtain-up. By then the foyer is already filling with ticket holders, and there's a rising wave of excited, expectant chat in the air as the clock ticks down.

All those interactions with Big Big Train listeners online, all those mail order and online sales – these will all be made real, made flesh, tonight. Here and now these self-styled Passengers are coming into their own. They've made the trip not just from across the UK – they've flown in from Italy, Sweden, the USA and South America, even Australia and New Zealand. Close friendships have been formed among them, and some have arrived in groups. The band's guest list for the weekend is packed with notable fellow musicians, including Louis Philippe, Christina Booth, Twelfth Night's Andy Sears, Pendragon's Nick Barrett, The Enid's vocalist Joe Payne, and Matt Stevens of instrumental proggers The Fierce And The Dead.

The sense of event in the venue is palpable, and the huddle at the merch table is crazy. Nellie Pitts is handing over T-shirts, mugs, hats, hoodies and badges at an overwhelming rate, as artist Paul Whitehead graciously holds court nearby. Somewhat taken aback by the thirsty enthusiasm of this event's untypical clientele, the Kings Place bar staff are earning their wages tonight.

Oblivious to all this, the musicians themselves are in their well-appointed dressing rooms, changing into stage wear and warming up. As their stage time approaches the atmosphere becomes charged with a cocktail of excitement and nervousness, and has its own avant-garde soundtrack. Nick D'Virgilio raps out paradiddles on a chair in a muffled tattoo. David Longdon soars through scales to warm his vocal cords. Rikard Sjöblom and Dave Gregory hit chord shapes and rehearse licks, getting brain and hands in perfect co-ordination. Pianos tinkle, trumpets toot, tubas parp. Employing an old fiddler's trick, Rachel Hall dusts her hands with talcum powder to keep them dry onstage. And all the while Gregory Spawton wanders up and down the dressing room corridor with his back-up Rickenbacker, running through the first few bass passages of each song, getting them pre-loaded into his musical cortexes. By this point, his nerves are burning.

"I wasn't losing it," he recalls later. "I wasn't sitting on the floor in a corner rocking backwards and forwards, but I was in a little bit of a muck sweat. Kathy had been front of house dealing with ticketing issues, and when she came backstage she reported that Nellie was frantically busy on the merch desk. Kathy was extremely nervous – in every respect we have been in this together over the years and she has as much invested in this as anybody. I tried to calm her down which, strangely, calmed me down, a bit."

With five minutes to go the band gather at the stage door and catch a glimpse of the lively sell-out crowd. The air is abuzz with the thrill of witnessing, and being part of, a rare and highly anticipated event. The eternal cheerleader, D'Virgilio calls everyone together for a morale-boosting, decidedly un-English huddle and team talk, ending with a joining of hands and a shout of 'Goooooo BIG BIG

TRAIN!' They're duly 'stoked' as the stage manager gives them a five second count and the house lights dim. And with that the eight members of Big Big Train take to their stage.

As captured on the subsequent live album *A Stone's Throw From The Line*, the effusive, full-throated cacophony of applause, whistles and cheers that comes from the audience takes the band aback. Without a note yet struck, the overwhelming wave of positive energy coming at them is such that David Longdon has to remind himself to breathe. But then he relaxes, the adrenaline kicks in, and he can begin. The roar dies down into an expectant silence.

"You're quiet," the singer whispers to the room.

"Make some noise!" retorts one wag in the audience.

You couldn't have scripted it better.

"Funny you should say that!" Longdon shoots back.

"Ready?" The roar says they are. The band kick into a strident *Make Some Noise*, and Big Big Train are away.

The previously ambivalent reaction to the single is but a memory. Tonight the song goes down to applause, cheers and whistles from a room that – the band can tell – is completely on their side from the off. Having dedicated *The First Rebreather* to absent friend Andy Tillison (who is recovering from a recent heart attack) Longdon introduces the band, and Dave Desmond leads the brass players onto their perch up on the balcony for *The Underfall Yard*.

As Dave Gregory picks out the song's knotty introduction Spawton looks out across the room and perceives a change in the atmosphere. The crowd now know they won't just be hearing the shorter, snappier pieces in Big Big Train's catalogue. Nothing is off limits, and they seem to appreciate that they're getting the good stuff, the

'Goooooo BIG BIG TRAIN!'

In full flight at Kings Place.

deep cuts. Also, the band's dearly held ethos of replicating the songs as faithfully as possible to the records is working, with Manners and Poole's meticulous sound preparation clearly paying off.

But the complex 23-minute piece that threw the band at their Real World rehearsal still isn't perfect tonight. At one point D'Virgilio loses his way a little and Spawton has to count him back in. Perversely, the moment gives the bassist a sense of self-confidence: here he is, the initiate performer helping the experienced sticksman back on track.

Bringing the first set to a close, the emotional rollercoaster of *Victorian Brickwork* gets the loudest appreciation so far. With the band bathed in soft, watery blue light, Rikard Sjöblom's searing guitar solo receives huge applause from a thrilled crowd, and Ben Godfrey's

melancholy trumpet tugs at the room's heartstrings. While Rob Aubrey is busy behind the mixing desk, he can see the audience reaction, he can see eyes filling with tears around him.

Back in the dressing room during the interval there's a good vibe, but there are niggles, and adjustments to be made. Dave Gregory thinks the first set was a little rough around the edges – they'll need to shape up in the second. He's also aware that the audience's enthusiasm is very real, and the sheer novelty value of them playing live is helping to paper over any cracks. ("The other frightening thing is that the whole thing was recorded and filmed," he says later. "How many bands have their very first concert of a tour filmed and released?")

Andy Poole is irked that, even after all the practice, they cocked up *Uncle Jack* and there was that missed cue at the end of *Victorian Brickwork*. That song has always been a challenge for D'Virgilio, who at this point is still reading his parts off music charts. He's also seasoned enough to know that you could rehearse for an entire month in a room, but playing on a stage is a whole different vibe and headspace – and all bets are off.

David Longdon too is aware that a performance is

Victorian Brickwork.

a living thing, and you have to think on your feet live and adapt. This is their first time before their audience, and in the opening half he gauged their reaction as he enjoined them to put their arms in the air, to clap their hands. He has worked out their requirements and now has a good idea of how far he can push them. For tonight at least, there are moments when the fans really just want to listen and soak up the music. He will calibrate his performance accordingly in the second half.

And the band kick that off half an hour later. Opening with *Kingmaker* could have been a gamble, but it works, with its catchy chorus and Sabine Reichhuber's projection working well. As with *Make Some Noise*, the current single *Wassail* transcends its recording and comes alive in the room. Here Longdon debuts his Green Man mask, and delves into the stage persona the prop helps him access ("I deliberately give myself over to whatever that thing is," he says, years later. "That character is him, not me. I'm not there, it's another thing.") A beautiful *Summoned By Bells* is taken out by the brass section. Longdon has drilled the

Summoned By Bells.

145

rest of the band to all turn their faces towards them up there on the balcony. It's a good, theatrical move, proving his consummate sense of stagecraft.

To the crowd, to his bandmates, perhaps even to himself, Longdon is a revelation. As the band hold the line behind him, he's simply in his element – not at all self-conscious, reading the room with good instincts, his back-and-forth with the crowd natural, unforced and completely in tune with the spirit of the event and the group he's fronting.

In *The Underfall Yard* he assumes the persona of a commuter, having been brought props including a bowler hat, briefcase and umbrella, standing as if waiting for a train. His flute playing adds to the Big Big Train tapestry too, and he brings the self-deprecating fun Andy Poole hoped he would. As he sings the *Make Some Noise* line '*We are young, got it all going on*', Longdon gestures with a flat, wavering hand that says, 'Okay, young*ish…*'

Hall and Sjöblom each bring their own attractive charisma to the band's stage presence. The former often

Rachel the singing violinist.

Rikard rocking out.

Dave Gregory, in his element.

sings and plays fiddle simultaneously; the latter switches effortlessly between electric guitar and Nord synthesiser, smiling and rocking out as he does it.

For the guitar buffs and XTC aficionados in the room, this is a rare opportunity to watch English maestro Dave Gregory in thrilling action.

D'Virgilio offers a hugely accomplished and tastefully short drum solo, and a lively *Judas Unrepentant* gets a standing ovation and a huge roar of approval. It's a highpoint that moves Gregory Spawton and its writer Longdon almost to tears. Introducing the penultimate song, the singer neatly puts it in context with the show's location. "Seventy seven years ago, a hundred yards away from here, Joe and Tommy set out on a great adventure and this is their story – this is *East Coast Racer.*"

Closer *Hedgerow* showcases Rachel Hall's violin chops, and as the band hit the song's final, decisive accent, Kings Place erupts. There's another standing ovation, and in

147

NDV drumming (and singing) up a storm.

time-honoured style the eight members of the band link up, enjoy a long bow, and bask in their hard-won moment of arrival.

After the show, they head out to say hello and thank the Passengers, who clamour to get an autograph, a selfie, or to just say hi. "The fans – young and old – were simply lovely to spend time with," Spawton wrote in his diary later, "and a couple more hours passed. Over the three Kings Place gigs, I found myself with incredibly generous gifts – wine brought over especially from Italy, a T-shirt from the States, a bottle of Elbow beer.

"Some attendees had travelled a very long way indeed and it was great to catch up with friends and fellow musicians such as Louis Philippe. By the time I got back to our hotel after the first show I was tired and very hungry. We got to bed at about 2am. I don't sleep well at the best of times but that night I was still awake at 6am."

"I felt very positive at end of that first evening," says

After the show.

With that first performance under their belt and the backline already set up, Saturday's soundcheck was a less fraught affair for the band and team. They used the time to hammer out a few kinks – some small (Rob Aubrey dialled in more of the audience into the band's monitor mix so they could hear their reactions better); some more significant (they ran through *The Underfall Yard*, yet again). The press were in again that night, including Dave Ling for *Classic Rock* and *Prog*'s Jerry Ewing, with the pressure on to earn positive reviews in those influential, taste-making magazines.

Andy Poole, "but I knew we had two more shows and needed to stay fresh and focused. We were aware we might be forgiven some first night nerves, but that we needed to step it up and be more confident on the Saturday."

French magazine *Koid9* were present at that Friday show, and gave it a glowing full-page review in their autumn issue. They praised each member individually for their skills, and admired how the band made their way through some fiendishly long, difficult songs. The writer concluded that the brass section was one of the elements making Big Big Train 'one of the greatest groups of the genre, and a facet that puts them in a niche nearly all their own'.

◆◆◆

And with the band feeling more confident the music went more smoothly, although seconds before stage time Rachel Hall did manage to spill her jar of white talcum powder down her new black dress. On the upside, she later received a wave of spontaneous applause for her soaring violin solo in the middle of *Hedgerow*. "It was a lovely moment," she says. "Even with the fans knowing what was coming from the recordings, I think there's a kind of emotion you get from placing a violin solo in a context where it wouldn't be expected, fitting with the journey or story of the music. When it works well I think it really connects with people."

The Saturday night was the best show for Dave Gregory, who did take a while to rediscover his own stage legs. "I get so tense. Tension produces nervousness and vice versa, it's a vicious circle. I completely fucked up a couple of my solos. I cheated my way around a few places, but there were certain dropped notes and things that people would have noticed. But then there are 12 other people on stage who cover for you – you might make a few mistakes but there's enough noise going on so that it won't stop the show."

David Longdon gives himself over to the Green Man...

Spawton noticed for the first time that, at the line '*She flies*' in *East Coast Racer*, several fans spread their arms as if they were wings and held them there, utterly swept up in the moment. Andy Poole, who had been worried about that 'inter-song banter', was particularly struck by how David Longdon had risen to the occasion live. "David was fantastic," he says. "That was the biggest revelation – that David was able to connect with that audience and draw them in."

"For me it was a huge learning curve," Longdon says, "from rehearsing to being on stage. I learned more about the Big Big Train audience having seen them and I was certainly wiser about what we were capable of. The fervour when we went on stage was surprising in a good way, considering we hadn't played live together ever. I hadn't done anything on that scale either – it was breathtaking. Greg noticed that on stage I have a few notes written down as memory aids. But I started talking about other stuff – off-the-cuff things when the adrenaline is going – and I like that. He and Andy were very nervous, which was understandable, but it was a big ask. Andy's gregarious in public, but he wasn't a showman – he sat and did his thing. Greg was incredibly shy at that point – to go on stage and do what he did [took guts]. A lot was expected of us, and they both rose to it. They hadn't seen me live so didn't realise how comfortable I was. But Nick is a very confident live performer, and he and Rikard were up for banter with me."

Spawton quickly picked up on the good stage communication between singer, drummer and guitarist. "I've seen bands where the members are talking to each other on stage," he says, "and it can feel like an in-joke with which the audience isn't involved. But because David, Nick and Rikard are all frontmen, they could talk to each

The bass player on acoustic guitar for Uncle Jack.

Andy on 12-string for The Underfall Yard.

other on mic and involve the audience. It's a band of leaders really. While I led the prep for the shows I had no experience playing, and Nick's vast experience came to the fore. He was a real live leader – his huddle and pep talk before each show really brought us together."

In his positive review of the Saturday night show for *Classic Rock*, Dave Ling noted that the tickets were rare as gold dust, and that fans had even come in from Australia

for this 'truly special gig': 'As you'd expect of a frontman shortlisted to replace Phil Collins in Genesis,' Ling wrote, 'the flute-toting David Longdon is an outstandingly charismatic performer.'

Once again, after the show Big Big Train met Passengers and friends and family alike. Rikard Sjöblom's parents and partner had flown over from Sweden for the show, and also there was Richard Williamson, Spawton's childhood friend and singer for his first band, Equus. Joining her brother Jerry was Big Big Train's new artist in residence, Sarah Ewing, marking the first time that the band – David Longdon included – had met her in person.

◆◆◆

By the Sunday, soundcheck had been honed to a tight 15 minutes. D'Virgilio led the band in their now customary pre-show huddle, and then they hit the stage for their matinée performance. Present were Spawton's brother Nigel, their mother Doreen and stepfather Will. When Will expressed his nerves before the show, Kathy Spawton was able to reassure him confidently that – three days in – everything was going to be alright.

As Danny Manners puts it, the band had 'audibly

Danny Manners at his keyboards.

relaxed' by show three, and after two nights of jitters Dave Gregory says, "I was just getting used to it on the Sunday show and thought I would just fly through the next performance. But, of course, we had to go home." By way of proof that the band were hitting their musical stride, most of the performances featured on *A Stone's Throw From The Line* (released in December 2016) would be taken from that Sunday performance.

"We played well that day," says Spawton, "*The Underfall Yard* was almost flawless, with Dave and Rachel in complete command. *Victorian Brickwork* was also nicely done, I thought. Rikard's solo in particular was a high point, bringing that mid-song ripple of applause, which is one of the best things a band can hear at a gig. David's voice was sounding well warmed up, and between them he, Nick and Rikard helped generate an easy, relaxed performing atmosphere and a good rapport with the audience. On that Sunday, David took off on a 10-minute ad-lib about his stage set-up, which led towards a ceremonial handing over of his ever-present chocolate bar to Sue Heather, one of our Facebook forum moderators, and a chocoholic."

Andy Poole was especially impressed by the way Longdon approached the fact that this was a Sunday matinée – an odd, decidedly un-rock 'n' roll time slot that might well have detracted from the event. The singer explicitly acknowledged it as such in the room, and suggested that (in an echo of his words to his nervous bandmates at the Prog Awards) neither the band nor they would be here tomorrow, and they should all just enjoy the experience, together. "But it was the way he said it," says Poole. "It wasn't patronising. The big relief came for me when we finished on Sunday. I remember David and I embracing in the bar on the Sunday and saying, 'Bloody hell, we did it! We nailed this!'"

Also present at the Sunday show was *Classic Rock*'s Managing Editor, Jo Kendall. Formerly *Prog*'s Production Editor, Kendall's an experienced gig-goer with a sensitive, objective ear for music. She has a vivid memory of that afternoon: "I remember thinking 'Wow, this lot are good', especially having the brass section with them. *Make Some Noise* was a jubilant opener but, at this point, to me David seemed a little nervous when performing. This might be why he had some props – some that don't seem to have seen the light of day again, such as the commuter's mac, briefcase and brolly. But what he did have was utter conviction. His voice was superb. As a friend said to me while we were watching him, 'He's really full on, but I like it!' I got emotional at *Curator Of Butterflies*. It's songs like this that connect very deeply, they tell a story that breaks your heart – the puzzling thing is you might not quite understand why it's doing this to you. I've now realised they have a knack for that. I didn't expect to be so moved that afternoon, but I was."

Uncle Jack knows...

Big Big Train at Kings Place.

Kendall's friend, the one who found Longdon 'full on', was in fact actor and Big Big Train fan Mark Benton. A well-known face on UK TV, he was introduced to Spawton and Longdon after the show, they got on, and he would go on to feature in a festive video for the band later on.

In another fateful meeting, Kendall's other 'plus one' that day was folk star and singer songwriter, Judy Dyble. A cult figure on the English folk scene since her Fairport Convention days, Dyble had always been on the periphery of greatness (she had once famously knitted onstage while Fairport's Richard Thompson traded guitar licks with Jimi Hendrix). She wasn't familiar with the band, but had kept in touch with Rachel Hall after she had worked with her, and had come to see what her friend was up to. "Judy was always very kind," says Hall, "I was touched when she attended. It was lovely to see her again."

Spawton and Longdon were delighted to meet Dyble. "When I was introduced to her," says Longdon, "I told her how I was a fan of that first Fairport record [*Fairport Convention*] and [Dyble's duo with Them's Jackie McAuley]

Trader Horne, and we got to chatting. It was great. Those gigs really did change my life."

For Dyble's part, she was taken with the band, and particularly Longdon's powerful voice. After years away from music she had recently started making records again. A few weeks later – with Kendall as intermediary – she and Longdon got back in touch, and went on to strike up an enduring friendship that would bear musical fruit five years later.

But for all these celebrity meetings, it was the fans that made the biggest impression on the band over the weekend. Here in the room, the reality of the Passengers' enthusiasm, affection and engagement touched Spawton and Poole. This was their first real taste of such an audience connection. But even the experienced Nick D'Virgilio could feel the love. "Just beautiful people all around," he recalls. "I think there's something about this music that people internalise. It speaks to them in a certain way. The subject matter is very English but all these people from all over the world get into it. I suppose it's similar to the way I got into early Genesis when I was growing up in LA."

"It was an absolute melting pot of people from across the world," marvels Spawton. "Each night the foyer was really big and full. We wanted to get out and talk to people because in many cases they'd made such an effort to come such a long way. That became part of the story of the shows."

He for one also noticed how the listeners' appreciation had varying contours over the three shows. Friday's house was raucous, excited at the sheer sense of occasion. Saturday's was more intense, leaning in and listening hard to the music they'd only heard on record before. The Sunday afternoon slot helped create a more relaxed vibe.

After that final performance, with an 'end of tour' feeling in the air, there was an emotional farewell as the members all headed their separate ways, each with their own sense of validation, and thoughts on a job well done over the weekend. "Kings Place was euphoric," says brass leader Dave Desmond. "It was unusual to be on the balcony, and it didn't quite feel we were part of the band, but that was purely down to lack of space on the stage. It was emotional seeing the live audience appreciating what you do. We were 13 people together playing highly complex music, and it worked. I'd had input from the start, so there was a little bit of me in there. I've had lots of highs through playing in the army, but, from a personal point of view, Kings Place was right up there."

"It was emotional," adds Rob Aubrey, "it really was. The brass tugged at the heartstrings every time they came in. Even being the guy behind the mixing desk, some of the moments were really choking. I don't think *A Stone's Throw From The Line* really quite captured the moment. Every night there were tears in the eyes. Kings Place was fantastic."

And Rachel Hall was happy and excited about it too. "Friday was the best time ever, because it was the first gig and there was a massive buzz, and some of my family were there. It was lovely to have a live audience to share the songs with, and the energy and the music on that night was quite amazing, it's one of my favourite gigs that I've ever played. When we first got back home, we were probably all ecstatic, having done three gigs together with that audience reaction and the sense of belonging and community that Big Big Train has. You realised that you're in more of a performing role now."

And for D'Virgilio, despite the technical exigencies of the set, the shows were "a magical experience. In the grand scheme of it all, a few mistakes are nothing. Everybody was pumped up and excited – we had a great cheering chant before we went on stage. Listen to those recordings now, every song was played about 20 BPM too fast because the energy level was so high all weekend, but it didn't matter. I was on cloud nine after that weekend."

Reviewing that Sunday performance, *Prog*'s Fraser Lewry called it 'very very special', and noted that: 'The band receive the kind of rapturous welcome more usually reserved for legends like Brian Wilson or Kate Bush […]

Longdon moves with the dramatic, sweeping exaggeration of an illusionist conjuring a series of increasingly unexpected animals from thin air, as if performing to an audience that's much larger than the one actually present.'

There was a much, much larger audience awaiting Longdon and the rest of Big Big Train, three years into the future and 500 miles away. But after their successful and expensive stage debut they now needed grist to their mill, fuel to their fire. They returned to the studio to crack on with their much anticipated new album, *Folklore*.

The band, the crew and the fans at the end of the final Kings Place show.

XIII

'Set a course for the stars, reaching out for the far things...'

WITH ALL THREE SHOWS having sold out, Big Big Train's Kings Place venture pretty much paid for itself. Sales of merchandise were beyond all expectation, and for once the band were headed into the black. Yet the financial rewards of the weekend were far outstripped by the artistic, and the personal. Kings Place affirmed in Gregory Spawton's mind that, 25 years since its inception, the band had truly evolved.

The shows and their Real World sessions had been a profound bonding experience for the band, but it still rankled with Spawton that he and his wife Kathy had been left to organise the whole thing alone. A 'BTFOOM' issue if ever there was one, Andy Poole's absence was noted with both disappointment and frustration, and the wedge between the two founder members drove in deeper. "The reality is Kathy and I had a world of pain," Spawton says, "and Andy did not lift a finger to help. I wasn't sure if he was being lazy or if he was completely oblivious. I sent him a snotty email later – 'You must have seen we were drowning?' – and he was stunned by the email."

"Greg said that coming up to the gigs he and Kathy were working flat out," Poole responds, "and that I never once asked what I could do to help out. Delphine, my soulmate, had died about two weeks before those shows and I had

that to deal with. I was also very busy learning all my parts, plus I had subsidence in my house and had to move out and find somewhere else to live. I didn't have any spare capacity. I wasn't quick enough off the mark to say that I had all these things going on."

"Probably he just wasn't aware," Spawton concedes now, "but it caused a major rift between us. I felt he had stepped aside when he should have stepped up. But then I never said to him, 'Do this, do that', and maybe I should've done. I probably am a control freak and put myself in that position – 'never complain, never explain… and then complain afterwards!' I was working, I had two kids, and it was all really stressful. We should've got some outside help, I know that now."

Big Big Train now headed down into *Folklore*, and it wasn't before time. The band's main income was from CD sales, and it had been three years since *English Electric: Full Power*. While Kings Place was a milestone for the group, it had taken up the time and bandwidth available to them. Also, the costs of the Real World sessions had made a serious dent in the band's accounts. The resultant *Stone & Steel* Blu-ray would help refill the coffers, but that disc wouldn't be ready for sale until the following July.

"Three years was far too long a gap," says Poole, "but

I don't know how we could have avoided it. I remember at the time being a bit tortured by it and asking myself how fickle the audience would be. Audience loyalty was slightly untested by us then. My concern was always that we were being overly ambitious. We had a timetable which suggested we would get an album out quicker. We weren't paying ourselves anything, and going to Real World and paying for the film crew had exhausted all our funds. It was worth doing, but it was a nightmare."

Just as Spawton saw Poole as a handbrake on the band's progress, so Poole often considered Spawton to be financially reckless, his cost/benefit analysis often way off beam. "And I wasn't necessarily wrong about some of these things," Poole says now. "Greg had a lot of confidence in what he was doing, but sometimes that was unfounded. He would want to book a back page advertisement in *Prog*, partly as a status thing, and I would question whether it would reward us with sales or grow the band. I would ask him where the feedback was that these things were helping, or whether we were just chasing promotional opportunities. We were still getting into the business culture of it and coming out of it being a hobby, so our relationship was going through a transition from being best mates to more about business, and there were niggles creeping in. I got knocked back for asking whether we could afford things or whether something was the best way of spending money. I wasn't being negative – I just wanted to approach things on a business footing.

"So there was a certain divergence between me and Greg around this time. By then we had been 'married' a long time and been through a lot. There were certain things about which we were less tolerant – things that you accommodate earlier on in a marriage start to become a bit annoying. David kept out of it, or was kept out of it."

◆◆◆

There was one more rare live experience for Big Big Train in 2015. Organised by their rock star son Francis, The Charlie and Kathleen Dunnery Children's Fund raises money for children's causes in the family's home county of Cumbria. That year, CKDCF's annual benefit concert was taking place at Egremont Market Hall on Saturday 24th October, and Francis Dunnery invited Big Big Train to headline. By then Nick D'Virgilio was back in the US, and Andy Poole and Danny Manners were unavailable. Spawton, David Longdon, Rachel Hall and Rikard Sjöblom were well up for the show, and worked up a short acoustic set as a one-off, pared-down incarnation of Big Big Train. Near the date they were informed that they had been bumped to second position on the bill, and on hearing the reason why they were delighted. Dunnery had played guitar for Robert Plant in the early '90s, and the Led Zeppelin superstar had agreed to perform at the charity show, rightly assuming top billing.

Mountains come out of the sky at Ennerdale Water.

The concert was part of a weekend long series of fundraising events, including a seven-mile charity walk around Ennerdale Water, a lake in the nearby Lake District. So on a soaking wet and freezing cold Saturday morning the four BBT members joined Dunnery, Plant and the other walkers for the hike.

"I really enjoyed the walk around the lake," says Rachel Hall, "and being part of the whole experience. The night before we heard from people involved in charities receiving support from the CKDCF. You could tell there was an immense sense of community spirit all around the room. It was nice to do an acoustic set; it was a little bit like an adventure I suppose."

Once back at the hotel the band dried off and snatched a quick rehearsal for their 20-minute set, comprising *Upton Heath*, *Uncle Jack* and *Wassail*.

That evening Dunnery opened the show, followed by his replacement in It Bites, John Mitchell, and then came Peter Jones, also known as rising prog talent Tiger Moth Tales.

As Big Big Train took to the stage to close the first half, Spawton had an odd moment. "I looked to my left and saw Francis at the side of the stage just bopping along to our music; this guy, so important to my musical story, was watching me play. And John Mitchell was the other side of the stage – it was like an It Bites sandwich! I found that quite moving."

In a parallel universe, former BBT applicant Mitchell could have been in David Longdon's shoes that evening. It could have been him working hard to win over 400 Cumbrian locals who had clearly never heard of the band in front of them. But by the end Longdon came good, and had the audience singing along to *Wassail*'s infectious refrain.

But spare a thought for Rikard Sjöblom. He was offered a last-minute guitar slot in Plant's band along with Dunnery and Mitchell but, frustratingly, he was unable to change his plane ticket from Sweden and couldn't make it to the requisite Friday morning rehearsal. "It would've been awesome," he says with a rueful chuckle, "as a

With Francis Dunnery in Cumbria.

Rachel and David onstage in Cumbria.

Zeppelin fan, plus I really loved the songs I was meant to play. He was doing stuff from the *Raising Sand* album he did with Alison Krauss, which is my favourite album of his. Robert was quite particular – as Francis put it to me he didn't want 'a fuzz metal wanker', just someone who could play with a bit of slapback echo. I was happy they asked me, and so sad I couldn't do it."

On the night, Sjöblom had to content himself with joining his three bandmates and the other performers as they supplied backing vocals for Plant's encore, Led Zeppelin's *Rock And Roll*. "That was great fun," says Spawton, who used to play that song with Equus back in

For one night only – BBT unplugged in Cumbria.

the day. "Robert was bloody great, he really was, and good fun too. At breakfast at the hotel we had a chat with him; he was interested in us and was really engaging. Rikard and I were as shy as naughty schoolboys, but David wasn't, of course. He was like, 'I'm a frontman, Robert's a frontman – we're going to talk as equals.' There was some Midlands chat, all quite puckish, and David asked him, 'So, what is it like to be Robert Plant?' And he replied, 'I'm 67 and my girlfriend's 30 – *that's* what it's like to be Robert Plant!' I thought that was such a hilarious response. The next day I got on the train home, thinking how my life had changed. I came back on cloud nine."

With Robert Plant.

❖❖❖

While Andy Poole hadn't fancied doing the Dunnery gig, he had been galvanised by the live shows, and couldn't wait to get stuck into *Folklore*. Now everybody had a clearer idea of what their roles were, of what each player was bringing to the mix. They allowed themselves until the end of 2015 to record and, with Rob Aubrey at the engineering helm, the band and their contributors brought the album to life across several studios.

Contributing to his first album as an official member of the band, Rikard Sjöblom sent his parts in from Sweden, his home becoming the latest extension of that catch-all, 'English Electric Studios'. Spawton, Danny Manners and Dave Gregory also got to work at their respective house-

holds. The other official newbie, Rachel Hall, became deeply involved with the string arrangements. Recording mainly at Ashwood Studios in Norwich near her Cromer home, she played some cello parts along with violin, and also directed a string quartet completed by Lucy Curnow (violin), Keith Hobday (viola) and Evie Anderson (cello). Dave Desmond's brass ensemble were now a vital part of the BBT sound. He, Ben Godfrey, Nick Stones, John Storey and Jon Truscott returned to lay down their brass at Real World.

Nick D'Virgilio had recorded some of his drums there, and worked up his other parts at the in-house recording suites at Sweetwater. David Longdon's vocals and Danny Manners' double bass were captured back at Aubitt.

Along The Ridgeway *at Real World Studios.*

Written by Longdon, *Folklore*'s title track was borne from the single *Wassail*. "*Wassail* was me looking back into English folk history and folklore," he says, "and the track *Folklore* itself shares similar chords with it. But again it's a bit different, exotic – there are some almost Arabic sounding lines in there, and that's me making it a bit more 'world music'. Robert Plant had been working at Real World, and had been making a [world-embracing] album called *Lullaby And The Ceaseless Roar*, and Elbow had been at Real World too [making *The Take Off And Landing Of Everything*]. These were artists we were interested in. Greg and I were egging each other on, as we do, the sparks were flying quickly and we were getting some interesting ideas."

By pure chance, months of writing resulted in a 50/50 mix of songs from Longdon and Spawton. The latter had been working on the typically grand, historically literate pieces *Along The Ridgeway*, *Salisbury Giant* and *London Plane*. "I knew what David was offering up and I was responding to that," he says. "We were a team. He had taken on some of the heavy lifting with the accessible tunes, so I decided to go down my own route."

As well as *Folklore* and *Wassail*, Longdon submitted a song about Winkie, a blue chequered hen pigeon that had received the Dickin Medal for outstanding bravery during World War II. Winkie's was an extraordinary, fabulous tale that fitted Big Big Train to a tee.

An RAF Beaufort Bomber had ditched in the North Sea in February 1942, having come under enemy fire on the way home from a mission over Norway. Trained by the military pigeon service (a real thing), Winkie was aboard with the crew. There was no time to write a message for it to carry before the plane crashed, but the hope was that, on release, the bird's homing instincts would lead it back to its loft in Broughty Ferry near Dundee, and its very presence might raise the alarm. And that's exactly what happened. Winkie flew the 120 miles home where, exhausted and near death, it was intercepted, some say by its owner, George Ross; others – including Longdon in his song – say it was loft manager Sgt. Davidson. Either way, the RAF base in Fife was alerted, the bomber's most likely coordinates were calculated, and a ship promptly despatched. The downed crew were rescued from certain, icy death, thanks to Winkie.

"*Folklore* was shaping up as a smooth album," says Longdon, "and went on to run together very well. When I wrote *Winkie* that was a reaction to that smoothness. I wanted something a bit jumpy and quirky and I thought the subject matter was very Big Big Train. It's very English, unusual but heroic – serious and poignant, but quite funny as well. It was a ripping yarn, and people think it's too silly or that it's music hall, but it isn't – it's still about a war hero, you have to be respectful, and play it straight."

Inspired by its titular cosmic event and the life of prominent British astronomer Sir Patrick Moore, *The Transit Of Venus Across The Sun* was a late addition to the record from Spawton. He was incredibly proud of and hopeful for it, but his initial demo earned a muted early reception and limited feedback from his bandmates. It was only when Sjöblom keyed into the song that enthusiasm grew within the ranks.

"I was really disappointed and wondered if I'd got it wrong," says Spawton now. "It's an odd piece which tries to get to the heart of a story, and subsequently it's become a live favourite for us as well. You never do know how a song will connect. Being a songwriter does make you vulnerable. You're exposing the inner workings of your soul and your mind to other people. It's not an ego thing really, it's more that you're looking for affirmation that you've done something good."

With melancholy brass and string lines, intense, chanted passages in 7/8 and its overall rising musical architecture, the song set an emotional storyline – mortality and once in a lifetime love – on a cosmic scale. *Transit Of Venus* would translate well in later shows, and became Rachel Hall's favourite song on the album. "I love the course it takes," she says, "from the opening brass section, and the way it builds to the guitar solo at the end. I'm especially a fan of the Latin chant in the middle, as I don't think it sounds like anything Big Big Train had done before."

During the promotional push for the album, Hall's insights on the workings of the band's main writers were also instructive: "Greg's very well organised and keeps everyone on track, and we definitely needed it for that album – there were so many of us! His musical directions are around melodic ideas, and then I would think of the best instrument [violin, viola, cello] for these ideas. Like on *London Plane* and *Brooklands*, melodic lines were developed and then put into bigger arrangements. David is the soul of the band, always having a laugh when we get together. He works differently to Greg, in blocks or chunks of strings, and is very clear how he wants it to sound. He likes big strings then solo lines. Because I know

David's hand-written lyrics to the Latin chant section of Transit Of Venus.

the instruments they both come to me, I score them and then send them to Danny, because if there's a problem with chords, Danny's straight on it. That's why it's so collaborative, it's like this chain of ideas. But there are no egos in the band, nobody I couldn't speak to if I have a question about what we're doing. Everybody's thinking about the songs."

Though Spawton had been mindful to not 'write for the road' after their debut live foray, he consciously did so on one of the songs. *Brooklands* was inspired by another quirky piece of British history – the tragic story of John Cobb, the racing driver who died on Loch Ness in 1952 while attempting to break the world water speed record. The ambitious 12-minute piece was intended as a partner track to the similarly epic *East Coast Racer*.

"David's demos are pretty complete," says Andy Poole. "Greg's are much 'sketchier', and *Brooklands* lost its way a bit. When I heard the demo I thought the 'lucky man' section was a really good hook, but there's too much flab around it and the verse is weak. I used to say to Greg that we should look at Elbow and what they were *not* doing – they're not noodling around for 20 minutes, they're delivering songs with universal messages that people get hold of and apply to their lives. Everybody piled in with parts and *Brooklands* got over-produced."

Each member of the full line-up was now playing and

contributing, all recording remotely and simultaneously. As Poole began to bring together all the parts coming in, he could see both the pros and cons of this working model. "*Telling The Bees, Salisbury Giant, Transit Of Venus* were all very strong," he says, "with the band working very well together, everyone pitching in with lots of good parts. But when the ideas were sketched out – when they weren't explicit when they went out to people – it wasn't clear whether a track was driven by guitar or keyboard, or where the dynamics lay.

"*Brooklands* is a good example. Danny and Dave would sometimes both send us good yet competing parts. We would try to accommodate them both, we'd get to the mixing stage and try to negotiate. Sometimes it worked well, sometimes it got messy. Early on Rachel had done some strings which she thought were going to be featured, Danny was doing a lot of keyboards, Dave Gregory was going for it, Greg had done a dominating bass part. It ended up a bit of a pig's breakfast."

Dave Gregory would have major issues with this recording system later on, but he still thinks that, "for anyone new to Big Big Train *Folklore* is the album they should start with. It's a good collection of songs, we were all in a happy place and there's good variety. *London Plane* is one of my favourite songs of Greg's, I love it, and I thought *Folklore* was a great single which deserved more attention. I wasn't so sure about *Along The Ridgeway* when I first heard it, but there's a magic to it that I discovered later. I love *Winkie* but wasn't happy with the production – it was a bit kitchen sink-y and needed some weeding. It's a great story and the way David told it was really good.

"In fact, I've never had a problem with any song Greg and David have sent me since *The Underfall Yard*. It's a bit

like Colin Moulding and Andy Partridge. If Colin brought up a couple of songs, Andy would be intimidated or inspired and always have to write four or five in response. I think the same happens between David and Greg – there's a bit of healthy competition."

Recording from home himself, Gregory found that having a fellow guitarist in Rikard Sjöblom, on stage and now on a full album, only served to improve his Big Big Train experience at that time. "The band got better," Gregory asserts. "There was still plenty for me to do – it wasn't like Rikard was stealing any of my thunder. On the contrary, I think we worked really well together, and he took some of the pressure off me. I still don't feel strong enough as a soloist to be a featured player on an album that lasts more than an hour. I'm really just a pop guitarist who got lucky. My solos usually didn't last more than eight or sixteen bars – suddenly I'm in a prog band as a featured player. I've never felt confident enough to carry a big band like Big Big Train on my own. Rikard is quite an inspiring influence on me. I can't afford to slack when he's around. The pair of us make a good team."

Before playing with Gregory, Sjöblom had only been vaguely aware of XTC, and subsequently bought all their albums. "Dave has his style of playing," he says, "and I wanted to bring something different. Having two different guitar players puts a mark on things, and for the most part *Folklore* was about trying to get my style of playing more into the thing. I did the solos on the end of *Transit Of Venus* and *London Plane*. Greg told us to decide between ourselves, he wanted us to make the parts our own, so Dave and I talked and he was the one who said, 'You take this one'. I was open, there was never any elbowing. Danny does the bulk of the keys and I had to find my place in that too.

"*Folklore* was a development from *The Underfall Yard* and *English Electric*. It's good not to stagnate or stand still, and with everyone playing and contributing parts it takes on a life of its own as well. Sure, parts I've contributed have disappeared, but that's okay. Even if it's a really nice part, it's not the end of the world. I can use it for another song."

Back home again in Indiana, Nick D'Virgilio was really pleased with the finished album, and the unique unit that Big Big Train were becoming. "*Folklore*'s a really good record," he says. "The band was really starting to take on this *thing* – you could see the flowers beginning to bloom. Our sound got bigger – on singalong tracks like *Wassail*. I love *Winkie*, and *Telling The Bees* is one of the best songs David's ever written."

A honeyed slice of English lore, the sweet and understated *Telling The Bees* bookends the album, with a story that reinforces the folkloric concept. "Someone in a review said that it has an 'inane' chorus," says Longdon, with faux outrage. "But it's a different end to an album from what we'd done previously. Greg puts a lot of thought into the sequencing of our records."

They recorded a promotional video for that song, with them performing it in another freezing cold venue – this time a barn near Basingstoke. They also made an accompanying video for *Folklore*'s title track. For this Longdon had a vision of a *Wicker Man*-like procession of

Telling The Bees *by Sarah Louise Ewing.*

people through the countryside, and suggested that the band should ask their Passengers to get involved in the shoot. They put a call out for extras on the Big Big Train Facebook page and, sure enough, on a cold, foggy morning in March 2016, a hundred diehard fans showed up for the shoot on St Catherine's Hill, on the outskirts of Winchester.

They had been sent a video of some basic choreography in advance – courtesy of a dance tutor friend of Longdon's. They would have to lurch uncannily towards the camera as if possessed by spirits of the earth, some kitted out in paganistic masks similar to Longdon's own Green Man visage. In the name of the cause, the fans gladly threw the shapes and gamely traipsed across the Hampshire countryside in the perishing cold. Their efforts were intercut with shots of Big Big Train themselves walking the fields, and also performing the song in that same Basingstoke barn. The results make for a thoroughly endearing moment in Big Big Train's history. Even if Michael Jackson had set his multi-million dollar *Thriller* video on a Hampshire campsite on a wet winter's day, it wouldn't have been a patch on this.

"David drove the video," says Spawton, "and it was brilliant fun, a blast. It was guerrilla film making too, we didn't get permission from anyone to do it, no bureaucracy. We had a drone up, the fans came from all over the country,

Folklore *procession in Winchester.*

"When we're all together, we get photos done..."

bringing their kids, and we all went to the local pub afterwards, about 100 of us all in our garb. *Prog* magazine covered the shoot, and by then we were getting more professional ourselves in terms of the way the press worked. Part of the planning from there was that, when we're all together, we get photos done."

In the lead-up to the shoot there was another slight butting of heads between Spawton and Poole, when Spawton went ahead and booked a venue for the filming, which cost the band £1,500. "I was starting to question certain things," says Poole. "I asked where the storyboard was and how the dance was going to work. What's really frustrating is that the *Telling The Bees* video, which is much better, just got slipped out after the album had been released, and got overlooked. But all that said, *Folklore* is still a very strong album."

Sarah Ewing's striking artwork, notably the blue/black cover image of a crow, enhanced the album's pastoral tone, and *Folklore* followed the brace of *English Electric* releases as another admirably coherent and sonically familiar symbiosis of form and subject. "I think *Folklore* has a good balance of songs," says Spawton. "It's a cross-section of what we do – a mix of accessible and complicated. It's a good jumping-in point. It's a very even album, but there possibly aren't that many moments with the tingle factor."

The week before the record's release – on 27th May 2016 – the band held a launch event at Real World. This took the form of an album listening party in The Big Room, and the band – minus D'Virgilio – played an acoustic set to 60 paying fans (their ticket price also including a copy of the album) and held a Q&A session too. Nellie Pitts had even arranged for a brewery to produce a Big Big Train Ale and a Wassail Cider. "That was good fun," says Spawton, fondly.

On the drawing board: Sarah Louise Ewing's cover artwork for Folklore.

"Nick beamed in on camera from his home, he was sat on this big sit-on lawnmower! It was a successful event, it did cost us money but we used it as a PR thing."

The prog press greeted the album warmly. In her balanced lead review for *Prog* magazine, Jo Kendall praised the album's 'twilit stories shared around a roaring campfire', while noting that Big Big Train's emotional range had perhaps narrowed: 'Whereas the previous *English Electric* sets are near-perfect articulations of modern progressive soul music, *Folklore* is a slightly more fantastical collection.'

The magazine also ran a four-page feature drawing on interviews with Spawton, Longdon, Rikard Sjöblom and Rachel Hall – her first in her official capacity as a band member. Notably, Bob Harris still remained enamoured with the band. On his Radio 2 show he had played *Wassail* on the single's release and, much to Longdon's delight, had read out the lyrics in his famed, hoarsely hushed tones. The DJ went on to playlist *Folklore, Salisbury Giant, The Transit*

Of Venus Across The Sun and *Telling The Bees*, and when Harris got his own show on the new, short-lived digital radio station TeamRock, he invited Spawton and Longdon to come in for a chat.

"We did the interview in his studio in his back garden," says Spawton. "He had *thousands* of records, and his son was engineering. We thought, 'This is mad!' There we were talking to this legendary figure – you know you're making progress when you're on that guy's radar. At the end he asked us the classic question – 'What is prog?' David pushed it my way with the words, 'He has you on the run, Gregory!'"

And as off the cuff as it was, Spawton's definition was a good one: "For me [prog] is a way of thinking which frees you up from the constraints of normal, popular musical routine. We're magpies, we'll dip in and out of different genres and bring them together to make our own thing."

"Progressive rock is a really flexible genre," Longdon added, "which allows us to extend certain aspects of the songs. We can develop themes and bring the themes back

'So tell me, what is prog?' With Bob Harris in Oxfordshire.

[…] A lot of thought goes into it, there's a lot of melody and counterpoint." And in closing the interview, Harris offered his own pithy definition that prog was "music of the open mind".

Folklore earned Big Big Train their first placing in the Official UK Charts. On the week of release they hit number 75 on the Albums chart. The vinyl edition (released once again by Chris Topham's Plane Groovy) entered the Vinyl Albums chart at 34, and they landed at number five in the Rock & Metal Albums chart. In a charming twist to the story, *Winkie* writer David Longdon was contacted by a representative of the Royal Society for the Protection of Birds. "He said, 'I understand you've written a story about one of our Dickin recipients,'" the singer explains. "I thought I was going to get fined. But no, he was delighted. I've been contacted by teachers about *Winkie* (and later for *Brave Captain* and *Ariel*) asking if it's okay to use these songs as teaching material. Of course it is."

◆◆◆

Folklore made it to lucky number 13 in *Classic Rock* magazine's Album Of The Year list in their end of year issue. The band had begun 2016 by appearing in *Prog* magazine's '100 Greatest Prog Artists Of All Time', a poll voted for by the magazine's highly invested readership. Yes topped the list, with Big Big Train landing at a creditable number 24, nestled between Hawkwind and Tool. And when the Progressive Music Awards were announced in June 2016, the band were nominated in three big categories.

Their weekend at Kings Place was shortlisted for Live Event of 2015-16, alongside others including a recent outing by Rush, David Gilmour's run at the Royal Albert Hall, King Crimson's UK Tour and also RoSfest, the major US prog festival held annually in Pennsylvania. *Folklore* was nominated in the Album Of The Year list which also featured titles by such acts as Hawkwind, Dream Theater, Haken and Russian duo iamthemorning. And in testament to how far they had truly come and their standing on the modern prog rock scene, Big Big Train were also in the running for Band Of The Year, putting them in the same category as noted artists including Crimson, Steven Wilson, Dream Theater, Riverside, TesseracT and Jem Godfrey's Frost*. This was a big deal.

Since they'd last been nominated the Prog Awards had been relocated from Kew Gardens to The Underglobe, a cavernous, characterful venue beneath Shakespeare's Globe Theatre on London's South Bank. Sweetwater sponsored a table for the 2016 ceremony and Nick D'Virgilio flew in as part of the team. This meant he could join David Longdon, Gregory Spawton, Rachel Hall and Danny Manners on the night. That year the awards were hosted by broadcaster and prog fan Matthew Wright. Jon Anderson was named 'Prog God'. *Master Of Time* writer himself Anthony Phillips won the 'Storm Thorgerson Grand Design Award' for his recent run of reissues on leading prog label Esoteric, and Van der Graaf Generator were honoured for their 'Lifetime Achievement'.

That trophy went to Manners' favourites Gentle Giant the previous year, but the keyboardist was still overwhelmed to be in the presence of the great and the good of the genre: "You're in a room with several of your teenage idols, people like Yes, Genesis, Van der Graaf. I remember Greg saying, 'Oh god – Peter Hammill's over there! I can't go and talk to him!' We all said, 'Don't be ridiculous!' We were almost pushing Greg towards him."

Spawton finally did pluck up the courage: "I spoke to

Peter, and to [Van der Graaf's drummer] Guy Evans too. We had a nice chat, and I told Peter what his music and words meant to me. He was a very sweet man, and it was another arrival moment for me. Nick knew Mike Portnoy, who was there. Like David, Nick's so good in those situations. And Rachel really enjoyed it, she really did us proud that night."

Hall remembers the night fondly. "Swanky parties and a room with an intense understanding of prog everywhere – both of these things were a little alien to me. And who would have put the two together?! I remember Nick was totally in his element, which was nice to see, and was kindly introducing me to a few people."

Spawton also found that other, newer artists were making a beeline for him. "I didn't know who all of them were to be honest, but the shoe seemed to be on the other foot. They were less interested in us as a band and more so in how we broke through. That was the repeat conversation: 'How did you do it? How did you get your profile this high?'"

Folklore was pipped to Album Of The Year by iamthemorning's *Lighthouse*, but to their delight Big Big Train's run at Kings Place won them the 'Live Event Of The Year' award, and soon after they were called back to the stage to receive the trophy for the big one: 'Band Of The Year'. Given the competition, and given how far they had come, they were overwhelmed. In three years they had progressed from Breakthrough Artist to Band Of The Year. "We were blown away," says Spawton. "Nick was particularly delighted, having come close at various points in his career to considerable recognition with Genesis, Spock's and then Cirque. He was genuinely excited by it. To me, it felt we were growing further as a unit."

The year closed out with the release of *A Stone's Throw*

The Band Of The Year at the Prog Awards, 2016.

From The Line, a CD souvenir of the Kings Place shows that had pushed Big Big Train onto this fresh new trajectory. Reflecting their standing in the wider prog rock sphere, the Real World film *Stone & Steel* was voted the year's biggest multimedia event in *Prog*'s 2016 end of year readers' poll. In the same survey, Big Big Train were pushed into second place for Band and Album Of The Year by the untouchably popular Marillion and their eighteenth record, *FEAR*. Longdon, D'Virgilio, Spawton, Manners and Dave Gregory were also placed in the top ten for their respective instruments. Given the premium that this genre places on musical virtuosity, this was no mean feat. And, as if to cap it all, even the *Bournemouth Echo* – Andy Poole and Gregory Spawton's local rag – finally wrote a few lines on them, having been utterly oblivious of their hometown band's travails for the past 16 years.

By this time Big Big Train was Spawton's full-time job. He had accepted voluntary redundancy from the council, knowing that this was his chance to devote his complete attention to a band that really was on the up. Truly gathering speed now, they were already on to the next record.

A teaser came from David Longdon, during an interview on the red carpet at the Prog Awards. "It's following on in the tradition of *Folklore*," he said. "It's concluding the songs that we've been writing around those themes. We want to put a full stop at the end of those types of songs. We've written a thing we call 'The Albion Cycle', which is a series of albums predominantly about England, and that cycle's coming to an end with *Grimspound*. After that, we're on to other things."

XIV

'Artists and dreamers and thinkers are right here by your side...'

"In the modern music business," says Gregory Spawton, "you can't drift for too long profile-wise, because people move on. We learned that from *English Electric*. We needed to be a fairly constant presence, to be seen to be out there offering stuff, so even the naysayers might give us a second chance having heard our name, yet again."

The year 2017 started very well for Big Big Train, with more trophies to add to their cabinet. In March, they won four of the top accolades at the annual Classic Rock Society Awards. David Longdon and Andy Poole represented the band at the ceremony, in Wath-upon-Dearne in Yorkshire. With Wishbone Ash's Martin Turner presenting, Longdon

CRS Awards winners 2017.

won Best Male Vocalist, Nick D'Virgilio took Best Drummer, *Folklore* was voted Best Album, and Big Big Train were named Best Band.

After *Folklore*, the original plan had been to release an EP, *Skylon*, as an *amuse-oreille* to keep the audience engaged until the next full album arrived. But the writing sessions for *Folklore* had been highly productive and there was plenty of material in the pot. *Skylon* itself hadn't quite worked with the album's theme, and had been parked. Two other songs, *The Ivy Gate* and *Grimspound*, had been lined up for *Folklore* but weren't finished in time for the release, and were held over. There was a charged creative atmosphere around the group at the time – ideas were coming in thick and fast, not just from Spawton and Longdon, but from their bandmates too.

"Writing an album is not a neat process," Spawton adds. "There are usually some leftovers, some beginning of new ideas, and once we started putting all these together it became clear we had a lot of potential tracks. David and I were talking about it and realised, 'Hang on, we've got another full album here', and so the record morphed. I think *A Mead Hall In Winter* was a significant step towards that."

That song had its roots in the *Folklore* sessions too. Spawton had asked Rikard Sjöblom to build some music around the acoustic guitar line of *London Plane*. Working on the fly, the guitarist proceeded to record a piece he christened *London Stone*, but his guitar was about a semitone out of tune with *Plane*'s original piano, so didn't quite match up. With no time left for a re-record, the piece thus missed the deadline for *Folklore*. But Sjöblom carried on tinkering, adding to Spawton's original acoustic guitar figure until he had a 15-minute demo of a whole new song, complete with proggy Moog and crunchy Hammond moments. Sjöblom didn't feel comfortable writing the vocal melody, concerned that he might miss the nuanced Englishness that was a BBT trademark. So Longdon worked on the top line and added flute melodies, with Spawton writing a lengthy set of lyrics for what would become *A Mead Hall In Winter* for the new album, *Grimspound*.

"*Mead Hall* was a great collaboration piece," says Sjöblom. "It was my own take on Big Big Train. I gathered my musical experience of playing in the band and tried to write for them. It's good to know that I can – and want to – write for BBT, there's space for it. It's not a closed shop. As long as everyone likes the material, it's open territory."

It was, literally, an accident that meant Dave Gregory had the time to contribute his guitar work to *Mead Hall*. He has been a Type-1 diabetic for over 50 years, and just before Christmas 2016 – as he was working his way through his recordings for the album – he was making breakfast when he suffered a hypoglycaemic attack. "I was racing to get food on the table because I needed to eat quickly," he says, "the insulin had kicked in and I'd underestimated the effect it was having. I tripped over a metal flight case and fractured my ankle in two places."

He was incapacitated, in plaster and on crutches for the following three months. "I had been struggling to meet the deadline for my guitar parts, but because I was laid up all my normal daily activities were curtailed, and I was holed up in my music room. I couldn't move, but I could play guitar and was able to finish off the work that I had let fall behind because of various other commitments. Had I not fallen, I might not have played on *Mead Hall*, and I would hate to have missed that.

"*As The Crow Flies* is a really underrated song too, and contains probably my best guitar playing. That track is a career highlight for me. When Greg sent it to me Danny had done a beautiful piano arrangement, and I didn't want to cover it up. But as I started noodling around, I started adding guitars and the piano became less of a featured instrument. Because I record at home and not in a professional studio, the guitar sound isn't always as big and warm as I would like, but I like the sound of the guitar on there, and the way it was mixed."

"I bloody love *As The Crow Flies*," adds Spawton, its writer. "It's a shame it was never really picked up on, because Danny's piano part on that is lovely. It emerged as such a strong piece of music."

Chiming 12-string guitars and plaintive violins open *Meadowland*, another folky Longdon/Sjöblom/Spawton co-write, whereas the multi-faceted jazz/prog rock instrumental *On The Racing Line* became one of the band's most animated workouts of the period. It emerged when Spawton asked Danny Manners for a musical prelude to *Folklore*'s *Brooklands*. The pianist set to work elaborating on that song's chord progression and, enlivened further by some heavy showcase drumming from Nick D'Virgilio, the piece proved Manners' genuine facility for the musical genre in which he now found himself.

Winkie – that odd anthem of wartime heroism and derring-do – was recent proof that strands of British military history ran deep in the DNA of the band, going back as far as their album *Gathering Speed*, inspired by the Battle Of Britain. Longdon had been thinking of writing something about World War I ace fighter pilot, Albert Ball. Ball is a local hero in Longdon's home town of Nottingham, where a statue of him was erected in 1921.

Longdon's late father had been in the RAF too, and the singer says that the eventual song, *Brave Captain*, "was about the relationship between the statue, my dad, and myself. You have to know the events in Albert Ball's life to get it. I think one critique later said, 'It's almost like Longdon's a little boy in the first part of the song.' Well, I am! That was the idea. The fact that Albert and my dad were both in the Air Force was the very human connection that drew me in. I saw him in connection with my dad.

Rather than literally telling his story I wanted the long atmospheric intro, more soundscapey, like a Brian Eno type thing, because we hadn't done anything like that before. We didn't need another *Wassail*. I want to push new ground rather than repeat things, and I think *Brave Captain* does that."

A Longdon/Spawton co-write, the album's title track considered far skies and deep time, contrasting the fleeting span of mankind and its civilisations against the infinite nature of the heavens. As was often the case with Big Big Train's finer moments, this stemmed from a conversation between the two men. Spawton had first become aware of Grimspound, a Bronze Age settlement on Dartmoor, during his Archaeology studies back in Reading. "It's incredible to think that people lived there once," he says. "I

Captain Albert Ball in the live film made for Brave Captain.

just mentioned it to David in passing one day, and he went away and wrote the lyrics. It had got him thinking, and this fed through to the idea of the crow's role in folklore as the carrier of souls. This connected some of the threads between the two albums – the crow became such a big figure for us, and began to creep into other songs."

Big Big Train's resident artist Sarah Ewing had picked up on the meaningful image of the crow for *Folklore*'s cover, and

Work in progress on the Grimspound *front cover.*

had also begun working on some material together, with a view to making an album in the near future. "Judy's voice is really interesting," he says. "You can hear the experience and wisdom, and when I started working with her I thought *The Ivy Gate* would make a good duet for us." Dyble was invited down to Aubitt from her Oxfordshire home, and she and Longdon recorded the duet with Rob Aubrey.

"I really dig *The Ivy Gate*," enthuses Nick D'Virgilio. "The way David brings in the female vocal, the subject matter – it's stuff I'd never think to write about. The way the English tell stories is really cool. But there's also some really heavy drumming on *Grimspound – On The Racing Line, Brave Captain*, which is really fun to play live."

Notable by their absence on *Grimspound* were Dave Desmond and his brass counterparts, who had been a fixture on the band's albums since *The Underfall Yard*. "We were working at a real pace," Spawton explains, "and there didn't seem enough time to factor in brass arrangements. But also I didn't want us to become completely defined by the brass. We sort of wanted to prove that the eight of

her striking, award-nominated art for *Grimspound* would revisit this, the bird this time in full flight and incorporating the Corvus constellation referred to in the title song. Ewing's distinctive illustrative style and eye had become another part of Big Big Train's creative fabric.

They were a proper, successful band in their own right now, and with their line-up set and all bases covered, there was no longer the need to feature prominent guest performers on their album, for either artistic or promotional reasons. But when Longdon came in with the bleak fictional folk tale *The Ivy Gate*, he felt they needed a mature female vocalist to sell the song. He could only think of one lady for the job.

He and Judy Dyble had kept in touch since meeting at Kings Place. Not only had they become good friends, they

Judy Dyble and David recording The Ivy Gate.

us could do it on our own. But in retrospect I would have preferred to have Dave's input on *Grimspound*. When we played *A Mead Hall In Winter* live subsequently, he retrofitted it with a brass arrangement, and it does lift the song to another level. So, if I had my time again, I would've slowed the album down by about three months and put some brass on there."

For Dave Desmond's part, he could understand the thinking at the time: "I got it. I just hoped people didn't like it too much without us! I was worried that maybe our involvement would become just an occasional thing."

Speaking to the band, the word 'Grimlore' comes up to describe this particular brace of albums. The conflation of the two titles reflects how, like the two *English Electrics*, they were considered as a pair. And while brass wasn't part of their shared palette, Danny Manners notes that strings certainly were: "We had a lot of strings on *Folklore*, and I don't think we were that successful with it. For that to work there has to be room in the arrangements for them, or they have to be very simple. It worked on *Salisbury Giant* because the idea of a string quartet was in Greg's mind when he wrote the original demo. On *Grimspound* Rachel is more to the fore, and it feels like a more confident album in terms of playing. I think it has a bit more clarity. With David's songs there's a template to follow, you know roughly what everyone's going to be doing and you're adding more performance to it. It's a lot more work to do Greg's songs, but the advantage is that you have a lot more freedom. Over time I got better at knowing what works with Greg's pieces, and he began to write with me, Rikard, whoever, in mind."

Here Manners touches on the point Andy Poole made on the recording of *Folklore*, albeit from a different perspective. "One of the difficulties with Greg's material," Manners explains, "is that, with everyone recording on their own at different times, you don't always know what someone else will be doing. It's quite exciting when someone comes up with something you hadn't imagined. There's a semi-random element, with the end result depending to some extent on what order people record in. Sometimes it's planned – if Greg thinks a certain song is more guitar-based he might try to get the guitarists to track their parts before the keyboards, or vice versa. At other times it's a bit more arbitrary. Generally we got quite good at avoiding clashes, but they did occasionally happen. I'd throw in some fantastic organ lick but someone else had played a great guitar lick, and one of them has to go. Sometimes I found that frustrating."

Folklore evolved over a few years, but *Grimspound* came together in a matter of months. Spawton for one found it to be, "an absolute breeze, the easiest album we've ever made. Looking back we almost repeated the *English Electric* thing of making two albums at once, but entirely organically. *Grimspound* came together so quickly and felt so natural and easy. It's a collection of songs that just happened. It's got elements of folklore, even if it's invented, like *The Ivy Gate*, but it's more diverse thematically and lyrically. I think people went back to *Folklore* after *Grimspound* because they began to be seen as two of a pair."

"I think *Grimspound* was definitely in reaction to *Folklore*," counters David Longdon. "It's everything *Folklore* isn't. It's a much more aggressive, very proggy sounding record. *Folklore* is a bit more pastoral and smooth, both in subject matter and tone, and my contributions to *Grimspound*, like *Brave Captain*, were in reaction to that. Prog is a rabbit hole that I can't always be going down, but 'to thine own self be true'. We were very self-aware, and *Grimspound* was us saying to our audience, 'Don't worry, we haven't forgotten we're a prog band.'"

And from his vantage point across the Pond, Nick D'Virgilio could see that "the production had got bigger and better, and there was more of a polish to the sound of the band as a whole. Greg and David allowed the rest of the players to add their elements to the music, to give their life energy to a particular piece of music. All of those little things really shine, and the whole product is growing into this beautiful piece of art."

The album also did something to put paid to the erroneous perception that Longdon wrote the short, catchy numbers, and Spawton penned the long complex stuff. An edit of the latter's stomping, catchy, Mellotron-rich *Experimental Gentlemen* was used as a single, and when Spawton read the comments underneath the subsequent video (recorded in The Wood Room at Real World), he got his first taste of the kind of vitriol once heaped on Longdon for the sin of writing relatively light, singalong, life-affirming rock songs.

"On Facebook our Passengers are quite sensitive and careful," Spawton says, "because they know we're around on the page. But on YouTube people are really blunt, it's a more raw feedback. But the criticism I saw was good for me. I began to see through David's eyes, to see what David had been through with *Make Some Noise* and *Wassail*. He's been the fall guy, completely unfairly, for when the band has been more accessible. He's taken a couple of low blows for his songs, which I don't think merit any attention at all, because he's also written songs like *Judas Unrepentant* and *Brave Captain*, which are firmly in the tradition of progressive rock music. It seems sometimes like anything

we release as a single people hate. Perhaps we should do a Led Zeppelin and not release singles…"

Albeit in an upbeat and accessible way, *Experimental Gentlemen* celebrated the Enlightenment values embodied by astronomer Charles Green, naturalist Joseph Banks and the other scientists aboard Captain Cook's vessel, Endeavour. Perhaps only in progressive rock could this song be perceived as being 'lightweight'. But Spawton was discovering first-hand what many artists – from Bob 'Judas!' Dylan to Steven 'No Longer Sufficiently Prog!' Wilson – also knew: as bands grow in stature, so a certain faction among their audience develops a zealously proprietorial sense over them, and over what their music should be.

"I've found that as you start to go up the food chain," Spawton muses, "you bring a dedicated fan base, but people are quite happy to kick the shit out of you with some brutal online commentary. Some of the stuff we read about ourselves is eye-wateringly rude, but you just have to ignore it or try to laugh about it. It's frustrating when you read one star reviews on Amazon. If you don't like us, fair enough. But I don't think any of our stuff is one star. Some of the English spirit is supporting underdogs, and in the progressive rock world we're probably not seen as an underdog anymore by some people. They may think we've 'got above our station'. I don't think that's true, but they may project an image onto us which is how they choose to perceive us. We're just trying to do the best with our music."

Despite such brickbats, the band's faithful fans fervently pre-ordered copies of the new album. When *Grimspound* was released on 28th April 2017 (less than a year after its predecessor) it replaced Deep Purple's *Infinite* at the top slot of the UK Rock & Metal Albums chart, and glanced just shy of the UK Top 40 itself, peaking at number 45. The reviews in the prog-friendly parts of the press and internet were positive. Writing for prog-sphere.com, Nick Leonardi suggested that their tenth album could be their greatest, and that: 'The group is at its most focused at this point, delivering a number of amazing compositions and coming very close indeed to progressive perfection'. On progarchives.com the band's early champion, *Feedback*'s Kev Rowland, reflected on the quarter century since he reviewed *From The River To The Sea*: 'Back in 1991 I said, "If you like Genesis (prog not pop), Galahad or Marillion, then this is the band for you". More than 25 years on, I am pleased to amend that, and just say that here is a band for lovers of all great music, whatever the genre. Superb.'

The album would hit number 17 in *Classic Rock*'s Best Albums Of The Year chart too ('It's ambitious without being overwrought,' wrote Fraser Lewry, 'and as beautiful as it is smart'). And while Dave Desmond was pleased for his friends, he was also just a little stung that they'd done so well without brass. He jokingly told Spawton that it felt like his lottery syndicate winning the prize while he was away on leave.

"Usually your fans all buy an album in the first few days of sale," says Spawton, "so you appear in the mid-week charts and then, come the end of week, you're nowhere to be seen. But this held up, and we suddenly had a Top 50 album in the UK. Of course you disappear very quickly after that, but it showed that the fan base was becoming more substantial. There are very few progressive rock bands today appearing in the top half of the UK charts beyond Steven Wilson and Marillion. The big unknown remained whether we could build on that."

◆◆◆

And with still more material in store, they weren't done for the year. "We thought it would be a ludicrously prog thing to release three albums in quick succession," says David Longdon, with a cheeky grin. "It's all fuel to the fire and adds to the legend. But I do think *Grimspound* would have been a much bigger album for us had *The Second Brightest Star* not followed so hard on its heels. I think that split the vote."

Released on 23rd June, just two months after *Grimspound*, *The Second Brightest Star* was envisioned as a companion piece to the previous two albums, and comprised songs that hadn't quite fitted the bill for either *Folklore* or *Grimspound*. Two of these were written by Rachel Hall.

"That was unexpected," she says. "Rikard had a solo gig in the UK and I decided to play with him. We were basically in Greg's living room in Bournemouth rehearsing for it. I had written this little tune and asked if either of them could work out what time signature it was in, because I didn't write it thinking about that. They're trying to work it out and Greg says, 'That's brilliant. Can we have that for Big Big Train?' Yeah, you can have it! So then I developed it from there, not very much because it's not a very long track. I did a demo of how it could work for the band and everyone put their little bit in."

As the band once again pitched in, Longdon conceived the folky song's title, *Haymaking*. Hall was initially wary, wanting to get away from folk music's clichéd attachment to hay and straw, but she relented. Nick D'Virgilio would go on to rely on this polyrhythmic tune when showcasing his extraordinary playing outside of the band. "*Haymaking*'s a great track," he says. "It's fun to play, the melody on the violin is really cool, and I've used that a lot on my own since. I use it to play along to, it's a staple for me at drum clinics, and I played it on Drumeo, this geeky drum website."

Still available on Drumeo's YouTube channel, the video – 'Nick D'Virgilio: Progressive Rock Drumming Tips' – remains a valuable, mind-boggling insight into his musical thought process. It's an object lesson in breaking down flummoxing compound time signatures, and making them natural, musical, and all with D'Virgilio's consummate swing.

Hall's other song for the record was altogether more haunting. *The Passing Widow* was a ballad inspired by multiple marathon runner and round the world yachtswoman Rosie Swale-Pope. This one wasn't intended for the band either, but as she wrote it Hall could imagine Longdon singing it. "So I sent it to him," she recalls, "and said, 'Look, I'd really like you to sing this if you like it. If you don't like it, it's absolutely fine.' Danny did a lovely piano arrangement after I sent him the rough chords, and the two of them recorded it live at Aubitt. We didn't go for a click track or anything, because that would have spoiled it. They played it together in a live situation, which was brilliant. I think that was what it needed to get that emotion into it. I recorded the string parts later."

Spawton remembers that Aubitt session well. "We were all watching Danny and David, and there wasn't a dry eye in the house. It's a little off piste for Big Big Train but such a lovely piece of music in my view. Rachel only sings one line, which was her decision. The rule we have in Big Big Train is that if you write the song, you produce the song, so she had the final say."

"I was surprised Rachel's two songs got on there really,"

says Andy Poole, "because they were very un-Big Big Train. I like them though." Back too was *London Stone*, Rikard Sjöblom's original acoustic guitar piece that led him to *A Mead Hall In Winter*. Co-written by Sjöblom, Spawton and Longdon, *Skylon* began life in the lead-up to *Folklore*, when Spawton's imagination was captured by the titular space aged structure ('*Like something from Dan Dare*'), which had loomed over London's South Bank during The Festival Of Britain in 1951.

"I wrote that around the time of *London Plane*," he says. "Skylon was an extraordinary piece of engineering. Just like David's lyrics say, it was '*After the fire, after the storm, Post-war London six years on*'. We were coming out of the post-war malaise, the Festival was about what Britain and the Commonwealth could still do, and it was scattered with these sci-fi things. Skylon would be an extraordinary thing to have on the Thames now – it would make the London Eye look unremarkable. But it ended up in landfill, or at the bottom of one of London's lost rivers. It's one of those very British post-war stories."

Another river, the Stour, inspired Spawton's sweet and jazzy *Leaden Stour*, which marked the return of Dave Desmond's brass troupe, while a personal experience led David Longdon to pen the album's celestial title track. While looking into the Corvus constellation for the track *Grimspound*, he had heard mention of 'the second brightest star'. He used the term in that song and it had stuck with him. He was a lifelong David Bowie fan, and it had a Bowie-like ring to it.

Settling in at home in Nottingham, Longdon had begun to feel on a more even keel in his personal life. He had hooked up again with some old friends, who convinced him to go to a school reunion at his alma mater, Kimberley

Comprehensive. "I was torn," he says now. "Did I really want to go? Anyway, I had a shower, got ready, and drove down. It was foggy and the moon was bright, and I'd had that line in my mind. And the reunion was great. We were all older, in many ways it was no time at all since we'd been at school, and yet it was also a massive amount of time. The song is all about that, and thinking about perspective over time."

When he heard Longdon's demo for *The Second Brightest Star*, Spawton immediately loved the song. "It's beautiful," he says, "I think it's one of his best ever. It's a little like [*English Electric Part Two*'s] *Swan Hunter*, hidden away a little bit but has enormous potential to be one of our best-loved songs. It just needs to be heard in the live environment."

Some tracks on the album revisited and enhanced music from the previous two releases. Developed by Danny Manners, *Terra Australis Incognita* was an extended arrangement of *Experimental Gentlemen*'s closing section, the languid circular motion of its chord sequence drawing on a relatively obscure Genesis song that Spawton had always loved – *Submarine*, the B-side to their 1982 single *Man On The Corner*, from the *Abacab* album.

Brooklands Sequence united *Brooklands* with Manners' tour de force *On The Racing Line*; *London Plane Sequence* saw *London Plane* with a fitting new introduction, *Turner On The Thames*. This same year the latter sequence went on to form part of *London Song* – a freely downloadable suite of Big Big Train's compositions inspired by London, completed by *Skylon*, *London Stone* and *Wassail* B-sides *Lost Rivers Of London* and *Mudlarks*.

"There are moments on *The Second Brightest Star* that I love," offers Dave Gregory. "It's almost a shame that the

London Plane Sequence wasn't done earlier, rather than putting it out as an afterthought. *Brooklands Sequence* works perfectly well, and then there's all these great new songs, like the couple from Rachel. I personally think we should have closed the album with the song *The Second Brightest Star* rather than opened with it. It's more a completist's album – a nice potboiler while the guys were busy writing for the next full album."

"It is a 'companion album' at the end of the day," adds David Longdon. "There's some good material on there, but I do think it diluted *Grimspound*'s impact, it had some of its thunder stolen. But that's what we did, and we learned."

With hindsight, Gregory Spawton agrees too. "We were struck with this idea of making a 'secret album', but yes, it was too soon. Looking online it looks as if listeners are moving on to the next thing all the time, but in practical terms they're absorbing things as they go, and I think we crashed into that 'absorption period'. It was a bit too much of an effort to grab attention, an attempt to seize some column inches. We should have given it six months after *Grimspound*, not six weeks."

After this three-record spurt of creativity, the song vaults were largely exhausted. But during the summer Longdon and Spawton came up with Big Big Train's first, and only, Christmas single. Longdon's *Merry Christmas* was a big, surefire festive anthem about the real meaning of the season ('*When did the ringing of tills drown the peeling of bells?*'). It came complete with Dave Desmond's Salvation Army-style brass arrangement, the sound of sleigh bells and The Chapel Choir Choristers of Jesus College, Cambridge.

The band made a fun and meaningful video for it too. Directed by Peter Callow and with Spawton's brother Nigel

With the Choristers of Jesus College, Cambridge.

among the cast, it featured the band members encased together in a vividly coloured snowglobe. Actor Mark Benton – whom the band had befriended at Kings Place – played a bedraggled office worker whose drab life was finally given warmth when he embraced the true sentiment of the season.

By way of a B-side, the song was backed by Spawton's darker, sadly nostalgic *Snowfalls.* "It came out exactly as I wanted it," he says. "We had always wanted to do a Christmas song and we found a gap in the schedule in the spring and summer. I was sat in July writing lyrics about snow. David did the heavy lifting and wrote *Merry Christmas,* a song which I think ticks the box for the progressive rock audience but has a good singalong chorus as well. It's a very clever piece of writing, and it let me write something a bit broodier."

But The Most Wonderful Time Of The Year is also The Most Competitive, and, due to a dwindling singles market and a storm of bigger names peddling their own winter wares, *Merry Christmas* disappeared like a snowflake in a blizzard. It was a rare and costly bomb for Big Big Train, who were so confident in its success that they had manufactured thousands of CD singles. This was a blip in what was otherwise something of a banner year for them. *Grimspound* and *The Second Brightest Star* had been warmly received and sold very well on CD, vinyl and digital formats.

And as the year began with a slew of credible awards courtesy of the Classic Rock Society, hopes were high for that September's Progressive Music Awards. Longdon, Poole, Spawton, Manners and D'Virgilio all attended the ceremony at London's Underglobe, where Big Big Train were once again in contention in three categories, including UK Band Of The Year (which went to Marillion; Opeth were named International Band Of The Year). *Grimspound* was nominated for Album Of The Year, but that trophy was taken by Anathema's *The Optimist,* and Sarah Ewing's celestially beautiful artwork for *Grimspound* lost out in the Best Album Cover category to that of Tim Bowness's

Lost In The Ghost Light. (However, her moody, evocative artwork for *The Second Brightest Star* would garner the band their sole trophy at the following year's ceremony, in 2018.)

While they left empty handed and a little disappointed that night, they were still on a highly productive and successful streak on their own terms. And they were making good on those lessons on being a constant presence, on being seen to be out there 'offering stuff'. Not only had they made two acclaimed albums back to back, but they were also gearing up for their second set of live shows, in another classy venue, in a swanky area of London town.

Tim Bowness recording with David at Real World in 2018. Tim's vocals featured on an alternative version of Seen Better Days *on the* Swan Hunter *EP.*

Mark Benton with Gregory and film makers Peter Callow and Steve French.

XV

'We tell our tales, we sing our songs,
while we have breath left in our lungs...'

BACK IN APRIL 1981, during XTC's last US concert tour, Dave Gregory performed at California Hall on the University of California Berkeley campus, near San Francisco. To this day he remembers it as the worst sounding venue he ever played in his life, followed closely by Cadogan Hall in Chelsea.

After Kings Place, Gregory had been looking forward to playing live with Big Big Train again, and when he was told that Cadogan Hall had been chosen for the band's next set of live shows, a memory flickered in his mind. Back in 2009 he had seen Marillion perform a memorable acoustic show there on their *Less Is More* tour. To those tremendously acute ears of his, Ian Mosley's snare drum was too loud, reverberating and dominating Marillion's imperious sound. "I was still really excited about the shows though," he says. "I thought we could pull it off, with enough time to prepare and rehearse."

With its sweeping, U-shaped balcony, the 950-seat venue originally opened as a church of Christian Science in 1907, and its resident orchestra is none other than the Royal Philharmonic. Much like Kings Place, it regularly stages events by artists from the fields of classical, jazz, folk and world music. But then Marillion had played there successfully, as had the likes of Al Stewart, Richard Thompson and Rick Wakeman, so it could accommodate rock artists of varying stripes. And as per the band's preference, this was a decorous cultural venue with seating, far from the sticky floor music circuit Big Big Train were trying to avoid.

Since Kings Place, the band had been looking to play a similar 'mini-residency' at a different but similar room in London. For a while they considered Union Chapel, a small but beautiful venue in Islington, but because of the neighbouring residential area, the chapel's volume limits are relatively low; the full, 13-piece BBT line-up playing anything *tutti* would have sent the decibel meter well into the red, so it was a non-starter. And besides, according to Danny Manners, "Union Chapel would have been great in terms of atmosphere, but a disaster acoustically. I thought it would be the perfect place to do *Victorian Brickwork*. But unfortunately it's got so much fucking Victorian brickwork that it would be a complete mush!"

Instead, Gregory Spawton and Rob Aubrey headed to Chelsea to scope out Cadogan Hall, and were taken with the impressive room. With confidence high that they could sell out at least two shows, they booked the venue for the Friday and Saturday nights – 29th and 30th September 2017. When the shows were announced, a year in advance, the ticket uptake was such that another show was hastily arranged for the Sunday, 1st October.

To get an idea of what the room could do, in February 2017 Spawton and Aubrey returned to watch a show by Brit Floyd. This world-renowned Pink Floyd covers band is well drilled, usually playing over 100 shows per year across the world, and they're well versed in adjusting to the random challenges each new theatre, club and auditorium throws at them. Aubrey remembers making a point of speaking to their PA engineer: "The venue had said their PA was loud enough, but Brit Floyd's sound guy said, 'No, you'll need extra PA in here'. It sounded good downstairs, but we made the fatal mistake of not going up to the balcony…"

◆◆◆

Spawton had learned a lesson from the onerous task of organising Kings Place. He was now aware of what he was in for and what needed to be done, and this time he drafted in some extra help. Besides her work on the merch desk, Nellie Pitts had some valuable experience in tour managing, and pitched in with tasks like arranging accommodation. The band had also become friendly with Stephanie Bradley, one of Marillion's inner circle. As their 'Convention Coordinator', Bradley was responsible for organising the biennial Marillion Weekends – the hugely successful fan conventions attended by thousands of that band's diehard fans. Nine hundred people in a restored London church held no fear for her, and she would prove to be an invaluable help over the weekend. And once again, Spawton's wife Kathy was hands-on, dealing with ticketing issues, notably the complex, fiddly matter of the guest list.

Despite the stress of getting the show on its feet, Spawton for one had been buoyed by the band's triumphant, award-winning live maiden voyage across town, and also by the reception of their recent recorded material, and the way the full line-up was gelling. He was hopeful that they could repeat their Kings Place trick. "I was my nervous self," he says, "but thought we would knock it out of the park."

And David Longdon was keen to get back out there too. "We had set the bar for playing live every couple of years," he says. "Then with sales of tickets for Cadogan Hall we realised there was excitement to see us live again, and that we needed to play regularly. We'd taken another few steps forward."

In the run-up to the shows, Longdon's life was moving forward too. His relationship with the mother of his children had finally ended. "I was heartbroken and it was horrendous," he says now. "Knowing something is inevitable doesn't stop the hurt when it finally happens. But with Cadogan Hall I had something to sink my time and energy into. I threw myself into those shows." In preparation, he had a successful operation for a troublesome hernia, and outside of Big Big Train he was working more regularly with his friend Judy Dyble, planning their own musical project, to be called simply Dyble Longdon.

It was because of Rob Aubrey's stint as Jadis's sound man that the engineer had met Andy Poole at all, back in the Joiners in Southampton in July '92. But even 26 years on (and despite all his achievements in the field) Aubrey was, by his own admission, still far more comfortable behind the desk at Aubitt or Real World than engineering a concert. "Doing the live gigs is a real stress for me," he says. "I hate the fact that after the gig there are so many opinions. You can't help but face those opinions, and I've struggled with that." Cadogan Hall was about to really test his mettle.

Meanwhile, Poole worked on the optimal stage placings for everyone at the upcoming show. This time the brass quintet would be able to fit onto the stage with the band. The set list would draw on the highlights of the last shows, but there was now an abundance of new material to choose from too. "The initial set list for Cadogan Hall included *Brooklands*," Poole says. "I didn't see how we could do both that and *East Coast Racer* – they were too similar. *Brooklands* would be a bugger to learn and pull off, and we were never going to drop *East Coast Racer*. For Cadogan Hall my big push was for *A Mead Hall In Winter* – I saw it emerge as a starring track, and Danny and I could divide up the keyboards. I think Greg was less keen on doing it, whether that's because the bass part was difficult or it's a big chunk of Rikard's writing. That set list was difficult.

We didn't want too many big numbers but, in a way, they're all big numbers."

Victorian Brickwork and *Judas Unrepentant* survived from the Kings Place set, and this time the show would open with the title track from *Folklore*, complete with a new, classically inspired overture written by Danny Manners. This would be pre-recorded and Rachel Hall would be first on stage, playing live over it. Also in from that album were *London Plane*, *Telling The Bees* and *The Transit Of Venus Across The Sun*. Poole got his way with *Grimspound*'s *A Mead Hall In Winter*, along with that album's *Meadowland*, *Brave Captain* and *Experimental Gentlemen Part Two*. The *Underfall Yard*'s *Last Train* and *English Electric*'s *Swan Hunter* would make their debuts too, while the rousing crowd-pleaser *Wassail* would close the show, hopefully sending the audience home happy.

The band convened at Real World for rehearsals the week before the shows, and Spawton remembers this time as another low in the deterioration of his relationship with Poole. "For the Cadogan week preparations at Real World, Andy effectively withdrew from everyone, at a time when we were all together in the eye of the storm. People didn't all sit around drinking every single night, but you should at least

Rehearsals for the Cadogan Hall shows.

spend an hour a day team building together when tools are down – it's really important. Andy would come back from the studio and disappear off to his room and not even say goodnight. I was angry because he appeared to be disengaging from BBT. However, I don't think that anyone in the band really picked up that there was an atmosphere between me and Andy."

For Rachel Hall, this period marked a strange time for the band. They were transitioning from playing smaller venues for the joy of it, and joining a larger world. It felt as if all eyes were now on them. "Suddenly the pressure was on a bit more," she says. "It was a lot more business-like: 'This is happening, these are the expectations, and we have to deliver on that.' I definitely felt more pressure with Cadogan Hall. As a band in general you always got the feeling that the next thing we did had to be even better than the last.

"The other thing I struggled with is that when you go to rehearsal, even though it's a rehearsal, it's filmed for archive footage. It sounds really ridiculous, but, as a female, I'm going to be in front of a camera and I don't know what's

Dusting off the Wassail *mask.*

going to be used. You kind of get used to it, but, by the point we got to Cadogan Hall, there was a lot of footage of the rehearsals going on as well. And I think that contributed to the overall pressure for this string of gigs, because everything was being watched. Everything."

◆◆◆

It was that first Friday that Dave Gregory could tell that all wasn't well: "When we set up on stage for the first time and started soundchecking I really got the shits because it didn't sound good. The building was designed for chamber orchestras, choirs and public speaking – it wasn't designed to accommodate drum kits and electric guitars, and therein lay the problem. Here I am in the room, in the real world, but everyone else has in-ears so they don't really have any understanding of how bad it's sounding. I thought we shouldn't panic just yet. I trusted that when the audience came in they would soak up the sound and it would change. But that didn't happen."

And there was much to play for. The band's profile was higher than ever, and so were expectations. The shows had

NDV working through lights and presentation with technician Sabine Reichhuber.

sold out, with Passengers on the way from across the UK and beyond. And there were some intimidatingly revered names on the guest list, among them Genesis's own Tony Banks, who was attending with that band's engineer, Nick Davis.

Backstage just before the Friday show, Nick D'Virgilio led the now traditional, morale-boosting BBT huddle. Rachel Hall emerged first, to warm applause, alone and playing soaring violin to the new *Folklore* prelude. With her in-ear monitors and new, wireless mic set-up she could roam the stage freely. She sounded great, and the mood in the room was high as she was joined by the band and they launched into the main track. Sabine Reichhuber had been commissioned once again, and throughout the evening her expanded projections and moody lighting would imbue the band's performance with a dramatic visual element.

In preparation for the shows David Longdon had been going to the gym to build up his cardio, and he enjoyed the larger stage, ranging across it energetically. But despite putting his whole, battered heart into his performance, and

David at Cadogan Hall.

whilst he could hear that the music the band were making was good, he could sense something wasn't right in the room. Throughout *Brave Captain*, *Last Train* and *Meadowland*, the energy wasn't coming back from the audience as he had expected.

Spawton thought it was all going well, despite the on-stage mix sounding a little drum heavy to him. D'Virgilio, Manners, Poole and Rikard Sjöblom were all in full flow. Gregory did his best to adapt to the sound, and Hall herself was having a brilliant time, her intricate playing charged by the sense of occasion. And then, during the last song of the first set, *A Mead Hall In Winter*, Big Big Train's first heckle came at them from somebody in the balcony, someone henceforth referred to by the band as 'Shouty Man'.

"He was shouting down to me halfway through," recalls David Longdon, "but I couldn't hear him. The in-ears block your ears – if you're not being picked up by the microphone, I can't hear you. But I could tell from his body language that it wasn't good. I just nodded at him. At the end of the song I hopped off the front of the stage and purposefully strode up to Rob at the back, and my exact words were: 'Hello Rob, I haven't got a clue what that guy just said. What's going on?'"

At some point, the speakers up in the balcony had been switched off. During the soundcheck, nobody in the team had gone up to check how it was sounding, and now all that those seated there could really hear were D'Virgilio's powerful, booming drums. "I didn't know anything about it, until Shouty Man blew his top," says Aubrey now, still embarrassed. There had been some discussion between band and venue as to the best way to incorporate the in-house PA system and the band's own. Aubrey says that

he's still not quite sure how the communication breakdown came about: "And besides, it was our responsibility. When we worked out what had happened, our monitor engineer Dave Taylor switched on their PA system upstairs and filtered out some of ours downstairs to make a makeshift mix. He ran around like crazy man in the interval."

Some other fans in the balcony had come down to complain to whoever they could, including Nellie Pitts in the foyer at her merch desk. (Pitts texted Aubrey throughout the first half but his phone was, understandably, set to airplane mode.) Kathy Spawton had been watching the show behind Tony Banks and Nick Davis. She went over to Shouty Man to ascertain exactly what was wrong. One audience member even pulled out his smart phone and sent his complaint directly to Gregory Spawton via Twitter, then and there. With the bassist mid-show and otherwise engaged, the tweet unsurprisingly went unseen until the evening was over.

Before the band re-took the stage after the interval, Longdon came on to address the audience to apologise for the sound gremlins. "We were five minutes late going back on and some guy was moaning about it," he recalls, "but we were trying to get the problem sorted. It's live music, that's the thrill and spill of it. It was exciting and different. It was out of the ordinary."

"Nick's a loud drummer," says Spawton, "and when he plays a gig he probably goes up another five decibels. But he backed off a bit in the second half because we weren't sure if the sound had been fixed. I remember as we were playing *East Coast Racer* Nick was really in the pocket – it was slightly pulled back and the groove was fantastic. That got a standing ovation, and the second half did go well. It started to feel as if we were battling our way through it, but the atmosphere afterward was a little sombre. It felt like being one-nil down at half-time in a cup final. We felt we needed to do two good shows and that otherwise reputationally it could be a disaster. If you do 100 shows a year and 10 get poorly reviewed, you've still got a 90 per cent success rate. But if you do just three shows a year and two of them get poorly reviewed… We were victims of our own lack of gigging really."

"That show was the first time the band had any adversity ever in my tenure with them," says D'Virgilio, "and it was good for us. You have to go through shitty times – in business, sports, music – and especially as a live performer. We needed someone to slap us down a little bit and bring us back to reality. But I have only good memories of Cadogan Hall. My wife Tiffany was there and it was the first time she got to know everybody. She did Rachel's hair and make-up, and became part of the BBT team. She fit in, and that was really important to me. And I remember going to do the drum solo, and walking out of the door to the big green light that Sab [Reichhuber] had made."

That other seasoned gigger, Danny Manners, was pretty sanguine about that night's false start. "The one saving grace for me – and it's totally selfish – is that I'd made various cock-ups that night. It was probably first night nerves, and knowing that Tony Banks was in. But Tony couldn't hear any of it anyway because, unfortunately, the sound was terrible. But I've done so many gigs where I can hardly hear anything; it's just one of those things. I knew Rob and Dave the monitor guy were doing their best to sort it out at the interval. Obviously you feel bad – you know some people have flown in from abroad. Visually Cadogan Hall's nice, but not the best place for prog. We met Tony [Banks] after the show and he was very gracious. Obviously we owed a lot to Genesis, but he said he could hear that we've also got our own thing going on."

Banks is one of the most prized and elusive figures on the progressive music scene, and it was a big deal that he had made the effort to show up. Stephanie Bradley came into her own here, as Spawton recalls: "I was chatting to fans after the show and then, suddenly, Stephanie grabbed me by the hand and said 'You need to meet someone, you need to come *now*!' She led me back into the auditorium where Tony and Nick Davis were kindly waiting. Stephanie was great – she realised it was important and that it was a photo opportunity, whereas of course I was just, 'Wow – Tony Banks!' Nick [D'Virgilio] had kept the lines of communication open over the years since his Genesis experience, and we were so pleased he did. And I think it was a big moment for David too, in coming to terms with

With Tony Banks and Nick Davis.

his past, and putting a full stop on it. It was really positive."

This was the first time Banks and Longdon had seen each other since that Genesis audition. "We had a chat about it," Banks recalls, "and, you know, he'd fallen on his feet. It seemed to work out, everyone was happy. And the gig was good – by that stage he had certainly learned how to be the frontman. He had his own personality."

As for the band itself, Banks – with his long, first-hand experience of the progressive scene – could see where Big Big Train were coming from. "In the early '70s we were lucky enough to get away with doing stuff that was quite novel. You could use strange chords, funny lyrics, different kinds of structure of songs and let yourself go a little bit, rather than feeling you've got to wrap everything up with two verses, a chorus and a middle eight. And I think that's the sort of legacy you get from the groups that have come since, Big Big Train being an example – more musicality, more adventurousness with the writing.

"When I saw the show, I felt that. That's why they're called a more progressive group. I don't hear very direct influences necessarily, I just hear that approach – of being prepared to try things and see where it goes. In this more commercial world nowadays you don't get that quite as much."

And while the evening ended well, Aubrey felt absolutely awful about the oversight. "I wish someone had just come and seen me about it at the desk," he says now. "I went to bed that night, and woke up thinking that it had just been a nightmare, but then realised it wasn't." He felt so rotten that he tendered his resignation to the band the next day, but this was declined out of hand.

"It was all of our responsibility," says Spawton. "Yes, he was the guy on the desk and he should have gone

upstairs but didn't. I'd watched him wandering around the auditorium. It was the right venue, but we did poor sound prep. From then on every bloody inch of a venue has been walked by Rob and Dave [Taylor]."

For the Saturday night Aubrey, Taylor and band worked hard to make the sound right. They took some of their own speakers upstairs to cover the people sitting behind the PA stacks, and put more speakers right at the back of the hall. To help with sound bleed between drums and vocal mics, D'Virgilio was moved back by a metre and the rest of the band forward by the same distance. At soundcheck Aubrey had people he knew and trusted spotted around the hall – especially the balcony – to confirm the quality of sound where they were. "We had to create a complete separate mix for the balcony," he recalls. "Upstairs had vocals, some instrumentation and no drums, which were carrying well from downstairs. That's all way beyond my mixing skills. Dave sorted the upstairs mix with his iPad. It was complicated."

Big Big Train's learning curve continued. The problem was fixed, and the next two shows went a lot more smoothly. For Rikard Sjöblom, order had been restored. "After the negative vibe of the first night I had fun, as I usually do when I play, and I always have fun with Big Big Train. It was a great crowd, Cadogan Hall was a much bigger venue than Kings Place, and this was only the second set of shows the band had done."

Manners says there was much that was improved on from their stint at Kings Place: "We'd made a bit more effort with the visuals. We'd learned a bit more about the theatrical and dramatic presentation of it. Kings Place was small and we were limited with what we could do. For example, some of the projections there didn't last for a whole song, just for some sections and not others – it doesn't work, because people wonder if the projector has packed up. And I'd written the *Folklore* prelude. With Rachel playing the solo against a backing track I'd put together, that worked well."

"There was a timer countdown behind the curtain," Hall recalls, "with a specific cue in the music for when I needed to start walking on for the intro. I remember one night standing next to Dave Gregory, repeating the words 'Shit! Shit! Shit!' before I stepped out, which I'm not sure was helpful to anyone else at the time, but quite funny to look back on. Although there was that pressure around that time, once on the stage I was generally fine. I think I've always been a performer at heart. Looking back at the things I have and haven't enjoyed about being a musician, what I always loved was the energy of performing with people, connecting with your instrument and with an audience."

Along with fan favourites like *East Coast Racer* and *Victorian Brickwork*, some of the new songs began to assert themselves. With its majestic mid-tempo movements and classic progressive moments, the dramatic *Brave Captain* captured the room. The 15-minute slab of *A Mead Hall In Winter* showcased the band members' individual skills and ensured the first set closed to rampant applause.

Like *Make Some Noise* at Kings Place, *Experimental Gentlemen* transcended its muted reception as a single and came alive in the room. "*The Transit Of Venus Across The Sun* came into its own live too," says David Longdon. "As with most of these things, I think our live albums are another window into our world, with the band playing material to the fans and getting the energy back from them. It's like a feedback loop, the energy snowballs, and that's the ultimate. Over a relatively short time Big Big Train became a serious live concern. Which is just as well really, as album sales are on the wane."

As for Dave Desmond, he was just happy for the brass to be on the same stage as the band. "We were taking up half the stage," he says with a laugh, "so when we weren't on there was this massive gap with empty chairs and music stands. Apart from the first night's sound incident, I remember the Cadogan Hall shows fondly. I could see the

Rikard during A Mead Hall In Winter.

Nellie Pitts at the merch desk.

The Transit Of Venus Across The Sun.

crowd properly this time, there was more of a connection, and the whole thing was a bit more polished than at Kings Place."

In another milestone, the band received their first broadsheet review. With Stephanie Bradley ensuring he had everything he needed, *The Times*' journalist John Bungey attended the Saturday night show, and went on to award the event four stars out of five. Suggesting that Big Train was the least inviting rock band name since Dumpy's Rusty Nuts, Bungey caught the tone of the band's recent creative arc over their last three albums. He praised their 'soaring epics […] firmly rooted in resonant melodic lines', and highlighted Sabine Reichhuber's visuals for *A Mead Hall In Winter*, which featured the frontispiece of Newton's *Principia Mathematica*. 'You won't get that at Take That,' Bungey asserted.

Big Big Train at Cadogan Hall.

So Big Big Train were back for good on the live circuit. Despite Friday's false start, Spawton saw that the band could sell out a larger venue, combat technical challenges head on, and play the songs as a full ensemble: "To stick with the football analogy, we won 2-1 in injury time. It was proof to me that there was now the critical mass to warrant a full tour. We learned some lessons, crucially to take nothing for granted and to select venues as carefully as possible, and then do everything you can in those venues to get the sound as good as you can."

And the other reviews for the weekend helped the band's profile further. Writer Kevan Furbank was at the Friday show for theprogressiveaspect.net. Singling out Rachel Hall, Rikard Sjöblom and Nick D'Virgilio for particular praise, he

NDV at Cadogan Hall.

summed up the evening with a reasonable assessment: 'It's fair to say that the sound issues came as a crushing disappointment to many, but thankfully the sound improved for the second half and, apart from a few issues with Rachel Hall's violin, it was the only jarring moment in an otherwise near faultless return to live work for the eight piece.'

In his appraisal for *Prog* magazine, seasoned music journalist Chris Roberts called Big Big Train 'the best British prog group of our times', and thought the show he saw was 'a triumph. This is big, big music [...] and it's what prog should be doing now. Blending the melodic beauty of Genesis with a tinge of Tull folk, revitalising it with elements of the post-rock drones of Mogwai or Sigur Rós...'

193

'All rise.' Dave Gregory at Cadogan Hall.

As for Dave Gregory, he never quite found his stride over the weekend because of his issues with the sound. But he did change his tune somewhat later when he heard Rob Aubrey's live mixes for the accompanying live album, *Merchants Of Light*, which used feeds taken straight from the soundboard across the three shows. "Rob did a marvellous job," says Gregory. "On the CD the concert sounds way better than it did where I was standing on stage."

Preceded by an EP release of *Swan Hunter*, *Merchants Of Light* was released the following July, 2018. It even included the Friday's groovy, in-the-pocket read of *East Coast Racer*; proof that, while the room had played havoc with the sound, the performances were still on point that night. The accompanying Blu-ray, *Reflectors Of Light*, also emerged to positive reviews the year after that, 2019, by which time the band had moved on to other, bigger things. "The days of the 'big live album' are probably over," Spawton reckons. "There will never be another *Seconds Out* or *Frampton Comes Alive!* – live albums are two a penny, but, although they involve a lot of work, they don't generate anything like the sales of studio albums. *Merchants Of Light* is really just a souvenir for those that were there."

While, perhaps unsurprisingly, *Merchants Of Light* only just breached the UK Top 100, John Bungey was on board for it, giving the record a four star review for *The Times*. The *Daily Express*'s Paul Davies awarded it the full five stars, deeming it a 'remarkable record' and praising Big Big Train's 'exquisite blend of melodious English folk prog sounds'. A quarter of a century into their existence, the band were getting print coverage beyond the usual, prog-friendly press – a rarity for a band of their stripe. Those hard yards were starting to truly pay off, but at a cost.

◆◆◆

Gregory Spawton and Andy Poole had once steered this thing together. Throughout the '90s (and with Ian Cooper pulling his weight in the early days too) Big Big Train had begun as a product of their close friendship, and a deep

Big Big Train at Cadogan Hall.

bond forged from their love of progressive rock. Beyond the band, Spawton and Poole had hung out together, gone to gigs together, dreamed together. They were more like brothers, and had affectionately called each other 'Bub' in correspondence. Now their band was selling albums, and selling out their live shows. From its humble beginnings in Poole's small Bournemouth flat, Big Big Train had evolved, expanded and refined itself. All of the ploughing on during the lean times had led to these rewarding years, but each

milestone also meant a slight adjustment in course. Along with their talent, each new member – David Longdon especially – brought their own field of gravity, and the group's axis had shifted accordingly.

"When we got the full line-up," Poole explains, "Greg and I said we needed to keep tabs on everybody, so there was an allocation – I would liaise with Danny and Rachel, and Greg would liaise with David, Dave [Gregory] and Rob. We didn't hear a great deal from Rikard and Nick.

And there were times when David would go quiet, and we wouldn't hear from him a great deal, or we wouldn't involve him in certain things. That was partly because he had his own shit to deal with, but also Greg and David were speaking a lot on the phone, and that was another bone of contention for me."

Another souring point for Poole was Longdon's work with Judy Dyble. He had seen them become friends since Kings Place, with Dyble contributing vocals to *Grimspound*'s *The Ivy Gate*. But when Longdon told him that he planned to make an album with her, Poole was concerned that this would both divert the singer's attention from Big Big Train, and use up songs that might otherwise make their way into the band's own catalogue.

"My next recollection," Poole says, "is learning from Greg that the album would be happening and that Greg alone had agreed for BBT/English Electric Recordings to fully fund the recording and release. Greg knew I would

Ben Godfrey, Rachel, NDV and David at Cadogan Hall, 1ˢᵗ October 2017.

raise concerns and likely objections, not least because no business case had been produced or considered for the project. So I was mightily peeved that any business good practice or protocol had been breached, albeit I understood the imperative to keep David on board the train. Greg informed/patronised me that Judy remained a prominent figure in the English folk scene and that the album would generate plenty of interest/sales from folkies who might then discover Big Big Train. I strongly disagreed.

"I remember emailing Greg and saying, 'That proves to me that you're just bending over backwards to accommodate David.' He came back with an equally stroppy email, saying how dare I suggest that. But I felt the bottom line was that Greg was scared, quite rightly, of David pushing off and leaving the band. He was such an asset, and without him we would have been pretty scuppered. I was annoyed Greg couldn't accept my email in the spirit that I was passionate about the band and was coming from a legitimate standpoint."

The balance of power in the band was now shifting. Poole was distrustful of Spawton's approach to the business aspect of the band, and began to feel excluded, demoted. As the interview offers came in, they were aimed mainly at Spawton and Longdon, with Poole covering important but less prominent duties such as pre- and post-production, graphic design, posting albums and merch orders.

Both Spawton and Poole could clearly see that the push and pull of band life had put a strain on their friendship, but they were also savvy enough to know they had a good – some might say wonderful – thing going. Band politics aside, Poole was thrilled at the reception from Big Big Train's growing audience: "We were clearly expanding our fanbase and it was exciting, having had Kings Place and Cadogan Hall and the aftershow experience of meeting fans."

But Poole could see that his position in Big Big Train had fundamentally changed. And Spawton and Longdon felt it too. Something, or somebody, had to give.

XVI

*'Good friends are made and sometimes lost,
a fellowship can fall to dust...'*

"RELATIONSHIPS FLOURISH AND HAVE THEIR TIME," says David Longdon, who knows a thing or two about these matters. "But sometimes love moves on, or something happens where we go down different paths. That's part of life. Surviving difficult things is sometimes easier than surviving success. Both have a massive impact on you. Every kick in the teeth can bond people together so they can move forward. But, equally, success can throw up different challenges."

When Longdon first came into the band's orbit for *The Underfall Yard*, Gregory Spawton had been a taciturn presence. Andy Poole was always the more outwardly friendly and sociable of the two, and he helped put Longdon at his ease as he got to work at Aubitt. "He was very friendly," Longdon remembers, "good company, very sweet and funny. I think the shift came when Greg and I started getting closer. Greg grew in confidence as the band grew. Big Big Train is a very supportive environment and he came out of himself, but I think over time Andy retreated. He went further and further to the background."

Spawton and Longdon had bonded over long phone calls between Shrewsbury and Bournemouth, making plans, getting to know each other. And they had their passion for songwriting in common too. Moreover, Longdon could never quite fathom how the Poole/Spawton dynamic worked, and just assumed there was a lot going on behind the scenes to which he wasn't privy. "But when I saw Greg was struggling with things, I asked him what Andy's role really was. Greg always wanted the comfort blanket or feeling of a band around him – no different to George Michael with Andrew Ridgeley in Wham! really. Greg always needed a companion."

"Andy was always very clubbable," says Spawton, "which offset my shyness, and that quality in him really helped as we introduced more people into the band. He could work a room, and I relied on him for the PR stuff, for the heavy lifting of dealing with people when I was less assured about it. But then I noticed that things began to change. As far back as Christmas 2013, at the Eastleigh shoot for *Make Some Noise,* I began picking up that there were issues. I could see that he was withdrawing. A pattern of absenteeism became more and more noticeable from this point on. Looking back, something had changed and maybe his heart was no longer in it."

There had been numerous flashpoints along the way: the difference in opinion over the giveaway of *The*

Underfall Yard; before and after the first Real World sessions; in the build-up to the Kings Place shows. Rob Aubrey still enjoyed Poole's company in the studio and on the band's curry nights, but had long stopped copying him on band-related emails. Spawton contends that Poole had started to take himself out of the loop with band matters, and this became a self-fulfilling prophecy.

But the two men went back a long way. With the existence of a limited company housing the band's business interests, the question of Poole's role within the group he co-founded was a professional matter, but it was also a deeply personal one. Spawton considered swallowing hard and living with the way things were. But by 2017, with Longdon now a third partner in the company and the band riding high on their new trajectory, Spawton came to the conclusion that Poole's position threatened the band's scope to flourish further, and the issue would need to be resolved once and for all.

With the Cadogan Hall dates in the offing, the issue was deferred to avoid any distractions. After the shows Poole went on holiday, and recalls that on his return Spawton called a band meeting in Oxford between the three men. "After Cadogan Hall, Greg had told me that he and David would spend the rest of the year writing the material for another album. By then he had moved the distribution over to [distribution company] RSK, so there wasn't much for me to do there. That's when Greg came to me and said we needed a meeting with David.

"In advance of that meeting I remember standing outside my house having a chat with Greg, who said that he and David no longer considered I was worth one third of the business. I could understand that, from the point of view of the songwriting and who had been doing the heavy lifting with the interviews. But there was all the stuff I was doing behind the scenes, working pretty long hours, which Greg wouldn't accept. Hand on heart, I was doing those hours and I don't think he appreciated how long it would take to do some of this stuff. Greg said: 'David and I need to know where you are with everything.' They'd been away talking about things, so I said I didn't even know what all their plans were."

Poole requested a formal agenda for the meeting. Spawton sent it to him and says that it clearly outlined that "it was very much about the future of the band and the roles of the three band members. So Andy was aware that this meeting was being pitched at one point of the triangle not pulling his weight. He had all the information he needed."

Held at the Oxford office of Spawton's brother Nigel, the meeting was fraught. Beforehand Spawton and Longdon were both nervous wrecks. They had both been involved in HR meetings in their own places of work, but this was completely different and on a deep, personal level. Whereas just a few years beforehand Spawton and Poole would travel pretty much everywhere together, they each arrived at Oxford from Bournemouth under their own steam.

Once in the room, Longdon assumed a chairmanship role, "because he could see I was quite agitated," says Spawton. "He felt as strongly as me but took it less personally. I took Andy's behaviour as an affront – he and I had a deep partnership and friendship, we'd gone through thick and thin, and he had withdrawn from all that. He was a friend and he had retreated. I was less frustrated with what he wasn't doing than with what he was allowing himself to become. By the end of the meeting I was this close to lamping him I was so angry, so frustrated."

There were no fisticuffs during the 90-minute showdown, but no verbal punches were pulled as the grievances were aired. "One thing that came up," says Poole, "is that when I was 50 [in 2013] Greg had asked me casually at his house where did I see myself in terms of the future of the band. I thought within five years we probably would have made all the albums we wanted and it would be winding down. I said that maybe at about 55 I would retire. It was a throwaway comment that came back to haunt me – that was the beginning of the end because Greg kept quoting it and saying I was leaving at 55. I hadn't said that. I was just anticipating where I would be or where the band would be and that it would be time to move on. Working up towards my 55th Greg was behind the scenes beavering away trying to manoeuvre things, thinking I would retire, and that the stuff I did needed to be re-apportioned or put out to other people."

"Andy had emailed me about retiring a few months prior to the Oxford meeting," counters Spawton, "so his expressed wish to be finishing work at 55 wasn't an isolated comment. Recollections may differ on Andy's level of commitment to the band and how much he was prepared to contribute. When it comes to Big Big Train and making music, I work hard and I am determined and driven. Not everyone is the same."

"Greg was merciless," Poole remembers. "He was hitting me with one thing after another. At one point David had to restrain Greg and tell him to stop it and that he was beating me into the ground. They said they had all these ideas and were cooking on gas and wanted to get on. They said they didn't think I had the passion needed to support them on that journey. By then I had had a bit of downtime which I was really enjoying, because I'd left the council and wasn't doing my day to day grind stuff. I sat thinking that I didn't have that passion at the moment. They were on a bloody rocket ship and I didn't feel I wanted to be on board. They tried to manipulate it into people asking, 'What does Andy do?' I said I did all the behind the scenes stuff, not the media stuff, so it was inevitable people would say that. They didn't accept that, particularly. And there were criticisms to undermine me, like about helping out with Kings Place."

With the two men coming from completely different perspectives, the argument went round in circles. In his chairman/referee role, Longdon saw that the conversation was getting too heated to achieve its aims, and suggested they cool off and speak another time. But before parting, Poole was presented with three options: Spawton and Longdon could buy out his one third share in the limited company and he could leave the band; he could stay in the band but cash out of the business; and the third option was to carry on as was – which wasn't an acceptable option for his partners. Poole said he would go away and think about it.

A month later the three met again in the café at Waterstones bookshop in Bournemouth. By that time the band had just accepted the biggest live engagement of their career, a festival headline slot in Germany, the following summer. Longdon suggested that Poole should stay on to take part in this milestone event for them, and then leave on a high, with an enhanced financial settlement for his third of the limited company.

"For a business that had never made a profit," says Spawton, "we felt the settlement was very fair. The meeting in Waterstones seemed to go quite well, Andy said he was moving towards playing the show we had lined up, but wanted to go away and think about it further. Then, a few days later, he suddenly toughened up his position and didn't accept that we had offered enough, and as part of that stance he didn't want to play the festival show. I don't blame him, but that increasingly wound David up."

"I was undecided at that point," notes Poole. "It wasn't as if it was up for discussion – the bit was between Greg's teeth. He wanted it resolved and me out of the band. David was more circumspect and felt very awkward about it, but at that point I was thinking that I just didn't feel very welcome in the band anymore."

With the ignominious prospect of becoming a session musician in his own band – paid a rate per album and gig – Poole's mind was made up, helped along by something Longdon put to him: "David said I should do what would make me happy, which I found helpful. Wlady [Poole's partner] was very supportive too, although she was quite wary wondering what else I would do. Also I'd developed arthritis in my hands, so playing certain guitar shapes was difficult. My mum was suffering memory loss and getting muddled, which was later diagnosed as Alzheimer's. And I was really enjoying not having day to day work stuff going on, so I thought maybe it was timely for me to go."

After some more financial wrangling and heated, 'Bub'-free email exchanges, Andy Poole alighted from Big Big Train at the end of 2017. Spawton went over to Poole's house to pick up some band stock that had been stored in his loft. Poole handed back Spawton's house keys, the ones he would use to let himself in to Casa Spawton to work on the records that had got them here, in the dining room or, as the Spawton kids had called it, 'Andy's room'.

Poole remembers now that, at the time, he "joked with several people that I was busy getting divorced from Greg and the band. The whole thing had soured. Now it feels completely right – I didn't have a great plan, but I thought there would be new adventures out there and things I could do."

The announcement of Poole's departure was made on the band's social media channels on New Year's Day 2018:

"Andy Poole will shortly be leaving Big Big Train. Big Big Train would like to thank Andy for the significant part he has played in the band's journey and we wish him well in his future endeavours. Big Big Train will continue with the seven piece line-up of D'Virgilio, Gregory, Hall, Longdon, Manners, Sjöblom, Spawton alongside the five piece BBT brass band led by Dave Desmond. For future live performance, the band has recruited an additional musician to assist with keyboard and guitar work. We will announce details in due course. We also hope to announce a UK warm-up show for our July 13th Night of the Prog festival appearance at Loreley. We expect the warm-up show to take place on July 11th. Best wishes Danny, Dave, David, Greg, Nick, Rachel and Rikard."

Andy Poole's posted a personal Facebook message, which he presented on a lovely old postcard that read simply: *'Dear All, It has been a long old trip aboard this train and now the time is right for me to disembark: I am ready for new and exciting adventures. Thank you to my fellow crew and passengers. I wish you a fabulous and fulfilling journey. Warmest regards. Andy.'*

"I think it all went pretty smoothly," Poole says now. "I was as determined as anybody for it to be like that. I did the postcard announcement which Greg liked. I came off Facebook straight away after leaving because I was only

on it for the purposes of the band. The comments from the Passengers were lovely, and they even did a collection for me, which was totally wonderful. I had no anticipation of anything like that. I never had a collection when I left local government after 25 years!"

Whether it was a throwaway comment or a conscious wish, it transpired that Andy Poole was indeed 55 when he left the band. The conditions were right, and, he says, "I think Greg was thinking that my departure would give him more control of the band. I remember one meeting where we wanted to get some things out in the open. I mentioned a few things about spending on videos et cetera, one thing that upset Greg was I said it was always 'jam tomorrow'. Greg said it was all about the money for me. I said it wasn't. I never thought it really mattered to Greg if the band makes any money. His mark of success for the band isn't that it turns in a big profit – for him it's all about album sales and profile."

Within the band, Danny Manners had a clear-eyed perception of what had been going on between its founders. "I did worry at one point that I was supplanting Andy in terms of keyboards," he says, "but he was always fine about it. He said he wasn't a career keyboardist, and for live stuff – even with software trickery – Rikard and I couldn't cover everything. But I missed him as much socially as musically, in a way more.

"When we were doing albums we'd work on them as they were coming together, we'd bounce ideas off each other. He'd pre-edit stuff before Rob got to it, or would be involved in individual parts as they got emailed in and identifying problems – 'Danny, Dave's done a solo at the same place you have!' But in terms of playing, there wasn't a role for him on the albums. He did pre-production and admin stuff, but, as the band grew, some of this began to be farmed out. When I joined, the band was still very much a cottage industry, with boxes of CDs piled up at Greg's house, and Andy would take a load down to the post office twice a week. The band has had to outsource stuff and become more professional since then.

"Relations between Greg and Andy had been deteriorating for a while, from around *Folklore* if not a bit before. Occasionally something would happen in the room, but more often I'd hear about it from one of them afterwards. It's a shame in terms of band leading, because when it was working they made a very good combination. Greg can be really obstinate, but he has a lot of drive – if he didn't the band wouldn't be here. Andy doesn't have quite the same drive but he is more empathetic, more sociable in some ways, and I think that's why they were a good combo, but it's also why they got frustrated with each other. And I suppose writing is another role that Andy didn't have. He said to me more than once he'd prefer in a way to be doing less proggy stuff. But the one thing Greg has never been is domineering about the writing. David came in and he wrote, Rikard, almost all the band has done some writing and he's been happy."

"I never had a vibe that something was wrong," admits Rikard Sjöblom. "They were never at each other's throats in front of anyone else. It wasn't really different after Andy left, but I did miss him. He was one of the first contacts I'd had within the band, and we got along very well. I remember once when I was over he took me out in his convertible around Bournemouth and we went to the beach for the day. That was nice."

"Andy leaving was a bummer for me," says Nick D'Virgilio, "because I liked him a lot, he was a cool hang. We had fun personally and had some great late night talks at Real World, and he did some of the textural things live. I was sad to see him go, but I'm very glad not to be involved in any of that drama. Being in a band can be really hard – it's like a marriage, and Andy and Greg were together since the beginning, so they have a lot of history. I can imagine that for them it was really hard. I'm far removed from all that, and happy to be because I have my own shit to deal with!"

For Rachel Hall, the band was changing at this time, "and it continued to change again beyond that point. Bands go through various stages in their journey and there isn't always a shared viewpoint between people. What's incredibly important to one person at one time can't always be what's most important to another, and conflicts of interest can't be carefully resolved without understanding all the factors leading to people's behaviours or decisions. That takes a bit of discussion that people might not be willing to engage in. It takes up time that a business might not have, and the momentum of the band and its next product has always been a key focus."

According to David Longdon, "Andy should be honoured for his role in Big Big Train. He made a massive contribution to the band in terms of its initial development and mooring up Greg when he was shy and insecure. Andy was that companion that Greg needed, he brought out the best in him. As Rob Aubrey said once, 'It's not so much Andy not changing, it's more that Greg has changed so much in a short time.' Greg has blossomed and has evolved in relation to the band's development, and I have too. But Andy diminished, and that's not his fault. It's not making him out to be a villain or somehow deficient. It was just the way it was. The band had reached a point where we couldn't justify that anymore and we had to address it."

"My only regret is that I didn't deal with it sooner," says Gregory Spawton now. "We should have had frank conversations earlier, and he might still be in the band if that had been the case. Working in a creative environment you're very emotionally engaged with each other – the 'divorce' from Andy was at least as stressful as my actual divorce."

With this traumatic issue now finally resolved, Big Big Train could re-group and try to move on. And they would need to get into shape quickly. In the summer of 2018 they would be heading to Germany, to play the biggest show of their career to date.

XVII

'Going strong, as beautiful as ever,
to show the world they're not alone...'

NIGHT OF THE PROG HAS BEEN one of Europe's leading progressive rock festivals since its inception in 2006, and certainly the most picturesque. Its regular setting is the Freilichtbühne Loreley, or Loreley Open Air Theatre – a stunning natural amphitheatre on top of the Loreley Rock, on the bank of the river in the beautiful Rhine Valley. The Rock is steeped in folklore of its own. One tale tells of a young lady who, driven to despair by an unfaithful lover, threw herself into the river there, and went on to haunt the place as a siren, luring sailors to their doom on the rocks.

The site certainly attracted promoter Winfried Völklein when he was scouting locations for his celebration of progressive rock, which has assembled some of the major names in the genre. Fish headlined the inaugural event in 2006, and as the event's reputation built year on year, Loreley went on to host dozens of heavyweight progressive groups – Jethro Tull, Asia, IQ, Marillion, Dream Theater, Anathema, Opeth and Yes (the Anderson, Rabin, Wakeman incarnation). Rikard Sjöblom played there in 2015 with his band Beardfish, and the year after both Nick D'Virgilio and Neal Morse reunited with Spock's Beard for a one-off European show at the festival.

A post-D'Virgilio Spock's were headliners in 2012, the year Big Big Train first popped up on Völklein's radar. He had been pointed their way by GEP's Marketing Director Peter Huth around the release of *English Electric*, and had watched them from afar with great interest ever since. "Their music is different to any other in the prog business currently," Völklein says. "They put so many different kinds of stories into their music, and they use instruments that are unusual in prog, such as the brass section. But the key point is that they are good composers. The trick is to combine harmony and difficult sections of a song properly, and they do that."

Völklein was aware that Big Big Train was a relatively untested live act, with only a handful of shows to their name. He had only ever seen them himself on YouTube, yet he was prepared to make a leap of faith. "I wanted to take the risk because I wanted to show prog fans that Big Big Train is the same quality as Camel, Steve Hackett, Marillion, and that they could perform as a headliner. I thought that there were maybe 1,500 people in the world who would simply not wish to miss this show, and also during the history of Night Of The Prog we have brought many unknown bands to fans here who didn't know them in advance. I just had a feeling it would work – I was very convinced about them and their ability to perform on stage."

Since their profile had risen circa *English Electric*, Big Big Train had begun to attract regular interest from festival promoters. Some had been pretty persistent, but all had been politely declined. The band had chosen to focus on building up their recorded catalogue, and were also still finding their stage legs together, so a festival slot felt some way out of their comfort zone.

But the Loreley offer came in around the time of the Cadogan Hall shows, and after Kings Place, when Gregory Spawton for one was more amenable to the idea. Völklein tried hard to reassure the band that, if there was any festival suited to Big Big Train, then his was it. "Finally I was able to convince them that we work very professionally," he says. "With all due respect to other prog festivals, on the technical side we are the Champions League, and I think every musician who has played our festival could confirm this. At other festivals [stage] changeovers can be an hour and a half. At our festival it's only 15 minutes. Some bands are nervous about getting changed over so quickly, but we make it work."

And so the date was set. On 13th July, Big Big Train would close the first night of the three-day Night Of The Prog Festival 2018, where they would be billed as co-headliners alongside Polish prog rock band Riverside. There would be almost ten months between the last Big Big Train show at Cadogan Hall and Loreley, so the decision was made to play a warm-up concert just before heading off to Germany. This would help the band get in the zone for their headline slot, and it would also help to break in Andy Poole's replacement, whoever that might turn out to be.

❖❖❖

Back in 2009 a friend suggested to Robin Armstrong that he should check out *The Underfall Yard*, by this 'new' band which might be right up his street. The budding English musician duly obliged, and absolutely fell in love with the record, *Victorian Brickwork* especially. "The complicated songs coupled with the brass was a winner for me," Armstrong says. "But I didn't think much more of it. There was a lot going on for me musically at that time – I was getting much more interested in doing music again. I was recording my own little experiments, which got progressively more serious to the point where I did my own album that year, *End Of Ecclesia*, which I tried to launch. I didn't get very far with it but got a few reviews which were all fairly positive."

Under his *nom de prog*, Cosmograf, Armstrong did better in 2011. His second album, *When Age Has Done Its Duty*, showcased his skills as a multi-instrumentalist, songwriter, vocalist and composer. Enhancing Cosmograf's credentials further were the guest artists he chose, including The Tangent's guitar whiz kid Luke Machin, Lee Abraham (who had also worked with former BBT singer Sean Filkins) and It Bites drummer Bob Dalton, whose parts were tracked at Aubitt Studios by Rob Aubrey. The engineer also mastered the record and, once again in the Big Big Train story, Aubrey became the all-important linkman. He suggested Armstrong should meet Gregory Spawton and Andy Poole, just socially. "It was a bit of a fanboy moment really," says Armstrong, "but we became firm friends straight away. They were interested in what I was doing and were complimentary about it. I run a vintage watches business and Andy had recently purchased an Omega Seamaster [a luxury diving watch], so we spent plenty of time talking about that, and I ended up servicing the watch for him."

Armstrong lived just 25 miles from Aubitt in the sleepy village of Waterlooville, and the tangential connection – and friendship – between him and band remained. Through Aubrey, Nick D'Virgilio ended up playing drums on Cosmograf's signature album, 2013's *The Man Left In Space*. Armstrong also managed to persuade Gregory Spawton into doing his first – and for a long while, his only – guest slot for another artist, supplying bass on that album's spacey instrumental piece, *The Vacuum That I Fly Through*.

The year after, Spawton would be there to provide moral support when Armstrong played his debut show as Cosmograf, joining The Tangent, Galahad, Frost* and others for the Celebr8.3 event in Islington, London. Rachel Hall would add some violin parts to his 2017 album, *The Hay-Man Dreams*, too. "We all kept being friends," says Armstrong, "with me crashing the BBT curry nights they have when recording at Aubitt. I was invited to Real World when they were making *Stone & Steel*. I was pretty friendly with all of the guys by then."

In December 2017, Armstrong got a somewhat mysterious phone call from Spawton, asking him to meet at the branch of Waterstones in the small nearby town of Ringwood. "It was all very cloak and dagger," Armstrong recalls. "I was shocked when Greg asked me to take over Andy's role on the live side, but I said yes on the spot. I'd admired the band as a fan, and it seemed incredible to be given that opportunity. I was filled with quite a lot of trepidation as well – I had hardly any live experience and the last thing I wanted to do was let them down. But, as Greg pointed out, he was inexperienced too. It was a 'helping each other out' situation from the word go, which

made me feel more at ease."

At first, for reasons of both cost and complexity, the plan had been not to replace Andy Poole at all, and rather adapt the songs and re-share his parts accordingly. But the band prided themselves on sticking to the sound of the recordings as closely as possible, and attributed much of the success of their other live outings to this approach.

Many of the string parts recorded on the albums were performed at gigs on keyboards, and Danny Manners felt he needed another player to continue to pull this off. Rachel Hall and Rikard Sjöblom already had their hands full with their violin and guitar/keys parts respectively; on tracks like *Make Some Noise* Poole had helped fill the sound with 12-string acoustic guitar.

When the requirements became clear, Spawton thought of Robin Armstrong as an ideal candidate. "We knew he was a capable multi-instrumentalist," says Spawton, "and that he would fit in well and be calm in a crisis. It came out of the blue for him, but luckily for us he accepted immediately."

So, like Poole, Armstrong would be playing keyboards, some guitar, and supplying backing vocals too. There was much for him to learn. The material was complex and he would need to multi-task – all the more reason for a pre-festival warm-up show. Under the terms of their contract with Völklein, Big Big Train could not play anywhere else in the European Union that year, and no other show could be in a large venue that might eat into the audience willing to make the trip to Germany for the Loreley slot.

By this point Big Big Train's merchandise manager Nellie Pitts had branched out further into tour management, working with bands including Frost* and French proggers

Lazuli. She helped Big Big Train in the hunt for a suitable room available just before the festival. Despite the relatively short lead time they secured The Anvil, a 1,400 seat concert hall in Basingstoke, just 60 miles from Bournemouth. They would play one night, Wednesday 11th July, and head off to Germany the next day.

While it may not possess the acoustics of Kings Place or the cachet of Cadogan Hall, The Anvil is still a modern provincial theatre, and for the band's purposes it was well situated for the imminent trip. The fact The Anvil was outside London was also reassuring to Völklein, who was consulted and consented to the show. Besides, given the venue's capacity, Spawton fully anticipated that they would be playing to a half empty room. To his genuine amazement, when the show was announced in January 2018, it sold out, and quickly too.

The Anvil/Loreley set list was culled from the Kings Place/Cadogan Hall shows, bringing together the band's monolithic, must-play pieces – *East Coast Racer, The First Rebreather, A Mead Hall In Winter, Brave Captain, The Transit Of Venus Across The Sun*. Also in were the anthemic *Folklore*, the irresistible singalong *Wassail,* and – something of a BBT deep cut – *Summer's Lease*, from *The Difference Machine*. They would also take their first live swing at *The Permanent Way*, from *English Electric*.

Rehearsals were set

The changing of the guard at Real World. As BBT were leaving for the Anvil show, Camel arrived for their rehearsals for Loreley. Robin and Gregory are pictured here with Peter Jones and Denis Clement of Camel.

up once again at Real World the week before the two appearances, and these went smoothly from the off. Despite the change in personnel, the band immediately sensed they were getting into a groove that had become familiar to them. They even worked in new ideas as they went along, rather than sticking quite so rigidly to the recorded arrangements.

At Loreley the band would have, for the first time, a full lighting rig at their disposal, and at Real World lighting/visuals designer Sabine Reichhuber had software that allowed her to pre-program the rig's exact movements, choreographed precisely with Big Big Train's set as rehearsed. "You could see her skills," remembers Longdon. "In Real World Sab was sitting there working with the computer program for Loreley's rig. Then at Loreley, she'd put the dongle into the lighting console and the lights automated as per her directions. It was brilliant."

On that stint at Real World it really struck Gregory Spawton how much the band had evolved. "On the first day we were playing really well. Every time you play together you move forward a few per cent, but I felt for the first time we could work on the fly a bit more. We all knew what we were doing far more than previously."

It wasn't quite such an easy ride for the new guy. In the lead-up to Real World Robin Armstrong had wondered if he hadn't bitten off more than he could chew.

"I started working with Danny on keyboard arrangements in January 2018," he says. "I was liaising with him – about 300 emails went back and forth between us – and we were working weekends and plenty of evenings too, programming keyboards. The bulk of the initial work was trying to decide who would play what and how much of Andy's work I should inherit. Andy had a different style of keyboard playing to me. He tended to favour left-hand chords and right-hand melody, whereas I tend to work the other way round. It meant a lot of the patches that had been set up for Andy were no longer very useable for me, so I had to take his templates and rearrange them to my own style and way of working. Some of Andy's plug-ins [music software] from Cadogan Hall no longer worked and had to be done again completely from scratch. There was lots of technical stuff to sort out before we could even get in a room together to rehearse.

"One of the challenges working with Big Big Train is that live they very much want to present every single part on the album without resorting to backing tracks. Typically on keyboards there can be 10 to 12 parts that have been layered up over successive recording sessions. It's an enormous job to unpick that. The easiest thing to do would be to simplify it and lose parts, but that's not good enough. Danny was very particular that all of those nuances were represented live. Some of the parts weren't so much challenging to play as challenging to remember. It was quite a complicated set – the sheer number of patch changes – and then to get over two hours of music in your head. That was the first wobble I had."

And then there were some contingencies that were completely beyond anybody's control. Like sport. On Saturday 7th July England beat Sweden in the football World Cup quarter-final, securing a place in the competition's last four. Their next game, against Croatia, was due to kick off at 7pm on Wednesday 11th, the evening of the band's warm-up show. "Well, who'd a thunk it?" Spawton wrote on the band's Facebook page. "England are through to the semi-finals of a World Cup and all is good in the world. Except for the fact that the match clashes with our gig at The Anvil, Basingstoke."

The band considered making their 8.30pm stage time later, but decided against it, given the potential of the game going into extra time and the transport problems which a late finish would cause their fans on a weekday night. The decision was taken that the show should continue as originally planned.

The Anvil marked the first time Big Big Train had a support band. Kicking off the evening were the Beatrix Players, a hotly tipped group comprising lead vocalist Amy Birks, pianist/backing vocalist Jess Kennedy and cellist Amanda Alvarez. The Players were a highly suitable entrée for Big Big Train. Their classy, classically orientated brand of chamber pop was progressive (Kate Bush's name regularly came up in the press for their acclaimed debut album, *Magnified*), and they too drew inspiration from historical figures, such as Catherine of Aragon.

On the night, as the Beatrix Players were winning over the room, Big Big Train prepared themselves backstage. *Match Of The Day* commentator and Big Big Train fan John Roder presented Spawton with a vintage England football shirt to wear for the encore, in the event that England beat Croatia. They lost, 2-1, and so the England top remained in the dressing room.

Big Big Train's show itself, however, was a winner. Leo Trimming of theprogressiveaspect.net was there and

Big Big Train at The Anvil.

observed that, despite some sound problems: 'This was a great performance of evocative and emotive music. Truly a celebration of a great band which has developed a very real sense of community with its fans.'

"The Anvil was a cool venue," says D'Virgilio. "It was good to have the warm-up – we were on the road. We were having the same crew join us more and more, we were hanging out with the brass guys, and we all became really good friends."

"I was really impressed by the theatre," says Dave Gregory, "and the crowd was lovely, really warm. It was our first gig without Andy and it wasn't a bad performance, but there were a few rough edges. It was the first time Robin had worked with us – he did a very good job under scary circumstances. It must have been nerve-wracking for him."

It was indeed. An unseasoned performer, Armstrong had felt the colour drain from his face as he took to the stage in front of the biggest audience of his life. "I did get

NDV at The Anvil.

a bit scared," he says. "I had some technical problems with the radio pack and I couldn't hear things as I had done in soundcheck, which was unnerving, and I made a few silly mistakes. Everyone assured me afterwards that no one really heard. I wasn't filled with elation at the end of the Anvil show – I wondered whether I'd done the right thing, because it had been a massive effort to learn everything and I was expecting a more euphoric finish to that gig. I felt I'd done better playing in the rehearsals and that I'd muddled through the show. It was a frustrating result compared with all the effort I'd put in."

To Rachel Hall, the show fulfilled its intended function well. "We'd been rehearsing for days, and The Anvil was a chance to find out where things could possibly go wrong and put them right for the Loreley show. For me, it did exactly that."

Hall had switched from her beloved acoustic violin to a new electric model. This would be much easier for Rob

Aubrey to capture at the sound desk, and its configuration meant Hall could also cover some of the music's viola parts more effectively. "That was a bit of a shocking moment for me," Hall says. "I've had my violin since I was 16, and I've played on the same instrument ever since. It's not a particularly good one, but it does the job for me. Going on with an electric violin – you've been fine through all that rehearsal you've done, and then suddenly you've got a completely different instrument in your hand. It's not even a violin really – it's a violin and a viola together, basically a square thing with five strings on it. So I had those anxieties at that gig."

There were no such anxieties for Rikard Sjöblom, an experienced live musician utterly at ease both in his own skin, and within the group. "When I'm playing I don't think much about what I'm doing, because – in the best situation – you know the stuff so well you don't need to focus, and it's more about delivering a performance for the crowd and having a good time with band. I always listen to the other guys, and if someone goes out on a little special treat and plays something different for just that night, that sets me off, in a good way. I don't like to only play what's written – I like to throw myself in a bit of limbo when I do a solo. The Anvil was a nice gig, but we were so focused on Loreley, so it was like a bonus. Robin's a great guy and he's a good and versatile musician. There was a lot for him to learn and he worked very hard."

To Rob Aubrey's ears, the sound coming at him from the Anvil stage was pretty good. The previous year he had been to a show by folk group The Unthanks at The Anvil, and thought the vocals hadn't cut through, so he attempted to mix Big Big Train's sound accordingly. But he later heard many comments from people saying that they couldn't hear the vocals from where they were sitting, and one particular comment didn't sting Aubrey so much as strike a chord.

"Someone said that 'Big Big Train need a sound

At the sound and lighting desks: Rob Aubrey, Sabine Reichhuber and video tech Markus Jehle.

engineer of the capability of Roger Waters' engineer',," he recalls. "I thought about it, and spoke to Greg and David about it afterwards. The thing is, we don't have the budget or the time that Waters has. And if his engineer – the best engineer in the world – came in to mix Big Big Train at The Anvil having the amount of time we had, I don't think he'd have done any better. Everybody has got to get quicker at setting up on stage. At The Anvil we'd been there since 9 or 10 in the morning but didn't start soundchecking until 4pm. We needed to get a bit slicker in that regard."

And their time-keeping could have been slicker too. One of David Longdon's overriding memories of the show is that they overran. "At the end of the show I'm literally having people take my jacket off me – we had to get a train that was leaving in 20 minutes. We got on that to London, then to a hotel, then we were up in the morning, over to St Pancras, then on the Eurostar to Germany. We were getting ready to spread our wings in continental Europe."

Longdon had performed in France with both Louis Philippe and The Gifthorse, but never in Germany. XTC had played a handful of shows there in their time, and The Anvil had filled Dave Gregory with confidence that Big Big Train would hold their own for the festival crowd there two days later. "But oh my goodness, *Loreley*!" The guitarist delivers the name with a deeply satisfied sigh. "From the moment the brass players came in we were off, and the crowd were with us all the way…"

◆◆◆

With Nellie Pitts once again handling the logistics, the 27-strong team of band and crew flew to Germany the day after the Anvil show. Due to a serious fear of flying, Longdon opted for the Eurostar, with Gregory and Kathy Spawton keeping him company. As they emerged on the French side of the Channel Tunnel, Spawton's mobile beeped with a message from Rob Aubrey. Stung from the criticism of his work in Basingstoke, he attempted to quit for the second time. When the band finally all converged at their hotel for their Night Of The Prog sojourn, Aubrey's resignation was, once again, rebuffed.

As the closing act of the festival's opening night, Big Big Train were the first band required for set up and soundcheck, bright and early on the Friday morning. Their hotel was a two-hour drive from the venue, so the band piled into their bus at 7am, were onstage by 9am and all set by 10am, with a full 12 hours to go until stage time. "It was a fantastic drive along the Rhine," Danny Manners recalls, "all those fairytale castles. The soundcheck went really well, kudos to Rob and the tech crew for that, because we didn't have three hours to soundcheck, we just had the one."

With a long wait until showtime, Spawton, Kathy and Nick D'Virgilio went sightseeing with Spawton's old friend Richard Williamson and his partner Claire, the five of them taking a leisurely road trip along the Rhine. It happened to be Kathy's birthday, and the mood was light. "That was great," says Spawton, "because as 'Mister Nervous Performer' I spent the day completely distracted and got back to the festival site for our Meet & Greet at 6pm, feeling refreshed and not having dwelt on anything all day."

Rock music, progressive or otherwise, is perceived in a different way in continental Europe than it is in the UK. Rock co-exists with pop and dance on mainstream European radio – it is enjoyed with an unalloyed, irony-free enthusiasm, and by a broader audience too. Whereas in Big Big Train's homeland the prog demographic tends to skew male and

Meet & Greet at Loreley.

middle-aged, in Europe the genre transcends age and gender. While some of their Passengers had dutifully made the long trip over, at their Meet & Greet the band met a refreshingly different, continental European demographic who were at Loreley to enjoy a weekend of prog rock music, and were open to hearing new sounds, maybe even a brass section.

In these environs and among these people, Spawton enjoyed a rare, transient sense of being a rock star. The event made Nick D'Virgilio – who had played Loreley before with Spock's Beard – all the more excited at the prospect of playing for thousands of people. David Longdon remembers that Meet & Greet well: "We were inundated. People were so excited. The number of young European men and women coming into the auditorium wearing BBT merch was noticeable. For the first time ever I had been warned not to walk in the audience, so I went and had a coffee on top of the hill."

Just two days before, Robin Armstrong had played his first show with the band. Now he was due to perform in front of a large festival crowd. "I was running on adrenaline by that stage," he says, "and was worried I was starting to

flag. The Real World experience was exciting, but I found it quite difficult to sleep, and the same after the Anvil gig. I was really struggling with lack of sleep. But I managed to get a reasonable night's sleep before Loreley, and the morning of the soundcheck I was feeling much more positive."

With dusk falling and co-headliners Riverside playing to the packed amphitheatre, time was ticking down to Big Big Train's slot. The 13 players gathered backstage to prepare. "Stage management at festivals is a very tough job," says Spawton. "We were told beforehand that nobody was allowed backstage apart from the band and crew – no wives, girlfriends or anyone like that because it was a very small backstage area. Ignoring the protocol, I had smuggled Kathy in, and when she was discovered it did cause a bit of a kerfuffle."

The festival generally ran like clockwork, but Riverside did exceed their allocated performance time by 15 minutes. This was a problem: Big Big Train had timed their set to two hours exactly, and had been made aware that there was a hard curfew – they had to be finished by midnight. Also there were a few jitters about going on after two much

David keeping a watchful eye on Riverside.

heavier groups, Riverside and (Big Big Train's former GEP label mates) Threshold; the crowd's audible approval for each band rattled the small backstage area.

With 4,000 tickets sold for the weekend, the place was already three quarters full. Spawton estimated that 500 or so of these people were hardcore Passengers who had made the trip – the others were new listeners, waiting to be impressed. Despite Win Völklein's confidence that they were up to the task, would Big Big Train's folk-inflected prog fall flat after all that chugging guitar energy? Would the Englishness of their offering, of Dave Desmond's brass section, really resonate with a European audience who had enjoyed a whole day of heavy rock and drinking? With moments to go, the members gathered backstage for their pre-show huddle, and as ever Nick D'Virgilio led them in the chant. Tonight though it wasn't the usual 'GO BIG BIG TRAIN!' For this special show the rallying cry was 'DON'T BE SHIT!', shouted *en masse* three times. From their positions in the front row, Kathy Spawton and Richard Williamson could hear this clearly.

Big Big Train walked onstage just after 10pm. It was 25 degrees, the sun had dropped over the Rhine and a gentle summer breeze blew through the amphitheatre. The audience filling it had been out all day in the summer sun, *feuchtfröhlich* and up for the party. 'Are you ready?' asked the ever undaunted David Longdon, as Dave Gregory summoned *The First Rebreather*'s intro figure from his trusty Les Paul Junior. Thousands of voices hollered back in the affirmative, and with that serious lighting rig bathing them in shafts of blue and red, Big Big Train were away.

BBT's view from the stage at Loreley.

It's a good few minutes before the bass kicks in on that song, so Gregory Spawton had time to look at 'the ego ramp', the runway stretching from the main stage and out towards the crowd. He wondered if Longdon would use it much. "I was just tuning up, getting ready," the bassist recalls, "and I looked up and David was already at the far end of it! He loved getting close to the audience. *The First Rebreather* went down really well, and then we did

Folklore and, of course, the brass section comes on. You could detect this wave of interest that there was a brass band playing."

"There was a real frisson," Dave Desmond recalls. "We did the extended opening to *Folklore*, and we heard the crowd cheer at the point Rachel stopped playing her solo part and the fanfare comes in. We thought they were cheering her, and they probably were, but it was still a nice, spine-tingling moment for us too. We needed to hear ourselves, and with the excitement of it all we blew louder than we needed to. It

was just very powerful – you got a sense as soon as the brass kicked in that they'd had a day of fantastic guitar bands but they'd had nothing like a brass ensemble."

Danny Manners' wife Sophie was sitting in the back of the amphitheatre next to Rob Aubrey's mixing desk. Manners recalls that when Desmond's section came on "Sophie heard some Germans say, 'What is *this*, a brass quintet?!' And I do remember the first brass entry, the crowd went absolutely mad. At the end they were saying, 'The brass is *fantastisch*!' And I knew David was going to

David on the runway: "I loved it – I wanted one in my house…"

lap this up. He has no fear on stage and really enjoys every minute of it. He and Rachel were both on the runway. I know Rachel really enjoyed it, and was really confident on stage. She was just great that night."

Hall recalls that, at soundcheck, "David and I both checked out whether the radio mics still worked that far down the runway. David knew he was using that runway! I wasn't so sure I would. I remember putting my make-up on and Nellie telling me I needed a bit more lippy – you know, one of those girly things women are honest with each other about. But I refused, on the grounds that I was there to play my violin tonight, not just to look pretty. I think that might have come across in the performance. I remember something had not quite gone to plan, directly before my *Mead Hall* solo. I thought, 'Perfect opportunity to divert attention – now or never!' and decided to go down the runway for the solo. I think it caught David by surprise.

"It was a buzz just to be on stage there that night, and we could see the audience really well, which you don't get in a theatre as much. With more space I was less worried about

She came to play – Rachel hits the Loreley runway.

moving around and getting in the way of David performing. On this occasion he was usually half-way down that runway! It gave me the security to be able to move around freely behind without any disasters of colliding or tripping him up. With the radio mic in this setting I was able to cross the stage to get to Rikard, or have communication with pretty much anyone in the band I wanted to at any time – apart from when I had to get to my mic to sing. It was a nice feeling."

"I loved that runway," adds Longdon. "It was the best thing ever and I wanted one in my house! Sabine even put some white tape on it and said, 'Don't go any further than that, because you won't be lit.'"

With Longdon, Hall and the entire band on such strong form, and with the large audience vocally onside, the show went like a dream. Sabine Reichhuber's classy visuals and sympathetic use of the lighting rig injected some traditional rock showbiz. With their non-language-specific singalong moments, *Summer's Lease* and *The Permanent Way* were well-chosen additions to the usual set. The quieter moments didn't feel like lulls, the audience's interest sustained throughout. "*Summer's Lease* was the track on the *Prog Spawn* CD," Longdon says. "It was the first track I'd heard by

Big Big Train, and I love it for that reason. It's one of my favourite songs of Greg's. That night, in one part we took it right down to the harmony vocals – '*Where did you come from? Where will you go to?*' – and it was a magical moment, it was hair-raising."

Rikard Sjöblom vividly recalls that moment: "*Summer's Lease* was beautiful. Even being a part of it onstage hearing my bandmates taking it down to the a cappella part, I almost forgot I was singing myself. I took out one of my in-ears to listen properly, and it was very silent among the crowd even though that's a quiet part. Then we took it back in with the full band, and it was just beautiful."

Although the band botched a short section of *A Mead Hall In Winter,* it still got thousands of arms swaying, at Longdon's behest, the singer then launching his tambourine

Feeling the buzz – Rachel, Rikard and Gregory rock out.

like a frisbee into the delighted crowd. And, for Robin Armstrong, Loreley was a much better experience than Basingstoke. "The Anvil had a very British audience feel," he says, "with the first three rows sitting staring intently at you with their arms crossed. At Loreley the crowd had been there all day, had been entertained by a number of bands and were pretty well oiled as well, so the dynamic was completely different by the time we came on stage. It seemed there wasn't much winning over to be done. Everybody was in such a party mood, it felt as if you couldn't do any wrong. They were very up for it and that helped to relax things. I was in abject terror though for the first half hour of the gig and I can't remember too much about it! As it went on it became easier, I had a really good sound mix, and by the end I was fairly euphoric."

Despite the midnight curfew, the band overran considerably. They finished the main set at two minutes to midnight, leaving D'Virgilio's drum solo and *Wassail* still to come. The drummer looked at the clock and at Spawton who, carried away by the occasion, nodded at him to proceed. It wasn't their fault they had gone on late, so to hell with the curfew. Spawton was also somewhat emboldened by the presence of Niall Hayden, the band's enormous roadie, standing solidly at the side of the stage. If the organisers wanted to drag the band off, they would have to get past this former firefighter first. But as it was, the extra time passed by, and Hayden was left undisturbed.

It had been 38 years since Dave Gregory's last big outdoor show, when XTC had been on a European tour with The Police in 1980. He was completely awed by this Night Of The Prog slot. "I would have to say that it's the greatest live experience of my entire career, and I can't imagine playing a better gig. Everyone played great – there were a few mistakes, including a colossal one in *Mead Hall*, but they didn't matter. Having such an amazing audience made such a difference as well. I don't think it could have gone much better. All of us felt that all the work we'd done, the slow build-up that had been simmering, finally

NDV's drum solo at Loreley.

had come to the boil. I felt a strong sense of fulfilment, both for the band and for myself.

"There's something about a summer's evening and live music. Outside, as an electric guitarist, you can turn the volume up and make a lot of noise without the same acoustic issues as in a concert hall or theatre. And there's a party atmosphere – people can go to the bar, dance and chat – it doesn't matter. There's more of a communal spirit to an outdoor audience. With Loreley, I felt this was where we should be all the time. A lot is down to Nick and the sheer force of his playing. The two most important people on the stage in a live band are the drummer and the singer. You need those vital elements if you're going to entertain a big crowd. David had the crowd in the palm of his hand. I felt really good for him having finally got to where he wanted to be without having to rely on another band to get him there. And Nick was in such a good mood and so confident. He just carried us."

"Loreley was fantastic," says D'Virgilio. "It's amazing considering the band had only done seven live gigs. At a

An epic, fantastic, 'orgasmic' night for the band at Night Of The Prog.

prog festival, people with passes aren't going to leave – they're going to stay to see what those headliners are like, and this band is good enough. After that first song we're sucking people in and by the end of the show we're going to convince them and recruit a lot of new fans. That's definitely what happened. David gave a great performance, he was a real lead singer."

"At Loreley we went out and *conquered*," says Longdon. "We grew to the occasion and filled the stage. It was a spectacle. Sabine's really good, but before we'd given her a

limited palette – having a great lighting rig notched us up again. Roger Taylor of Queen said that the bigger the audience got, the bigger the band got, and we could do bigger venues too, because we have that drama. It's doing something on that scale but making it feel intimate as well. We met lots of new fans after the Loreley show, and I think we converted a lot of people."

Rob Aubrey was a veteran of Night Of The Prog, having presided over the sound there for bands including IQ and Sound Of Contact. "I'd had a few disasters there

David passes the vocal baton to NDV at Loreley.

before," he says, "but with Big Big Train it was a lot smoother. From the first moment David was down the catwalk because he had a radio mic, and Rachel came out her shell so much, she was straight down the catwalk too. She was like a different woman. They really rose to it and the audience really loved it. The moment the brass guys came in there was a murmur – 'Oh, this is something really different and special'. Certain people have been disparaging of the brass guys, asking 'What's the point of paying a lot of money to have five guys on stage when you could do it with tapes or samplers?' Well, you wait until they start playing – the audience melt. Admittedly it's expensive, but it's part of the show. Loreley was great for me."

Aubrey had a friend – an engineer from famous Dutch prog venue The Boerderij – walking around the auditorium and feeding sound intel back to him at the desk. "He was encouraging me to enjoy myself and made me a bit more at ease," says Aubrey with a laugh. "I would love to do Loreley again knowing what I know now. It was a big success for the band but I was too nervous to enjoy it. The following night people said the Camel sound man produced one of the best sounds they'd ever heard. But he had four people on stage and I had 13!"

Coming offstage, for Gregory Spawton there was only one word for the night. "It was *epic*. The backdrop, the stage, the arena itself. It's the most prog thing you can imagine, it's like playing a gig at Helm's Deep or something. If a dragon had flown over, you wouldn't have been surprised. Yes, *Mead Hall* went wrong and we fluffed the link between Danny's keyboard solo and *Judas Unrepentant*, but I thought then that we could probably win over any audience. It was *orgasmic*. It was one of the best things we've ever done, and might be the best thing we ever do. It was a massive step for us. I'd love to play there again."

Backstage there were joyful hugs after a job well done, another milestone marked, and the group headed back to the hotel to celebrate together into the early hours. Hall had taken full, happy advantage of the white wine on their rider, and – much to Gregory and Kathy Spawton's amusement – spent the drive back asking their taxi driver to repeat his obscure German name. "I'm not sure he was amused," says Hall now, "and I shamefully still can't remember his name…"

Yet amid all the happiness, something niggled at the band's remaining founder. "My one regret was that Andy wasn't there," Spawton says. "What a shame he decided not to stay on for that show, because David and I could have announced from the stage that it was his last show, and it would have been such a spectacular send-off. I'd like him to have seen it, to have experienced that sense of arrival, because he'd earned his part in it. I know in recent years we were no longer close, but I felt that by turning down that gig he denied himself a last amazing moment, which he deserved to have."

("I did have the option to do the show," Poole says now, "and I don't know why I didn't, I probably should have done. I was away, I made a point of not being around. I was busy enjoying myself with Wlady and my dog…")

So Herr Völklein's punt worked out well. Night Of The Prog was a big success for him that year. With some 4,000 people attending, it narrowly outsold the previous year, when a crowd of 3,800 gathered for Mike Portnoy, Marillion and Yes Featuring Jon Anderson, Trevor Rabin and Rick Wakeman. "Riverside put on a tremendous

David: "At Loreley we went out and conquered..."

performance," Völklein says, "but nobody left after them, and Big Big Train really delivered. I was convinced they could, and they did. I'd like to bring them back again."

And, naturally, after the high of the gig came the comedown, each member dealing with it in their different ways as, back home, they settled back into their routines, jobs, lives. Loreley taught Robin Armstrong about a whole new world he hadn't been exposed to before. "I don't think I fully understood the euphoria and value of it. I came back from Loreley and was on a high for a week, but then inevitably I crashed down quite badly and suffered a few problems mentally after that. I got problems with anxiety, not caused by the gig itself, but witnessing something that I'd dreamed of doing since I was 16, then finally achieving that level of exposure to a huge audience, and then coming back to reality. That was a bit of a culture shock."

Rikard Sjöblom would top up his adrenaline the day after the band's set, when he took to the Loreley stage again for his Saturday afternoon slot leading his own group, Gungfly (Beardfish having split in 2016). By then his BBT colleagues were already spreading out across the world. Nick D'Virgilio flew home to the US, Longdon was on an early Eurostar home to the UK, and Gregory and Kathy Spawton used the opportunity for a 'mini' grand tour of their own. They took the train to Cologne, and to Germany's oldest city, Trier, to look upon the Porta Nigra, the Basilica of Constantine, and other works of the Romans from the days they laid claim to the land.

Big Big Train were spreading their wings, and plans were already afoot for their first proper tour. It was only right that their next musical voyage should embrace ideas of travel, adventure and enlightenment.

"Loreley was one of the best things we've ever done. It was a massive step for us..."

XVIII

'Sate our urge to see the world,
to make us feel alive, so alive...'

"I ABSOLUTELY LOVE *GRAND TOUR*," says Rikard Sjöblom. "Musically it's really strong, I love the songs, everyone's playing is top notch and David is singing his heart out."

By their sheer presence, Sjöblom, David Longdon, Nick D'Virgilio and Rachel Hall had often led Gregory Spawton to proclaim that Big Big Train was a band of frontmen. And thanks to those same performers it had evolved into a band of singers. With four such strong vocalists in the fold, it made sense to make the most of this aspect of the BBT sound. Whereas Longdon's multi-tracked harmonies on *The Underfall Yard* were all him, he now had three bandmates who could pull off complex, quasi-operatic choral parts in the studio and, crucially, live.

When he suggested that, for the Loreley show, they take *Summer's Lease* right down to its vocal harmonies in parts, he was keying into this major strength. "I like [Crowded House/Fleetwood Mac's] Neil Finn," Longdon says, "and Lindsey Buckingham's a genius, bless him. I'm a big Crosby, Stills, Nash & Young fan too, they inspire me. Harmonies are powerful. Human voices singing together – there's something really raw and emotional about it. It just gets you like brass bands do, the old bottom lip starts to go. Things were in progress with *Grand Tour* by the time we got to Loreley, we wanted the harmonies in. And the theme, that's always between me and Greg – we'd both read and see things, then compare notes, and the ideas come."

For their twelfth album the band's quintessential Englishness was refracted through a European lens, and their historical bent was given a continental twist. From the 17th century until the early 19th, well-heeled young British, European and, later, American debutants would broaden their minds with travel. In the spirit of empiricism, they would take in culture, arts and science as they journeyed across the different countries of Europe on the 'Grand Tour', which usually culminated with a stay in Italy. An aristocratic precursor to 20th century Interrailing, this rite of passage inspired work from some major minds – Francis Bacon, Goethe and Dickens among them. It is held that Mary Shelley had the idea for *Frankenstein* while on her own Grand Tour with Percy Shelley and Byron.

"But we didn't want to be too literal," says Spawton. "I did a lot of research on the Grand Tour and there wasn't a single route. There was a pattern but people visited different places, so we weren't too precise about it on the record but followed a general route down to Rome, and then we head off into the universe with the song *Voyager* and then return home, hopefully, fairly triumphantly. The album was a metaphor really. It's art following life – we were reaching out into the world and wanted to take the music on its travels as well, in the way that the band is becoming a bigger concern. For David there was a sense of being more alive – he'd been through some difficult times, and part of the album for him is being more alive, haymaking and seizing the moment."

Following the album's prelude, the Francis Bacon-inspired *Novum Organum, Alive* was Longdon's hopeful, well-crafted paean to the life-enhancing qualities of meaningful travel. With its Mellotron hook, major-key chorus, rich vocal harmonies and infectious guitar and synth solos, it would be both a catchy ignition point for the album, and was almost machine-tooled as a concert opener for the accompanying tour dates. It also reflected a rebirth and rejuvenation in the singer's private life. In the four years they had known each other, he and Sarah Ewing had

Sarah Louise Ewing's artwork for Roman Stone.

become close friends. By September 2018 (fittingly, as they attended that year's Progressive Music Awards together) they realised they had fallen in love, and the couple made their relationship public the following March.

Over 13 minutes and five parts, *Roman Stone* saw Spawton on well-trodden thematic ground, broaching the rise, glory and fall of the Roman Empire. This song was also ripe with four-part vocal harmonies, a stirring guitar solo from Dave Gregory and Rachel Hall's plangent violins, and, having been absent from *Grimspound*, Big Big Train's brass section were back too.

The quintet had been an integral part of the band's success at Loreley, and the show had cemented their place in the band's soundworld. "They really are a significant weapon in our armoury," Spawton says now. "The brass absolutely sets us apart from almost anybody else out there. But it's like deploying your cavalry – you bring them in at crucial points rather than overdoing it, in the same way that you don't want 10 minutes of guitar solos."

David Longdon's own tempestuous 14-minute epic, *Ariel*, brought together the worlds of Shakespeare, Percy Shelley and Byron in cinematic style. Its highly literate/literary theme was set within an eight-part song cycle, a masterfully executed, densely layered piece that showed how far this band line-up – honed now by the years and their live experiences – had really come. "It's different," says its writer. "It didn't follow the usual format. Some people refer to it being operatic or even musical theatre because there's lots of singing in it. It has some real moments, but I wanted that to be a storytelling thing. There's a lot of words, it tells a story and I'm proud of that one."

Similarly deep musically, *The Florentine* was Longdon's cheerful, thoughtful tribute to Leonardo da Vinci, a

The BBT brass ensemble at Real World, October 2018.

Shelley's funeral, an illustration for Ariel *by Sarah Ewing.*

subject well suited to prog rock's intelligent, all-encompassing lyrical legacy ('*A polymath that did not fit the paradigm*' [...] '*Detailed delineations, observations precise*' [...] '*Your notes, fine drawings and designs are bound in codices voyaging through time*'). But the song wasn't without its challenges. Once again the issue arose of having to accommodate the numerous melodic ideas pouring in from the international branches of English Electric Studios. Rob Aubrey remembers feeding all these into his Pro Tools system at Aubitt, throwing up the faders, "and there were two solos at once – one from Danny and one from Rikard. They were both brilliant, I didn't know how it was going to work. I asked David, 'What are we going to do?' And it was actually very simple – we just extended the song. We looked for an alternative drum part from Nick and extended it, so there's a keyboard solo then a guitar solo. This is prog, after all…"

"But we don't try to endlessly cut and paste or extend songs for the sake of it," Longdon stresses. "I struggle with the expectancy that, just because something is lengthy, it's somehow got merit. Sometimes when I listen to progressive rock bands' extended compositions, it can be woeful – if it's not well done, don't do it! A song should be as long as it needs to be. It's got to flow through, and we spend a lot of time getting the balance right. With *Grand Tour* most of our time was spent listening over and over, getting the transition right from one section to another."

However it happened, Rikard Sjöblom remains delighted his guitar contribution made the cut for *The Florentine*: "I'm very happy with that one. I'd been trying to do more guitar work where you don't hide behind a lot of distortion, fuzz or effects. I was going back to the idea of 'What does a Fender Stratocaster sound like when you just plug it in and play it?' I wanted that solo to be natural, just playing nice notes one after another. I love *The Florentine*."

The close two-part harmonies on the song's strummed verses came from Longdon and Nick D'Virgilio, a renaissance man himself as he earned his first songwriting credits for Big Big Train. Drawing on his love for jazz fusion, the instrumental *Pantheon* came with jarring atonal chords and complex non-diatonic progressions from the Mahavishnu Orchestra/Tony Williams Lifetime playbook. And yet the piece was recognisably Big Big Train, with Longdon smoothing its edges with soothing flute, Rachel Hall channelling her inner Jean-Luc Ponty with some fusion fiddle, and the brass band mollifying ominous passages with their proletarian tones. Here and throughout the record, this was the classic BBT sound but pushing out into new, exploratory territory.

"It wasn't important that I end up writing for the band," says D'Virgilio now, "and it's only important now because the stuff I've contributed is being accepted and enjoyed. I just threw stuff out there. From my vantage point I guess Greg wanted to give me the opportunity. Now I'm contributing even more, and it's very rewarding." The drummer also offered up the music for what would become that gentle intro piece *Novum Organum*, and *Theodora In Green And Gold*. He sang the latter song's middle section himself, Longdon wrote the melody line and Spawton contributed lyrics inspired by the titular Eastern Roman empress, whom he had seen depicted in vivid mosaics in the Basilica of San Vitale in Ravenna, Italy.

Spawton's other 14-minute piece, *Voyager*, took the premise of travel, discovery and the quest for knowledge to its interstellar extreme. The song had started life back when he and Longdon were working on their *Hope* project, the

prog opus planned in a hot tub in Wales and shelved just prior to *Folklore*. NASA first billed the Voyager program as 'the Grand Tour of the Solar System', and Spawton's early drafts of the song went under the name *Grand Tour*, then *Merchants Of Light* (later used as the title of the Cadogan Hall recording). Now renamed and completely revamped, *Voyager* emerged as one of the most replete and defining progressive pieces performed by the band to this point. Emotive and grandiose, it included some truly dazzling interplay between the musicians, notably a synth/guitar duel between Danny Manners and Dave Gregory, both on blistering form.

"In the early days," says Gregory, "I'd get sent a new piece of music and Greg or David would say, 'We want some guitar here, a solo here,' whatever it may be. In recent years it was more, 'Just send us some stuff and we'll pick and choose what we want.' *Grand Tour* started the same way, but there were more people involved – Danny, Rachel, Rikard. Nick was writing songs, everyone was pitching in. So my role kind of got watered down a little bit. I was second-guessing what everyone else was doing. Especially with our way of working remotely. With *Voyager*, I didn't even care if they used it or not, but I just really wanted to play over those chords and in that time signature. So I sat down, and I wasn't thinking how to reproduce it on stage – it was an opportunity to be flash! So that's what I did. They liked it, and I'm proud of it, it's exciting."

Like *East Coast Racer* and *Brooklands* before it, *Voyager* dealt with the relationship between mankind and machine, and was in keeping with the writer's enduring, romantic fascination with the vestiges of humanity's incursions into the environment – those long exhausted mines, those ancient settlements, and now, probes lost to the depths of space.

The strings for the song were recorded at Abbey Road, the most famous, and most expensive, recording studio in the world. The opportunity arose through American producer Mark Hornsby, a good friend and colleague of Nick D'Virgilio's at Sweetwater, and subsequently a friend of the band. Hornsby had put together sessions with an elite, 17-piece string orchestra for another project, and he told Big Big Train that if they had any material for the orchestra to record then they were welcome to participate.

Spawton's strings were arranged by Danny Manners and Rachel Hall, with arranger John Hinchey converting them to scores for the musicians. (If you look closely at their charts in photographs, you'll see the song is still entitled *Grand Tour*.)

Rachel in the control room, Studio Two, Abbey Road.

The orchestra was recorded in Studio Two, best known as The Beatles' room, and conducted by Rick Wentworth. A 'real character' according to Spawton, Wentworth had composed the score for cult British movie *Withnail & I*, and had worked with Roger Waters on his 2002 opera *Ça Ira* and his 2014 film of *The Wall*.

During the sessions, new string parts were also recorded for *East Coast Racer* and *Brooklands*. Along with *Voyager*, these re-orchestrated songs are – at time of writing – due to emerge on a release called *Ingenious Devices* in 2022 or 2023. "When you're a rock musician who can't really read music," says

Recording strings at Abbey Road, conducted by Rick Wentworth.

Rick Wentworth and Danny Manners at Abbey Road.

Spawton, "you need an interlocutor in that situation between yourself and the orchestral musicians. John and Mark were a godsend, they really helped in communicating with the orchestra. Hearing something you first knocked up with some samples suddenly played in a great-sounding room by a top-end string section – that's another one of those 'pinch me' moments."

Grand Tour was guided safely back to earth with the majestic, brass-laden coda *Homesong*, returning the listener to the real world with the comforting sound of birdsong. "We didn't want a radical change of direction musically," says Spawton. "We wanted a change of scenery, and although there are a couple of curve balls from what we'd done before, *Grand Tour* did build on the current infrastructure of the sound of the band."

Although he later thought it could have used some more pacy numbers, as *Grand Tour* came together early in 2019 Spawton considered it a collection of the band's best songs, and had high hopes for it. "The core test of material for us has always been that 'tingle factor' – it's the whole

purpose of what we do. You've got to find the combination of chords, melodies and words that deliver the moments that only music can, where people go 'Wow!' or have an emotional connection. I think there are several of those on that album."

"Greg and David do so much research," offers Sjöblom. "It's one of the things I've always liked about their writing, on *Grand Tour* but also back to songs like [*English Electric Part One*'s] *Summoned By Bells*, which gives me goosebumps. Speaking as a songwriter myself, I always tend to go towards how I perceive the world, and my feelings, these inner journeys. So I'm jealous of the way they can take a subject and use it for a song."

But despite Rachel Hall's high-impact string contributions to the record, she was beginning to struggle. "There were nuggets of things within the songs I managed to put myself into," she says now, "and listening to it, there's a lot on there. I did it, almost, in a state of not really being there.

Equus rides again: Gregory with his old bandmates Phil, Simon and Richard, who sat in on the Abbey Road recording session for Grand Tour.

"I was at a time in my life when I was working flat out to keep my teaching business going in a remote part of the country, in conjunction with the band. Recording deadlines were tight, and the writers knew what they wanted from me and what role I would play. As my parts were on acoustic instruments, they were required to be played in a studio environment, booked specifically for that purpose in a small window of time. It was the same for the brass and for David's vocals, but others were able to record more in chunks at home when they felt like it. When you've had intense connections with your instrument and music, one of the things that's most troubling is when you can't feel anything anymore, and this album was the start of a sense of loss, at what perhaps had begun to feel like a production line of parts for albums. But nevertheless I was there doing what I'd always done.

"After the sessions I'd always collect what was recorded from Rob on the hard drive, and spend time selecting the parts to send back to him for final mix. Detail was everything in this band. Parts had gradually become more exposed within the mix than certainly they were when I started the journey with them, and Rob knew what I was looking for within the performances."

NDV and Danny (with Kathy Spawton and Tiffany D'Virgilio) in the Abbey Road canteen, April 2019.

When it finally emerged on 17th May that year, Big Big Train became a Top 40 band. *Grand Tour* landed at number 35 in the UK Albums Chart, and was only beaten to the top slot of the Rock chart by the new, self-titled album from German metal gods Rammstein.

And *Grand Tour* was an album to behold. Sarah Ewing's impressive hand-painted cover depicted Apollo (the Greek/Roman god of, among many other things, music). Ewing envisaged the album's sumptuous accompanying booklet as a journal of someone who had undertaken the Grand Tour itself, and crafted it using only techniques and pigments that existed during the mid-19th century. The band's ever-dependable vinyl agent, Plane Groovy's Chris Topham, was reluctant to include the album's ambitious, complicated, and expensive booklet with the vinyl edition, but economies of scale meant that, ultimately, each unit could be produced affordably. Topham ordered a run of 1,500 units – 1,000 on black vinyl, 500 on cream – and they sold out quickly. As the band's vision had grown, so their artwork and media had grown with them.

Online and in print, the reception to *Grand Tour* was warm. In his five star review for *The Express*, writer Paul Davies judged it to be a 'magnificent opus', noting the parallels between the Renaissance period addressed and the rebirth of progressive rock itself, at which Big Big Train was near the vanguard. While putting just three stars their way, *The Times*' John Bungey still referred to the band as among the most convincing of the modern prog crop, saying the album was 'as ambitious and intricate as anything they have attempted'. In his two-page review for *Prog*, veteran writer Mike Barnes called it an 'extraordinary album', praising its scope, the performances, and the lyricists' storytelling power.

Behind the scenes at the Grand Tour *photo shoot.*

At the following September's Progressive Music Awards, *Grand Tour* would be voted Album Of The Year, winning out against stiff competition from nine other releases from artists including Steve Hackett, Haken, Dream Theater and Gong.

The plaudits across the prog rock press, online and in print, were plentiful that year. For online music magazine thefirenote.com, knowledgeable writer Scot Lade made a compelling list of 2019's most impressive, progressively inclined albums, His rundown gave ample proof of how healthy the scene was. Among better known names – IQ, Opeth, Focus, The Flower Kings, Banco Del Mutuo Soccorso – were Ukrainian act Karfagen, Norway's Jordsjø and Spock's Beard offshoot Pattern-Seeking Animals. *Grand Tour* topped Lade's list and, referencing the album's many cultural influences, he pinpointed just why it worked so well as a piece: 'Big Big Train have expanded their sound in accordance with their larger world view. This is the record they've been working towards. This is the record where Big Big Train have finally come into their own and sound like no one else – except themselves.'

The high-minded, US-based cultural site popmatters. com maintained that 'no-one does this sort of sound better'. *Classic Rock* included *Grand Tour* in its list of the year's best albums, and although Opeth's brilliant *In Cauda Venenum* was named Album Of the Year in *Prog*'s Critics' Choice and Readers' Poll, the magazine's readers voted Big Big Train the Band Of 2019. They also named David Longdon Best Male Vocalist, with Gregory Spawton, Danny Manners and Nick D'Virgilio all featuring in the Top 10 lists for their respective instrumental categories.

◆◆◆

The winner of the 'Unsung Hero' category in *Prog*'s Readers' Poll that year was none other than Nellie Pitts. She had proved her tour management mettle in 'herding cats' by getting the entire Big Big Train team to Loreley. "That was my baptism of fire as their tour manager," she says. "Loreley was really nice, there were loads of people there and the band went down very well. It was a pivotal point for them, I think. In Greg's mind it proved that they could play live outside of London – I'd pestered him about that too, told him that if you just keep on playing London shows you're going to upset fans elsewhere. Now he could maybe see it was feasible to take BBT as a whole and put it in other places."

So when it came to organising the next set of UK shows in support of *Grand Tour*, the band didn't hesitate to recruit Pitts. After the stress that single-venue live shows had exerted on him, Spawton was grateful to delegate a multiple-venue, six-date tour elsewhere. "And Nellie worked really hard," he says. "She did all the booking, and it's such a bloody difficult thing, routing the shows, working out the capacity of the venues, the percentage each venue takes of the merch sales – there's so many things to consider."

Robin Armstrong was once more enlisted to play keyboards/guitars with the band, and Big Big Train undertook a week of rehearsals at Real World. Dave Gregory remembers that they also had to work very hard on the set from home. "For about two months I was in my room, rehearsing with the music charts. Real World was always such a luxurious place to rehearse, it was lovely to have five days there. It all came together remarkably quickly."

They worked on a set comprising five songs from *Grand Tour*. The evening would open with the rousing *Alive*. *Theodora In Green And Gold*, *Homesong*, and *The Florentine* were present, the latter giving D'Virgilio a welcome opportunity to come down from his drum riser and join Longdon centre stage. *Voyager* would be given a cosmic sweep by an evocative film from the band's new visual artist Christian Rios (a D'Virgilio find), who had also worked with prog supergroup Transatlantic. Also in the set would be Rachel Hall's showpiece *Hedgerow* (with Hall's vocal contribution notably enhanced), *Folklore*'s avian epic *Winkie*, *Grimspound* showstopper *Brave Captain*, and the must-haves – singalong pre-encore tune *Wassail* and, to close, *East Coast Racer*.

"*East Coast Racer* was always the very last song in the set," Dave Gregory remembers, and as he describes this particular moment, he lovingly re-enacts every movement contained within it. "At the climax I'd play the chord while running all three of my fuzz pedals and my treble booster, then I'd tilt gently towards the amp, and this big swell of feedback slowly arrived. David would put his hand up, we'd all stop, and everything just vanished. It was my favourite moment of the show."

The talented English folk/prog outfit Sweet Billy Pilgrim were the support act for the Grand Tour, which opened on 26th October with Big Big Train's very first show in Scotland. The Queen's Hall in Edinburgh is a converted church with a large balcony sweeping around the 900-capacity room, and when he first set foot into the impressive space, alarm bells went off in Spawton's mind – it reminded him of Cadogan Hall. And indeed, there were some sound problems during set up, but Rob Aubrey, Dave Taylor and the team knew what to do, and the sound worked well. According to the review for theprogreport.com, Edinburgh was 'a superb show [...] an evening of amazing music'.

Given that this was their first official tour, tickets sold well. The group traversed the country, taking in Newcastle's City Hall, the Victoria Theatre in Halifax, The Riverfront in Newport (the band's first incursion into Wales) and Birmingham Town Hall. "It was our first time on the road travelling together," D'Virgilio recalls, fondly. "Me, David, Sarah [Ewing] and Tiffany piled into a little sedan and we drove hundreds of miles up and down the country, it was like a real band thing. There was camaraderie, a little drama, money was being spent, some people got a little uptight. But that's the type of shit that's supposed to happen! When we showed up to this beautiful theatre in Birmingham, Greg's home town, he was on cloud nine. It was a sold-out crowd, the band gelled, and he was so happy."

"From my point of view," says Spawton, "I'd gone from the YMCA in Sutton Coldfield to Birmingham Town Hall – quite the journey. It was full of my mum, family, schoolmates and bandmates – Equus were all there, and we nailed it. It was so exciting."

Dave Gregory had always loved Newcastle City Hall. He'd played there before, twice with XTC and once with singer/songwriter Aimee Mann. "There were so many live albums recorded there," he says. "I've got an amazing

The Queen's Hall, Edinburgh, 26th October 2019.

Soundcheck at Newcastle City Hall, 27th October 2019.

Birmingham Town Hall, 30th October 2019.

recording of the Small Faces there, in '68. I think it's the Geordie audiences – they either love you or hate you, and if they love you they just carry you away. They're phenomenal."

"At the Edinburgh show," David Longdon recalls, "in that beautiful little church, people were pleased to see us. It was brilliant to be playing in Scotland. And then in Newport, people were so pleased we'd come to play Wales. But why wouldn't we? Of *course* we'd play Wales. I remember it got a bit scary at Halifax, when I came out after the show and people were queueing to see me. There was a tap on my shoulder and somebody told me, 'You need to go, *now*.' I wasn't sure what was going on, I think it was getting ugly with the bouncers, who were making people leave. So I had to spin on my heels and go.

"All the shows were different. The audiences

were different in the way they interacted, and that's great – those variations make it interesting. Usually with prog, it's complicated music. I remember Alex Lifeson said when Rush go on tour he would rehearse until he could more or less play the songs and read a newspaper at the same time. We rehearsed a lot before. Three months before shows I'll start singing through the set, gradually getting into it, the stamina of it, the recovery. The body gets used to the routine of gigs. At about 4pm it starts making you really tired, you start shutting down, and you think, 'I'll never get

on stage, I'm exhausted!' The body works out that, come 8 o'clock, it's going to have to give you a massive rush of adrenaline, so it starts to save its energy for that, and by the time you're on stage, the adrenaline's there again. My voice held up, but you never know. I loved that tour."

Danny Manners also enjoyed the sense of the band being on a full tour: "Six gigs in a row was luxury for us. I got better, and the band did. That was the tour that I felt, 'Yes, I've got this down now.' When I made a mistake I shrugged it off, and I went in with a better frame of mind

Birmingham Town Hall, 30ᵗʰ October 2019.

236

– I was more confident. Hackney was the best one for me. That was the best I'd played with the band. Again, we relaxed into it – it was a very relaxed experience."

Captured on the subsequent concert film and live album *Empire*, that triumphant, sold-out show at the 1,275-capacity Hackney Empire in east London was the last night of the run. Steven Wilson dropped in to the soundcheck to wish them well, and an old hero of the band, Genesis's Anthony Phillips, was in attendance for the show, which D'Virgilio also remembers as a real highlight. "By

the time we got there the band had gelled and we were on fire. We could have easily kept going. Meeting the Passengers at Hackney and on the whole tour – it was just fantastic."

"I always liked talking to the fans," says Rachel Hall. "You remember certain faces, and it gives you some sense of being part of something, beyond it being an experience from your own perspective. It's always nice to see happy people. If they had been rude it would have been different, but most people were very respectful and pleased to be

Danny Manners and NDV, Hackney Empire, London, 2ⁿᵈ November 2019.

237

there. I've always enjoyed being sociable where I can, since I've spent many days at the computer working with audio files. The event of people coming together for the same reason is kind of a beautiful product in itself."

"A lot of the Passengers did tend to get a bit starry eyed over Rachel," says Dave Desmond with a smile, "and over Dave Gregory too. But not with us sadly – most of them walked straight past the brass guys, and that's fine! But the whole tour was

Rikard, Birmingham Town Hall, 30th October 2019.

great. Newport was smaller and had a good atmosphere. Edinburgh was really tricky acoustically. Halifax was great because it felt like brass band territory – there's a history of brass bands there and we'd all played there before with army bands."

Throughout the tour Desmond, Paul Hawkins, Nick Stones, John Storey and Jon Truscott – resplendent in their customary flat caps and waistcoats – again had their moment in the spotlight during the 'drum and brass' solo section with D'Virgilio near the end of the set. It was an amusing bit of shtick that – along with David Longdon's twinkle-eyed dramatics and the hirsute, smiling, head-banging Rikard Sjöblom – offered a wryly fun, warmly human astringent to the arch, highbrow musical moments

freighting the *Grand Tour* album itself.

"I remember the long hauls in a minivan with most of the band," Sjöblom says, "and the nice camaraderie between us all. You could hang out with anyone in the band and have a good time, and it's not always like that. I had a great time, staying in a lot of funny places. There was one hotel, we arrived very late and the bar was closed, but they quickly opened it for me and a couple of the brass guys who wanted a late-night beer."

As the tour reinforced some friendships within the band, and their strength as a live act, it also served to affirm the strong relationship between BBT and their hardcore fans. The Passengers phenomenon had become well known in the prog community, so much so that filmmaker Philip

BBT, The Riverfront, Newport, 1ˢᵗ November 2019.

than the band needed, but with their first choice venue – The Sage in Gateshead – already booked up, it was the only remotely suitable place available in the area at the time. The band ended up playing to a quarter-full room, but City Hall's hire charge had been predicated on the maximum potential audience size. The discrepancy between the two figures – and other expenses such as the substantial filming licence fee at the Hackney Empire – put a deep dent in the band's finances.

Also, there were 13 musicians in the band, and their tech team and retinue pushed the core team to over double that figure – 28 people had to be moved and accommodated across the country. Add to that the transportation of gear, the hiring of projectors, the Hackney camera crew – any Big Big Train tour was going to be costly. "The tour was very expensive," concedes David Longdon. "It's a big endeavour for a band of our size, and it could've bankrupted us easily. But it was a great thing to do. It was good to take the music out and play. It's not all about

Briddon contacted the band to request that he and a small crew fly over from Australia at their own expense to document the tour. Released in August 2021, the resulting film – *The Journey Of The Passengers* – features footage of the shows plus interviews with many of the fans who flocked to the tour from across the world, each gladly explaining what makes them so invested in Big Big Train.

But despite this documentary, largely healthy attendances and strong merch sales, the *Grand Tour* tour still wound up losing a great deal of money. The 2,000-capacity Newcastle City Hall was much larger

Rachel Hall, Hackney Empire, London, 2ⁿᵈ November 2019.

'Sate our urge to see the world, to make us feel alive, so alive...'

BBT on the 2019 tour.

the money – it's about having life experiences, about doing stuff, it's about the adventure. It goes back to having to speculate to accumulate, and we got a great deal of goodwill out of it. We're trying to grow the band, and we know that the way to do that is to play more shows."

With that in mind, even before that tour, plans were in progress to make 2020 Big Big Train's most ambitious and exciting year yet. It was time to take the band across the waters to the USA. Since its maiden run in 2004, The Rites Of Spring Festival – better known as RoSFest – had built a reputation as one of the most prestigious progressive rock festivals in the States. Spawton had a longstanding gentleman's agreement with its founder, George Roldan: if Big Big Train ever played North America, then their debut show would be at RoSFest.

And the band were good to their word. Their headline appearance at the festival was scheduled for 9th May 2020, at Sarasota Opera House in Sarasota, Florida. Other shows were lined up in Canada (Toronto, Montreal, Quebec City), New England and New Jersey, with this North American jaunt closing with a show in D'Virgilio's base of Fort Wayne, Indiana, in Sweetwater's state of the art Performance Pavilion.

Then, into July, Big Big Train were set to return to the UK to play the historic music club, Friars. Now based at the 1,200-capacity Waterside Theatre in Aylesbury, Buckinghamshire, the club (and its famous promoter David Stopps) played a crucial part in the early careers of David Bowie, Genesis, Queen and a plethora of other major British rock acts. Symbolically, this show would be a big deal for Big Big Train, with Spawton and Longdon particularly excited about the prospect.

The band were also booked for another festival, the Ramblin' Man Fair in Maidstone, where they would headline the prog stage. Even if only a small section of the projected 15,000 attendees were open to the genre, they would still be playing to thousands of potential new fans. And they were slated to cross the Channel again, with major shows in Holland and Germany, prior to their trip concluding – like the old Grand Tour itself – in Italy.

But, of course, none of this came to pass. No sooner had it begun, 2020 came to a shuddering halt, and the entire world with it. All plans – for Big Big Train and for everybody else – were derailed. And, in so many ways, things would never be quite the same again.

Robin Armstrong at Hackney Empire, 2nd November 2019. This was his last show with Big Big Train.

XIX

'None of the old rules apply, we're into the not knowing...'

"Big Big Train are very sorry to announce the postponement of the band's shows in the United States and Canada in May due to the coronavirus and following the cancellation of RoSFest. [...] The band's UK and European shows scheduled for July are currently still scheduled."

Official statement on bigbigtrain.com, April 2020

"We have of course continued to monitor events regarding coronavirus. With the restrictions that have been entirely understandably imposed by European governments, in conjunction with the promoters of our six shows in July we have bowed to the inevitable and been forced to cancel these concerts."

Official statement on bigbigtrain.com, May 2020

As THE SHEER SCALE AND GRAVITY of the COVID-19 pandemic became clear, governments across the world grappled with rising infection rates and fatalities. In the effort to curb the virus's spread, country after country locked down, and the lives and liberties we all took for granted slid into the recent past. One of the many casualties was the live music scene, which collapsed almost overnight. Given the human and economic costs of the outbreak, the consequences for Big Big Train were not tragic, nor were they uncommon. Nonetheless, the band's touring plans were drawn reluctantly into the sidings, with their North American dates cancelled and then, inevitably, the UK and European shows too. And there were more shocks to come that year.

Straight after the Grand Tour, Robin Armstrong had made the decision that he could no longer commit to playing live with the band. "The preparation and rehearsal required to play at this level is insane," he told his followers on Twitter, "and there just isn't enough time going forward to fulfil all the requirements for BBT whilst forwarding my own music ambitions with Cosmograf. I'd love to be able to do it all but I have to earn a living too as well as indulging my passion in music. So, sadly the show at the Hackney Empire was the last time I'll play for Big Big Train."

As valuable a contribution as Armstrong had made to the recent live shows, his amicable departure was about to pale into relative insignificance. The Loreley show was a career highlight for Dave Gregory, but there were a few issues weighing on his mind. Over the past few years he had quietly come to feel that, as the band had expanded, his role had contracted. "My guitar did help to shape the sound of the band," he says, "up until at least the tail end of *Grimspound*. That's when I started to feel my stuff was getting a little bit watered down.

"Our way of working meant that, for example, Dave Desmond would've done a brilliant piece of brass arrangement where you had decided it was a guitar track, so your guitar would either be rejected or buried under all this of brass. Greg came to favour the brass because it became integral to the sound, and fair enough – Desmond is brilliant and all the brass players are absolutely top notch. I defer to that decision. But my incentive throughout the *Grand Tour* album was diminishing."

Still, the guitarist enjoyed the Grand Tour itself, despite the modest confines of the minibus the band travelled in. "I didn't mind because there was a hotel at the end of the day, you could get out and freshen up. Because it was a short tour, it was bearable. And the fans made up for anything – the reception you got, even at the more sparsely attended concerts, the fans were super appreciative."

The tight budget for the planned North American tour meant that there would not be the money to accommodate the entire band and crew in hotels every night. Instead, everybody would be split across two high-end Nightliner tour buses as they travelled through the US and Canada for the two weeks of the trip. This was a red line for Gregory. He was 67, and in a storied career he'd already had experience of those seemingly endless routes between the states. "Nightliners are the best way to see America," he says. "I've done overnighters on them – occasionally you're expected to, because of the distances. But after one night everybody can't get off the thing fast enough. You want to have a shower, freshen up, and don't forget you're expected to put on a demanding, two-hour show at the end of that day. The reality is different from the dream – never underestimate the value of peace and quiet on tour. If you want me to work for you, the very first thing you have to provide me with is a bed for the night. It's not like I walked out in a huff. I didn't *want* to go."

Dave Gregory dug his heels in. He could not tour with the current plan in place, but that plan was the only way to make the North American dates remotely financially viable. There was a failure to agree between what could now, regrettably, be called the two sides. So, after 11 years of playing with the band, the time had come for Dave

Dave Gregory.

Gregory to leave Big Big Train.

"This has not been an easy decision for me," he said in his press statement in March 2020, "but after careful consideration I have concluded that I would prefer not to tour internationally with Big Big Train. […] I am proud of the role I have played within Big Big Train and have enjoyed the last decade with the band immensely. I look forward to remaining associated with Big Big Train in the future."

"Dave wasn't being a prima donna," says Gregory Spawton now. "The guy's got diabetes and he's a certain age, and in effect he was saying he needed a hotel room every night, and we just couldn't afford it. The tour bus would have been for three nights or so at a time, punctuated by a hotel on our days off. I haven't toured that way, but I'm not unaware of the unpleasant aspects of it – if you've got 15 blokes on a bus and light a match, it's going to go up! It's not something I was particularly looking forward to myself, but that was the only way to make the trip stack up. I love Dave, I love his talent, and he's also an incredibly stubborn guy – you don't persuade him about anything. Instinctively I suppose I always thought there'd be an end of the road with Dave. To be honest we got further with him than I thought we would, and I'm so glad that we did – he made a huge impact on Big Big Train."

Speaking about it almost a year on, in April 2021, Dave Gregory pores over a list of the songs to which he contributed his top notch virtuosity. It runs to over 70 titles. "All these 'bonus' tracks," he notes, with some marvel, "*Seen Better Days*, *Lost Rivers Of London* and *Mudlarks* – it's magical music. God bless Greg and David – they were always writing, always pushing ahead. It's great quality stuff, some of the most gorgeous things ever written – why

aren't they better known? I can't cast aspersions. Greg's a brilliant artist, and David too – his artistry, as well as his brilliant voice, has come on leaps and bounds. There's nothing I regret working on."

In these strangest times, Rachel Hall also reassessed her priorities. Outside of the band she had a portfolio of other jobs, including as a violin teacher. But there were only so many hours in the day. The band was a time-consuming yet ultimately part-time entity, and she realised that she too had given all she could, and had come to the end of her tenure. "It's been over eight years since I started recording for Big Big Train," she wrote in her leaving statement that October. "How time flies when you are making music! After much consideration, I am no longer able to offer my commitment to the band and will be embarking on a completely new journey of my own. Much heartfelt thanks to the Passengers for your kindness and support. I wish my fellow band mates good luck and future success."

She also left a video message on the band's Facebook page, warmly thanking the Passengers for the many kind messages she had received on the news of her departure, and raising a glass to them, and to music. In a blighted year, the UK was just one nation waking up to the courage, compassion and expertise exhibited on a daily basis by its health workers, across the NHS and beyond. Hall revealed that she had been working in a care home since leaving the band, and was planning to continue a career in the healthcare sector.

Speaking in April 2021, Hall remembers some 'really lovely gigs' on the Grand Tour, but by the Hackney Empire show she was struggling. She was suffering from insomnia, and her anxiety was being exacerbated by technical problems with her electric violin and in-ear monitors.

"When I see the film of Hackney, if I look at it as a product of the band, I'm proud to have been a part of it, and it sounds fantastic. I guess it would have been nice to have played another gig had the pandemic not happened, but I was ready for a break and to move to the next part of my life.

"I've always known that, working with such talented writers and musicians, the collective work was something

Rachel Hall.

special. I think in time I'll be able to look back to that part of my life and see what was achieved, and be happy that it's been well documented by what we've produced together. If I ever have children or grandchildren, at least I have a good-quality recording to show them!"

Although not made public until October, Hall actually resigned in March, but graciously agreed to hold off from making any announcement until the remaining members could soften the blow of this sad news with something more positive for the fans. And then, when Danny Manners handed in his notice in July, he also agreed to keep it private until an amenable moment for the band.

This third blow, Manners says now, had been coming for a while. "I'd been thinking about it in 2019. I'd been thinking that I really must get some solo projects going. Dave and Rachel's departures made a difference – I was very sad to see both of them go. When Rachel left, Greg did say to the rest of the band, 'Okay, is everybody else committed?' And I did um and ah about it. I said I was considering it, but was committed. But at the back of my mind I knew I couldn't do my own projects and be in the band, and there's my IT career too.

"Big Big Train's a big time commitment. The keyboard parts are complicated – it's fairly dense, detailed music. Partly I feel I ought to be quicker at doing it all, but I need time to improve my own skills, and realistically my own projects won't happen if I were to stay in Big Big Train. The shows had been cancelled by then, which meant I wasn't leaving them in the lurch – I would have done the gigs. Covid itself wasn't the reason for leaving, but it does heighten the sense of *carpe diem* – better get on with things. I haven't had any second thoughts since. It's been perfectly amicable. When I Facetimed Greg his reaction was, 'Fuck!' David was gobsmacked and disappointed, but he was lovely about it. We go back a long way. It must've been a blow after Rachel and Dave. The last eight years had been great – I would never have thought I'd have been in a prog band."

"Losing Dave was a big thing for Danny," says David Longdon. "As a friend and musician I'll miss Dan being in the band, but we're adults and I'm still friends with him and Dave. I knew them before. I love Danny dearly, he's a very bright man, a deep thinker, and an incredible musician, but he doesn't get things *done*. I would be very surprised if there was a Danny Manners solo album, because he'll just talk himself out of it. There comes a point where you have to commit to an idea. I've learned that. It's not arrogance. 'But could this song be better?' 'No! The song is done, and it goes like *this...*'

"I met Rachel through BBT, and I remain friends with her. The touring life for her had been quite hard. The upheaval didn't seem to go well with her. I remember saying to her on the tour, just rhetorically, 'Are you sure this is good for you? Is this the right thing for you to be doing?' She's become a nurse, rather than a peripatetic music teacher, and I hope it brings her peace of mind."

Rachel also remains close friends with Rikard Sjöblom.

"I didn't know that she and Danny were leaving," he says. "I've tried to think back to see if I did know – or even about Dave – but no, I didn't. Covid shifted people's view on what was important in life as well, I think. Dave, Danny and Rachel are fantastic musicians and great people as well. I will miss them being in the band."

"It'll be strange without Danny and Rach," reckons Nick D'Virgilio. "Danny's fantastic – a great ear, tons of chops, those will be missed. Rachel has a nice aura about her onstage. There were some nights on

Old friends – Danny Manners and David Longdon.

tour when she clearly wasn't as comfortable as on others, but when she's really comfortable and really on it, she's *killer*. In Loreley, she was seriously great. She has a mellow demeanour, but gives this edge to the performance. Rachel was cool, a really beautiful person."

The Hackney concert film, *Empire,* was released on Blu-ray in November 2020. In their four star review, *Mojo* – a well-respected British music magazine one step removed from the progressive rock press – hailed Big Big Train as 'the standard bearers of new UK prog'. By this point *Empire* was no longer just an HD memento of Big Big Train's first UK tour – it had gained a fresh, valedictory context. Now it was partly a tantalising throwback to the halcyon year before coronavirus restrictions annihilated the live music sector.

Mainly though, it was a bittersweet celebration of Big Big Train's first 'classic' line-up. *Prog* magazine's review of *Empire* summed up this sentiment: 'There's a tinge of nostalgia then, even sadness, in seeing this chapter in the band's history come to a close. The next is yet to be written, but let *Empire* show that by 2019 Big Big Train could hold their own with the very best of them.'

As well as the trauma of these personnel setbacks, there were some nasty, lingering accounting problems that needed to be dealt with once and for all. Settling these, along with the expense of the Grand Tour and the collapse of the North American/European shows, meant that finances were now looking precariously thin. What an emotional see-saw this was: the career highs of the band's *Grand Tour* cycle; now soul-crushing lows in the dumpster fire that was 2020.

By April, Gregory Spawton was disenchanted, running on vapours: "I'd already had a conversation with Danny when he was first thinking about quitting, and it seemed he'd come back on board, so the second time it came completely out of the blue. And because everything else was falling apart – the financial stuff, the tours cancelled, the members leaving – it was beginning to feel that this was it, that we were over."

On top of all this, David Longdon was now caring for his elderly mother Vera, who was suffering from vascular dementia, at home in Nottingham. And he had another gut punch to withstand. Over the past few years he had poured heart and soul into Dyble Longdon, his collaboration with Judy Dyble. The two worked closely together, her focusing on lyrics and vocals, him rendering her words into a rich musical tableau that drew on folk, prog and art pop.

With his own production smarts and multi-instrumental skills at the heart of the project, Longdon also brought in some select guest artists – Gong's bassist Dave Sturt, Isildurs Bane trumpeter Luca Calabrese, and each and every one of his Big Big Train bandmates. The record positively vibrated with twanging guitars from Dave Gregory, beautiful strings from Rachel Hall, and Danny Manners' plangent pianos. Rikard Sjöblom even flavoured the record's 11-minute centrepiece *France* with accordion – the first instrument he'd learned as a child.

Dyble had long suffered from emphysema and – at her insistence – the pair had raced to get her vocal performance captured for the record while she was still capable. After Big Big Train's Hackney Empire show that November, she confided in Longdon that she had been diagnosed with lung cancer, and, on 12th July 2020, she succumbed to the disease. Sadly, she would not get to see the many plaudits the Dyble Longdon album *Between A Breath And A Breath* would receive.

On its release in September 2020, *Mojo* leapt on the album, awarding it four stars and calling it a 'wonderful swansong from Fairport Convention's original vocalist'. The record landed at number four in the newly launched UK Folk chart, and received airplay by DJ Mark Radcliffe on his folk show for BBC Radio 2. But after the project was completed, as the vinyl run quickly sold out and the good notices poured in, Longdon felt nothing but numb, still shell shocked by the loss of his friend.

He had last seen her at the hospice, the day before she died. Later, at her funeral, he gave the eulogy, speaking affectionately about the funny, bright woman he had come to know well since their first meeting at Kings Place, five years before. "We'd become so close," he said later, "really good mates. She was a very wise person. I'm really proud of the album we made."

The ructions in the Big Big Train camp had also given him real pause for thought. "I can't lie – I thought about leaving Big Big Train, about knocking it on the head. When the other guys were leaving I thought, 'Should I? Do I still really want to do this?' And the answer was, 'Yes, I *do* still want to do this.' Greg said, 'Are you still into it?' Yes, I am. We need to move on. There are bands that get things done. We forcefully make things happen. Necessity is the mother of invention, it's not a bad thing. We come across as being studious, but there's a brutal element of energy to us too. We throw ourselves into the process, and something always seems to come. Now it would be the four of us – Greg, Nick, Rikard and me. The doors were off. And I liked that."

Spawton himself had also come close to calling it a day. He recalls that his wife Kathy – ever his staunch ally and the voice of reason – put a great question to him. "She asked me, 'What else are you going to do? This is what you've done for 30 years!' We had invested so much in this and it felt like, just as we were really getting somewhere, we'd derailed. I was hitting my head against a brick wall, and really needed a holiday. Kathy and I took two weeks in Naples and I totally cleared my head, of the band, of everything. By the time we got back I thought, 'Okay, let's get on with it.' And David was really good. When the chips are down he's a really good mate, one of those people you can rely on."

Throughout this turbulent time, from their homes in Nottingham and Bournemouth, via phone, email and Facetime, Spawton and Longdon had each other's backs. They kept communicating, kept propping each other up, and kept planning all the possibilities for a band now boiled down to its essence as a quartet. As for the other two players involved, Big Big Train's onward journey had never been in doubt.

"This is the best band I've been in," says Nick D'Virgilio, "in the way it's run, the people and the songs. When I got the email from Rachel to say she was going I replied: 'Is anybody else leaving the band?!' David and Greg wrote back: 'No, we're still going dude!' We're really just getting started. We're all a bit older, we've been doing this a long time, and achieving success at our age is so cool. I want to ride this wave as long as we can. It's a big world out there, and there's a lot of people listening to progressive music. We're a prog band, we go for it, and we're all happy with that. It's a fun ride. I hope we keep going for a really long time."

The only solo album among D'Virgilio's raft of credits at the time was his 2001 release, *Karma*. Then, in June 2020, English Electric released the UK edition of the follow-up. *Invisible* placed the drummer front and centre as lead vocalist and songwriter, and featured contributions from some heavyweight talent from the world of prog (King Crimson bass legend Tony Levin; Dream Theater's keyboard wizard Jordan Rudess) and rock (Cheap Trick guitar great Rick Nielsen; Mr Big shredmeister Paul Gilbert).

Invisible was seen in the drum, rock and prog press where D'Virgilio is a familiar name, but the worldwide moratorium on live music prevented him from taking it on the road and fully connecting with his audience. "It was a strange year, not being able to play live," he says. "If you're not out there playing it's hard to keep people engaged, because there's a lot of music out there, a lot of noise, so it's hard to reach new people. But *Invisible* was well received and I'm thankful for that. It got me motivated with writing for Big Big Train. I started work on another one, and if I can keep that wave going in conjunction with BBT, I would be happy with that."

Somewhat stranded at home in Sweden, Rikard Sjöblom could relate to all this. As a solo artist and lead vocalist/guitarist/keyboardist for Beardfish and, now, his own prog trio Gungfly, he was well versed in keeping numerous musical plates spinning at once. Gungfly's album *Alone Together* appeared in September 2020 but, with venues closed and the aviation industry all but grounded, they were unable to support the release with live shows. When it came to Big Big Train that year, despite the unexpected shift from septet to quartet, Sjöblom was keen to proceed.

"I was very much on board," he says, with a shrug emphasising what a no-brainer the decision was. "I never thought they were going to bring it to a halt – of course we were going forward. Though I didn't know in what way. A band is a combination of the people in it, and when you take someone out, it changes stuff. It's gonna be different, but it'll still be great. We talked early on and they asked me if I'd be willing to record guitars and keyboards. Of course I was – I do that all the time with Gungfly, it's something I've always done, so it's not a strange habitat for me. If I record guitar for a track I will get ideas for the keyboard too. They kind of work hand in hand for me."

And two other vital factors came together to fuel the renewed Dunkirk spirit within the band. After 30 years, Big Big Train finally had their first manager. A lifelong prog rock aficionado, fanzine writer and subsequently a sometime contributor to *Classic Rock* and *Prog* magazines, Nick Shilton had been at the band's Astoria gig, a lifetime ago now, in 1996. He had followed the band with interest since, watching them evolve from shaky beginnings into the kind of outfit capable of producing *The Underfall Yard*. He was utterly won over by *English Electric*, and when the band played Kings Place he bought a seat in the front row, flying into London from a family holiday in the South of France for that one night, returning to his (tolerant) wife and children the first thing next morning.

A qualified solicitor and company director, Shilton had invaluable experience as a finance lawyer, hard skills in matters such as contracts and negotiation, along with a good sense of the typical challenges facing a prog rock band in the 21st century. He knew he could make a difference. At a meeting a while after Kings Place he told Spawton and Andy Poole that if he could ever be of any help at all with business advice, they should let him know.

In 2018 Shilton had sold his shares in the legal recruitment company he founded 15 years previously and was in a position to commit fully to a career in the music industry. He and Spawton incorporated Kingmaker Publishing, with the goal of producing books of interest to the progressive rock community in the future. A year later, Shilton formed Kingmaker Management, and Big Big Train were one of the first bands to sign up for his services. He began optimising the band's Heath Robinson-esque infrastructure, professionalising three decades' worth of DIY admin, goodwill agreements and 'back of a fag packet' contracts into something more streamlined.

Through Shilton, by summer 2020 Big Big Train had support from major booking agency United Talent (with David Gilmour and King Crimson among their other clients), and big-league entertainment promoters Kilimanjaro Live. As and when the live circuit was resurrected, the band would be ready to resume in earnest. Also, much to Spawton and Longdon's deep relief, Shilton ensured that those Damoclean accounting issues were finally resolved once and for all, with the band's finances placed on a much more solid footing.

That second boost for Big Big Train came directly from that group of people who had helped them before, who had shared their finest moments, who gave the whole damn thing its meaning. The Passengers. In January 2019 the band recruited Steve Cadman as their Website/Digital Manager, and he was tasked by the band and Shilton with creating a fan club on steroids – The Passengers Club. For an annual membership fee, Big Big Train's inner circle of listeners could have exclusive online access to otherwise unreleased film footage, music, photos and blogs, with fresh content served up every two weeks.

The website, thepassengersclub.com, was launched on 14th February 2020. Its first additions included early demos – of *Merchants Of Light* (that *Hope*-era progenitor of *Voyager*), an abandoned love song called *Capitoline Venus* and an early version of *Curator Of Butterflies*, all annotated by Gregory Spawton. Among the video footage was a report from David Longdon at Playpen Studios in Bristol, as he completed work on *Between A Breath And A Breath*. From The Big Room at Real World, Longdon, D'Virgilio, Sjöblom and Rachel Hall could be seen practising the vocal harmonies for *Theodora In Green And Gold* in the run-up to the Grand Tour. The band had been mindful to document their progress over the years, so there was plenty of material to mine.

The 'Bub' had bubbled back up in the healing relationship between Gregory Spawton and Andy Poole. Passengers Club members were treated to ancient, unearthed camcorder video of BBT circa 1990 – with Poole, Spawton and Ian Cooper playing an instrumental version of early composition *Jas* in the splendour of Poole's Bournemouth living room. There was even a blurry clip of Big Big Train ploughing through *The Shipping Forecast*, at that Astoria gig back in '96. Perhaps contrary to expectation, Steve Hughes' groove was solid and sober, but the performance proved just how far Big Big Train had come as a live band in the two intervening decades.

The Passengers Club became an immediate hit with the fans. The band members were amazed and heartened by the groundswell of support. "Without The Passengers Club it would definitely have been over," Spawton asserts. "It brought in a substantial amount of money, out of nowhere really. So while we were haemorrhaging cash on one side [due to the 2020 tour cancellations], we had this unexpected cash coming in on the other. But it wasn't that so much as the response. The uptake by the fans was such that it gave me a real shot in the arm. It reminded me why

I was doing this, who we were doing this for, or with. So there was a yin and a yang; there was good stuff happening alongside the bad."

The wheels were moving again in what was, on paper at least, Big Big Train's 30th year. In the teeth of some true adversity, Real World beckoned once more.

◆◆◆

As soon as it had sunk in that the tour wasn't happening and the band line-up had changed for good, Spawton did what he did during earlier bad times, even *Bard* times – he picked up his Takamine 12-string and wrote. "The Passengers' response helped me realise that there was a professional requirement for me not to wallow in it all, and to get my head down and write. David had invested a lot of time in Dyble Longdon and didn't have many songs ready, and Rikard had just done the Gungfly album, so I kind of knew the load would fall on me, which I actually kind of liked. It was like the old days. So I wrote, and once you're back in that process you remember why you want to do music. I found solace in the fact that there were some good tunes."

Dwelling on themes old and new, these contemplative songs took shape through home demos, and gained solid form in a week of recording sessions at Real World in November 2020. Spawton and Aubrey arrived on the Monday, with Longdon joining on the Wednesday. However, due to ongoing restrictions on global travel, Sjöblom and D'Virgilio were unable to fly into the UK. Instead, temporary mixes of the material produced over the week were sent to them, with Sjöblom working at his home studio in Sandviken, and D'Virgilio at Sweetwater.

A work of vaulting ambition, Spawton's sprawling prog rock piece *Atlantic Cable* was inspired by the first telegraph

Gregory Spawton and Rob Aubrey at Real World, 2020.

wires laid beneath that ocean in the 19th century. In the febrile 21st, nationalism, isolationism and a strain of anti-intellectualism had gained new traction in public discourse, but here was a celebration of the value of communication between peoples and countries, and the achievements of science and technology. Complete with some of the band's most intense and knotty instrumental passages to date, *Atlantic Cable* could also be seen as a reflection of the band's desire to reach the USA themselves. Hands across the water, indeed.

Dandelion Clock was a gentle, melancholic tune about time's passing, regrets and 'could have beens', while *Endnotes* was, a rare thing for its writer, an anthemic and highly personal love song inspired by his wife. Its last line reverberated with a phrase harking back to the beginning of Big Big Train's whole long journey: '*On the water the driftwood breaks free/On its way down the river to the sea.*' The brief, haunting piano instrumental *Headwaters* even took its title from the river's opposite end – its source. If the band was bouncing back, its recent existential troubles had certainly fed into Spawton's subconscious, and had him reflecting, taking stock.

When he delivered his first demo to his bandmates, the advantages of Big Big Train's new, slimline formation began to kick in immediately. "I sent out *Atlantic Cable*," he recalls. "I'd written the first few minutes as a piano piece, and Rikard said, 'Can I do it on organ?' He did, and what he came back with lifted it up a level. He put in some big organ bass notes I wasn't expecting, which made me throw out my own bass part and go somewhere else entirely with my bass pedals. For me it was a 'hairs on the back of the neck moment', at the sense of size, and that's all down to Rikard, his arrangement of my tune. It excited me."

After *Between A Breath And A Breath*, Longdon's song folder was all but bare. There were, however, two promising pieces remaining from the *Hope* days. One was called *Pagan Times*, a big, bright song written by Longdon about a community in Orkney years before 2020. "I was in a period of mourning, of grief for Judy," he says, "and I told Greg, 'I can't write.' He said, 'We have to have something from you on the album. *Pagan Times* is a great tune, so why don't you write new lyrics to that?' So I did, and I wrote about the pandemic. It's me being slightly crippled, in shock with the pandemic."

Now retitled *The Strangest Times*, the song's upbeat, major-key melody ran counter to its downbeat allusions to lockdown, social distancing and 'the PM's 5pm address' – all references to which the entire British public had become wearily accustomed. "I don't want to write another song like *Ariel*," Longdon says. "The music has to change – I can't be doing the same thing. To me *The Strangest Times* sounds like a Who track, or Elton John."

Sjöblom leapt on the song with fresh fervour: "I had so much fun doing that one. David told me to do my best Elton John piano. I'd always played Elton's stuff. When I was younger I was a bar pianist, and I'd play *Rocket Man, Goodbye Yellow Brick Road, Tiny Dancer*, so *The Strangest Times* was all Elton's rhythmic style and palm glissandos. The only thing I was really missing was the oversized glasses!

"I feel personally that I contributed more of myself to that album than ever before, and that feels very good. David and Greg trust me, but still there's always some anxiety about recording parts for an album, especially doing it on your own in your own studio. The pressure can get to you – it can creep in and you feel like you're doing the same thing over and over. There's so much lather-rinse-repeat music in the world, and I don't want to end up there. I want to be creative and do new stuff. You always have to push yourself to get the best out of yourself."

Written by Spawton, the other fragment of *Hope* was originally entitled *Edmund Ironside*, after the 11th century English king. Spawton rewrote the lyrics, and now it was called *Black With Ink*, and the multi-layered, proggy music therein now espoused the history and value of libraries, of common knowledge shared in Man's common cause: '*We*

253

see the same stars/Walk the same ground/Lit by the same sun/We could be one.' And when Longdon sang his sole brand new composition to Spawton down the phone one evening, the pair knew they had the album's title track.

"*Common Ground* is about Sarah [Ewing] and I," says Longdon. "It's a love song. Sarah coming into my life changed everything. She makes my life better. When we became a couple, when we could first be together properly, we were in Avebury – very Big Big Train land, on the Ridgeway, on the Chalk Hills, amongst the ancient stones of our ancestors. It was a real moment because we were finally together and we could move forward in life together. We were finding our common ground. These are not historical songs. They are about real people, they're about my life."

Buoyed by the reception for *Invisible* and inspired by a major highlight from Genesis's catalogue, Nick D'Virgilio had also been working on his own contribution to the pot. "I set out to write the band's quintessential instrumental," he says, "our *Los Endos*, the song we'd close concerts with." Clocking in at just under eight minutes, D'Virgilio's *Apollo* was a festival of prog, a masterclass in brainy, '70s-fuelled rock that picked up where his Grand Tour piece *Pantheon* left off.

"Nick had been working on it for a long time," says Spawton. "He'd always wanted to do an instrumental with the impact of *Los Endos*. He sent me the first minute a year or two ago, and he eventually found his way to the end of the track. It's a great eight-minute tune, and we knew people wouldn't be expecting that from what's usually a vocal-heavy band."

D'Virgilio's other song for *Common Ground* was *All The Love We Can Give.* "It's my Bowie/Bryan Ferry/Roxy Music thing," he says, "with a little prog mixed in. It's not a complete left turn, just some new flavours. All bands need to do that, I think." The song's positive vibe chimed with the album's overall insistence that – in the face of all adversity, within and without – love is the answer: *'Decide to save another/Make it right to love each other/Making a heart grow stronger/It's the better way ahead.'*

◆◆◆

By the time Hall and Manners' departures were announced in October, Big Big Train could sugar that pill with news of *Empire*'s imminent release, and of the band's work on their thirteenth studio album. For *Common Ground* the four remaining members would be joined once again by Dave Desmond's brass band. Desmond, Nick Stones, John Storey and Jonathan Truscott were augmented by trumpeter Stuart Roberts, and they gathered at Real World in October – each member the requisite six feet apart – to record their parts for the album. "I'd been sent the demos over lockdown," Desmond says, "and I'd been working on them. After wondering if anything was ever going to start again, it was great to get recording, and great to see Greg and Rob. When Greg sent me *Endnotes* he said that they'd like an overture for it, so it was lovely to flex my arranging muscles. The songs were very strong."

"When I was doing my parts for the album," says Sjöblom, "a couple of times I did think, 'What would Danny do? I might've gone there, and tried to search for Danny's vibe, especially the piano. The same with Dave [Gregory] – both men are iconic in their way of playing, their choice of notes and sounds, and where to play. Dave inspired me since the first time I played with him, but I have a style of my own too. I figured we'd bring other people in as we went along, and – sure enough – here we are."

As well as the album, they held out hope that in the near future there would also be live shows, and, for that, Big Big Train would need some fresh new hands. Besides this band, Nick Shilton's Kingmaker Management also represented Dave Foster. Born and raised in St Helens, Merseyside, this affable and highly adept guitarist had been a face on the UK prog rock scene for years, through his work with The Reasoning, Panic Room and as part of The Steve Rothery Band. He cut his teeth in the '90s with his enduring cult prog outfit Mr. So & So, and continued into the 2010s with The Dave Foster Band, his collaboration with enigmatic Dutch singer Dinet Poortman.

In January 2020, just before the world stopped, Gregory Spawton attended a Dave Foster Band show at London's Dingwalls venue, a date on the group's brief tour in support of their acclaimed album, *Nocebo*. Spawton was impressed, but thought no more of it. Then, as the year progressed and plans disintegrated, it became clear that Big Big Train would need a second guitar player for any rescheduled live shows. Foster's name came up in the conversation, and he was invited to audition.

"I sent videos of me playing *Folklore* and *Wassail*," he says. "It was a really nice way in. You want to know that you connect with what you're doing, and I already really liked Big Big Train's material. I watched them in Halifax [on the Grand Tour] and was blown away. I've always been a massive Dave Gregory fan, and I was amazed by Nick D'Virgilio and Rikard – great musicians."

Some other new musical talent was drafted in for the record. Spawton had long been a fan of acclaimed British folk band Lau, and admired the accomplished skills of their fiddler, Aidan O'Rourke. BBT's graphic designer (and Fish bassist) Steve Vantsis knew Lau and made the introduction. O'Rourke supplied his string work to the band from his studio in Scotland.

As had so often been the case in Big Big Train's 30-year story, Rob Aubrey was the conduit to another new contributor, whose talent he had noted

Dave Foster.

years before. In the late '90s Kent-born Carly Bryant had recorded at Aubitt as a teenager in a duet with her sister, and she returned to the studio in 2016 as part of an all-female wedding band. A music graduate, Bryant sang and played guitar and particularly piano, to an extremely high level.

As well as making records under her own name, she had lived and performed in Paris, and between 2017 and 2018 toured the world with Brazilian supergroup Os Mutantes. With its roots in the politically active *Tropicália* movement of the late '60s (a scene that also prominently featured Caetano Veloso and Gilberto Gil), that band had an enduring, culturally significant profile in Brazil and beyond, and a huge following to match. In 2018 Bryant joined them in their native country for their headline slot at the massive João Rock Festival, where they played for an ecstatic crowd of over 60,000 people.

By the time Rob Aubrey got in touch to sound her out about Big Big Train in 2020, Bryant was settled in Dungeness, where she had founded The Marsh Choir, a wildly successful 500-strong collective whose honorary members include Dame Judi Dench and Joanna Lumley. "I got this random message on Facebook from Rob," Bryant recalls with a smile. "'I don't know if you remember me, I work with this interesting outfit called Big Big Train – look them up and see what you think?' I did, and I wasn't sure at first, wasn't convinced it was for me. I hadn't ever worked with stuff like this, but I couldn't leave it alone in my head.

"Then Rob sent me *Empire*. Usually I'd skim through things, but I watched the whole of it from start to finish, then watched it again straight away. I knew then that this was something I wanted to get involved in. They sent me the entire catalogue, then that summer they asked me to

Carly Bryant.

record myself playing the piano for *East Coast Racer* and the synth solo and organ for *The Florentine*."

Spawton and Longdon were delighted by the performances Bryant sent them, as they were by Dave Foster's audition. They were excited at the prospect of having two such strong new voices in the mix and decided that, as well as inviting Foster and Bryant into the touring band, they would also include them on the new album itself. Foster was asked to add guitar parts to *The Strangest Times* and *Atlantic Cable*, while Bryant was sent the piano music for the song *Common Ground*. So there was an exciting sense of hope and new horizons when, on Saturday 28th November, the pair arrived to join Spawton, Longdon, Aubrey and team for the last two days of recording, at the studio that has loomed so large in the Big Big Train story.

On the Friday, having laid down most of his own vocal parts for *Common Ground*, Longdon sat in the quiet of his room at Real World, and ruminated on all that had happened this year – to Judy, to the band, to the world at large. He was, he said, still trying to come to terms with it all: "But being in the band, being here in Real World – it's alright for me not to be okay. I can suspend my fears here. This year has tested us. But I think Big Big Train are a good band. I have faith in the band. And we have more to do."

Gregory Spawton and David Longdon at Real World Studios, 26th November 2020.

XX

'All that was lost is found, back from the deep...'

Real World
Saturday 28ᵗʰ November 2020
(About 5pm…)

In The Wood Room's vocal booth, Carly Bryant is behind the microphone and in her flow. Her diction is crystal, her harmonies precise. Her eyes are closed, one hand is pressed to her headphones, the other moves in time to the song – the choirmaster conducting herself. She hadn't expected to be adding so many vocals to the record, but her hosts have been so taken with her that, while she's here, they've been finding plenty for her to do. And she's up for it.

After she leaves here tomorrow, Bryant will start getting into a new daily routine. She'll get up at 8am and spend three hours learning new material from the set list for Big Big Train's live shows. Then for another three she'll recap what she has already learnt. Only then will she move on to her 'day job' work for The Marsh Choir, as well as the music and sessions for her next album with her own band.

"I have to learn Big Big Train's music off by heart," she says in April 2021, while deep into her practice, "so it sinks in and sounds good and confident, and so I can relax into the performance. I learned *Master James Of St. George* in an hour, fine, but then *Atlantic Cable* took two weeks to

get into my ROM. The keys aren't crazy, and the acoustic guitar in the middle is nice, but the singing is syncopated. The level is high in that band. I don't want to be the weak link."

She will also start mugging up on progressive rock itself. On Gregory Spawton's recommendation she'll read *A New Day Yesterday*, the recent, near-definitive history of the genre by author and *Prog/Mojo* contributor, Mike Barnes. She'll be reminded of her affection for Genesis and ELP, will fall head over heels for King Crimson (who remind her very much of Os Mutantes), and will feel she has 'wasted her life' because she hasn't listened to anywhere near enough Yes. (Andy Poole and Sean Filkins would surely approve.)

Beyond the vocal booth's glass and across the studio floor, Bryant's addition to *Dandelion Clock* pours from the monitors mounted on Rob Aubrey's mixing desk. He scans the Pro Tools screen, multi-coloured waveforms scrolling right to left in time, capturing the performance. David Longdon is beside him, watching, and producing. Bryant finishes her part, her eyes open, and she smiles out through the glass, inviting any notes. Longdon pushes the talkback button on the desk – he wants her to channel her inner chanteuse, to try and sound a bit like Jane Birkin. Bryant replies with a giggle that, when she lived in Paris, she got mistaken for Charlotte Gainsbourg so often that, in the end, she didn't even try to argue with the people who stopped her in the street. She just smiled and gave her best *faux* Charlotte smile for *le selfie*.

Aubrey re-cues the music, and Bryant delivers her part as requested. It's perfect, and Longdon stabs the button again to tell her as much. She does the part once more, almost identically, so it can be double-tracked on the final record. Then it's on to the next, and this goes on until *Dandelion Clock* has grown from a good demo into a living, breathing thing.

Gregory Spawton has been here since Monday. All of his bass, bass pedal and guitar parts are in the can. Now, as the day winds down, he uncorks bottles and pours red wine into glasses. Underneath his laconic demeanour, his mind is simply fizzing. He's been so impressed with Bryant. Tomorrow, he decides, he'll ask her to layer up harmonies on *Atlantic Cable*. She has also played him some of a proggy opus she started writing in Las Vegas while on tour with Os Mutantes, called *Welcome To The Planet*. Spawton loves it, and has asked her to work it up into a demo. He's already thinking of ways to keep her interested in the band from now on. It's a similar sense of excitement and anxiety to the one he felt over a decade before, when David Longdon took to Aubitt's booth for his fateful first session for *The Underfall Yard*.

Spawton hands a glass of wine to Dave Foster, who's on the control room's sofa, taking it all in, and getting into the tune. He may be a serious guitarist, but Foster runs on good English humour, and is generous with fun anecdotes. After one Steve Rothery show, he recalls, he walked into a lift full of German people, who were – for some unlikely reason – all humming the theme tune to the very English '70s

UK sitcom, *Terry And June*. Over the day he has revelled in Real World's impressive array of highest-end vintage gear. In The Big Room earlier, he pointed at a particularly battered box set into the impressive desk (a Pultec tube equaliser unit, as it happens), and said to his new friends, with marvel: "It blows me away that that – *that!* – is worth *more than my car!*"

Foster has already supplied his guitar parts for *The Strangest Times* from his home studio in St Helens. Tomorrow – Sunday – he'll sit in The Big Room and record his contributions to *Atlantic Cable*. "I live in the world of Tool and A Perfect Circle," he says, "and I've told Greg to rein me in, because I could easily bring in too much heaviness." A seasoned player who recently played to thousands of people on Rothery's world tour, he is unfazed by the demands of the average session. But then *Atlantic Cable* isn't your average rock song.

"I've sat in sessions with blues rock bands," he will reveal, months later, "and I can do that stuff, you know, in my sleep. But that Sunday at Real World was something

Dave Foster and Rob Aubrey recording Atlantic Cable.

259

else. They're all lovely people, but I didn't know them, and I was given a chance to play over a moderately complicated solo section. I was there in this massive room with Rob, Greg and Chris [Topham] watching me, and I was thinking, 'Why am I getting so nervous?'"

With lawyerly reserve, Nick Shilton monitors Saturday's progress from a discreet corner of The Wood Room. He knows to keep out of the way of the band's creative process, but with his prog fan's ears he can hear this new record coming together nicely. Shilton's workload – and that of Steve Cadman – is quietly building up too. Cadman has been stoking the fires of The Passengers Club, and the label's upcoming schedule is filling up. *Common Ground* is set for release in the third quarter of 2021, the remixed and remastered edition of *The Underfall Yard* will land in March, and, in the fullness of time, *Ingenious Devices* will finally offer the full fruit of those Abbey Road string sessions.

Also on the English Electric schedule is a reissue of David Longdon's long deleted 2004 solo album *Wild River*, with work already proceeding on the follow-up. *Door One* is expected to feature saxophonist/flautist Theo Travis (King Crimson/Steven Wilson/The Tangent), prolific drummer Jeremy Stacey (Crimson/Robbie Williams) and, on bass, one Steve Vantsis.

Not to be left out, Gregory Spawton is set for his own album too. Under the moniker Germander Speedwell, he will produce a set of songs to be performed by a host of guest vocalists, with Peter Hammill, Stackridge's James Warren, and Longdon all pencilled to contribute. To Spawton, Big Big Train's 2002 release *Bard* may well be a relic of bleak times, but that long-deleted record has, over the decades, become a curio amongst the Passengers. The year 2022 will

be its 20th anniversary, and the plan is to give it a birthday reissue, with some judicious edits and re-records to remove the worst of any remaining BTFOOM moments.

And then there's the Loreley show. Big Big Train's triumphant headline set at Night Of The Prog was recorded by the festival's multi-camera crew, and work will soon begin on an edit for a Blu-ray release of what remains their biggest show to date. Winfried Völklein has already been

Clare Lindley.

sounding them out about topping the bill once again at a future Night Of The Prog. The BBT camp are also working on the rescheduled North American and European tour dates, in the event that the pandemic is controlled and the world can once again ring to the sound of live music. In the frame to join as tour violinist is Clare Lindley, who replaced Rachel Hall in Stackridge when she moved over to Big Big Train.

The Wood Room is dominated by Peter Gabriel's own, beautiful Bösendorfer grand piano, the one he takes on tour. Earlier today, within just an hour of arriving at Real World after her long drive from Kent, Carly Bryant was seated at its keyboard, with David Longdon nearby with his acoustic guitar, and the two began working through *Common Ground*'s title track. They were both nervous at this first meeting, gently sussing each other out, building up a good working dynamic. Soon they were at ease and smoothing out the tune's deceptively fiddly time shifts ('Is that part in 7?' 'Let's see… no, it's 6') and sharing out the harmony lines ('Oh, you're going for that one? Okay, then I'll go *here*…').

With Longdon wanting it 'gospel-y', they approached the song in numerous ways, tweaked a few sticking points until – in a creative atmosphere both light and constructive – the song began to flow as if it had just been unearthed, intact and fully formed. "It's a bit like an IKEA bed, isn't it?" quipped Longdon, to Bryant's immediate laughter. "You keep working on it until it comes together."

When bidden, Foster and Spawton joined in on acoustic guitars, and by mid-afternoon an acoustic arrangement of *Common Ground* had emerged complete, captured on camera (and subsequently released across the band's social media in August 2021). "You've clearly worked on this," a delighted Longdon told Bryant as they wound down. "I really like what you've done – and you've asked all the right questions." Bryant was pleased too, her smile a 1,000-watter. It was hard to believe this was the first time the two had met, let alone played together.

"Watching Carly and David working on that," Rob Aubrey says later, "that gave me some tingles on the back of my neck for sure. And you could see the attitude of the guys – David and Greg were very happy.

Finding common ground in The Wood Room.

These new people they've brought in are really talented musicians. It's definitely the start of a new chapter."

Throughout the Saturday, Longdon is pleased with the way the music is progressing, and is in his element producing *Common Ground*. Earlier he added his own vocals to *Black With Ink*. The smile is returning, as is the twinkle in the eye. And if Spawton's songs for this album contain allusions to Big Big Train's beginnings, Longdon goes one further, with this intriguing flight of fancy:

"I've been thinking, what – or when – is 'Point Zero' of Real World being here? And of us being here? And Greg and I being how we are? I've traced it back to Peter Gabriel wearing the red dress in Ireland [National Stadium, Dublin, September 1972]. Genesis had done an album, they went into [Charisma label head] Tony Stratton-Smith's office and he said, 'With all the will in the world, you're earnest boys hunched over 12-strings. Who's going to notice that, really?' Peter went away and thought about it, and that night – unbeknownst to the rest of the band – he went onstage in his wife's red dress. With a fox head on. And Tony Banks kicked off – he would've vetoed it. And it made the cover of the *NME*! That's an artistic statement. Then they made *Selling England By The Pound*, Greg hears his brother playing *Dancing With The Moonlit Knight*. Peter's career keeps going, he leaves Genesis, does his own thing, and Real World comes about. Would all this have happened if he hadn't worn the dress? So, thank you Peter! And your lovely wife Jill, for the dress…"

David Longdon in conversation with Peter Gabriel at Real World Studios, 3rd November 2021.

The sky is dark outside The Wood Room now, the 'Record' light is finally off, and the Saturday is done. Soon all will head to the canteen, for dinner, for conversation, for the chance to get to know each other. But for now everyone has a drink in hand, and there are cheers all around to new friends and to a good day's work. Smiling, Longdon turns to Spawton and addresses him directly. "It's been a great day, Greg. *Resurgam*!" The two clink and raise their glasses, to the day, to the band, to the onward journey.

Endnotes

'All that is gone and done,
all that is yet to come...'

MORE THAN ONCE DURING THEIR FRIENDSHIP, David Longdon and Gregory Spawton discussed what should become of the band if the unthinkable were to happen and one of them was no longer around. Both men were in complete agreement on the subject – each of them would want Big Big Train to continue without them. But neither they, nor anybody else, could have foreseen how soon this would become a real consideration.

◆◆◆

In April 2021 the reissue of *The Underfall Yard* – the album that marked the start of Longdon's journey with Big Big Train – hit number one on the UK Rock Albums chart. That same month he and Sarah Ewing got engaged, and they made plans to marry the following year.

Then, on 30th July 2021, *Common Ground* entered the UK Albums chart at number 31, making it Big Big Train's second Top 40 hit, and their highest charting record to date. Given that the band's line-up had changed so dramatically since *Grand Tour*, the reception from fans and press was reassuringly favourable. In his balanced critique for *Mojo*, writer John Bungey gave the album three out of five stars, saying that 'Melancholy has never sounded so seductive'. In his assessment for *Uncut* magazine, Johnny Sharp awarded the record seven out of ten, labelling the band a 'neo-prog institution'.

With the live music scene predicted to emerge from its enforced stasis in 2022, Big Big Train announced their rescheduled tour plans. Starting with UK shows in March, they would play 40 concerts, with a string of shows across Europe and their first swing at the US and Canada. These

David and Sarah, April 2021.

were exciting times, the optimism in the BBT camp spurred on by the prospect of this extensive run of gigs, and by the fresh, revitalising presence of Carly Bryant, Dave Foster and violinist Clare Lindley.

After the fruitful process of making *Common Ground* they now had new writers in the fold, and were already cooking up another set of songs. They carried on recording, primarily at Aubitt but also at Real World and the musicians' respective home studios. Initially there was talk of a quick follow-up EP to *Common Ground*, but this soon evolved into an LP.

Welcome To The Planet took its title from Bryant's art-rock opus, the one she had shown Gregory Spawton during her time at Real World. Within Big Big Train's own musical hothouse, the song had quickly grown into a majestic, melodic and delightfully eccentric piece strewn

Big Big Train, 20th October 2021.

with flute, big choral harmonies, bombastic brass courtesy of Dave Desmond and the boys, and an assured lead vocal from Bryant herself.

Dave Foster also made his debut as a contributor to the band, co-writing the jubilantly breezy 11/8 piece *Made From Sunshine* with Longdon (Longdon and Lindley proving a strong vocal combination here). Nick D'Virgilio supplied the insistent, suspenseful and oddly catchy *The Connection Plan* (featuring violin from Derek Reeves, of the Fort Wayne Philharmonic) and drum showcase *Bats In The Belfry*. Rikard Sjöblom turned in a highly proggy, accordion-rich instrumental of his own, *A Room With No Ceiling*.

For Spawton's part, he channelled the more traditional BBT sound on *Oak And Stone* – a restrained piece chiming with 12-string acoustic guitar – and *Lanterna*, initially conceived as an extra section of the already sprawling *Atlantic Cable*. He also revived that lovely unused ballad, *Capitoline Venus*, while his pop-rocker *Proper Jack Froster* brimmed with references to those wintry childhood days sledging in Sutton Park, its sweet nostalgia cut by dark memories of his parents' stormy, doomed relationship. (When released as a single in December '21, the song would be graced by a beautiful animated video by Swedish artist Love Andreas Gson Fagerstedt.)

The only time this whole new line-up was ever in the same room together was in London, on 20th October. They did a press shoot with photographer Sophocles Alexiou, as well as group interviews with Jerry Ewing for *Prog* and Dave Ling for *Classic Rock*.

A week later Spawton, Longdon, Bryant and director/producer Tim Sidwell headed to the magnificent All Saints' Church in Lydd, Kent. It could hold 2000 people, and, in non-pandemic times, this was where Bryant would conduct The Marsh Choir. On the day of filming though, it was just Bryant and Longdon, performing a beautiful acoustic arrangement of *Welcome To The Planet*, with Bryant on piano, Longdon on flute. Duetting in harmony, the pair's vocal chemistry had already come on since the year before, and that first day they set to work together in The Wood Room at Real World. While at All Saints' Church, the three members also recorded a track-by-track commentary for the upcoming album, to be aired on their social channels and The Passengers Club. The tone here was notably informal and relaxed. These were three friends, quick to laugh, and chatting about their craft.

Longdon hadn't contributed any complete songs for *Welcome To The Planet*. While still deeply involved with the band, by this point he was pouring much of his considerable compositional energy into *Door One*. Musical contributions came in from Jeremy Stacey, Steve Vantsis, his old friend Gary Bromham and Theo Travis (for whose 2021 solo album, *Songs From The Apricot Tree*, Longdon had added a haunting vocal performance, on the song *Brilliant Trees*). He worked on his record industriously, passionately across the year with engineer/co-producer Patrick Phillips, with sessions at Playpen Studios in Bristol – where he had worked on Dyble Longdon's *Between A Breath And A Breath* – and at the sanctuary of Real World.

In mid-November Longdon spent time at Playpen with Phillips, laying Stacey's drums into the *Door One* mix. By the time he left the studio for home, on Thursday 18th November, the album was really coming together. Longdon was extremely pleased, engrossed and enthused. This was his project. He had total creative control over the work, no compromises.

Then there was Big Big Train. With new faces, another Top 40 album under their belt, another strong record scheduled for release in January and their first major international tour hoving into view, the group he fronted was set for an exciting next chapter of their own.

And, of course, there was Sarah, with whom he had finally found true love, and contentment. When she greeted him on his return to Nottingham, David Longdon was a happy man.

But this happiness was cut cruelly short. In the early hours of the Friday morning Longdon fell at home, and sustained serious injuries. He was rushed to hospital and put on life support. Later that day, Sarah was joined at his bedside by Gregory and Kathy Spawton, Nick Shilton, Longdon's old friend Simon Withers, his daughters, Amelia and Eloise, and their mother. The day after, Saturday 20th November, Danah Cadman – an invaluable member of the BBT team and close friend to Sarah – joined Gregory and Kathy at the hospital to offer Sarah all the emotional support they possibly could. And that same afternoon, with just Sarah with him, David Longdon died. He was 56.

◆◆◆

When the news of his death broke, the tributes poured in. Bereft fans deluged Big Big Train's Facebook forum with condolences for his family, friends and bandmates. They offered moving, fond testimonials to the man, with many posts accompanied by a treasured selfie taken with Longdon after a BBT show. Loved ones, the band, and the community around them struggled to come to terms with the sudden, unfathomably tragic nature of his loss.

In a moving eulogy, a shell-shocked Gregory Spawton recounted how David Longdon had changed his life, and eloquently summed up his talent: "Over the last decade or so we shared many adventures together," Spawton wrote, "and now those adventures are over. […] David was an alchemist. He made my songs shine with his extraordinary voice and presence and he drove me on to write better songs. He helped me feel more comfortable on stage and to step forward out of my comfort zones. In every respect he enriched my life and made it for the better.

"Many have spoken of David's exceptional kindness and thoughtfulness. Even more notable to me, however, was his loyalty. He always had my back, and when times were difficult he would be there with the right words at the right time. I loved him like a brother.

"David's world was full of love, his love for others and theirs for him. In particular, his life was hugely enriched by the love of his partner Sarah and his daughters Amelia and Eloise. The strength and fortitude that these three women have shown throughout the harrowing circumstances of the last few days has been extraordinary."

Nick D'Virgilio addressed his tribute to Longdon directly: "I am really sad that there could not be more for us to accomplish together. We were just getting started. Just know that your art, your voice, and your smile have brought so much joy to so many. If legacy means anything, that is a good legacy to have. Rest in peace my kind and talented friend."

"David was a dear friend of mine," added Rikard Sjöblom, "like a brother. He was a fantastic musician and the best vocalist I've ever worked with, but most of all he was a fantastic, loveable human being who I will miss for the rest of my life. Thank you for everything, brother Longdon."

On his own social media, Dave Desmond posted a link

to *Leopards*, from *English Electric*, one of the first Longdon songs the band had recorded. "You were an INCREDIBLE talent Dave," Desmond wrote, "and such a very kind, loving, caring, interesting and hilarious man. It was such a treat to spend the other evening sitting with you […] and to see firsthand the sincere love and affection you and Sarah shared for each other. Rest in peace my friend."

In his tribute, Danny Manners recalled how he had met Longdon, how their friendship had led himself and Dave Gregory into the Big Big Train story, and he spoke of his qualities as a man: "[David] would talk fearlessly and directly to musicians of high renown, but equally modestly and decently to fans, or to the studio cleaner. Those same qualities were the secret of his impact as a singer, I think. He possessed a lot of vocal technique and control, but you were never aware of it, or of him putting on an obvious performance. He seemed to be able to convey emotion directly and simply through his voice, without any self-consciousness. It was a rare quality, and proved the spark that lifted Big Big Train to the next level.

"David also had a wicked sense of humour, which you could depend upon to puncture any possibility of self-importance on his own or anybody else's part. He was always very generous in his encouragement to me to overcome my natural tendency to perfectionism and procrastination, gently reminding me that life is short. […] He was a thoroughly decent, lovely bloke, whose too early departure is very hard to bear for fans, bandmates, friends and family, especially his two daughters, his partner Sarah, and his musical brother Greg. Perhaps we can console ourselves a little with the thought that he left at a point in his life where he had found true personal happiness, and musical fulfilment and recognition. Love you, David."

And Dave Gregory praised his friend's 'relentless creative energy' and 'phenomenal voice'. "You also provided me with the opportunity to grow as a musician," he wrote, "as the song material, from both you and Greg Spawton, became ever more ambitious and expansive. I'm grateful for the artistic nourishment it gave me, the work you put in truly inspiring.

"I can't leave without mentioning the banter! Never malicious, always hilarious, it ran like a thread behind any conversation regardless of how serious, and with it you kept our spirits high. […] But right now, my thoughts are with those closest to you, especially Sarah, and your daughters Amelia and Eloise for whom I wish courage and strength in coping with their incalculable loss. You leave this world a better place for the gifts you brought to it and will be remembered forever. Goodbye, old friend."

In the press, outlets ranging from the *NME* to *The Guardian* ran the news story online, while *The Times* printed a full-page obituary in the newspaper, with journalist Dominic Maxwell outlining Longdon's rise to prominence with Big Big Train. The December issue of *Prog* magazine featured a four-page tribute to the star, and that same edition was also notable for containing the results of the 2021 poll, wherein the readers had chosen their favourite music and musicians over the year. There was some solace to be had here. Big Big Train were named Band Of The Year, *Common Ground* was voted Album Of The Year, and Spawton, D'Virgilio and Sjöblom all ranked highly in their respective instrumental categories. The titles of Male Vocalist Of The Year and Person Of 2021 went, of course, to David Longdon.

◆◆◆

Also in that issue was one of many warm reviews that *Welcome To The Planet* received in the run-up to its release on 25th January 2022. (While briefly hitting the Top 10 in the midweek chart on the strength of pre-orders, the record entered the final chart at number 44.) The album was understandably seen through the lens of Longdon's loss, but *Prog* critic Gary Mackenzie also found much to enjoy: '*Welcome To The Planet* has solid Big Big Train DNA, real heart and great performances [...] Although the next destination on Big Big Train's journey is unclear, it must surely still be informed by David Longdon's legacy.' *The Sunday Times*' review was short, but sweet, noting how Longdon's 'grainy, innately musical voice gives songs such as *Lanterna*, *Capitoline Venus* and *Oak And Stone* a pastoral beauty that is unbearably moving'.

And, fortunately, Longdon had been captured up close while laying down his innately beautiful vocal for *Capitoline Venus*. Back in July, he had given four complete takes of the song in the vocal booth at Aubitt, with a camera locked off and recording him. Released on BBT's socials the week after the album came out, this was Longdon's final performance for Big Big Train, at the place where 12 years before – almost to the day – he had first come into their world, which had been forever changed.

❖❖❖

At her fiancé's hospital bedside, Sarah Ewing had reminded Gregory Spawton about his pact with David Longdon. David would, she told him, absolutely want the band to continue. The subject came up again at Longdon's funeral, held on 6th January in the Amber Valley in Derbyshire, attended by family and close friends. (The order of service included a piece from his *Wild River* album called *On To The Headland*,

Uncle Jack from *English Electric Part One* and David Bowie's *Life On Mars*.) And with 2022 dawning, and the initial shock of bereavement slowly subsiding, that abstract 'what if?' scenario was now a very real dilemma for Spawton.

"The few times we talked about it," he recalls now, "David was absolutely adamant that we should carry on if something happened to him. I always said to him that I was really not sure we could. And to be honest, for the first few weeks after he died, that's how I felt. But when Sarah made it clear that David had also told her that he would want the band to continue, it made me more comfortable about it. I feel that we've very much got his consent to do that."

The UK and North American shows scheduled for the first half of 2022 had been cancelled in the aftermath, but there were other, longer-term considerations, both artistic and pragmatic. There was the question of David Longdon's legacy. For friends, fans and family alike, there was comfort to be had in having him immortalised through the band's recorded catalogue. But it was important to ensure that the songs he wrote would still be performed, and heard by audiences new and old. For the band, there would be consolation in performing the songs to which Longdon had contributed – there's cathartic power in playing music with such meaning. And, as individuals, as songwriters and musicians, Spawton, Nick D'Virgilio, Rikard Sjöblom and BBT's new recruits all still had artistic impulses to express, perhaps more now than ever. And for the fans, the Passengers, having the band play on could only be a positive thing.

And so, on 11th February, their manager Nick Shilton posted a statement from the band on their Facebook page, revealing David Longdon's wishes: "After careful consideration, and with the active encouragement of

David's partner Sarah, we have decided to honour David's wishes.

"Big Big Train will therefore seek to continue as a band and will perform live and release new music in due course. More specific details of the band's line-up and planned activities will follow in further announcements, including an opportunity for fans to celebrate David's life and musical legacy."

On 22nd March Big Big Train and Kingmaker Management hosted 'an evening celebrating the life of David Longdon' at Kings Place, London, site of BBT's live debut with Longdon nearly seven years before. Here band members, past and present, were joined by the BBT team, their close circle, and figures within the music industry to remember Longdon, to reminisce, mark his achievements, to shed a tear maybe, but also to recall his sharp, big-hearted sense of humour, and laugh again too.

At time of writing, Patrick Phillips is supervising work on *Door One* to ensure that, once completed, it is as close to its creator's vision as possible. A release is tentatively scheduled on English Electric Recordings later in 2022.

And as for Big Big Train, they are left with the unenviable task of replacing the irreplaceable, while moving into the future, and writing the next chapter in their remarkable history. Over 30 years in, this story of a rock band isn't over yet.

Author's Acknowledgements

I WOULD LIKE TO THANK Nick and Gregory at Kingmaker for trusting me to tell Big Big Train's story so far, and for their counsel and encouragement along the way. I am indebted to Nick for the reams of initial interviews he conducted in preparation for this book, and my gratitude and apologies to Gregory for the many, many hours spent together on the phone/Zoom/Skype piecing together details from the last 30 years; any inaccuracies in this regard are all my own. I am very grateful to Professor Geoff Parks for his diligent proofreading. Geoff, you are, quite literally, the don.

Thanks to all the interviewees here for your invaluable contributions. Special appreciation must go to all the members of Big Big Train past and present for patiently enduring hours of interrogation. The music you've made continues to make the world a better place for your army of fans around the world. Speaking of which – to all Passengers everywhere, your passion for music and especially for this band is a wonderful, life-affirming thing that remains a pleasure to witness. This book was written with you firmly in mind. Thank you.

Things just wouldn't be the same for me without *Prog*'s Jo Kendall, Natasha Scharf, Russell Fairbrother, Dave Everley and the magazine's incredibly knowledgeable roster of contributors. The same goes for Siân Llewellyn, Polly Glass, Ian Fortnam, Fraser Lewry, Scott Rowley and the team at *Classic Rock* – it's an honour.

A very special thank you to my friend, the shy and retiring Philip Wilding, for getting me into this game in the first place. And to the 'Nabob Of Prog' himself, the indefatigable Jerry Ewing – thank you for everything you've done, for me, and for the music.

Mum and Dad, Hywel, Lloyd, Luigi, Mikey, Piers – thanks for bearing with me, in general really. And to my wonderful wife Claire (who's more of a Britpop girl, but that's fine) – when David and Sarah spoke about finding true love and happiness together I understood what they meant, and that is because of you. It doesn't really cover it, but thank you. I love you.

This book is dedicated to the extraordinary talent that was, and always will be, David Longdon, but I also offer my own work here as a tribute to Linda Tredgett, in loving memory.

Grant Moon

Photography Acknowledgements

THE AUTHOR AND PUBLISHER WOULD LIKE to thank the following sincerely for their kind permission to use their photographs in this book:

- Sophocles Alexiou – pages 255, 256, 260 and 264.
- Erick Anderson – page 229 (top).
- Robin Armstrong – page 214 (bottom).
- Kain Dear – pages 138, 139, 140, 141, 143 (left), 145, 147, 148, 149, 150, 151, 152, 154 and 156.
- Bo Hansen – pages 234, 235, 237, 238, 239 (bottom), 240 (top left) and 241 (top left and bottom).
- Niall Hayden – pages 166 and 173.
- Michael Heller – pages 184, 185, 186, 188, 190, 191, 192, 193, 194, 198, 208, 210, 211, 212, 214 (top), 215, 216, 217, 218, 219, 221, 223, 232 and 246.
- Simon Hogg – pages 159, 161 (top) and 181 (bottom).
- Willem Klopper – pages 97, 111, 116, 143 (right), 144, 195 and 244.
- Neil Palfreyman – pages 146, 153, 196 and 247.
- Geoff Parks – page 180.
- Lorraine Poole – page 160.
- Martin Reijman – pages 236, 239 (top), 240 (top right and bottom) and 241 (top right).
- Wayne Smith – page 61.
- Steve Somerset – page 85.
- Chris Walkden – pages 137 (top and middle) and 171.
- Richard Williamson – page 261.
- André Wins – the front cover and pages vi, 220 and 224.
- Simon Withers – page 136.

Every reasonable effort has been made to trace copyright holders, but if there are any errors or omissions, the publisher will be pleased to insert the appropriate acknowledgement in any subsequent printings or editions.

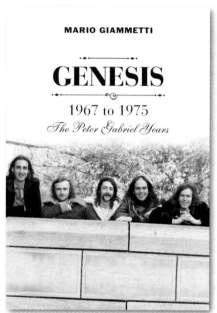

'A must for all fans who are interested in early Genesis. I thoroughly recommend it.' – STEVE HACKETT

'Essential for anyone with more than a passing interest in the band.' – PROG

'Much of the tale is told in quotes gleaned from extensive, frank interviews with the players… This is close to definitive.' – MOJO

'Reverent, well researched. Bejewelled with photos and souvenirs, this encomium will be hard for any believer to resist.' – CLASSIC ROCK

'The post-Gabriel period mined in impressively obsessive detail. This is a substantial and fascinating read.' – PROG

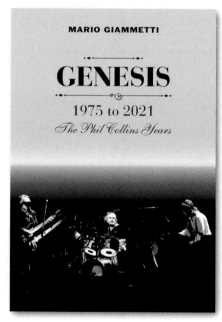

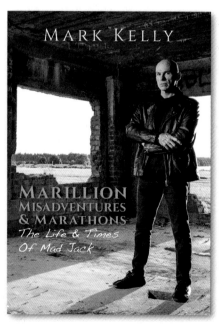

"Mark Kelly deserves so much credit. An incredibly gifted musician and composer, he has now written a book that is compelling reading. It's rare to find such honesty in a book like this and undoubtedly it was written from the heart." – RICK WAKEMAN

"An immensely enjoyable and entertaining romp through 40-plus years of prog history." – PROG